CROSSTOWN

CROSSTOWN

a novel by

Loren W. Cooper

XENO

Book design by Selena Trager

Library of Congress Cataloging-in-Publication Data

Names: Cooper, Loren W., author.
Title: Crosstown : a novel / by Loren W. Cooper.
Description: Pasadena : Red Hen Press, 2017.
Identifiers: LCCN 2017011703| ISBN 9781939096029 (softcover : acid-free paper) | ISBN 9781939096012 (e-book)
Subjects: LCSH: Time travel—Fiction. | Reality—Fiction. | GSAFD: Science fiction. | Fantasy fiction. Classification: LCC PS3603.O582665 C76 2017 | DDC 813/.6—dc23
LC record available at https://lccn.loc.gov/2017011703

The National Endowment for the Arts, the Los Angeles County Arts Commission, the Dwight Stuart Youth Fund, the Max Factor Family Foundation, the Pasadena Tournament of Roses Foundation, the Pasadena Arts & Culture Commission and the City of Pasadena Cultural Affairs Division, the City of Los Angeles Department of Cultural Affairs, the Audrey & Sydney Irmas Charitable Foundation, Sony Pictures Entertainment, Amazon Literary Partnership, and the Sherwood Foundation partially support Red Hen Press.

First Edition
Published by XENO Books
an imprint of Red Hen Press
www.redhen.org

For my daughters, Isabella-Grace and Abrielle,
both just setting their feet on the Roads.

And for my wife, Jac—
a better traveling companion could not be found.

CROSSTOWN

INTRODUCTION

D EAR READER: What in the world are we doing here, you and I? Why am I writing an introduction to a novel that is perfectly capable of launching itself without one? Why are you reading this introduction, when you could just turn a page or two and start to enjoy Loren W. Cooper's engaging story? What in the world compels you to read this false start when the real thing lies so near at hand?

Actually, I should be asking the question like this: What in the worlds are you doing here? In a parallel universe, you aren't reading this introduction, but have jumped right to the first page of *CrossTown*, or to the last page (since in that universe you always need to see first how a novel is going to end), or are thumbing through the middle pages to read random paragraphs so you can decide whether this feels like the sort of novel you will enjoy.

In one universe, you are reading this introduction because you are a compulsive completist and consider that if you have not read every word of a book, from the copyright notice to the designer's note about the typeface, you have not read the book. Or in a different reality you are reading this introduction because you are riding the knife edge of possibility, unsure whether you are going to read this novel (thus ending up in a left-branching universe) or pass it up (a right-branching universe).

To the completist version of yourself, I make this promise: this introduction won't go on much longer. I want to hurry you along to the main event. But bear with me just a little longer while I address those versions of you that are on the cusp of reading this novel or not.

In some universes, you have opened to random pages to discover what sort of novel this might be, and you have found words that suggest science fiction: hard vacuum, nanotech, clone, radiation, actinic, supernova. But a random sampling of vocabulary has also yielded terms typical of genre fantasy: vampire, faerie, pooka, plate armor, sword. And in the midst of these you may have come across a word to confound all of your familiar genre associations, the word Brylcreem.

CrossTown is a fantasy novel, but it is a fantasy story played out on the largest possible setting. *CrossTown* encompasses all of space and time, but all the possible spaces and times, as well as all the impossible spaces and times of mythic imagination. It ranges from the territories where many possiblities converge—the thrumming capitals of existence—to the hinterlands and hinterwhens.

This is also a detective novel, with its fee-for-service hero who has a murder to solve. It is a novel about alien minds, a novel that tickles our sense of wonder, that succeeds in stretching the reader's perception and effing the ineffable, while at the same time being the story of a sorcerer whose ambition is to become an ever more powerful wielder of magic.

I have seen this novel develop over the course of many years, and I have always been impressed by how it manages to succeed simultaneously in so many existing traditions of storytelling while ordering reality in a new way. I mean, wow!

CrossTown is full of thrilling action, of hidden agendas, of narrow escapes. It is, in short, a lot of fun. But it's also a new version of one of the stories we need to tell ourselves again and again:

The hero, wearing one of his thousand faces, seeks the elixir, in one of its thousand forms, and ends up being surprised, elevated, bereft, and consoled. And we, as readers, take that same journey through heights and depths to arrive at contemplation. This is a novel that offers its own answer to the question of what we are to do with the gift, the privilege, of our human birth.

My advice, Dear Reader, in whatever universe you occupy, is that you read on.

—Bruce Holland Rogers

CHAPTER I

A CCIDENTAL TRAVEL happens all the time.

Vincent van Gogh had lived in CrossTown long enough to be familiar with the concept. "It must have followed someone home, Zethus. Caught someone's coattails at a crossroad, perhaps. Came in like a fever, picked up off the street. The building never had a history of haunting."

I studied the façade of the building from the edge of the road. Vincent stood next to me, shifting his weight uneasily from foot to foot. "If not the place, what about the people?" I asked. "Any budding warlocks in residence?"

Vincent shook his head. The motion exposed the scar of the wounded ear under the loose tumble of long red hair. "Nothing like that. The Old Woman wouldn't have it. Not in her building. It might have chosen us as easy pickings. The ones who have already moved were the ones with children. I was the only one in the building who had any contact with a working sorcerer. I had to talk fast to get the Old Woman to agree to that."

I looked at the violet will o' wisps floating along the edges of the smooth asphalt lane. A light mist fell down through a pastel smear of sky and darkened the asphalt. The violet globes were a Wayshaper's mark. Their presence assured that this Road had been tamed to prevent a resident short on power and knowledge from absently crossing into some distant possibility during a casual trip to or from the local grocer or bookstore. Such places hold a strong attraction for CrossTown residents needing security and safety in their travels.

Unfortunately, the markers provided no assurance as to what or who might wander along that Road. Particularly in CrossTown.

The brownstone looked, to the untrained eye, virtually identical to its blocky brethren on either side. Seen through the eyes of a sorcerer, the mark on Vincent's building was obvious. Gusts of wind chased rills of moisture across the blacktop to the granite foundation of the apartment building, but the wind died before it touched the walls of the building. The water fell away to black pools standing at the base of the wall. A dull, oily sheen smeared the surface of the water where it trickled over the stone and pooled on the cement like runoff from a slaughterhouse floor. Rows of corbels brooded over darkened windows like heavy brows hanging over the empty sockets of a skull.

Vincent had called on me to hunt down the source of the mark on that place. "She could have invited a priest," I told him. "Someone she had a better liking for."

Vincent cleared his throat. "She doesn't like any in the spirit business. But she's desperate enough to let you take a shot, based on my recommendation."

I raised an eyebrow. "Desperate enough to pay?"

"We all chipped in," he said stiffly. "We share the burden of payment."

"Price of a profession, Vincent," I said mildly. "I should give my services away no more than you should give away your paintings."

A pair of soldiers strolled by on patrol, horsehair crests nodding in the breeze, bone-hilted ritual daggers crossed in the smalls of their backs, bulky machine pistols slung at chest level over their ceramic armor. Vincent watched them cross to the other side of the street before they reached the brownstone. "You'll have your silver," he said without glancing away from them to meet my eyes. "Once the job is done. Once the building is clear. The Old Woman told everyone you would be cleansing the building today."

That's the bulk of my job. Call it spiritual pest control.

I stepped away from Vincent and turned down the walk to the front entrance of the building. I didn't expect any more useful details out of him. Knowledge helps most in these situations, but what Vincent had told me was scanty and general. Nightmares. Oppression. Hints of madness. Signs of a psychic parasite, but not specific enough detail to narrow identification any further.

The door gaped open like a hungry mouth. The darkness beyond the doorway thickened, eating the light. I paused on the threshold, studying the doorway, and felt Blade rouse, the Legion stirring restlessly behind him.

Blade's voice came to me like the rustle of steel sliding in a scabbard. "Strengthen the defenses?"

I considered the implications of waking my Legion of Bound Spirits before responding. "No. But stay ready. This one looks powerful but not subtle. Let's see what he's made of. Be prepared if he turns out to have unexpected depths."

I stepped through the door's shadowy mouth. The air took on a taint of decaying flesh. Miasma curled around me, heavy with a rotten strength, but Blade walked with me, stayed within the bounds of body and soul, and stood watch at every door of my spirit. No simple taint could make its way past the first Captain of my Legion.

I stepped across the threshold and onto thin gray carpet. I called the White Wolf out of the sleeping Legion. I loosed him enough so that he came to stand before me, his icy blue eyes burning into the artificial night. Only another sorcerer or a creature of the spirit would see him clothed in his hoarfrost fur, the arctic chill of his breath wreathing his head, his eyes like banked coals as he met my gaze and waited.

I nodded past him into the darkness. "Lead me."

Lips edged in black curled away from icicle teeth. "And take him?"

"Not yet." I cocked my head, listening to the whispering flow of power through the house. "Bring him to bay."

A deep current ran through that place, heavy with the coppery scent of blood. A film of decay settled over everything within the building. I thought the blond wood panels covering the walls bore a layer of dust and filth until I stepped close enough to see light that should have reflected off the polished surface fading into the walls.

The power in that place hated life and order and cleanliness.

I felt that power tremble when my Wolf's hunting call drifted down the hallway. As the current of power contracted and localized, the source drawing back to itself much of the strength it had built on a foundation of fear, I walked on down the hallway. Overhead, long fluorescent lights fought a losing battle against what from the corner of the eye appeared to be clouds of gnats. Only another sorcerer would have heard the whine of the alien power buzzing overhead or the baying of my Wolf trailing through that place, and only another sorcerer would have heard the White Wolf's bay thicken to a deep, throaty growl.

He had found my prey.

I made my way quickly through a door and up an open stairwell. A hissing voice rose through the growl. I exited the stairs and started down a long hall toward the White Wolf. Baying, he reared at an apartment door. The power running through the place crested like a wave rising before it crashes down with all of its weight and strength. A sudden roar shook the floor under my feet as the door facing the White Wolf exploded outward and the White Wolf vanished in a cloud of debris.

I steadied myself with one hand against the rough plaster of the wall, not quite losing my footing as the building swayed. A rolling groan of stressed timber swept through the hallway like a vast exhalation. A cloud of dust and pulverized plaster choked the hallway. A sour, carrion smell rose with the dust. I covered my nose and mouth with my sleeve, breathed through my mouth, closed my eyes to slits, and waited for the dust to settle. After a few moments, once the visibility had lightened to a gray haze, the White Wolf emerged through the wreckage of the door and stalked back to where I stood waiting.

The building settled and steadied and the gathered power faded, leaving only the stench behind. I knew that the attack had been loud enough that even Vincent would have heard it from the street. From his perspective, it probably sounded as if I were demolishing the building.

I hoped it didn't happen that way. I hoped the thing I hunted wasn't that strong.

The sickly-sweet smell faded as the localized power thinned away to a trace. My quarry had escaped my hound. I set my hands on my hips and looked down at the White Wolf. "I'm disappointed in you."

The White Wolf sat back on his haunches and gave me his best flat stare. "He was waiting. And stronger than you thought. Strong enough to shake my grip. Not terribly refined, though. And he seems tied to a physical strategy."

I shook the dust from my long coat pointedly. "I noticed that. So did everyone else in the neighborhood with ears to hear."

"There's no need for sarcasm," he snapped.

"Did you discover anything useful?"

"He was never human, but he's using a corrupted human form."

"Corrupted human? Corporeal?"

"Corporeal enough to give you problems. I'm surprised he hasn't taken the fight to you directly."

I shook my head, ignoring the wicked gleam in the White Wolf's eyes. I had begun to develop a feel for the nature of my prey. The deliberate and heavy evocation of mood indicated a broad sadistic streak. "This one feeds on fear," I said. "He has no interest in killing."

"Not yet."

I gave the White Wolf a stern glance, which he shrugged off with wolfish indifference. It has been my experience that the shackles of enforced service rest uneasily on nature spirits. "Have you caught the scent of any old trauma in the building?"

"Like a murder?" he asked, grudging respect audible in his harsh voice. "It's a nice thought, but even though this thing is wearing a corrupted human form, it doesn't have a human source."

"So, what did it taste like?"

He laughed a wolf laugh, tongue lolling. "Corrupted flesh. Human flesh. But that was a mask. Underneath that . . . something wild. Something thriving on the lack of protection in this place. Something quite inhuman but fascinated by all things human. A taint of the Fae."

I rubbed my chin as I considered. "Nothing better than that?"

"He was fast, strong, and waiting, though he wasn't ready for me. I managed to get a piece of him, but when he shifted out of there, he had plenty of power left to cover his tracks."

The White Wolf turned, and I followed him down the third floor hallway. The floor gave under my tread, a soggy feeling like stepping on flesh. Jaundiced light bled from incandescent bulbs burning in yellowed glass globes set high on the walls in both stairwell and hallway. Shadows played around my feet like swarms of rats.

The door where the White Wolf had triggered the trap had vanished, along with a considerable part of the doorway. The force of the trap had pulverized the globe of the light on the wall across from the door. A crater opened in that wall at about chest-height, breaking through the drywall and into the timber and brick of the outer wall. Only traces of the door frame remained. The hole in the plaster across from the doorway gaped wide in a grimace filled with splintered studs like broken teeth. Had I been standing in that doorway during the attack, I would have become a large stain on the remaining wood and masonry.

The White Wolf turned through the splintered remnants of the doorway, but I hardly needed him to guide me. I could still see the overlay of power wreathing the place like dirty smoke. I stepped into the room. Through the past I heard the distant murmur of old voices. No furniture stood in the room beyond. Empty light sockets stared down at the bare hardwood floor. The sharp tang of cleaning chemicals hit my nose, and the gleam of freshly scrubbed wood met my searching gaze.

To my sorcerer's senses, a sweaty perfume of fear lay heavy on that room, despite the efforts to scrub it away. I would have bet that the last tenants had moved for a good reason. I followed that scent of fear, and saw the White Wolf sitting in the middle of a large, empty room at the back of the apartment.

Cautiously, I opened my sorcerous awareness further. The shock of sudden images hit my mind—*fear, and the sense of being small and vulnerable in a large and hostile world, alone, loved ones dead but still walking and talking with some other thing inside, features sloughing away from familiar faces like ill-fitting masks, skin rolling away from bodies like old laundry to reveal something jagged and alien underneath, and the voice of a dead man whispering words too awful to hear*—and I pulled back instinctively from their fading strength.

"This was the nursery."

The White Wolf flinched as I straightened and glared at him. "I'd figured that much out for myself, thank you."

I could feel Blade bristling within me. "He fed here. He fed on *children*."

"No wonder they moved," I said into the silence. "The children's nightmares would be growing worse, night after night. Children's dreams are powerful things. They gave our visitor a chance to get a handle on this world, as well as allowing him to build a tremendous power reserve from their fear. But he's not here now."

The White Wolf looked at me sidelong. "This isn't his lair. This was simply the best place for him to lay his trap."

"So where is he, then?" I turned in an angry circle. "He has too heavy a presence here to track through all of this. And you said he wasn't subtle."

The White Wolf's icy eyes narrowed. "I said he wasn't refined. He's not a native of this place. He's not at home here. That doesn't mean that he is without a plan. Or that he can't lay a trap, for that matter."

I nodded. "And the trail led you up." I turned, and felt the White Wolf at my back like a chill breath of arctic air. I paused, lowering my head. "Would you contest your service, then?"

His momentary silence held a strong undercurrent of calculation. "No. But I would warn you. He may be out of place, but this one is strong. Terribly strong."

"Strong enough to take me, you think?"

A low whuff of air curled over my shoulder. "You've surprised me before."

I laughed. "You're actually concerned."

"Just trying to bring you to see reason." He sounded affronted. "Most of the Legion lies dormant. Perhaps you should awaken them."

"And risk the distraction of my roused host, with no prey at hand to give them? I think not."

He said nothing else as he followed me down the stairs, but I could feel his disapproval like a gathering storm at my back. Good. If he were angry enough, perhaps he'd take his frustrations out on the opposition.

The stairs creaked underfoot, the oppressive echoes of childhood nightmares fading as we descended. I kept my ethereal senses extended, analyzing the framework of power that ran through the square of the building like a decaying vine threading through a sagging lattice. But this spirit had a crafty touch. Brooding shadows pulled me in several directions at once. In every apartment I felt sure a trap would be waiting, carefully prepared and lovingly fed on the fears of sleeping innocents.

I knew better than to play that game.

I descended to the ground floor and searched through the apartments, looking for a weak spot in the fabric of decay that draped the building. The White Wolf stalked cautiously at my side; Blade stood ready at the edges of the stillness-in-motion that I had long ago fashioned into the stronghold of my spirit. I deliberately stayed away from the active traces of my enemy that ran through the shadows of that place like blood thickening in the veins of a corpse. I sought the places between shadows until I found what I needed in the kitchen of a corner apartment.

The curtains had been drawn back from the windows, though the light faded before it touched the clean hardwood floor. Shadows clustered there less thickly than I had seen in the rest of the building, and the taint that lingered there held its position grimly and with effort. Every utensil in the kitchen stood neatly racked. The broad expanse of white stone countertops gleamed with diligent daily scrubbing. That kitchen had all the hallmarks of a finely tuned machine running smoothly under a firmly assured hand. I wondered if it was the Old Woman's kitchen.

I glanced at the White Wolf. "Perfect."

His eyes sparkled impishly. "My faith in you is restored, oh master."

"If you ever lose the sarcasm, I may just expire of shock."

"And what will you use as bait for your trap?"

I reached to a round glass container racked among many on one polished counter top, poured out a handful of the fine grains within, and carefully sprinkled the salt into a neat white circle on the smooth surface of the floor. "You said that he had little finesse, remember? So I will deal with him head on. I will not bait him to this place, but rather I will hale him here to answer me."

"Bold." The White Wolf sat back on his haunches. "Could be dangerous. What if he's too strong for you?"

"If he's too strong for me here, away from all of his prepared places, then subtlety will do me little good in the end," I said mildly. "Don't you agree?"

He muttered a snarl under his breath, but did not answer.

I set the White Wolf to guard. Then I relaxed in front of my circle of salt, ready to begin my summoning.

Words and gestures are for the crowd, really. Sorcery is a matter of will, aided at times by symbolism. My summoning was less than flashy. To an outside observer, it would probably have looked as if I'd gone to sleep on my feet.

Through half-open eyes, I saw the shadows in the room grow and twist, as if cast by bare, gnarled trees bowing before a great storm. The darkness grew heavier, and with it came a wind—a roaring gale that tore doors from cupboards and scattered the contents across the room. The unnatural fury smashed containers sitting quietly on shelves, and flung fragments of glass about the room like a malevolent whirlwind. Through all this rage, no fragment touched me, and not one grain of salt was disordered.

I leaned forward and spoke quietly to the circle. "It does you no good, as you see. I am protected."

The wind died, and two carious, yellow eyes opened in the empty air in the middle of the salt circle. "Who are you, who would dare summon me?"

I grinned, bowed mockingly. "You might think of me as a sort of spiritual thug, a kind of ghostly gun for hire. I am a sorcerer. My name is Zethus. And you are?"

The eyes flickered, as if lit from behind by a candle flame. I had to crane my neck to look up at them. "Fear itself."

He spoke in the voice of the whirlwind. The building shuddered to hear him speak. I reached into my pocket, drew out a pack of cigarettes, shook one out, and lit it casually with a flame I called to dance from the tip of my left thumb. I puffed out the flame, leaned back into the empty air, pulled my legs up, and floated there, supported by the White Wolf's power over the air. "I doubt that," I said. "Sorry. I'm all out of fear today. Would you like some tobacco?"

Golden eyes glared down at me through the rising wisps of smoke. "Foolish mortal . . ."

I took a drag and let the smoke curl out of my nostrils. "You're right. Probably not."

Some cultures say that tobacco protects by some innate power in its essence, as if the addiction in it were a live thing to be commanded. In my opinion, tobacco is an aid in these dealings more as a part of the ritual than anything else. If a practitioner can casually light a cigarette and take an insolent puff or two, it expresses a level of confidence that can be nothing but off-putting to the foe. So much of sorcery is confidence. Besides, tobacco often helps cover the smell of an opponent, and this can be no small thing in many cases.

The golden eyes closed, and when they opened, a ragged form misted into view behind them, growing visibly more solid with each passing instant. Jagged lines crisscrossed the angular body the spirit had taken, painted in raw flesh. The lips of countless wounds gaped as he shifted his weight. Muscles and ligaments and tendons could be seen writhing through the fissures like snakes when he moved. Dark drops of blood spattered the floor like rain and streaked his body in black ribbons.

I glanced at the circle of floor ringed by gleaming white salt and watched the blood begin to pool. "The whole Jigsaw Man routine's been done, you know. You should relax. Think of this as an interview."

The golden eyes blinked. "What?"

"An interview." I took another considering drag on the cigarette, then leaned forward in a friendly way. "Look. I've been sent to bring you out of here. And while I do that, I'm evaluating you. I want to see if you have what it takes to join my Legion. I want to see what you're made of." My gaze flicked back to the cascading blood. "Besides discarded body parts, I mean."

He reared back and brought both fists crashing forward. His hands stopped above the salt as if they'd run into an invisible wall. Blood sprayed out around them, outlining the curve of the salt circle and running down to join the blood lapping at the edge of the salt without actually touching it. "Insolent sorcerer! I am of the Wild Hunt, Blood and Bone! Though I have gone far from my haunts, still I will have the respect due me!"

He slammed his fists into the barrier again. This time the building shook with the impact. I glanced down to see a dark spot creep into the white curve of the salt.

I straightened my legs to stand once more on solid ground. "No more time to play," I said curtly. "You're too dangerous to add to the Legion. I'd like to introduce you to someone. Several someones, actually. The Captains of my Legion. They're here for . . . well . . . you."

He raged on as I spoke their names, but as they came, a silence grew around the circle. "Blade."

At my right hand rose a tall, hooded form, face a dim blur beneath the hood of his cloak. He held a sword upright in his hands, and the blade burned with white fire.

"Shadow."

A hulking silhouette of absolute darkness slouched into place at my left hand.

"Bright Angel."

Across from Blade at the far edge of the circle of salt, two brilliant semicircles of light opened into an angel's wings. The face could not be seen through the flames of the wings, but a burning sword as red as blood swung loosely from the angel's right hand.

"Bane."

Across from Shadow, a gaunt, manlike shape as pale and hungry as bare bone stepped out of the gloom, silver eyes dimly lit from within, thin lips drawn back to expose jagged teeth.

I watched the four edge in around the silent figure of my prey. "And for his part in the hunt, I give an equal share of the kill to the White Wolf," I said, snuffing the cigarette between thumb and forefinger with a quick twisting motion and closing the ritual.

I could hear the Wolf's claws clicking on the tiled floor behind me as I reached out with my foot and with one swipe broke the circle where the blood had eaten away at the line of salt.

I turned away, a great wind buffeting me from behind. A roaring as of many voices rose to shatter the silence. Then, abruptly, all became still. I turned and surveyed the wreckage of the kitchen, the glass and the scattered salt, as the sun broke through the windows. Of the blood that had filled the circle, not one drop remained.

I met a subdued Vincent outside. He transferred the fee to my account without any questions. He did not doubt that the spirit had gone. I knew without looking back at the building that the pall had lifted, that the stone façade of the brownstone no longer wore the face of death, and that the water ran clean over the stones of the building.

I checked the account, validated the transfer, transferred a small portion back to the sending account, and showed Vincent the transaction. "For the kitchen and the hall. You'll know when you see them."

He nodded wordlessly. I shook Vincent's hand one last time, and to his credit he did not shy from my grip. He had lived in CrossTown long enough to know what it meant to be a sorcerer. That's why he had called me, after all.

I tipped my hat and left that place behind me. Within, I could taste the contentment of my Captains and the White Wolf. Even so, a taint of rot and copper hung at the back of my throat. We needed to take the time to relax a while and digest our most recent conquest. First things first, however; I had a personal piece of business that would not wait, not even on digestion.

CHAPTER II

ALL ROADS may lead to Rome, but they pass through Cross-Town first.

Roads and streets run like veins and arteries through the beating heart of CrossTown. Each runs through all manner of distant and not-so-distant possibilities.

There's a theory in modern physics that posits a universe for every decision we make. Each time we choose, right or left, vanilla or chocolate, high or low, we split into separate universes. A vanilla me here, a chocolate me there, a rocky road with pistachio me somewhere else, and some poor lactose intolerant me further down the line. The dominant me is my subjective reality. In CrossTown, the probable mes collapse into the dominant wave, but all those wandering Ways continually wash other alternate lives, lives meant to be lived in CrossTown, up on its jagged shores.

The names of Roads are choices; the turning and branching of Roads are choices; Roads are physical manifestations of their builders' decisions. Think of Roads like Loxis Falangos and Agiou Nikolaou in my home town of Thebes, flowing together to become Epameinonda. In one possibility, Loxis Falangos dominates, and Epameinonda doesn't exist. In another, Loxis Falangos takes the lead. In a third, Loxis Falangos flows into Epameinonda, and Agiou Nikolaou never carried any merry wanderers on its narrow back.

Think that's unique? Name a town. Take Longfellow and Hawthorne in Saint Louis, Missouri, which flow together, meld, then reappear as separate streets. In one possibility, Hawthorne is the single remaining street. In another, Longfellow takes the name of the blended road. The other Road, the Road not chosen, wanders off through possibility. In Eugene, Oregon, Tenth Street vanishes into a hill, then reappears on the other side. Broadway murders Ninth and has hidden its body and killed its name. In Frankfurt, as with many old cities, Roads change names as they run merrily along, belying their age by twisting and turning like young byways through narrow spaces, desperate to keep their figures trim, caught in a race for eternal youth, spinning off alternate possibilities like dream factories. Every city, every town, as it grows organically, has or develops such Roads.

Everywhere, every place and every time where man or something like him has lived, Roads run into one another, branch, disappear here and reappear over there as if they were quantum tunneling. They run, meet, part, cross again, and form a bewildering Mandelbrot set of linked probabilities.

Beware the Road outside your front door, for it is both old friend and passing stranger.

All those choices, all hooked together, comprise a vast sea of possibility. A knowledgeable traveler can ride the currents in that sea to unimagined destinations. And an innocent, all unknowing, can trip over an errant probability wave and find himself or herself or itself somewhere quite far from home, quite far from ordinary. Even in the distant places, away from Cross-Town, it's surprisingly easy for a traveler to take a wrong step and vanish from his known, small world into a strange place in a larger world. Sometimes those travelers wind up in CrossTown, to stay or to pass through to some other destination waiting in the wings.

CrossTown is the crossroads of probability.

I took a WanderWay from OldTown through CrossTown's Psychedelic Quarter, knowing I had crossed over into the mainstream districts when the outlines of the Way stopped wavering and the sky eased back to hues less painfully bright and no longer maliciously shifting. The markers remained, of course, the violet globes of an anchored Way promising security and stability. High priced real estate lined the Way, towering into the sky. The stiffer the prices and the more crowded the land, the more we tend to build up or down, no matter what our place or time of origin.

People pressed around me, mostly core human stock but mixed through with everything from Faerie Breeds to a gaping pair of Yushrub Bushmen. I shook my head slightly at their conservative trims and swaying progress. They were so obviously yokels that I'd be surprised if they made it past the block without losing most of their hard-earned berries, or picking up a blight from some local hard case. My step never faltered, of course. In CrossTown the rule of survival never changes: it's every sophont for him/her/it/themselves.

That's the major reason I make my home on the outskirts of CrossTown, rather than somewhere in the direction of its stony heart. That, and the lease is cheap. The question of living somewhere other than CrossTown has never been a serious consideration. The advantages of the Ways are too tempting, if you have the will and skill to grapple with them and bend the Ways to your own purposes.

I brought my mind back to the business at hand. I glanced down the endless street at the usual snarl of traffic, sighed, and searched for an open byway—something small, something unmarked and unanchored, a Road less traveled. A few more feet, and I saw what I needed: a small straight path opening between two brownstones, stinking of musky decay and stale urine, fading off into a settling gloom. A tall figure in a full cloak that almost concealed curving arm spurs, wearing a wide-brimmed slouch hat pulled down over his features, stepped into the alleyway ahead of me and faded into transparency after three steps. An impatient traveler like myself.

I followed him onto the unanchored Way, but when I extended my senses the Road thrummed to the deep Gothic hum of NightTown. A WanderWay has restlessness at its heart, a blind questing desire to roam. A WayShaper can guide that desire. The traveler before me had left the Way linked to Night-Town, so I called up a different rhythm from the Way, a mix of tunes and times faster and livelier than NightTown's patient song of the endless hunt.

The smells in the place I was looking to find would have a harder edge than NightTown's, less earthy, with the sharp taint of chemicals and old pollution biting at the back of the throat with each breath. The sound in that place never quite died. When all else faded away the subsonic hum of power snaking through conduits would set a man's teeth on edge and make him long even for the sharp staccato of gunfire just to drown out the inhuman pulse of the place. Vendors could be found there, selling every kind of ware, so long as all the impersonal power of technology lay at the heart of the goods.

The Way responded, turning toward my destination. I took two quick steps, my shoulders hunching slightly as TechTown burned into place around me. Flowers of light opened on all sides, cajoling, pleading, commanding, all in the name of an economy that never slept and under the auspices of a culture that spent its most powerful communication techniques on advertising. The streets were remarkably bare of pedestrians. In TechTown, the skies bore the brunt of the traffic snarl. Between the vast heights of TechTown's superalloy towers snaked layers of flyers, so thick that it has been said that night in TechTown outshines the day, despite the harsh light of the naked sun.

I turned left, strolling down the block toward a small familiar door. It slid noiselessly aside before my hand even brushed its matte black surface. Inside, Joseph Cartaphilos met my eyes, jerked his head toward the side counter, and gave his attention back to the only other customer in the shop. I leaned against the side counter, studying them.

Joseph's customer, a small pale man, shook his head. He wore a purple, mesh muscle shirt and plastic pants. The curling white traceries of cheap implant surgeries covered every exposed inch of skin. "That's not what I'm looking for," he said harshly.

Joseph looked sincerely apologetic. Joseph always looked sincere. It was his gift. "That's what you're paying for. You want current military reflex boost wetware, you pay current military price."

The small man cut his eyes toward me, a snarl curling his lip. His face went slack (his version of thoughtful) and then he nodded sharply. "I'll be back."

Joseph gave him a cheerful smile and secured the door behind him as he left. "Zethus. I've been expecting you."

I gave him a curious look. "Oh? I didn't think I was so predictable."

"It's a little less between visits each time," Joseph said with a smile. "You're developing a reputation." He reached beneath the glass cases, manipulated something, and pulled out a small box. He placed the box on the counter. His eyes on my face, he flicked the lid up. "That what you're looking for?"

My breath hissed between my teeth. I ran one finger lightly down the barrel of the injector. I paused on the single ampule. "Is it a ten?"

Joseph spread his hands. "Hey. I know your current balance better than you do. It's a ten. You wouldn't come for anything else. One golden hour for each year of rejuvenation. Ten golden hours for ten years of life. You're actually slightly ahead of the silver curve right now. You must work your ass off."

I gave him a tight grin. "I'm motivated." I closed the lid carefully and caught his eye. "Make the transfer."

"Done." He cocked his head curiously. "You mind me asking why you do this? Not that I'm complaining, of course. I love a loyal customer. But you've no fondness for the sparkle of Tech-Town or the things we have to offer. I know there are more . . . traditional . . . paths to get what you want. Paths you should be more comfortable with than this. Less expensive paths."

I tucked the box safely beneath my arm. "I have no great love for the life in this place, that's true enough. But those other ways you speak of have costs of their own." I met his eyes squarely. "I know those costs too well to think them any less expensive in the long run."

He pursed his lips as I turned and stepped through the opening door. Blade stood ready, though I did not believe I would need him.

The other man had waited for me, of course. I expected that. He was fast. Worse, he was enough machine that it took me longer to touch his will than I had anticipated. He landed a glancing strike with the edge of his hand to my left temple before I managed to shut him down. Even though I rolled with it, for a few moments I saw nothing but star-shot darkness. I found the wall of the shop and braced myself until the ground steadied under my feet. I leaned back against the cool stone of the tower wall and looked at my attacker. He swayed where he stood, his eyes open and unfocused.

My eyes moved past him to a tall man in a brown cloak who had stopped to regard us both. Beneath the cloak, I knew, he wore a habit as severe and plain as his outer garment. Under that he would be wearing NeoTemplar composite armor, standard equipment along with the variety of weapons he always carried about his person.

The tall man's dark eyes met mine. "Witch."

I rose to my feet slowly. "Knight Commander Vayne."

A number in my Host bristled or quailed, depending on their nature, as he weighed me with his eyes. "Feeding your habit, I see."

Suddenly sweating, I retrieved the box from the ground where it had fallen. I'd lost track of it during the attack. I flicked the lid back. My legs went rubbery with relief as I saw that the ampule remained unbroken. Shaking my head, I pulled the injector out and fitted the ampule in place. I didn't intend to take the chance of losing it again after coming so close to seeing more than five years of hard labor vanish in a single foolish instant.

Vayne's voice thickened with distaste. "You could have the courtesy to indulge your vices in private."

I met his eyes as I triggered the injector and felt ice hit my veins. "You don't have to watch."

He gave me a grim smile. "Yes I do. I still bear responsibility for bringing you to this place. Your sins weigh on me, but one day I will see your soul brought to the light."

I leaned my head back against the wall and smiled as I felt the substance of my purchase spread through my body. A tingling intensity built, an earthy pleasure like a long, slow orgasm, and when the wave passed, the small pains had faded, or at least diminished. Even the throbbing in my head became little more than a memory. "Does your debt weigh so heavily on you, then?"

"A debt is a debt," Vayne said sharply. "I would, of course, prefer to return your favor by saving your eternal soul rather than your miserable life."

"Then you shouldn't take such offense at these treatments. The longer I live, the more chances you have to convert me."

Vayne frowned. "I do not care to be mocked. This unnatural extension of your allotted span is a defiance of the will of God. It gives you nothing more than an opportunity to stray further from the path of righteousness. Your dependence on this drug is a weakness. Not unlike your dependence on that horde of captive demons."

I flexed and stretched, caught again in the wonder of youth renewed. "Damn, the little pains add up so slowly, you forget them until they're gone."

Vayne's hard features suddenly relaxed, and he laughed. "You never listen."

I gave him my best rolling two-step. "Would you rather waste youth on the young? Just let me continue as a cheerful pagan and potential convert for a while longer. You know I am no enemy of the Faith."

"Only by example," Vayne growled.

I neatly tucked the injector and empty ampule back into the box, and tossed the package into a nearby recycler. I turned to my attacker, who still stood loosely, and gave him a single silent command. He folded like an empty suit of clothes.

I grinned at Vayne. "Maybe someone will relieve him of the burden of any loose cash, and he'll wake up a wiser man."

Vayne looked down at him unsympathetically. "I doubt he'll gain any wisdom, though he may lose some cash, if he's foolish enough to be carrying any."

"So were you just passing by, or what?"

"I had an errand to the local Chapter, but I have been trying to find you. You might as well know. Some old friends of ours are back in town. They've been asking about you."

My eyes narrowed. "Whitesnakes?"

He nodded.

I allowed myself a brief pungent editorial, then sighed. "The sons of bitches are persistent, I'll give them that."

"Banishing their Avatar gave you a certain . . . prominence."

My lips twisted. "You mean I'm still number one on their list of people to do." I gave him a sideways glance. "You're in their top five, you know."

He gave me a feral grin. "I always wanted to be popular. Just means I don't have to look as hard for them. I don't like cultists. Give me an honest unbeliever like yourself any day."

"You're becoming corrupt. Too much philosophy. Perhaps one day I will convert you."

Vayne snorted. "Not with your arguments." He gave me a direct look. "Watch your back."

"You as well." I watched him walk back down the lonely street, and disappear down a narrow Way.

A strange man, Anthony Vayne, Knight Commander of the Knights of the New Temple. He'd been my ticket into this land of wonder and wastrels, introducing me to my Master in the Ways as a favor for having helped him out of a sticky situation in a desolate place, back when I'd first lost my way and found myself on the outskirts of CrossTown. From what I'd heard, he'd been around CrossTown for as long as any could remember. He undoubtedly came from down a Way where man's allotted span was considerably longer than it was where I came from—which gave him a certain comfortable room to talk about my desire to stretch what few years I had. I had to admit, though, that in the light of his unexpected depths, I occasionally found myself tempted to curiosity about the faith he followed.

Broke again, feeling ten years younger (guaranteed by warranty) than I had before I'd come to TechTown, I set my feet on the path Vayne had taken, but I chose a different Way. I cut off quickly into the narrow mouth of an alleyway unmarked by anchor lights. As I strolled along, I reached out to the fabric of the Road with senses tuned to years of wandering the Ways. That particular path had been so well used that the Road ahead blurred with myriad destinations. The opposite of the safely anchored main Ways, a wild WanderWay like that small alley could dump an unwary traveler into any one of thousands of variant possibilities.

I touched the living murmur of the Road and ran my senses across it like a bow across the strings of a violin. The Road responded to my touch, throwing up countless promises: smells of rich, spicy food and the sound of low laughter on a quiet summer evening; the full moon riding high in the velvet sky, fat and bright and rich; the quiet lap of water in a cold gray harbor empty of ships, the evening sky dark with the threat of a squall; the sun rising over a hillside house of glass and steel, the lights of the City, father of all cities, spread out below like the fading glitter of fool's gold, the illusion fading but not yet out of reach . . .

I shook my head, pulling back from the promise of the Road, and played a careful, familiar tune, soothing the wild Way and turning it toward a place full of the scent of rain and wet wood, the sound of the storm stalking through the forest on cat's paws to curl around the cold chimney and scratch gently at the cracking paint of the too-thin wooden doors. Ragged wisps of cloud opened and closed against the stars, teasing me with the glimpse of a clear night, and the lights of the city were no more than a bright fog off to the west, while the voice of the wind swallowed all but the sharpest sounds of the bustle of that place.

I took my first step down that Road as my destination solidified, felt the temperature drop, and smiled. I raised my face to taste the rain, letting my long coat catch the wind and spread behind me like the cloak I no longer wore. The house rose before me out of the rocking clasp of the trees, and the gate flapped in welcome. I crossed into the yard, stopped to secure the gate—reminding myself again to fix that damned latch—and paused to run my hands across the silky cold heads of my jade spirit dogs. They slept peacefully, dreaming light dreams of the hunt and the kill at the end, their slumber undisturbed by any visitors.

I took my front steps two at a time. Mine was a small house, clinging to the edge of CrossTown in a patch of woody real estate secured only by my will and the anchors I had built there over the last few years. When winter came, the wind always found whatever chinks I had missed the summer before, but it was private and it was mine, and that was all that mattered to me. Not least of the benefits of having the skills of a WayShaper is the ability to carve lebensraum out of amorphous possibility. The rural nature of my neighborhood meant there were no other dwellings in immediate proximity to my own, and I liked it that way. Chimereon, my closest neighbor, was a carnivorous serpent-goddess whose realm extended into a forest much deeper and darker than my own quiet patch of woodland. That stretch of wild lands buffering my place from her temple suited us both. We had exchanged visits when I first came to stake my claim out at the edge of her realm, and she turned out to be good company, with a mutual interest in chess. I hadn't seen her for some time. Good fences, good neighbors, and all that.

The front door opened at my touch. As I stepped over the threshold the lamps flared to cold brilliance and fire leaped in the hearth.

"Welcome home," Silver said quietly.

I shucked my coat and tossed it casually across the back of an overstuffed chair, sprawling and split from years of shaping itself to my body. "Anything happen while I've been away?"

"Nothing much. A couple of stray dire wolves from Goblin-Town. The riders were most apologetic." Silver's voice had no more inflection than usual, which is to say, none at all. A mote of light danced at the edge of one wall. Silver's voice radiated from that. Everyone should have a housekeeper like Silver to watch over the grounds while they're away.

"Any damage?"

"None to the property. They were too smart to cross any boundaries. Terrorized the local wildlife a bit. Nothing serious."

I sat and pulled off my boots. "I'm surprised Chimereon didn't take umbrage."

"She was out hunting. I would imagine that's the reason the goblins were so apologetic. No one wants to be on the bad side of that daughter of Quetzalcoatl."

I laughed. "She does take her cold-bloodedness to an extreme. Any messages?"

"One moment."

I sat back, stretching while he checked with the Bank of Hours. He would also have the water heating and let me know when it was ready for my shower. My muscles were loosening, relaxed as the rejuvenation treatment continued to work through my system. A hot shower would be a nice way to help that process along.

"Four messages," Silver said abruptly. "One from Chimereon. One from Grimly Carvebone. One from Eliza Drake. One from undisclosed source. And your balance has been updated."

My eyes narrowed. "Undisclosed source? What's the disclosure fee?"

"More than your current balance."

I frowned. "Chimereon's message is predictable, given the Goblins and their unruly mounts. She probably wanted to know if I had any axes to grind that she could add to her own. As a courtesy, of course. Carvebone would be one of the Goblins, yes?"

"Correct. And the Lady Drake will undoubtedly be extending the usual invitation."

I closed my eyes and pinched the bridge of my nose. "Undoubtedly. I'll give her one thing: she's persistent. What's my current balance?"

"One golden hour, twenty-seven silver hours, thirty-four iron hours, and three bronze hours."

I opened my eyes, my frown deepening. "Not that I'm complaining, but that's one gold more than I thought I had. Have you been holding out on me?"

Silver refused to be baited. "With the message you were advanced one conditional golden hour from an undisclosed source."

"Open the message."

On the wall across from me, a vertical line of light flared to life, and then turned sideways. Distinctive black calligraphy flowed across the white background silently:

To the human sorcerer known as Zethus, I send salutations. The advance you have been given is conditional on meeting my messenger at Sidelines Altaforte within one hour of opening this message. You are bound to nothing beyond this meeting by the deposit to your account.

Silver closed the display. "That short text is all that the message contained."

I sighed and reached for my boots. No rest for the wicked. "Trash the Goblins' message. They're just trying to drum up some support, now that they know who they crossed. Chimereon can deal with them as she sees fit. I'll look at her note later. The messenger will already be traveling to Sidelines Altaforte, I would imagine."

"You don't suspect a trap?"

"I can't turn down the fee. And since that message had all indications of a Faerie invitation, I certainly would not rule out the possibility of a trap. But Nuada Silverhand's more subtle than that, and I have more favorable than unfavorable contacts over past the fields we know, so it's worth the risk."

"And the message from Eliza Drake?"

I thought about my earlier conversation with Joseph, about the prices paid for immortality. I'd had conversations with Eliza in mind since then. I'd known her a long time. I'd met Eliza Drake originally while I had been on a job for my Master in the Ways, Matthias Corvinus. Eliza had her own skills in WayShaping, as well as other abilities in the domains of life and death. Those abilities were rare among vampires, and that gave her a certain independence. She also had to deal with certain limitations, due to her circumstances. Undeath isn't a free ride. Vayne, of course, didn't approve of Eliza. Eliza had become too comfortable with darkness for Vayne's taste, but I didn't share Vayne's prejudices. "Save it too," I told Silver. "Always keep your options open."

"As you wish."

I stood, pulled my coat around my shoulders, and walked out into the wind, deciding that I must have imagined the distaste I had heard in Silver's voice at the last.

CHAPTER III

THE IDES of March had come to Rome, and Caesar had that hunted look in his eye. I watched the odds shift in the top left corner of the big screen as he descended the steps of Pompey's Theater, and idly wondered what the variation on this particular line of possibility might be, down some distant Way.

Senators poured down around him, and Caesar's eyes rounded with fear as he saw the glitter of knives rise above him. Surround sound clearly delivered the scraping of the blades on bone, the dull impact of hilts meeting flesh, and then the crowd pulled back and parted for a tall, muscular man who wore his toga with spare elegance.

Caesar's eyes dimmed as they rose to the man standing quietly on the steps above him. Caesar's Latin remained terse and elegant down to his last breath. "Even you, Brutus?"

Brutus snorted, looked past his dying leader, and caught the eye of the waiting centurion. The soldiers opened ranks, and two burly legionnaires manhandled a cursing Marc Antony out into the open. Brutus nodded once, and the centurion drew a *pugio*. Antony's struggles grew frenzied and his cursing took on a shrill edge. The centurion took two long steps and thrust the wide blade up under Antony's ribcage. Antony stiffened, and bright blood burst out of his mouth. When he stilled, the legionnaires dropped his body to the cold stone. The centurion turned, his men reforming ranks under his watchful eye, and set his century in motion. Brutus watched the senators pick their slow way down the steps, dripping blades dangling, forgotten in many hands, careful to avoid the blood pooling around the two bodies, and he smiled.

I nodded and took my eyes away from the screen. A Brutus with the conscience and political instincts of a Stalin. Down that particular Way, Octavian wouldn't see his nineteenth birthday. The development of Rome would be interesting without Augustus.

My gaze ran across the weapons hanging from the walls: racked swords and splintered lances from the First Crusade; broken shields from the fall of Byzantium; automatic rifles from frozen Chozen with the butts split from having been used as clubs in close quarters. Between these Momento Belli hung scraps of parchment bearing quotes from Dante and Pound, and over the door the infamous image fluttered: a headless body holding its head before it like a lantern, the eyes in the head burning with a rage bright enough to light the way. Bertrans de Born had come a long way from Altaforte, but at least his place felt homely to him, and he kept to his main interest, making considerable money from the side bets on all manner of conflict.

No one had an eye for conflict like Bertrans de Born.

Bertrans had done well for himself with that eye of his. Analogues and parallel possibilities across the Ways are a dominant gaming variant in the gambling subculture of CrossTown. The complexity of betting on alternative personalities in variant possibilities, like a Rome dominated by a sociopathic Brutus, brings an appeal that outshines something as mundane as a horse race. Also key to the common interest is the ephemerality of those distant shifting possibilities. The closer you get to CrossTown proper, the more alternate possibilities are absorbed into the massive probability wave of the CrossTown timeline. Doppelgangers can exist in CrossTown, but they have to be far enough removed as analogues not to collapse into the subjective timeline of the dominant probability. Bertrans had a gift for sifting through the distant Ways and finding situations skewed slightly, subtly, and unpredictably to draw his clientele.

I scanned the room, looking for my client. My gaze flicked past men and women of all types, some not even clearly mainstream stock, though in the dim shadows of the bar even an experienced observer like myself could have some difficulty separating cosmetics and bodymods from uncommon genetic variants or simple supernatural beasties. In the distant motion of the crowd I caught glimpses of the familiar sight of a werewolf on the make and the burning lure of a vampire on the hunt, but even the denizens of NightTown did not move in isolation, for I noticed the humming cameras of Calvar Trueheart flying a search pattern above the crowd. I spotted his armored form leaning on the bar. He seemed to be casually hitting on a cat-breed waitress, his Aryan features lit by flickering holo feeds, his gaze never straying too far from the camera pickups. In his sparkling blue eyes there lived a certain hope that some hapless creature of darkness might cross over the line and make themselves available to be featured on the next episode of *Paladin's Progress*. Posthumously, of course.

I shook my head in disgust. Just the typical CrossTown sports bar crowd, and no sign of my client. I glanced at my watch. I'd give my contact one more minute. Times weren't that hard and I didn't need the work that badly.

A glimmer of motion caught my eye, a sparkling luminescence dancing like a candle flame that had lost its wick. A mental tingle swept across me as I felt Blade shift to strengthen his barrier, my first line of defense. I turned my head slightly, narrowing my eyes and then smiling as I recognized the emerald glitter of my mentor's chief servant.

I allowed my sight to shift over to the spiritual more heavily, the sparkling, green cat eyes now clearer than the dim, dancing figures drifting along the dance floor like a dream. "Sapienta. What news?"

As always, I could taste a touch of laughter in Sapienta's voice. "Matthias Corvinus requests your presence, at your earliest convenience. If you will be delayed, meet him down by the sea."

Down by the sea meant down in DeepTown, at his retreat in the caves. "How important is it? I'm supposed to be meeting a client at the moment."

"Important enough for him to send me to find you. Important enough that he wants to discuss the matter face to face." Sapienta paused. "Is this a long term job, or a short one?"

"Haven't met the client yet," I said with a shrug. "All I've seen is a gold deposit at the Bank of Hours and a note requesting this meeting."

I caught a spark of speculation leaping in the cat eyes. "Gold. A respectable sum for a dangerous job. Princely just for a meeting. And he said at your earliest convenience . . ."

I frowned. "Is that all he said? Nothing else?"

"Important, and your earliest convenience. And down by the sea if you're delayed. I leave the interpretation up to you. I have delivered the message. I must go."

And like a candle flame that has been blown out, the dancing emerald glow vanished.

I glanced around the room once before shifting my sight back to the physical, deciding that this client had pushed the matter as far as possible. I'd even refund the fool's deposit, all but the hour I'd wasted here, of course. Last I checked, I was rated over a silver myself.

As I shifted back, I caught a glimpse of a looming figure solid against the shifting backdrop of the crowd. Blade rang a warning in my head as I let all but the usual light overlay of my active spiritual senses slip away. "I know. I see him."

He had the height of a Sidhe lord. He wore his human form like an unaccustomed suit of clothes, flowing across the dance floor and through the crowd with inhuman ease and grace, painting his illusory body lightly over every motion. His course carried him relentlessly toward my table. I could feel the soldierly elements of my personal Legion scrambling to the alert.

Looking past him, I locked eyes with the vampire, who had glanced up from the sappy smile of his victim/date to follow the movements of the newcomer. Fangs flashed at me briefly, and then the vampire no longer stood there and the door flapped in the breeze. Perhaps the vampire knew something about the messenger that I didn't.

Perhaps he had a bladder problem.

I shifted my gaze back across the table, and the newcomer smiled down at me, his hand coming to rest on the back of the chair across from me. "Zethus?"

I nodded. "Have a seat."

He pulled the chair out, but extended his other hand. I rose grudgingly, and let his long fingers curl around mine. His skin felt cool and dry, with no hint of the power within. That made him all the more dangerous.

Blade had every defense raised. Behind him I could feel the bulwark of the others. Even the Sleepers wrapped in their prison of curves stirred in their slumber, and it had been many years of weirdness since the last time that had happened. I had not added my own will to the defenses yet, for that would have been discourteous, but neither did I call my Legion down from the walls of my spirit.

He took his hand from mine, and sat across from me, smiling slightly. "I apologize for being late. The Way was . . . difficult."

I didn't see an easy response to that, so I didn't make one.

His smile widened. "Are you ready?"

My eyes narrowed. "I haven't agreed to take the job, yet."

He shook his head. "That's not what I asked. We'll get to that soon enough. But first, are you ready?"

I had been trying to place him, knowing he stood high in the ranks of Danu's Children, yet not identifying him. But that question stirred something. I recognized him. My will burned along the borders of my mind, but even here, if he had come for me, I did not think I could successfully resist him. "What is your name?"

He laughed. "You know me, do you not?"

I leaned forward, looking into those eyes that shaded quickly from blue to black, and searched for a glimmer of starlight. "What is your name?"

The shape of his face changed, rounded, the cheekbones becoming less prominent, and the eyes darkened, though a glimmer rose within their midnight depths. "Do you want to ask that question, Zethus?"

We played an old game, as old as mankind, old even when I walked the green earth, and if he had come for me, then I had little hope of challenging him. "What is your name?"

His features finished shifting, and for but an instant I looked into a face mirroring my own. Then he leaned back, his mask slipping back to the lean, aristocratic arrogance he had worn when he had first walked into this place. His smile showed too many teeth. "Why, I go by many names. Some call me Halfjack, for my duties ever take me between the mortal realm and my own, and some call me Shadowjack, for the same reason. But you, sorcerer, you may simply call me Jack."

I kept my voice low. "Mr. Fetch, what could you want from me?"

He leaned forward, swallowing his smile. The expression in his midnight eyes chilled me where I sat. For an instant, I felt the touch of Death, and my Legion of Captive Powers shuddered as the walls of my spirit rang under the hammerblow of his gaze. "Do not call me that in this place, man. Do not call me by that name ever."

I pulled my eyes away from his with effort, shaking my head as he leaned back and grinned at me. I didn't even try to match that grin. We knew where we stood. I had broken his gaze. That would be about all I could manage. He could take me any time he wanted me, Legion and all. Death looked out through those laughing eyes, and I was no immortal, in spite of my TechTown years. Not a good moment for my ego.

I hate bargaining from a position of weakness.

I drew in a deep breath, met his eyes deliberately, and put my hands flat on the table. "I repeat. What could you want from me?"

His eyelids drooped lazily. He studied me as a cat watches a mouse. "Why, mortal man, I want to take you on a journey, of course."

I started to push my chair back from the table. He held up one long, thin hand. "Relax. It's not what you think. In this case, I am messenger and guide. The deposit was just for this meeting, and those funds are yours. But there is someone I represent who has a job for you. Answer me one more question. Of your Legion of Captive Powers, how many are Fae?"

I glared at him. "Is this a trick question? I haven't made Fae my specialty, and work for the most part out of CrossTown. A few have Faerie origins, as I'm sure you know, but most are local, or from down distant Tracks. I've taken every one of them fairly, in single combat . . ."

"I'm not questioning the legitimacy of your prey," he said. "But the fact that you have a mixed Legion, the fact that you do not specialize, the fact that you are old and experienced but not weary, and the fact that you are of a stock most mortal, all give you particular . . . credentials for the job at hand."

I looked at him suspiciously. "And what is the nature of the job?"

"Call it pest control." He grinned. "More I am not allowed to tell you. You will have to speak with your employer to find that out. I am simply a guide. I will take you there and bring you back, unharmed. I was instructed to tell you that you have not committed to anything if you follow me. And there is another forty-nine hours in it, just to hear the proposal. All gold."

I licked my lips. That offer touched my greed, so I knew the job would be dangerous. And Fetch himself to guide me. But Corvinus wanted to talk to me, and he said it was important.

"How soon would we leave?"

"As soon as possible. The Tides favor the Summer Country right now, so for every minute spent in CrossTown, five will have passed on the Other Side."

I pulled back deeper behind the walls of my spirit for a moment, and contacted Keeper. "Do you have a current download of the Temporal Tidetables?"

Round, violet eyes blinked, then Keeper grunted. "Yes."

"Faerie to CrossTown?"

"Five:One."

I might be able to do this and still make it to Corvinus without irritating him unduly. As a colleague in a somewhat rarefied profession, I owed Corvinus respect. As my onetime sponsor and Master in the Ways, I owed him more than that. But he had said at my earliest convenience, and he understood business.

"I'll accompany you into the Summer Country and listen to the offer."

"Excellent," he said. "And the transfer has been made to your account. Shall we go?"

I rose as he did, and followed as he led the way out through the crowd. Outside, a yellow cab driver cussed a horse and coach in a cockney accent. The horse didn't look impressed, and neither did the scaly coachman. Jack walked with a long, even stride, and I stayed close as he turned from the glitter of the anchor lights and down the shadowy recesses of a WanderWay. Shadows curled around us. His hand caught my elbow and steadied me as a great rushing murmur surrounded us, and the world spun sickeningly underfoot.

He pushed me forward, and we stepped out of the shadow of rearing golden trees, through lush grasses an impossible shade of green that whispered around our feet, and into the soft, directionless light of Faerie.

CHAPTER IV

FETCH LED me up a twisting path marked out through the grasses by waist-high stones staggered at ten foot intervals. Trees stretched up and around us. As we continued I saw that all the local wood had golden foliage and bark of burnished bronze. To the north a darkening came over the distant trees, and even from that range I could sense the independent hostility of that place.

It is wise to pay attention to such feelings in Faerie.

The path wound out through the whispering grasses. I could hear laughter ringing in the light breeze that rose up around us as we walked. The trees clashed their metallic leaves rhythmically, not quite in time with the wind, and while I could barely discern the intonations of speech, the words eluded me. Something about Faerie always left me feeling like a slightly dull child, overhearing but not quite understanding the adult conversation passing over my head.

I dogged the heels of my guide. Slowly the trees drew away around us, until I beheld the glorious span of a Faerie castle. Tall, narrow, glittering like a polished jewel, the castle had a delicately, sharp, crystalline feel to it. Conservative architecture, for the Fae. A stream of shining water reached out of the distant hills to hold the castle in a crooked embrace, then stretched silvery fingers off down through the grass and into the golden forest.

The path we trod led us down and along that water. As we walked into the brighter light, out from under the shelter of the trees, I saw that a dark shadow flitted along at Jack's heels, though the light remained directionless. I cast no shadow, not even a pale shade. And when we came to the stream, I could see Jack's profile clearly in the bright waters, as if they were a mirror, but according to that chuckling brook, he walked alone but for a thin twisting distortion like waves of heat dancing above a fire. No reflection of mine stared back.

"This land doesn't recognize me."

Fetch glanced back at me. "I thought you had been here before."

"Twice. Once as Aengus' guest at the Dagda's court, and once as Oisin's guest at Lugh's court."

"Where you offended Silverhand."

I shrugged. "He was drunk. So was I."

Jack grinned like a wolf. "Drunk or not, he remembers."

I smiled wanly. "Holding grudges seems to be a hobby of Powers."

"It is," Jack said seriously. "And you should be complimented that Silverhand feels you worth the trouble. Regardless, both times you were a guest, and the masters of those lands extended the courtesy of recognition. In this case, the master of this land isn't going to the trouble, and you have neither the age, nor the power to make much of an impression on this place."

I snorted. "Thanks. So I'm not a guest, then?"

Jack shook his head, long hair falling across the midnight depths of his eyes. "You are a prospective employee."

"I'll have to remember that, and be suitably insolent," I said.

Jack chuckled. "You already have more than enough insolence for any two mortal sorcerers."

I couldn't think of a witty enough reply to that, and I wanted to appreciate the sight of the castle spires rearing over us, parting the distant puffs of cloud like mountain peaks, so I said nothing.

Movement stirred at the gates. A figure in ornate full plate armor stepped forward. A squad in similar armor stood erect around the gates. More armored forms stood unmoving on the battlements.

I looked at Jack, cocking an eyebrow. "Gothic plate?"

"The master of this place has certain fond memories of high chivalric romances," he said with some amusement. "It would be wise to remember that. Address her as Lady."

"You're kidding."

The knight chose that moment to salute us both. "Well met, Messenger of Death. I see that your errand met with success."

I glanced at Jack, to see if his teeth were grinding, but he wore a deliberately pleasant expression on his face. "Puck, why don't you and your little band of tricksters find something else to do?"

Merriment colored the voice issuing out of the helm. "I thought you knew. Same as you, I'm working off a debt. Though the torment of this place is almost worth it such times as this, oh Messenger of Death, when I have the chance to have a little fun with her Ladyship's guests." The helmet swiveled toward me. "What about it, buddy? Best two out of three?"

"Not unless you're part of the job. I don't work for free."

A moment of silence ensued. I had the impression that Puck was busy reexamining his first evaluation of me.

Jack stalked on past Puck. I followed, my stride more relaxed than his. I knew of Puck, prankster extraordinaire, and while I wasn't surprised that he had wound up in a position to owe someone service, I was amazed at the thought of anyone successfully enforcing his payment of such a debt. Then I thought of someone successfully demanding the cooperation of Fetch. I decided then to stay on my best behavior with the Lady.

We stepped through a rainbow of flowers that wreathed the dropped drawbridge, while below brilliant colors of myriad fish burned through the clear, sparkling waters of the moat. Beautiful, like all things of Faerie, and like all things of Faerie, every flower had its poisoned thorns. In the depths of those clear waters I could see golden fish swimming lazily through the clean, white lines of stripped bone.

We stepped out of the light and into the glittering light of the keep itself. A gentler sparkle relieved the stress of Faerie's relentless light, and countless diamond pinpoints shone against umber stone as if some Faerie craftsman had stolen pieces of star-filled evening to hang as tapestries in the Lady's hall.

I felt Blade twitch, responding to my rising concern. I had seen the splendor of the Royal Sidhe courts and the power of Faerie Principalities, and this place was second to nothing I had seen. I opened my senses slightly. Instead of the overwhelming roar of the competing essences of many Sidhe Lords and Ladies, I felt instead a controlled threnody, like a subtle and mighty choir of voices all raised in orchestrated gentle lamentation. My sorcerer's sight adjusted as we walked, tuning itself to the harmonies of that place. The movement of inhuman, ghostly wraiths swam around Jack and me through currents of power like the fishes in the moat we had passed over. They danced a choreographed routine in time to the unheard music of that place, attending to errands and tasks I could not fathom, but that I knew must exist by the very purpose of their motion.

I began to understand what I had walked into. The metallic taste of fear rose in the back of my throat. I clamped down on the stirring Blade. "Stay low, but wary."

I felt his response, as well as the gentle awakening of the other Captains of my Legion. It gave me some reassurance, empty though it might have been, to know that they were ready. Even waking the Sleepers would have been of little help in that place.

We crossed through the entry hall into a vast room. Huge spheres turned ponderously in distant corners, dappling everything in the room with silver light. She waited in the center of the room, bathing in the light. Her arms opened wide. She turned slowly, suspended in thick tides of brilliance. I tried to think of how she might be described. More than merely inhuman in her perfection of form and feature, looking upon her could only be compared to looking on some vast and overpowering phenomenon, like the explosion of a star. Of course, the fact that I could taste both degree and kind of the power radiating from her like light from the sun may have had something to do with that.

As she turned to face us, clothed only in the light, I felt not the slightest stirring of lust. Mortal terror can be a remarkable anti-aphrodisiac. I had never looked on such raw power unveiled, though I had seen glimpses of it in Lugh. But then, Lugh had bothered to be subtle. She opened her eyes, and looked into mine. I shivered and deliberately dropped my gaze.

That was the most difficult thing I had ever done.

When she spoke, her voice reached out to stroke each nerve ending in my body individually. With effort, I deliberately recalled what I had seen swimming in her eyes before I had torn my gaze away. Down boy. Black widows had nothing on her. "Zethus. I am pleased that you have come here to me."

"Lady." I swallowed, thought about a cigarette and quickly discarded the idea. I didn't think I could pull it off, and this wasn't the time for half measures. "What could you possibly want from me?"

She laughed. "I need a human sorcerer, Zethus. You come highly recommended."

I pulled my hat low, risking a quick look from under the brim. "I hate to tell you this, but I can't do anything for you that you can't do better. I've never met a Fae sorcerer before, but you have more power and control locked away here than I have ever seen. Lady."

She dimpled. "Why thank you. The clarity of your vision confirms my selection of you for this task. But as you said yourself, my power is locked away here. I am a creature of place, Zethus. I need your human mobility. And more than that, I need your human immunity to the fires of the bones of the earth."

I nodded, though I had never heard iron described in quite that way. "What do you want done for you?"

"A small thing. A trifle. I have a nuisance on the border of my demesne that I would be rid of."

My eyebrows shot skyward. "And you want me for this?"

Her teeth gleamed like pearls, small, even and slightly pointed. "You have unique qualities I wish to use."

I nodded encouragingly. "Like a lack of sensitivity to the presence of iron."

A hint of disapproval touched her perfect features, like a cloud moving across the face of the sun. "On the border of my domain furthest from the heart of Faerie, the flesh of the earth has pulled away from the bones. That place is . . . uncomfortable for my servants, and limits my vision. For us, the flames of the Mother's fiery birth still rage in the bones of the earth."

I relaxed slightly. "You have a pest control problem. I would expect that this spirit has no trouble with iron, and reason to bear you no good will. Is it a ghost, by chance?"

She smiled. "You mean the spirit of a mortal man, clinging to this place with a strength born of desperate fury and a hot thirst for revenge?"

"Something like that." I kept most of the dryness from my voice.

"Then you know my problem."

"Your messenger told me fifty golden hours for hearing the proposal. How much to complete the job?"

She waved one hand casually. "Another fifty to join the first."

I kept my voice steady. "Anything special I should know? Ghost of a sorcerer, ghost of a saint, that sort of thing?"

She shook her head slowly. "As I told you, my sight is limited in that place. I have little direct knowledge of the nature of this ghost. Will you do this for me?"

I tried not to let naked greed show on my face. Fifty golden hours was the reason I had delayed Corvinus. One hundred golden hours was a princely sum—nearly a century of hard labor for a Silver like myself. A job like this meant more than that, even. It could change my rank with the Bank of Hours from Silver to Gold. No more scraping for rejuvenation treatments and slowly losing ground against the inevitable hand of time. One Hundred golden hours could buy me more than a mortal lifetime of rejuvenation treatments. I knew the job couldn't be easy, not if she were offering that kind of compensation, but then I never had been given the opportunity to earn that kind of compensation.

I licked my lips, already considering how to attack the problem. Scout first, case the situation, determine what additional resources I might need . . . "I'll do it. When do you want me to begin?"

Her face closed off to a mask of ice. "You have fifty hours to complete the task."

I felt a sinking sensation in my innards. Trapped by my own greed. "You said nothing of a time limit."

She continued speaking as if I weren't even present, all pretense at courtesy abandoned. "I will take you as far as I can. Beyond that, it's up to you."

One hand lifted. I felt the world twist around me even as I sputtered protests. Too late, of course, to do me any good. The exchange and contract would already have been registered with CrossTown's Bank of Hours. As well as providing an equitable means of exchange in the chaos of CrossTown's measureless economy, the Bank of Hours acted as a nearly inviolate keeper of transactions. Break a deal registered through the Bank of Hours, and you can't transact with them again. Ever. Crossing the Bank was a one-way ticket out of CrossTown's economy of service.

I looked up at barren, red-streaked hills, and cursed my avarice. If I didn't meet the terms of the contract, more than my fee would forfeit. Indemnities could be crushing, given the size of the fee.

Corvinus had always reminded me to read the fine print. I was young, as CrossTown sorcerers go, with no more than a hundred and fifty subjective years in that place, and already I had earned my way to a silver rating—in large part because I had been willing to brave hazards. I had been one of the lucky few whose skills transposed well into CrossTown's peculiar economy of services, since no matter what shore of the seas of possibility you find yourself washing up on, sorcerers of any significant strength are a rare commodity. But I needed to be ranked higher, I needed to move further faster, because only a Gold could afford to live comfortably and pay for the regular seeds of immortality.

A shadow fell across my path. A hand dropped to my shoulder. "I have to say, I'm impressed with your strength. Most don't display that much composure in a private audience with Titania. All but the Lords of the Fae don't handle themselves as well as you did."

My mouth twisted. I had handled myself right into a deadly situation. The presence of Fetch was no accident. "What now?"

One long finger indicated the path before us that wound up into the hills. "Your prey lies there. I will wait here until you return, or until fifty hours have passed in this place. And then I will come for you."

I looked into his eyes, and found what I expected. If I took too long, Jack would provide the indemnity. I had no illusions about evading him. He would find me, eventually, and take his due.

I turned away from the amused patience in his face and set my feet on the path into the Iron Hills.

CHAPTER V

A WIND as thin and cold as the blade of an assassin's knife whispered through the bare hills. I turned the collar up on my long coat, wishing I had dressed more for warmth and less for style, and listened. The wind spoke in a soft, mysterious voice that trembled at the edge of comprehension.

I detected no taint of any spirit. I shook my head disgustedly. Any hope of a quick and easy end to this had already died an untimely death.

I touched Blade, confirming that he stood ready at the doorways of my spirit, his forces marshaled to repel any sudden spiritual attack, then called on the White Wolf. "What do you think, hunter?"

"I think you've lost your mind, accepting a deal like this," the White Wolf snarled. "Do you have any idea how many square miles of rusty land we'll need to search?"

I couldn't find it in me to upbraid him for his insolence. He was right, after all. "Call up a pack. Use what resources you need to search this land in sections."

The White Wolf reared back, his black eyes widening. "You trust me that far? Or are you that desperate?"

I dropped the veils that cloaked my will and regarded him without pretense.

He crouched, bowing his head and tucking his tail under his belly. Hoarfrost whitened the ground at my feet. "I will do as you say."

I felt nearly a third of the Legion rise to follow as the White Wolf flung himself into the air. Others stirred restlessly, Faerie spirits uncomfortable in the presence of so much iron. I calmed them, my will turning slowly inward around the most uneasy, pressing them down to somnolent quiescence.

My attention turned to my interior world; I had no warning of an external attack. The first blow fell as an explosion of heat behind my right ear. I turned and fell back, the world spinning around me, my vision narrowing to an enormously wide and solid figure, rushing at me with all the freight train irresistibility of an avalanche. I tried to raise my hands in futile defense as his clenched fist swelled to fill my sight . . .

. . . I looked out into the darkness. A solitary figure rose from the ranks. Blade stood as straight as his namesake as he mounted the steps to the central tower where I took my accustomed seat, overlooking the expanse of the fortress of my spirit. A place of power I had built over the years of memory and hope, the fortress of my spirit served as the center of my will. All sorcerers had such a place of power deep within their own psyches. Even as my enemy had taken me physically, I had retreated within to my only remaining safe place.

Cold fire burned in Blade's eyes as he knelt at my feet. "I failed you. I failed to account for the merely physical."

I shook my head, wincing, an echo of the pain remaining even in this place. "The White Wolf and his searchers missed him. I believe he had defenses of his own. He was prepared."

"You suspect a trap, then?"

"Oh, I'm certain it was a trap." I smiled mirthlessly. "I'm simply debating whether the Lady Titania was a part of it."

Blade's burning eyes narrowed. "You think perhaps she acted in the interest of Silverhand?"

"Difficult to say." I examined the assembled Host, counted the empty ranks of the White Wolf's searchers, and noted that the White Rose had taken her own gentler forces and had begun the difficult work of speeding up the natural healing processes of my body. A sweet, light scent rose with the White Rose's ministrations. I pushed the distraction aside and focused on the matters at hand. "Not with Silverhand's knowledge, I think. He has always preferred the more straightforward path. But as a peace offering, perhaps. Or a gift. Truly, I do not understand the Lords of the Sidhe well enough to be sure. You knew your brethren better than I ever will. What do you think?"

"We do not have enough pieces of the puzzle," Blade said. "But I do not see Silverhand's direct presence in this."

I sensed the locks on the doors of consciousness weakening. I took a last moment to reassure Blade. I didn't want his guilt over his fear of iron to interfere with his duties. "Watch well, Captain."

He bowed. I took my leave, rising up through the smoldering layers of awareness, toward the light of the waking world. I steeled myself, fighting resistance to my awakening, laying my will on the barriers until the locks burst open and the doors of consciousness stood wide before me. At the last, my body fought against an early waking, my limbs responding sluggishly.

Pain strengthened as I awoke, until ragged streamers of heat curled through my head and neck. Under that rose the light, floral scent of the White Rose, working gently to ease the source of my pain.

I waited until I could feel the position of my limbs as I lay sprawled on my back against the cold surface of the hills. I did not stir, but opened my eyes slowly to narrow slits. Without turning my head, I spotted my attacker taking his ease on a nearby rocky outcropping.

He grinned at me, revealing a mouthful of pointed teeth. "You're a sneaky one."

I opened my eyes fully, blinking against the light and the pain. My head pounded like a kettledrum in a Tchaikovsky composition. The side of my face felt hot and swollen. I studied my captor, a blocky humanoid the height of a very large man, with narrow, carnivorous features and dead, gray skin. He wore only a jaunty cap, colored the dull, rusty brown of dried blood. His eyes were narrow, ruddy slits, and his hands were the size of shovel blades, the broad fingers tipped with thick, yellow nails like claws.

I licked my lips and said nothing as my pain slowly diminished. I tried to stir, but a powerful force held me trapped and immobile, my limbs held to the rock as if pinned under some vast, unseen weight. I reached for the Legion. They lay beyond my touch, invisible bonds barring more than my limbs. I took a moment to consider before answering him coolly. "Actually, I thought my approach fairly straightforward."

"Not your approach. The insurance." He indicated the swirling patterns visible where my sleeve had ridden up to bare a forearm. "If I hadn't felt them so strongly, I might have made the mistake of killing you and releasing them. And I think those are not restricted to the merely spiritual."

I realized then that my senses had not been bound. Though I could feel the White Wolf running back to me on wings of the air, I could not sense my adversary on any level other than the physical. He had defenses against sorcery. "You have the right of it," I said. "The Sleepers are my insurance policy. That kind of insurance doesn't work unless everyone knows that they're there, so I advertise them. And you are also right about the nature of the insurance. Once wakened, the Sleepers wouldn't need to find your soul to take you apart. Though they would track it down anyway, after they had finished with your physical shell. The Sleepers have broad . . . appetites. Tindalans are thorough. Even if you've given your soul into the safekeeping of another, your Soulkeeper cannot have hidden your essence well enough that the hounds could not find it."

His grin faded. "Tindalans? How many? A pack?"

"A swarm," I said modestly. "And the command on them isn't literal. Leaving me to die of exposure or starvation will still have them howling out after you. And they'll be hungry when they awake."

"As I thought," he said heavily. "I'll have to send you away rather than re-dye my cap. Pity."

I swallowed. Redcaps were not gentle in acquiring the blood they used for dye. The Tindalans had been a fortunate threat for me more than once. Acquiring them had been something of a graduation exercise in Corvinus's eyes. I thought of them as a practical badge of honor. In this case they had proven their worth once again. I would undoubtedly have been a source of hat dye had I not had them, and I had higher ambitions than that.

The redcap looked up, scanning the sky. I could hear the Wolf howling his hunt in the distance. "Time we moved."

I would have called to the Wolf, for the hunters' absence reduced my strength sorely, but I still could not touch anything beyond my immediate senses. I tried the strength of my bonds as the redcap rose from his rock. "Who's your keeper?" I asked casually.

He laughed. "I never bothered with one. I'll take my chances not owing allegiance to any Power or Principality. I haunt the fringes. I prosper well enough, in this place, outside the reach of any Faerie Lord or Lady, free to seek my prey as I will. I will admit that you'll be the first to leave my hills alive. My usual visitors provide me fresh meat on a regular basis, and give me blood for my cap. Mortal blood is best. It keeps the sting of iron fully at bay. But any blood will do."

"Ah," I said politely. "And I thought it was a fashion statement."

He cocked his head. "What did you plan to do with the Gold?"

I heard the capital, and wondered what he meant by the reference to the Gold? Buried treasure? Redcaps weren't known for keeping anything humans find of value, except as a lure. Didn't seem to matter much now. I gave him a look of polite inquiry.

"Don't bother dissembling," he said. "They all come for the Gold. It provides me with plenty of opportunity to keep my headgear well dyed, so I can't complain. Good bait means less hunting. But you've thrown a kink in that, sorcerer—you and your Tindalan insurance—so I tell you what. I'll do you a favor. I'll set your feet on the right path."

He tensed. I held myself ready. I felt the physical bonds ease as he pounced. I threw myself against the barrier and sent one great call to the White Wolf. I pushed the message through in that moment of weakness before the bonds fell on me once again. Physically, I had no chance to resist the redcap. His speed and strength surpassed me to such a degree that he handled me as easily as I might handle a small child.

The breeze grew ragged. I heard the White Wolf's distant howl, but the redcap moved swiftly over the broken ground. The rough hills blurred in my eyes as he tucked me casually beneath one powerful arm and swarmed across the face of the rocks. He traveled like that for some time, until I began to feel the distant pulse of a WanderWay. I felt the first stirrings of hope. The call of the Road grew stronger with his progress. As I thought to reach out and touch the power in it, he came to a stop and threw me roughly to the ground.

I looked around—up at the high, gray walls stretching above me, brushed lightly with scabrous patches of lichen, and down at the land falling away from me. The redcap had dropped me at the edge of a long, steep slope. The cliff stretched down into the distance at an angle that veered only slightly from the vertical. The shape of the hills drew together to join in a straight descending trench which bisected the slope and ran out of sight toward infinity.

That trench spoke in the seductive voice of a WanderWay, promising nasty possibilities. I closed my eyes and called again for the Wolf, trying to punch through the redcap's remaining binding with every ounce of will at my disposal. I had never seen a vertical Way before, but I had sudden suspicions about the redcap's intentions.

He confirmed those suspicions when he kicked me over the edge of the cliff. The winds rose about me. The howling of the Wolf became a part of the voice of the winds. I felt my rate of descent slow as the Wolf's hunters streamed down around me, lending their strength to the White Wolf as he bent the winds of that place to his will. My rate of descent continued to decrease. I reached out to the Way. It resisted my shaping, locked to its destination, the path a well-worn groove of old, dusty footsteps, all pacing inward. It was a one-way path, a unidirectional flow, a turnstile through a locked gate. I might have been able to fight it and redirect my course if the redcap's bonds hadn't still lay heavily upon me and had I been walking rather than falling down the length of it. As it was, my divided attention cost me any chance of diverting the Way from its set destination.

Dust rose as the ground rushed up to meet me. The winds of the White Wolf pulled the air from my lungs even as they cushioned the shock of my fall.

I slammed into the ground and lost my breath. I spent a few seconds in timeless agony, trying to relearn how to breathe. When I recovered my breath, the air of the place—stale and dry as it was—tasted as sweet as that of any cool mountaintop. I spent those first moments concentrating on the redcap's weakening bonds. It took a little work to shatter them away to nothing. As the last traces of the bindings fell away, I realized that I could sense nothing of the White Wolf or his hunters. They had vanished.

CHAPTER VI

THE IRON HILLS were a verdant, pastoral paradise compared to the place the redcap had sent me. A flat, dusty plain stretched before me, a wall of cliffs rising at my back, cut by a single, vertical line in the red-gray stone. Slanting rays of yellow-brown light illuminated the plain, filtered through layers of dust that hung on the still air and coated my throat and lips. The air tasted flat, as if old, tired, unbreathed by any living, vigorous thing.

I stood on a narrow ridge of stone that stretched, straight as an arrow, from the line of the vertical cleft in the cliff behind me out into level ground. Except for that slender path of bare stone, black vines sporting thorns as long as my little finger curled over every visible bit of earth like an enormous dumping ground of military surplus razor wire. In the midst of those vines I could see movement. Small forms crawled lazily among the thorns.

That path had all the possibility of an arranged marriage. I'd need more to work with before I could leave that place through WayShaping. Someone—perhaps the redcap, though I doubted that from his comments and from the feel of the age of the place—had locked down the Way in that place, killing its impulse to wander. Even without that obstacle, I refused to leave without tracking down the White Wolf and his pack of hunters. Though they had eased my fall, they had vanished instead of rejoining the Legion after I hit the ground.

I pulled a kerchief from an inner pocket and tied an impromptu dust mask over my mouth and nose. The dust faded all visual detail into a brown and yellow blur after about a hundred yards. I eased my senses toward the spiritual and extended my awareness gently. I sensed nothing of the White Wolf and his entourage. He had not sought his freedom, since the bonds I had laid on him so long ago remained unbroken, but the traces on all of them lay slack and lifeless. I frowned, puzzled. The traces would not linger if the White Wolf and his pack had been destroyed. To seek freedom they would have had to sever the bonds. I had never before run across anything quite like what I felt then.

I found myself noting a few other disturbing elements. First, the vines and the forms among them did not register as having a spirit I could touch. That was a bad thing. I could touch no will around me, not even the smallest spark of hungry life. That told me that the movement I saw originated most likely with machines. Having no living spirit to touch, machines were immune to my sorcerer's influence. The place felt more and more like a prison, given the elements such as dead Roads, sentry machines, and the choking absence of life.

I sensed one other thing, perhaps the most disturbing of all. Ahead, straight down the path of stone that lay before me, I could feel a vast, muted power, like the glow from a great fire burning over the horizon. The closest experience I had to anything like that would be the luminescence of a Tindalan swarm. A very big swarm.

"Rose? Blade? Angel? Any ideas?"

The Bright Angel's voice had all the music of the stars themselves. "Look for the Wolf and his pack ahead. That power would mute any lesser radiance."

"And I feel the possibility of a loosening of the Way in that same direction." Blade's voice was expressionless.

I winced, knowing that he still blamed himself for his moment of inattention with the redcap. I explored ahead, along the length of the Road with my WayShaper's sense, and felt a thin, confirming pulse. "Limited, but perhaps our ticket to freedom?" I asked Blade.

"Our only visible option, at any rate," Blade agreed.

"What of the vines, and the crawlers among them?" The usual floral scent of the White Rose sharpened with her asperity.

"No life, no will," I answered. "Machines, most likely. This place is dead. Perhaps the machines and vines are the lingering weapons of some ancient war."

"Or the guards to a prison. Does it not bother you that this place is so well suited to your vulnerability?" Rose asked. "You cannot touch these machines directly. They will be immune to any but the most indirect of our powers and most of your physical forces went with the White Wolf."

"That's why I'll need you to give me physical boosts as necessary," I responded. "And yes, it seems that this redcap was entirely too prepared. Whether Titania merely delights in killing human sorcerers or is trying to make points with Silverhand is irrelevant. We have to survive this place before worrying about that."

"And then worry about Fetch," Blade said gravely.

"One impossible thing at a time. Unlike you, I'm only human."

I heard a few chuckles at that. Tightening my makeshift mask against the omnipresent dust, I began walking briskly toward the distant glow and the dim promise of another Way.

The machines took notice of me before I'd covered a thousand paces. The first sign came when the movement in the vines became a rippling wave of motion that exactly paralleled my course and speed. Shortly after, I saw a small, dark insectile machine scuttle out onto the edge of the road on too many thin, spidery legs. A high-pitched whine slid across the edge of my hearing as the camera cluster dominating the torso spun and focused, tracking me as I walked. The optimist in me hoped quietly that all of the machines were for observation only, but the realist in me pointed out—with as much relish as a bully kicking down a small boy's sandcastle—that such design specialization probably indicated swarm tactics and narrow roles for each small machine.

The realist in me can be a colossal prick.

I kept my eyes peeled for warrior drones and had the White Rose and Shadow set some of my limited reserve forces to work on readying adrenaline boosts. Their working had a taste both sweet and bitter. I would have preferred a steed of the air, but any forces I had capable of that kind of manipulation had departed with the White Wolf. I followed the ridge toward the living pulse of a possible Way I could feel in the distance. The dust thickened as I walked through an increasingly yellow light, the cast of old parchment.

The machines grew bolder, skittering out along the edge of the road in clusters of two to four. I watched them out of the corner of my eye. All had generally insectile or arachnid shapes, with long, thin legs supporting elongated or globular bodies, but I could identify several distinct types. In addition to the cameras of the observer machines, I saw what might have been folded blades, possibly small powered saws, and other bundles that may or may not have been various implements of destruction on worker or soldier types. The machines could have been a construction or maintenance crew, specialized for various tasks, rather than hunter/killers designed for swarm tactics. Based on long experience and cultivated cynicism, I drew my own conclusions, construction not high on the Pareto of likely functions.

Ahead I could feel that otherworldly presence looming on the horizon. The limp bindings of the White Wolf and the elements of the Legion he had taken with him led in that direction. I decided to move before the machines had me completely trapped, gave Shadow the nod, and watched the motion of the machines slow to almost nothing. I ran, pushing through air that was suddenly as thick as molasses. The machines moved more slowly yet, dropping away into the hanging dust. I did not doubt that they would track me. I couldn't stay boosted long: while boosted, I consumed my body's resources at a frightening rate. I could literally starve to death in minutes, though metabolic shock would get me long before that, despite the White Rose's buffering efforts.

I made the best of my opportunity, driving on down the ridge and through the thickening dust to a place where the light faded to a golden glow. I could feel the proximity of the Way, could even see where it split off from the ridge, but I could also feel something else. A powerful presence loomed into the clouds above me.

I could see the clouds of dust bent and twisted into a great vortex. The noise and the wind would have been terrible had I not been accelerated slightly past the normal flow of time. The regard of the presence at the heart of the storm fell down over me like a towering wave. In the moment of contact, I tasted something of its composite nature. Golden light fell down through the umber body of the whirlwind. The core of the vortex rippled toward violet. The air tasted of electric rage. Looking up through the muted light at the pent fury of the winds, I knew where the White Wolf had vanished, and I had a sudden suspicion as to what the redcap had meant when he had spoken of "the Gold." Call it what you will, that storm had more than a physical presence, drawing free spirits to itself and locking them into captivity in its raging heart.

What fool would have sought this thing out, in its furious solitude? The redcap said there had been many seekers after the Gold. He had been ready for a sorcerer. If a sorcerer managed to bind such a force to his service, he could increase his power considerably. But under the shadow of that mighty tower of wind, I wondered at the magnitude of foolish ambition that could tempt a man to pursue such a course. I personally wanted as little to do with that thing as possible. The Tindalans had been bad; this looked worse.

And I had other problems to worry about. Like Fetch and Titania and unfulfilled contracts.

I reached the mouth of the Road before allowing Shadow to drop me back into phase with the natural flow of time. I staggered as my body paid the price for thwarting the natural order. My guts churning and my limbs trembling, I had no chance of resisting the full force of the Gold's rage.

I hadn't realized how powerful it would be. I threw myself flat on the ground against the hurricane winds. The freight-train cacophony shook the earth. The wind howled like a chorus of damned souls. Dust abraded my skin as the winds ripped at my clothing. I had to hold the loose tail of my coat bunched under my arm to keep from losing it to the winds.

I reached instinctively for the White Wolf, though he had gone from me, and I felt the slightest response in return. I called to that response in desperation, convinced that without some way to tame the wind I would never live to walk the Road that lay behind the Gold.

I could feel the White Wolf fighting, giving me tremendous resistance, even more than when I had originally taken him. When I tightened my grip he fought with me, against the hungry force that sought to pull him back into itself. The resistance I felt came from the Gold, not the White Wolf. Behind the White Wolf I felt the elements of the Legion I had sent with him reinforcing his effort. With that I drew on Bane and Shadow and Bright Angel, leaving only Blade and his forces to man the fortress of my soul. Shadow anchored my will, Bright Angel wove strength into the strand that joined the broken elements of the Legion, and Bane struck past the battle into the heart of the Gold.

I felt its shock. In the moment of its surprise, the Gold's grip failed on the White Wolf and his party. I ripped them free and used the White Wolf's strength to calm a bubble of winds around myself.

The Gold reared above me, its winds a thunderous extension of its rage. The ground shook as it searched for me. While the White Wolf's bubble of winds flexed under the probing attention of the Gold, I reached desperately for the glimmer of possibility I had felt beyond its monstrous girth. Cupping metaphorical hands around limited possibility, I blew on the embers of the Way and kindled a destination from the smoldering ruins of the fading possibilities of that place. I felt a barrier then, an anchor that held the Way shut. I smashed through the barrier with a strength born of desperation as the Gold bent toward me, and I fled that place.

CHAPTER VII

THE WAY shivered under my feet, fighting my control, so I took what options I could find and hammered out a course on the hard-packed surface of limited possibility as I fled along in front of the Gold. The thunder of my pursuer diminished as I twisted and turned through narrower and narrower paths, until the Way became a thin track in the middle of a verdant savannah of rolling hills and clumps of deciduous trees. The winds weakened as I ran. Its earth shaking growl faded to a distant rumble.

The Road twisted like a living thing under my feet. I passed on through the shards of the barrier and came out from under the shadows of storm clouds into a warm sunlit place lush with new growth, the air heavy with the smell of water and free of choking dust. The last traces of the Gold's distant howl fell to a shimmering whisper and then vanished as the Way closed behind me. As the buffeting winds fell away, the drop in pressure felt like a momentary vacuum. My coat fell slack against my back and legs. I could taste grit in my mouth and feel the sandpaper rasp of fine dust against my skin as I moved. The last echo of the Gold's winds fell to the soft sigh of a gentle breeze. The acrid taint of stale air in my lungs vanished before a warm, lush breath of life as I breathed in air that tasted like a lover's mouth.

The warm, humid air, blue skies, lush green of the grass, the shyly budding leaves of the trees, and the throaty calls of birds in this new land were a far cry from the place I had fled. I had stepped out of a demon's dance on Bald Mountain and into the chorus of the Rite of Spring.

I wondered at the place I had left behind, the dead prison and its singular prisoner. I shivered in the broad light of day. I shuddered away from the thought that I had freed the Gold in breaking that last barrier. Certainly it had seemed to follow me down the Way. Its winds had reached out after me, though I had apparently lost it behind me. Good for me, bad for anyone it happened to blunder into. I had never encountered anything like that before, a storm with a spiritual center, and I hoped never to do so again.

I tested for alternatives down the limited possibilities I could find in the track where I stood, looked down the branching courses of the traveling Way. I bit back curses when I saw that the Way ran ominously close to the realms of the Fae. I needed more alternatives than that back-country track could give me. If I could find a crossroad, I could look for options, but I would have to both move quickly and with care. Fetch would be waiting to pick up my trail. If I found the proper Way, I would run through places that played to Fetch's Faerie weakness to iron until I could build a proper foundation I could use to pull myself out of this mess.

If I had unintentionally cast myself into the role of Reynard the Fox, I would at least play it to the hilt.

Beyond shaking Fetch off my trail, I had to have more information. I had to understand the reason Titania had trapped me—if it was the old grudge with Silverhand or something else. The only other batch of hostiles that came to mind was the Whitesnake cult, but the Whitesnakes had no friends among the Fae any more than they had friends anywhere else. I had been surprised that enough Whitesnakes were still around to present any kind of threat. I certainly wouldn't expect them to be able to muster enough forces to do more than put some ragged cultists on my track, so I didn't see any connection there. I needed to talk to Corvinus. I needed to understand if my old master had any insight into Titania's motives for setting me up as Fetch's meat. As for the contract itself, time would be passing swiftly in Faerie. I knew that my time would already have been up by the time I found my way back. Titania would be loosing Fetch on me soon.

I took myself along the track, twisting the simple Road under my feet to move more quickly through that reality than could any traveler bound by the limits of his horizon. Humped, gentle hills crowned by low trees with leaves like dusty green enamel bowed to the broad, brown face of a mighty river. I paused at the riverbank, considering my choices. A river could present access to a great many possibilities. No track made by man can compete with a river in majesty and maturity as a RoadWay, but for that exact reason I doubted the wisdom of using it as my Way. The wild, unbroken spirits of great waters call to like wild powers such as the Fae. The waters before me flexed great, sinewy muscles under a mask of imperturbable calm. The feral spirit of the river, though it cloaked itself under a smooth muddy surface, would not be one to trust lightly.

My hands clenched as I considered how my foolish greed had bound my course and narrowed my path. I worked my way up and down Roads along the riverbank until I found a bridge crossing the river. I could hardly contain my delight at the parallel iron tracks running out of the hills, down over the bridge and into the distance. Here lay a path alien and inimical to the Fae.

Smiling for the first time since the end of my conversation with Titania, I sauntered out onto the bridge. That track had its limitations as well, but I could begin to move in the right direction. The bars of iron lying across the black wooden timbers thrummed as I danced across the bridge in short, irregular hops from tie to tie. The thrumming grew in intensity and a grumbling rhythm built behind me.

I turned to see the broad, indifferent face of the massive locomotive that ran on those tracks, a black cloud of heat and fury crowning the brow. I touched the possibility of the Road in an attempt to surf a wave of possibility ahead of the train. I hoped to catch a wave that would carry me forward far enough and quickly enough that the onrushing train would not be a threat, but the possibility in the Road eluded my touch.

Snarling, with no time to question the strangeness of it, and no time to ready the aid of the Legion, I took Hephaestus' name in vain as my dance steps metamorphosed into the desperate staccato of flight. The thrumming of the rails grew until the rising thunder behind me consumed them. A shrill, whistling scream cut through the thunder like a metal raptor's shriek, and I flung myself off the bridge and into a nest of brambles that ran down to the riverside as the train's passage hammered the air.

For those who have never climbed up a muddy riverbank covered in blackberry bushes in the remnants of a suit never meant to endure the stresses of physical battle, I might recommend it as a character-building experience. I can't say that I'd recommend it in any other way. Slimy footing willfully attempted to bring me to my belly with every step; thorns covered my only available handholds, maliciously clawing into folds of clothing and exposed skin. Every step became a matter of focus and will. And as the landscape clung to my clothes and my body with every misstep, so did I leave skin and blood and patches of cloth behind. Once I made it to the top of the hill and freed myself from the last clinging tentacle of the brambles, I eyed the track with newfound ambivalence.

I added "taking a leisurely bath" and "acquiring a new set of clothes" to my list of things to do.

I hadn't walked railroad tracks often enough in the past to be fully cognizant of the fact that any pedestrian is little more than an ephemeral obstacle to traffic. I filed the lesson away, brushed ineffectually at my ruined coat, and studied the tracks. I needed a good jumping off point for a solid Way away from the Fae, and I needed to understand why the Road had failed to respond as it should. I would have expected that I had enough experience by that time that a little thing like an imminent threat would not have interfered with my concentration enough to keep me from using the Road.

Touching the iron Road's currents of probability, I noticed that the skeins of possibility in the Road had been ripped and torn to lifelessness. I studied the damage, pushed my senses down past small hamlets surrounded by farms to a mining community where the note grew discordant. The Road had been damaged. Something had ripped up the tracks, a destructive force unexpected in that place and time, able to destroy not only lives and homes and schools but also able to touch and destroy the possibilities in the Road. Something like a storm with a spiritual presence.

"It did escape, then," said a still small voice in the back of my mind. The thought so echoed my own that it took me a moment to realize the White Wolf had spoken. The fear in his voice, the disturbed quiet like the aftermath of a violent storm, betrayed how deeply his short captivity had affected him.

I thought again about the barrier I had broken to flee the Gold's prison. I had shaken the Gold off my trail, but it was still dangerously close. Did it hunt me now that it had broken free? Had it blocked the path deliberately? Whoever had imprisoned the thing must have known that the Gold could travel the Ways. Apparently, it could also manipulate them. Was it hunting me? Trying to trap me? Or was the destruction a byproduct of its madness? I looked to the White Wolf for answers. "Tell me what you know."

"It took us early, but it had trouble digesting its conquest," the White Wolf said in that same subdued tone. "It's an ancient thing, made now of the broken pieces of lives and memories swallowed over the ages to keep itself alive. The man who gave it life trapped it there, and went first to feed it. The thing that became the Gold was some kind of machine, I think, but also more than that: a TechTown kind of monster, a machine with a soul. Its memories were old and buried, and we were not yet completely absorbed and so I did not know the Gold fully, but I knew that when it woke to the need and blind hunger of life, the man was there. And the machines were there. It controlled the machines—had been built to be their master. It took the man, as it's taken every other life that came before it in flesh or spirit. It came to bind even the winds to its madness, ravaging out along the Roads, until at last three WayShapers imprisoned it. They lost their lives in the effort. Now all that's left of it is need and blind hunger. And rage."

I didn't have any answer for that. "Can you find it?" I asked. He hesitated before answering. "I am afraid."

I rocked back on my heels. I first thought of compulsion, my mental hand twitching toward a conceptual whip. But I have never had the need or desire to rule so strictly through overt domination. I prefer loyalty to fear, when I can have it. "What about the track? The Gold's not subtle. Can you track it indirectly? I can't afford to risk losing you to it again. I don't want you to approach too closely. Make for me a steed of the air, and I will follow close behind. I need to know if it hunts us. I need to be able to chart us a course out of this."

His eyes brightened at the prospect of close reinforcements. "I will find it," he said. "What happens when I do?" He whuffed out a heavy breath. "We'll see if together we can bring it down. It has its own Legion, you know. It does not simply devour, but also binds."

"We'll do what we have to," I reassured him. "We may not need to confront it directly."

The steed of the air rose before me in a rippling heat shimmer of impatient motion. I drew my legs up and over its broad back, furry with dust kicked up from the tracks, and then the strength of it swept me off to course my hound's trail. We flew down the tracks, toward the destruction I had sensed through the Road. A neatly groomed, compact roan pulling a covered buggy along the dirt road paralleling the tracks gave itself to a generous paroxysm of hysterics as we shot by. I couldn't see the driver under the rounded canopy, so perhaps I went unseen by him as well. If not, he would have some tales to tell at the local tavern.

The White Wolf's howl held a measure of hate as it came drifting back, and as I crossed over a gentle hill and saw the wake of the Gold, I understood why. Smoke drifted among hills of rubble; men with black faces rose from the shelter of the mine shaft to pick through shattered stone looking for traces of their families. And when the brick and stone had been lifted away, the light fell gently down over small, limp and twisted forms. Rough denim and gingham cloaked the worst of the wounds inflicted by the Gold in its passage. I looked away. Perhaps the damage had been incidental.

I had told the White Wolf we might not have to confront the Gold directly. Three WayShapers had died trying to bind the thing. And if the Wolf feared it enough, when I faced it, my Legion might be divided. The risk would be great. I wasn't sure I wanted to take that risk. Perhaps I could find a path that did not cross the Gold's. Perhaps it would find its way to Faerie, and return a little of the madness it had brought here. I didn't need the distraction of the Gold. The way I figured it, looking over the ruin of the town, someone else could deal with the Gold while I dealt with the more personal problem of Fetch.

I looked back down into the ruins of a red brick schoolhouse. A man's face caught my attention, a face weathered by hard years sifting a life out of the depths of a hostile land. The man's eyes, fathomless and dark as nuggets of coal, searched the horizon as rough hands worked gently, pulling brick and stone and splinters of wood and pieces of mortar away from a small, unmoving form. Those eyes looked through me, unseeing, as the hands continued their deft, gentle movements, and it seemed to me that miner was looking for answers that lay past the horizon, in the heart of the uncaring whirlwind, in the underpinnings of creation itself.

Creation had lost its voice in that moment, overwhelmed by destruction. Mute, all glory had no answer for that unvoiced question as to why such things happened. No one and nothing could say why children had to die. Something shifted within me, there on my steed of air, and I understood that I could not evade this responsibility. In escaping to this place, I had loosed a monster. I had broken the barriers on the Way and freed the Gold from its prison. Releasing the Gold laid on my shoulders a heavier burden than my own fate—I could do no less than my all to bring the Gold's threat to an end.

If I didn't provide that miner at least that much of an answer, his unvoiced question would haunt me for the rest of my days.

I tried to ignore the whisper of fear in the back of my mind. Three WayShapers had bound it. They had all died in the binding.

I would have to take another approach. Binding it to a location would take too long, and expose me to the force of its winds. I would have to bind it spiritually, break its will. How many sorcerers had died going after the Gold? Its Legion would be a rich prize, but would also make it incredibly dangerous. And none before me had succeeded. I wondered if they'd had nature spirits to bind its winds, or if the Gold's will was simply too strong for them. I thought of the White Wolf's fear. And then I set myself to my task.

I hunted along the trail of the Gold's destruction, running through a wake of havoc stretching across the verdant countryside. The ruin of a farmhouse, the destruction of a copse of trees, razed towns with names like Gorham and Murphysboro and DeSoto and Annapolis marked the Gold's footsteps. Always in its wake drifted the ruins of lives, and the dead.

I couldn't let this thing spread out across the Ways. And I couldn't just trap it again, not if it had taken three WayShapers to trap it before. The Gold had a spirit, so I could try to bind it, but I had never faced such raw power before. I'd have to divert a considerable part of the Legion just to protect me from the power of the Gold's winds. I'd have to find its heart and strike for that.

I ran fast enough, far enough, and long enough to begin to glimpse the rising cloud of its dust. I called to the White Wolf. "Can you mark its passage? It seems to almost be aiming for these towns."

"Not almost," the White Wolf snarled. "It's hungry. But it's moving so fast. I don't know how long it will take to catch it."

"Can we get ahead of it?"

"You want to face it now?"

"I must. Can you face it with me?"

"I . . . don't know if I can. And I am not alone in this." Fear weighted his voice. "Those of us once caught in the Gold's influence will hesitate to close with it again."

Could I risk facing this monster and its own Legion while driving my own? I thought not. I considered the nature of my enemy, and my allies. "Protect me."

"What?"

Shift the focus, I thought. Use his fear. "The winds will be a significant threat. Take the forces you had when the Gold took you the first time, and chain the winds."

"What about its hunger?" he asked slowly.

"I will face its hunger," I said. "All the rest of the Legion will face its captive spirits. Can you stand against the strength of its winds?"

He stiffened. "If you can stand against its hunger, I can stand against its winds."

"Lead me, then."

The White Wolf led me off the trail of destruction, the steed of the air increasing the pace until I had to close my eyes and turn my head from the wind's force. We moved at a ferocious rate, traveling with such speed that I could only cling to my steed and trust the White Wolf's guidance. We had to move faster than the Gold by a roundabout path, since it appeared to be traveling with a single-minded determination that followed the straight line of the railroad tracks which took it from town to town. I felt us slow. I opened my eyes to see a stretch of empty fields.

The spring sunlight had grown strangely soft and pale. With that I knew the White Wolf had succeeded in bringing me into the course of our quarry. We stopped in a large field as plowed and bare as the destruction behind us. I descended to the ground, dismissed my steed to free the White Wolf for his preparations, and began rousing the Legion. I called my Captains to me and set them to stir the full host of my conquests.

The Gold came on as a storm spreading across the sky, having picked up clouds on its journey. The first raggedness in the wind warned me. Then the rains came from light streamers of cloud, falling softly like tears through pale, tinted light. The wind grew steadily stronger until the noise of it rose to a familiar rumble, like a mighty river in full flood. When my prey crested the trees, its heart still burned a dark, resentful yellow-brown, but crimson, midnight blue, and ash gray swirled around its edges. The light fell through it as if through the stained glass of a cathedral.

It descended as a swarm of captive lives. I sent the Legion up to meet the swarm. The forces clashed with a silent, raging roar. In a battle of shades, nightmares rose to devour hallucinations. In a war of ghosts, undead will crushed disembodied awareness. I saw them all, the whole of my Legion, sweeping up to close with the host of the Gold, each wave of them following behind one of my Captains. Only the White Rose and her gentler forces remained with me, anticipating the time when her support would be needed. The White Wolf and his forces fought the winds to a standstill, so that I stood in a compressed bubble of calm. My ears felt stuffed with cotton as the pressure soared around me, but I ignored fleshly discomfort. I stood below, watching the spiritual conflict and waiting for the true enemy to appear.

Blade staggered in the midst of the battle. Bane rose to support him, only to fall back as golden light rippled across the broken clouds. The winds rose with a roar. Fragments of wood and metal came scything toward me out of the heart of the storm. The flying debris exploded without touching me as the White Wolf stood to his duty, bending the winds to his will. I felt then, rising through the heart of the storm, a thing of pain and rage and hunger, a thing as much to be pitied as feared. But I had no pity left. I brought my will to bear and grappled with the monster at the center of the storm.

The Gold fought without subtlety. In a hot tempest of hunger and fury, its strength strove to tear my will into pieces and consume me. I plunged into its depths, searching for its center, trying to find and smash whatever lay at its heart.

The power at the heart of the Gold filled my senses, a maelstrom of light and heat and motion and implacable appetite. The pure, wild nature of that power would have torn at my defenses even without being focused on me, but a will had guided the fury and directed its force. That desperate will brought all of its hunger and all of its strength to bear on me. I shuttered the doors of my spirit as much as I could and drove blindly on, unwilling to present anything other than a moving target for its rage.

I felt stretched, thinning under the strength of the assault. Doors in my mind, barred against invasion, were battered down by the onslaught. Hungry winds poured fury through the doors, eating into my will, bringing pain, and even more frightening, a consuming numbness as they advanced.

The storm peaked, the walls of the fortress of my spirit thrumming with the wrath behind the winds, the White Wolf's protective bubble bending in around me. Then I felt it falter, and I knew that my Legion had cut away some crucial part of its force. I drove further into its depths. Walls of color surrounded me, waves of motion rose about me. Then at last I burst into a small, still place, and I knew that I had found the heart of the Gold.

I touched it with my senses, to learn its nature and discover its vulnerabilities. What I found there shocked me. At the heart of that fury and monstrous hunger cried a small thing, blind and deaf and tormented by endless solitude. I thought of the story the White Wolf had told me, and I decided that however awful the death of the man who had created this thing, it had not been awful enough.

I tried to reach that small, blind, and lonely presence, to speak to it, to ease its pain if I could, to ask it to let go if I could not, but its walls were too high, its barriers too thick—it was too weak, and I was not strong enough. I would only fail in the attempt to bind such a thing. Failure would mean my death. I wondered, had I the strength to control it, if I had the monstrous cruelty to extend its pain only to enslave it to my will—but I didn't, and so the point was moot.

Instead of trying to bind the heart of the Gold, I pulled it to me and cradled it close as I severed every tie that held it to the continual torment of its continued existence. Then I broke the walls of its solitude on the rock of my will, giving that innocent monster peace the only way I knew. Holding it to my heart, I felt its breath blow out loosely around me and fade away to nothing.

I fell back out of the storm, through the ragged streamers of the last few elements of my Legion as they descended on the broken pieces of the Gold's Legion. The Gold's Legion was more of a mockery of a Legion, as all that remained after I had brought its rage and pain and fear at last to an end were the parts of the monster held captive to its failed attempt to reach out and break down the barriers of its intolerable solitude. I fell to my knees in the dust, looking up to watch the clouds wisp away into nothingness. The winds died away without a whimper of protest. Debris rained down over the landscape where the murderous storm had raged.

I watched the shredded white blossoms of a flower fall gently down like the pieces of an unfulfilled promise. I grieved, not only for its victims, but for the madness in all of us that brought something like the Gold into the world and left it to its pain and loneliness. I had no more answer for the Gold than I'd had for the miner in the town behind me.

If I had been a poet, I would have wept.

"Everyone alright?" I asked the Legion quietly as I gathered them in.

I received an equally subdued, collective assent.

I rose to my feet, searching for the Way I needed. I could feel a path calling to me, just past the hedgerows and over the fence, strong with the scent of possibility. I bent, picked up my battered hat, dusted it off against my leg, and went to answer the call.

CHAPTER VIII

ITOOK the hard Way, which meant the short Way, to the outskirts of CrossTown and home. I knew that Fetch would be looking for me. The Gold had not met even the imprecise description that Titania had given me of the spirit I had been contracted to banish from her lands. In any event, the contract seemed to be little more than a formal way of declaring me to be fair game for Fetch. The lords of Faerie tended to act by their own seemingly capricious set of rules, but even an outsider like myself could recognize an assassination attempt.

I still did not know if Titania had something personal against me, liked taking out the mortal competition, or had simply chosen to use me as a counter in some game involving Silverhand and his vendetta, though I leaned heavily toward the last. I did have certain reservations, though. If she had wanted to eliminate me, she didn't have to take this roundabout route. Something more lay behind her game.

At any rate, I had no intention of making things easy on Fetch. I traveled through realms dominated by cultures heavy in the use of iron, often on thin Roads paralleling iron tracks on which ran a vast array of machines, usually large and belching smoke or something worse, generally traveling in a considerable hurry, and always composed of iron. The air went from a smooth country vintage to something harsher, something that bit lightly at the back of the throat with the taint of technology. I followed that scent, though I had no taste for it, skirting the edges of cities that glowed with light and more illusory promise than Faerie itself.

The Road that I traveled curved in toward the TechTown side of CrossTown. I had no problem with that at all. I debated dropping by home, but Fetch would doubtless be waiting there to pick up my trail. Lying low in TechTown for a while might not be a bad thing, but I wouldn't be able to hide forever. I needed to talk to Corvinus. Aside from the fact that he had asked me to reach him earlier (an invitation I had accepted) he might have been able to give me some advice about my current situation.

I had options of my own, of course. I knew that I couldn't take on Fetch or Titania or Silverhand directly, but two out of three wouldn't be leaving Faerie, so if I stayed away from Faerie I'd at least improve my odds. As for Jack, I could involve Eliza Drake or Chimereon, both Powers in their own right not necessarily friendly to Faerie—but I didn't want to owe either if I could possibly help it.

Sometimes living in CrossTown seems to be nothing more than navigating a tangled web of obligation. My particular web had enough tangles at that moment, thank you very much, without adding further complication.

The Road broadened before me, opening out to nearly limitless possibility, and I knew I had arrived at the environs of CrossTown. The Way had always been difficult there, easily leading one astray. Learning how to navigate the treacherous shoals of CrossTown's sea of probability is the first and most difficult task for those learning to travel the WanderWays.

I found the frenetic pulse of TechTown, a thin electric line burning hot through the snarled alternative Ways of high technology. I set my foot on the path to TechTown, then doubled over as sudden weakness spasmed through my limbs and darkness rose before my eyes. I fought the malaise, summoning Blade to me through a connection gone tenuous.

I felt Blade move, felt something focused and sharp and powerful cut through the barrier thickening around me. Then it dropped away as if it had never been, and Blade walked with me. I paused on the Road, shaken, and then moved aside hurriedly as a blur whipped past me.

"What was that?" Blade asked softly.

"A hovercycle, I think," I said as lightly as I could manage.

I felt disapproval leaking past Blade's personal barriers. "You know what I mean. The wall I felt rise between us. What happened?"

"Good question." I called to the White Rose. "Anything wrong on the physical side?"

"Nothing that a proper diet and a less stressful occupation couldn't resolve."

"Everyone's a comedian."

"She's right, though," Blade said thoughtfully. "Whatever that was, it wasn't physical."

"It came from inside." The White Wolf rose from the depths to dog my heels.

"Some lingering effect from the battle with the Gold, perhaps?" I asked. "Fatigue?"

The White Wolf snorted. "Fatigue it was not."

Blade responded more slowly. "I agree. It wasn't simple fatigue. Though it may well be some lingering infection from the

Gold. You were isolated there. The Gold had a considerable Legion of its own that fell to us. Through us, you absorbed that Legion. There could be problems associated with the assimilation of that large and varied a force. And you haven't rested since your conquest before that. The Jigsaw Man, Vincent's ghost. You need to take some time to settle the new powers down."

The White Wolf grinned. "True. Rebel presences could explain much. Perhaps your Legion is no longer of a mind. One of the hazards associated with sorcery, I would say."

I stopped to regard him. Shadows crisscrossed the ground around me, falling from vehicles riding the air above. I had reached the edges of TechTown's maze of traffic. "And where would you stand in the event of such a rebellion?" I asked the White Wolf softly.

I felt Blade at my side, waiting . . . and the White Wolf laughed. "I'm not fond of captivity, that's true enough, but what I just felt did not have the flavor of a simple desire for freedom. Underneath it all was a desire of its own, to consume you, to consume your Legion. I want no part of something like that. Reminds me too much of the Gold, but with more malice than desperation. That scares me."

"There's truth in that," Blade noted. "There's also a certain amount of deception."

I rubbed my forehead with a hand still slightly shaking. "I would expect no less."

Reaction had begun to set in. All of a sudden I had to consider evading Jack or dealing with him while my Legion was divided. I thought of Shadow and Bane. Both powerful, independent spirits, either could have been responsible for the barrier. Either could have been testing me. Or it could have been something new, something taken from the Gold.

CROSSTOWN

I brought up subtle barriers of my own, distancing the Legion from the three of us. "I need the two of you to investigate this. Root out the Rebel."

"You suspect . . ." Blade began.

". . . Everyone," finished the White Wolf. "Otherwise, why the barrier? And why the two of us? Because we're unlikely to work together, you and I. We're both aware of the suspicion, aware of one another—if one of us was responsible, it would be difficult to pull off another attack without the other being instantly on guard."

"What about the defenses?" Blade did not sound pleased. "Who will you trust?"

"Bright Angel can take responsibility for the defenses. And I will be watching."

I let the barrier fade, and they nodded and faded from conscious perception. Bright Angel came to me when I called, wings of light folding around her. "Why has Blade pulled his forces from the walls of your spirit?"

"You felt the touch of darkness?"

"How could I not?"

I nodded. "Blade sweeps the inner defenses, searching for a cause. I need you to man the outer walls."

Bright Angel cocked her head, her gaze searching my soul. "You have your own defenses engaged. You suspect the Legion of rebellion."

I smiled fondly in spite of myself. "I feel safe with you guarding me, as always. However, I fear infection from the Gold."

Bright Angel nodded slowly. "I can understand that. You took on more than you ever have with the conquest of the Gold's Legion. But be aware, that may only have provided an opportunity for any who had been waiting. Not all the Legion loves you."

"Sorcery isn't about love. Sorcery is about domination."

Bright Angel shrugged. "Not that the two are necessarily mutually exclusive—but that is my point. Spirits are more than tools, as you know, and some may yet nurture a desire to again be free."

"You?" I asked quietly.

Her head bowed. "I am . . . content in this place and in this role. I fear you, perhaps I even love you a little. I would not see you come to harm, if only because of the protection you have given me in exchange for service. In spite of that, I will never forget what it means to be free."

I said nothing as she turned and went up to the watchtowers of my soul. Thus braced within and without, thinking deeply on the twin subjects of freedom and rebellion, I crossed over into TechTown proper.

Skirting between buildings that stretched to the clouds in a gloom only increased by the traffic above, I dodged a holographic, barely dressed shill for a strip joint. Her ample, illusory flesh faded before the assault of a mercenary recruiting ad. I left the two of them grappling behind me, keeping an eye peeled for further animated advertisements.

I thought about Anthony Vayne and the Knights of the New Temple, and grinned at the thought of Fetch following me there. The Templars practiced all forms of combat, including spiritual combat, as many a hostile spirit or Faerie lord had found to his dismay. On equal ground, I would probably still put my money on Jack against the Templars. Only a fool would tackle him within the environs of Faerie, but in the Knights' own hallowed grounds, Jack would be on the defensive. At that point, all bets were off.

CHAPTER IX

THE DOORS to the NeoTemplars' Temple in TechTown stood wide, open to all, as the doors to any decent temple should be. Entering the vast open space of the public worship area was easy. Fortunately, I hadn't come in the midst of an active service. Though surcoated brothers militant patrolled among the columns, none moved to stop me as I strode toward the small door unobtrusively set behind heavy curtains hanging across the back wall. I pulled the curtains aside and stepped through into the vestibule that separated the public area from the private. A stocky Knight Brother looked up from his desk as I entered. One hand dropped below the surface of his desk.

It warmed my heart to see proper caution. "I'd like to see Anthony Vayne."

The Knight Brother looked at me skeptically. "Anthony Vayne? Knight Commander Anthony Vayne?"

I nodded.

He twisted uncomfortably in his seat. I wondered idly if he wore a hair shirt under his habit. "He doesn't have much patience for interruptions."

"I'm not saying that he'll be glad to see me. But he'll want to know I'm here."

He reached for the phone. I studied the walls of the vestibule—bare alloy done over lightly in institutional gray—the walls of a fortress, an asylum, or both. When Vayne opened the door leading from the back, his face looked more grim than usual. "Zethus. How long have you been back in town?"

"Just arrived."

He gestured for me to follow him inside, holding the door open for me. The smartlocks all answered to palm print, and we both knew I wasn't on file and wouldn't be unless I joined the Order. I didn't see that happening any time soon.

I followed Vayne through a brightly lit corridor and up a lift tube. When he led me into his working office, I relaxed gratefully in the plush chair he kept for guests. I took time, as I always did, to study the paintings. While they looked to vary from sharply defined realistic landscapes to abstract smears of color, I knew that they were all true to the places he had been. I had been to many of those same places. They had been accurately captured by a master's eye. I had seen his work before: I had even caught him painting once. The easel stood inconspicuously in one corner of the room, draped with a white, silk cloth.

As far as I knew, Vayne always painted from memory. He considered it an exercise in discipline as well as a recreation and release.

He sat across the desk from me in the straight-backed, hard-seated chair he reserved for his own use. "I suppose you know that you are currently the legal prey of a certain well known Faerie Hunter," he said.

"That's why I came here. To see if you could put me up for a while."

I could read nothing in his face. "I don't think that you should stay here. It may be larger than you think. Someone's placed a bounty on you. Fifty gold."

I blinked. "What?" I held up a hand as Vayne opened his mouth. "I know, I know. But it doesn't make sense. It wasn't in the contract. Jack doesn't work that way."

"The bounty was placed by the Whitesnakes," Vayne said.

I blinked again. "You're kidding." I looked at his face. "You're not. How much bounty on you?"

He shook his head.

My eyebrows shot up. "None? What, they spent all of their coppers on me? They should be at least as annoyed at you as at me. Fifty gold seems not only a bit extreme, but a bit beyond what I'd have expected them to be able to scrape together. They didn't have a pot to piss in or a window to throw it out of after we banished their Avatar. The Whitesnakes find a banker? None of that makes any sense. And I don't see a Whitesnake bounty making the difference in my staying here. You'd like the bait, and the opportunity to come to grips with them again." I met his gaze directly. "You're not telling me something."

His lips tightened. "You need to talk to Emerantha Pale. You can use my phone here."

"That's generous of you," I sneered. Then I sighed. "Ah, hell, I'm sorry Vayne. I didn't know, and you're right. I really don't want the Order in the middle of all of this."

"You don't understand." He touched something behind the desk, and as a holographic interface blossomed before me, he rose to his feet and left the room.

I placed the call, wondering why he wanted me to talk to Pale. She was a colleague of Corvinus's and head of the Practitioner's Union in CrossTown. It couldn't be good news. On the other hand, Emerantha had known me for as long as I'd been Corvinus's apprentice. We had always been friendly.

I didn't have to wait long. Light crashed in on itself like a collapsing wave, and Emerantha's features sculpted themselves from the foam. "Zethus. Are you calling from the Knight Commander's location?"

I nodded.

"If that's not secure, nothing is." Her eyes were bright against the pallor of her skin. Emerantha's albino features might have seemed shocking on someone else—on her they looked good. On the other hand, the skin of her face drew tightly across the bones. I had not seen her show stress before. "What have you and your mentor been up to, boy?"

I let the boy crack slide, since I detected not the slightest hint of humor in her expression and tone. "What do you mean?"

"You know damned well what I mean. At least you had better."

I closed my eyes, waited a slow five count, breathed deeply, and only then opened my eyes to meet her sharp gaze. "It's been a long, bad day. I've had both cultist and Faerie hits put out on me today. I don't have the patience for games. What's going on?"

Emerantha's lips twisted. "Were you and Corvinus working on anything . . . special? Anything particularly valuable or dangerous, say?"

"I haven't worked with the Raven for a while now." I frowned. "He left a message this morning for me to reach him at my earliest convenience. I wish I had. I might have saved myself some trouble. But I don't know what he's working on. Why don't you ask him?"

Emerantha held my gaze, probing steadily with her eyes.

I leaned forward. "What's going on?"

She sat back slowly. "So you haven't heard. There's no easy way to tell you this. Corvinus is dead."

"I received a message from him this morning . . ."

"So you said. That makes you the last person we know of to have communicated with him before he died. Other than his murderer."

"He was killed." I could hear the tired bitterness in my voice, as if from a distance.

"It was obvious and very messy. NightTown style. A hit."

I mentally reviewed her questions. "And you suspect me?"

Emerantha sighed. "No. Particularly not with the recent difficulties you've been having. Besides, when we tracked your subjective timeline against the killing, witnesses placed you in Sidelines Altaforte. You've been too busy to kill anyone. But I wondered if they were connected—your problems and his."

I thought about the Whitesnakes. "I don't see how they could be." I again considered what she'd told me. "NightTown style? Knives? Ceremonial? Cultists?"

A slight shake of her head dismissed the idea out of hand. She and Corvinus had been friends for a long time. The tightness in her face was the only trace of the grief and rage and stress tamped down inside. "Something ripped him apart. Took considerable strength. Blood everywhere." The words came out of her in short, forced bursts. "No witnesses. No sounds. No nothing."

"Who investigated the scene?"

"We did. He was one of ours, after all. CrossTown Territorial Police took over after that, of course."

"You tested for Power." It was not a question.

"Naturally," she said curtly. "It was clean. Some odd traces, here and there, but nothing more than expected in the abode of someone like Corvinus. Less, actually."

"No Faerie taint?" I asked sharply.

"The only remarkable thing was the overall lack of traces we found. We found nothing distinctive." She gave me a wan smile. "It would have been an easy answer, at least."

It would have raised as many questions as it put to rest, I thought. "Why the question about what we might have been working on?"

"The place was torn apart," Emerantha said grimly. "So was his workshop downstairs. I suspect that someone was looking for something. You're one of the few Corvinus trusts . . . trusted. You've worked with him over the years on other projects. Your perspective, power and mobility have given Corvinus more options than he had before he took you as apprentice. If he were engaged in something major, it would not have surprised me to find he had pulled you in."

"A robbery? You think Corvinus was killed in a robbery?"

"No simple robbery." She paused, biting her lip as she thought. "You and I both know the precautions Corvinus took. It would have been difficult to break through his defenses. Everything was down. No alarms were raised. That takes entirely too much power for my comfort. So someone or something with power enough to break through Corvinus's defenses and do it quietly had to be involved. Even more concerning, something had enough power and subtlety to remove and block all traces. Even temporal traces. No scrying was possible. The place was swept clean. Given all that, you know and I know that something big had to be behind the attack. This wasn't spontaneous. This was planned. And you know Corvinus. Always exploring.

Always digging. Always researching. When I heard that you were being hunted, I started looking for a tie between Corvinus, you, and his attacker. Seems a little much for the timing of the bounty on your head and Corvinus's murder to be coincidence, don't you think?"

I didn't answer. I was busy thinking. I knew it wasn't Silverhand—he was pissed at me, and he could be a vicious bastard, but he wasn't the kind to hit Corvinus to get to me. No Faerie traces had been found. I had a momentary picture of the Fae and the Whitesnakes working together and snorted in disbelief. Not even my wildest paranoid fantasies could go that far. No self-respecting Fae would stoop so low.

I thought about Emerantha's questions, then looked up at her sharply. "What have you heard?"

She looked taken aback by the abrupt question. "What?"

"You heard me." I glared at her. "What have you heard that Corvinus might have been working on? What did you think I might know something about? Are you trying to solve a murder, or reconstruct his research?"

Her eyes narrowed at the last. I wondered if I had gone too far. "Listen, boy," she snarled. "This is how it works: you look for a motive that fits the facts. The involvement of power fits the facts. Reconstructing his research might tell us who would want it."

I stood, my gaze locked on hers. "There are a couple of other possibilities, aren't there? It could have been done from inside the defenses. Corvinus could have summoned something and lost control of it, right? Or he could have let someone in, someone he knew and trusted, like an old friend or a former apprentice. Given my skills, given my familiarity with Corvinus's captive powers, it might be possible for me to cover my tracks thoroughly, right?"

We were scowling at each other at that point. Then Emerantha raised one hand. "You're right. I apologize, but I have to push this. We did consider that possibility. We checked as well as we could to find any traces that the murderer might have left or any clues to the killer's identity. I've never seen all traces eradicated like that. Even old layers of Corvinus's working in the house were removed. We investigated and found nothing on you, or me, or the half a dozen other people Corvinus might have let into his sanctum. Why am I investigating any common research the two of you might have been doing? Because I know for a fact that Corvinus had developed something. He as much as told me that he had a living inquiry running that could rewrite CrossTown history, and I still don't know what he meant by that. He seemed to think it was important. Maybe someone else did too. Maybe someone thought it important enough to kill for."

"Who else knew?"

She shrugged. "You, I would have thought."

"That might be what he wanted to talk to me about," I said.

"Likely," Emerantha admitted.

I sat back down. "So what now?"

"The CrossTown Territorial Police have locked down Corvinus's place, hoping that someone or something will show," Emerantha said. "I'm checking with the base of practitioners, but so far those willing to talk have nothing to say, and not one of the rest has the connections to be suspicious. And then there's you. If this happened because of something the two of you were working on—that is to say, if you're lying to me because of an oath or some misplaced sense of loyalty—it might behoove you to remember that you could well be the next target of the killer, if what was sought was not found. Worse, you may be telling the truth, and the killer may still be seeking you."

"What do you want from me?" I asked suspiciously.

Emerantha Pale grinned in spite of herself. "You remind me of Corvinus, at times. You've been associating with him long enough that some of his habits rubbed off on you. I want you to come in. I want you to place yourself under the Union's protection."

I considered before shaking my head. "Nope. You want bait. I don't do bait. There're already too many sharks in the water, with no guarantee that you'll hook the right one."

"Go off on your own, and you might wind up as cut bait," she warned me.

"I'll take my chances."

She signed off without another word. I watched the air over Vayne's desk fade to normalcy, sat there and stewed for a minute. "Vayne!"

The door opened soundlessly. "If you still want refuge, I'll give it to you."

"No. You're right. I need to keep moving."

"Vengeance should be left to He who owns it."

I gave him a tight smile. "I'm more concerned about survival than vengeance right now. And as I recall, He helps those who first help themselves."

Vayne snorted laughter at that and I looked at him crossly. "What?"

"Nothing." He smirked. "It's just that when pagans start quoting scripture I figure that I'm more than halfway there."

I left him to his amusement and hit the street. I needed to formulate a plan. I needed a refuge that wasn't known to every

Tom, Dick, and Emerantha. I needed to avoid CrossTerPol's intervention. I thought about my vices and I came to an internal resolution. For a man dodging bounties and unknown killers, NightTown would be considered an unusual place to hide, at the very least.

CHAPTER X

THE WANDERWAY from TechTown to NightTown can be surprisingly short. Of course, that Way passes through some extraordinarily rough neighborhoods. Not one of my favorite routes. So I took the long route, through DreamTown. It seemed like a good idea at the time.

I got lucky. The first shot missed.

I had been strolling down a thoroughfare in a mixed crowd of revelers (revelry being the primary business of DreamTown) assured of my safety by the simple expedient of losing myself in the throng. I kept turning over what little I knew of Corvinus's death in my mind. I decided abruptly that at the first opportunity I'd have to do some investigating on my own, try to find some evidence to confirm or contradict the information Pale had given me. I was admiring the long crimson sunset, complete with a drawn out green flash obvious to everyone who even glanced casually in that general direction, when something spang!ed off the wall next to me, showering me with chips of brick and mortar.

Now for a guy who'd just found out that he had a price on his head, I had not to that point been remarkably bright. My reflexes, however, were pretty good. I dove for the cover and possible escape of a nearby alleyway.

In the narrow confines of the alleyway, something shiny and metal rose up on too many legs and leaped for me. I reached for the possibility of escape, and felt the resistance of anchors on that Way. I smashed through those anchors in an instant of strength driven by desperation. The time it took to drop the anchors blocking my Way, however, let the killer's drone reach me. It literally knocked me out of that reality and into the next.

The machine stabbed me twice, once in the leg and once in the body as I fell to my back. I put a spread hand on its slick metal carapace. It rose above me in a blur of slashing legs. I braced myself and threw it back, taking shallow cuts all along my arms and shoulders.

It landed on its side in the black mud, and rolled over with three lampreys already burrowing into its hull, their dull gray skins beginning to fluoresce, displaying brilliant patterns of living light as they consumed the power plant driving my attacker. The killer drone rose and managed two staggering steps toward me before collapsing. The mud around it came alive as more lampreys hit the area. The smell of ozone built in the air, coiling electric fields bristling hairs all over my body.

I did a little collapsing myself, as the White Rose did her best to keep me healthy. I had used quite a few resources lately. My body seemed a frail vessel for my survival instinct. Even the steady touch of the White Rose faltered, her sweet scent lost in the earthy taste of blood and iron. I needed a place to rest and recuperate. But first, I needed to make sure that the lampreys were enough to finish the job on my metal attacker.

I regained enough focus to see the thing's mechanical legs twitching spastically as more lampreys came writhing up out of the mud and into its hull. Bubbles of displaced air made a continuous soft popping as more and more lampreys rose to the area looking for scraps. The ultrasonic whine of teeth eating through alloy hide set my teeth on edge. That particular killing machine wouldn't be going anywhere any time soon.

I had found an old salvage yard on the edge of TechTown a long time ago and used it a few times. The lampreys wouldn't touch anything without a power source, but they were hell on machines. They occupied a valuable niche in an old dumping ground for obsolete military hardware. I suspected that they had been put together some time back by a skilled bioengineer from TechTown, or perhaps by an ecomage for hire.

I grunted as I bent forward, shifting my weight onto my good leg.

"And what do you think you're doing?" the White Rose snapped.

"Making sure that your good work isn't wasted," I responded mildly. "Or don't you think that anyone skilled enough to have anchored a Road might be able to track through it?"

I called up Shaper. He came to my mind's eye as a glittering fabric of color. "You need me?"

"I need to make myself less like myself."

"You mean a disguise?" Shaper laughed. "Human?"

My lips twisted. "Human and male. Similar build, same center of gravity. I haven't played this game enough to keep my reflexes in anything too radically different."

"You're not making this easy." He paused as he considered, then brightened. "I have it!"

"What?" I asked suspiciously.

"Age."

"I don't like . . ."

"Exactly." If he had hands, he would have been rubbing them together. "Anyone who knows anything about you knows how averse you are to aging. Not that it's uncommon, but you're obsessed. Point is," he continued hurriedly as I scowled, "that no one will look for you as an old man. And all you have to do is look old and different enough. It would take deeper searching to penetrate what I have in mind, and who will look for you under a wrinkled face?"

I thought about his proposal. It made sense. It wouldn't work against Fetch, but it might help with some of the crowd of bounty hunters out to collect fifty easy golden hours. I nodded abruptly. "Do it."

I felt my flesh crawling over my bones. Sharp pains stabbed me in my joints, forcing me to stoop. I watched my hair grow down over my eyes and fade to gray colorlessness. It took a certain amount of effort to hold the disguise in place, but that effort could yet pay significant dividends—if it worked.

The White Rose protested this use of valuable resources that she needed for the healing process, but I forestalled her. When Shaper had completed his task, I sent him back to the depths of the Legion.

"The situation's more serious than you thought," Blade said quietly. He stood beside me on the walls of my spirit as I lingered and thought about my next step.

"This doesn't change anything," I answered. "I still need to hide out for a while."

I had planned on going to ground in the Canyons of Steel. Bordering TechTown and NightTown, the Canyons of Steel were a maze of ruined technology, stalked by mutants, killer machines, old warbots, androids, cyborgs, and other things I didn't care to spend time around. It did have the advantage of being highly unfriendly territory for the Fae, however, and not comfortable ground for the Whitesnakes, either.

The attempt on my life had changed my perspective. Hiding in a den of potential bounty hunters, most of whom had machine resistance to sorcery, sounded more and more like a bad idea. The enemy had the initiative. I needed to take that away and reduce their advantages, not add to them. I had been thinking with the Fae in mind, not focused on the price on my head. The Whitesnake bounty had become as much of a threat as Fetch.

"Are you sure you want to go this alone?" the White Wolf asked suddenly.

I turned to regard him. "And upon whom would I risk bringing this plague?"

"You do have a standing invitation in NightTown," Blade said.

"No," I said without hesitating. "I can't afford to owe anyone else."

"She has a certain . . . hunger for your company," Blade said. "I understand your reluctance. But in her place of power, she has influence over the forces of life and death. Even Fetch would be uncomfortable there. I doubt he would seek to face both you and Eliza Drake in her own territory. She would be glad to give you shelter. And the Whitesnakes would not dare to hunt you in that place, though some of the hunters might."

What Blade said made sense. I didn't want to deceive Eliza by visiting her on false pretenses, though her invitation had been open for quite some time. I did regard her as a close enough friend that I wouldn't lie to her. On the other hand, if anything did go down in that place, her aid would be invaluable. Her retinue was well able to take care of itself. It was worth considering.

If any of my hunters appeared in that place, I could wind up in Eliza's debt if I needed her aid. I wanted to avoid that. Paying off that kind of debt could easily be the first step down a path toward becoming Eliza's vassal. I enjoyed being around Eliza, but on my terms, not hers. She was a vampire after all.

Blade's argument put me in a quandary. The machines of the Canyons of Steel would be a constant threat to me. Eliza Drake could provide refuge from the Whitesnakes and Fetch, but her help could carry a heavy cost.

I might have been forced to choose the more evil of the two hazards. I smiled. Eliza Drake would definitely be much more attractive company than a bunch of surly cyborgs, and I have always enjoyed the company of dangerous women.

They don't come much more dangerous than Eliza Drake.

There are many ways to become acknowledged as a Power in CrossTown, but all those ways boil down to outlasting one's enemies and becoming a landmark in the myriad, shifting landscapes of that complicated place. Eliza Drake had seen many enemies come and go, and her place on the edge of NightTown had come to reflect her presence to the extent that her domain shaped itself to her desire. The land reflected her will. That made her truly formidable in that place—and Eliza was plenty formidable without her environs rising to her aid.

I limped forward, despite the White Rose's admonition that she had not yet completed her work, and took a path out of there that took me past some of the wilder combinations of Night-Town and TechTown. Skirting the Ways to the Canyons of Steel, I hurried as well as I was able, keeping my collar turned up, my hat pulled down, and my face averted. I hoped that the rich petroleum smell of the mud would cover most of the scent of blood. NightTown had too many occupants with a taste for blood.

The ambush in DreamTown had been a pretty good trap, as traps go. The sniper might have missed deliberately, or simply provided insurance, but either way the would-be assassin had taken advantage of my weakness by employing a mechanical ally without a spirit to bind. Anchoring the WanderWay had shown more preparation than I liked to consider given the short time the bounty had been active. On the other hand, the price on my head was fifty golden hours, and it could have been active since the night before without coming to the notice of either Pale or Vayne. I had been fortunate that the assassin had possessed less skill than I at the more esoteric aspects of the Roads, or that he had spent his money on cheap anchors—if the assassin had been a "he."

I staggered on, over the border of NightTown, taking routes as tangled and inconspicuous as I could manage, looking for the lands of the Lady Eliza Drake.

CHAPTER XI

MY WOUNDS had closed and faded to sullen aches by the time I reached the outskirts of Eliza Drake's estate. My appetite had reached a cannibalistic intensity.

Dark, lush trees heavy with black fruit covered the grounds of her holding. The sun never shined there. Only certain lichens grew under the trees, taking sustenance from the minerals of the rocks and moisture from the dew. The trees nourished themselves on blood, or so I had been told. I walked cautiously through the trees, down a well-worn path lit dimly by a pale glow rising from the lichens.

That landscape hadn't occurred naturally. Eliza could shape the Ways. Old in the powers of the vampire kind, she could also touch the life and growth in living things and twist it into new forms. She had the same touch for death, or so I had heard. I believed what I had heard, considering the size and nature of her estates and her retinue. On the other hand, in all the time we had spent together I had never seen any sign of her overt power, though I had a feel for her considerable ability to mold the Ways.

The path divided, one branch continuing on into the forest, the other leading to an enormous manor house, every window ablaze with light. Music filtered out and into the night—the sounds of fiddles and pipes predominating. Inside, I felt certain, someone would be attempting a jig.

I had decided to be circumspect with Eliza. Cautious but truthful. It seemed the safest course I could live with.

I walked up to the brick portico and gave the chain a good hard pull. I didn't know if Eliza would be at this particular manor or not (she had a few), but I figured someone here would let her know of my presence one way or another. The door opened after a brief pause, letting a rush of light and music come roaring out into the night.

A woman stood in the doorway, dressed in crimson—even the ribbons in her hair were bright red. The red went well with her pale skin, green eyes, and dark hair. She looked me over disdainfully.

"Your fangs are showing, Teila," I told her mildly, letting Shaper's façade slip away.

She laughed. "Zethus! It's been a while since you've graced us with your presence. It looks like it's been a rough day." She smiled and beckoned me into the house.

I wiped my feet and stepped carefully across the threshold. "Is Eliza here?"

Teila nodded and closed the door behind me. "She's upstairs. She'll be happy to hear you've accepted her invitation."

I had expected that the unread missive from Eliza had contained a more recent invitation, in addition to the standing invitation she had extended to me. She was a socialite, like most of the vampire kind, constantly sending numerous invitations of one sort or another. Some were less dangerous to accept than others.

I let Teila take my filthy, ragged coat and my battered hat. She disappeared into another room. When she returned, she paused to lay fingers on the rents visible in my clothing. "You need a new suit."

"A seamstress would be cheaper."

She laughed, linking arms with me. "Let's go inside."

I raised an eyebrow. "Aren't you planning to let Eliza know that I'm here?"

"Already done, my dear." She gave me a wink.

"Ah."

Teila, predictably enough, led me to the bar. On an enormous expanse of gleaming floor a number of people, mostly human in appearance, danced to music from a band whose shapes had a tendency to ebb and flow with the harmony. The gray horse on drums kept up a complicated roll of precision percussion, but the six-foot rabbit on fiddle stole the show, his long ears twitching in time.

Teila leaned close. "No one plays Irish like the Pooka."

I nodded and rested my forearms on the twenty-foot long, polished, dark wood bar. It had been a long day. Events were beginning to catch up with me. I forced myself to remember that Eliza Drake's was not the place to relax my guard, no matter how warm and comfortable the surroundings seemed.

I looked down the length of the bar, past the bartender, who gave me a friendly nod. Couples nestled together at tables set strategically around the parlor, absorbed in the pleasure of the moment and the delight of the chase. I wondered idly how many of the guests wearing human guises still retained their humanity. A lone human at a party in NightTown can quickly find himself classified as an hors d'oeuvre.

A man wearing white ruffles under a black evening jacket sat down at my other side, and proceeded to study me in a rude manner. I returned the favor. Not one black hair strayed from its appointed place on his head; his features were dark, narrow, and vaguely Spanish; his clothing and jewelry were expensive and meant to look it. When he spoke, his voice was cultured and what he thought sounded menacing. "You're a little out of your depth here, aren't you?"

I had never been fond of smoothies, con men, or ladies' men. Call it the thug in me. This son of a bitch seemed to be trying for all three. I don't like to be threatened, and I hadn't had the best of days. "Who are you?" I snarled in return. "Other than a major stockholder in Brylcreem?"

He flinched, then his lips curled back from his long, pointed teeth. The Legion bristled as I sneered at him, but I relaxed as a delicate hand drifted down from behind me to pull back the sleeve of my ragged shirt. "See those marks? That's a captive Swarm of Tindalans. If you managed to get lucky and kill him before he ripped what little remains of your soul out and bound it into a pile of dog shit, where it belongs, the Tindalans would tear you apart, inside and out."

His eyebrows shot up as he looked past me. "Is this to be your treat, tonight? I hadn't meant to poach. Though I thought you had more refined tastes."

A dark woman in white eased into view, her full mouth smiling. "I don't recall inviting you, Emory."

He smirked. "I go where I please. I don't have to beg for scraps from your table anymore."

"Then why are you here?" the dark woman asked, ice in her voice. "There's nothing here for you, Emory. Find your own kind, if you can. Hunt your own grounds. Don't leech off mine."

"Leech, is it?" Emory's nose wrinkled in a snarl, his lips drew back to show his extended fangs. With his eyes smoldering like red coals, he suddenly didn't look like such a ladies' man. The bartender leaned across the bar, a pale light rising in his eyes. Emory's glance shifted between the dark lady, the bartender, and me. Finding no sympathy or fear in any of our faces, he turned and left in a swirl of coattails.

A number of the people in the room stopped to applaud politely as the dark lady called after him, "That's right, Emory— you go running back to momma."

She turned to look at me, her eyes sparkling. "I'm glad to see you, Zethus, even if you are looking a little scruffy. It's been a while."

"Not so long, Eliza," I responded gently. "Last winter—subjective."

The shade of her eyes darkened. "Here, it felt like an eternity," she said.

The bartender set a wicker basket on the counter.

"Ready for a picnic?" Eliza asked, cocking her head at me.

I felt a sudden chill. "How much do you know, Eliza?"

Her smile faded. "I've had a basket waiting, ready to go, every time I've invited you."

I picked the basket up with my left hand. "Well then, we'd better not let this one go to waste."

The moon had the rich color of glacial ice. Fat and full, it washed the glade with pale light. I pulled velvet blankets out of the basket and spread them out over a bed of thick, soft lichen. Eliza had chosen the spot, of course. We settled there under the trees, watching the moon. She drank wine while I ate a steak sandwich and a couple of firm, juicy apples, washed down with sweet red wine.

As I finished, Eliza grinned at me. "You were hungry. You're on the run again?"

"It's not an everyday thing," I sputtered.

"For some people it's not." She ran a finger lightly down my cheek. "For others . . ."

I looked at the wine, as dark and rich and red as blood, and set the cup down. "Corvinus is dead, you know. I have the Fae after me and a bounty on my head."

"I heard about Corvinus," Eliza said softly. "The Whitesnakes involved there as well, do you think?"

I yawned. "I'm not sure yet. I don't know enough."

She put her arm around me, gently turned me, and pulled me back against her. "Relax here for a while. You're safe with me."

Curiously enough, I was and I knew it. I could trust Eliza. She was a creature of her word. My concern with Eliza wasn't due to a lack of trust; I feared more the price I might pay for enjoying her company too much.

I relaxed, easing down until I could pillow my head in her lap. She rubbed the back of my neck with one hand and picked up my right arm with the other. "And what is your answer tonight?" she asked me quietly.

I felt a thrill of fear and desire work its way up my spine as she softly kissed the veins of my wrist. "My answer is the same, I'm afraid. That immortality comes at too high a price."

I wanted life, yes. I clung to life, and youth. But I loved all that the worlds could offer, as well. I had no desire to accept any bargain that limited me so severely. I wouldn't give up the sun for anyone, not even Eliza. So she always asked, and my answer never changed. Every choice has a price. It's good to understand that before signing any contracts. I wished I had kept that in mind when I had dealt with Titania.

Then there's the diet. I understand vampires don't manage too well on blood that isn't human. Something about needing to nourish themselves on more than simply the blood, but the vitality, the experience, the heart, mind and soul. I wasn't particularly comfortable with the idea of anyone else paying the price for my extended life. I didn't bother myself with anyone else's choices so long as their choices didn't threaten me directly—Eliza had to live with herself, and made what compromises she felt necessary. But I could control what choices I made, and the prices I paid.

Besides, I loved the hot, juicy texture of steak in my mouth, the crisp, tart snap of a firm apple, the warm, golden crunch of fried chicken, and the cold, smooth glide of ice cream. The idea of a liquid diet for eternity didn't appeal to me.

In spite of all that, my breathing came with difficulty as she kissed my throat, the chill of her lips hovering over the pulse of the blood before she drew back and looked me in the eye. "I would not be such a harsh mistress."

"That's not what I fear," I told her firmly.

She smiled sadly. "I know." Her mouth moved to mine, and time passed as we danced together, under the shade of the trees and in the light of the moon. Later, I felt the day catching up with me, and I grinned up at her. "No tricks, now."

Her eyes smoldered in the shadows. "I'll never take advantage of you, you know. When you fall to me, it will be of your own free will."

Still grinning, thinking about temptation, I faded to sleep.

CHAPTER XII

FEAR, RAGE, and sudden isolation drove me from pleasant dreams to madness. I reached into the darkness with all the strength I had in me, seeking to break bonds I could sense but not touch.

A slap shocked me awake, bringing the metallic taste of blood to my mouth. I opened my eyes to see Eliza silhouetted above me, open hand drawn back to deliver another blow. I rolled away from her and to my feet in one motion and looked out into the shadows and moonlight of Eliza's glade. I felt the ingathering power welling up within me. Trying to contact the Legion felt like fighting an eiderdown quilt, but I could feel the White Wolf reaching through from his side. I stood in the tangle of blankets and gave some direction to the power surging up through me.

That power called to the storm clouds roiling in the darkness above. Lightning flashed down, blowing one of Eliza's trees to splinters and nearly deafening me with the hot crackling fury of the strike. More power rose up from the fortress of my spirit, so I molded it, the White Wolf's paws over my hands like spiritual gloves, and hurled it from me.

A mighty wind swirled around the mossy bed where Eliza stood next to me. It whirled, rose to the clouds, then dropped back in a funnel to touch delicately to earth less than two hundred paces away from us. The funnel uprooted trees and smashed them down against their fellows in a fearsome display of strength. Then, as abruptly as it had all begun, the winds subsided and peace slowly descended on the forest. A swath of destruction had cut through the middle of Eliza's glade. Thick, dark red droplets seeped from split trunks and broken branches.

I felt Eliza's hand run along my shoulder. "Trying to impress me?" Her expression and tone were light.

I shuddered and turned away from the carnage. I fought nausea. "Digestion problems, I think. It's never been this bad."

She started rubbing the tension out of my neck. "Tell me about it."

So we sat back under the trees, looking out over the wreckage of the lightning and the wind, and I told her about my recent encounters. At the same time, I held a discussion with Blade and the White Wolf.

"It's from within." The White Wolf didn't look happy.

"But it's not focused." Blade's expression was even less cheerful.

"What does that mean?"

"I can't isolate it," Blade said grimly. "There's a single force behind it, something that would be as happy to see you dead as anything else, but the source of the attacks . . . it doesn't feel like one entity. It feels spread out."

I thought about that. "That would fit with the Gold's technique: every member of the Legion absorbed a significant amount of unfocused energy when we took down the Gold's legion. What if it's working through them?"

"It doesn't feel like the Gold," the White Wolf growled. "And that's not the only problem."

"Explain."

Blade answered first. "I agree with the White Wolf. It doesn't feel like the Gold's work. There's a consistent element of deception here, and considerable subtlety. Do you remember the dream?"

I fought back a shudder. "Not clearly."

"The dream was twisted, and you were slowly cut off from your surroundings by mounting filth," Blade said. "Deception and decay were not tools the Gold used. The Jigsaw Man, Vincent's ghost, was another story. The attack was subtle. The dream turned and bound you, and a barrier rose between you and your own Legion, and then something called up power from the Legion."

That startled me. "From the Legion."

The White Wolf snarled assent. "From myself among others. It felt as if my own power had gained an independent will."

"You're communing with your ghosts," Eliza said.

"We'll finish this later," I told the two of them, and gave her my full attention. "My apologies."

"No need for apologies," she answered. "I can understand your concern and need to investigate. What happened?"

I shifted uncomfortably. "Good question. I consumed some considerable power recently—more at one time than I ever have before. I think that may be causing me some problems. I may have an internal insurrection brewing."

"Bad timing," Eliza noted, her gaze sharp and attentive. "You need to quell that insurrection before you're too deep in the process of dealing with your hunters. You have too many distractions now—this matter of the Whitesnakes, Fetch on your trail, and all the rest. This time you were with me. I felt your power rousing and woke you, which wasn't as easy as it could have been. Considering the damage to the trees, I'm glad that you had enough control to redirect what was called. Next time you might not be so lucky."

"You have a point." She seemed a little stiff, a bit more rigid where her body brushed against mine. I knew how she felt. Neither of us had any particular inclination to reveal too much to anyone else, and what she had seen left us both a little uncomfortable.

I spared a glance for the devastation. Tiny, naked humanoids, their pale skin lambent in the moonlight, were emerging from the shadows to lap at the fluid seeping from the broken ends of branches with long, thin tongues. I shuddered and looked away.

"You should stay here until you have laid this matter to rest," Eliza said. "I can protect you from Fetch. His strength is death and age—I can resist him. I could teach you to resist him as well, if you would let me bring you over into the Night. Together, we could face him down. I would help you, if you would let me. Is the price really so high? It's not such a bad existence. And I would make the passage easy for you."

I smiled at her, thinking of what it must cost her to make that offer outright. I traced a line down Eliza's cheekbone from eye to mouth, and denied her gently. "You never give up, do you? This isn't the way for me. I want it all, you know. Life, youth, enough power to be independent. And I don't want to pay too high a price."

"You don't know what you're risking," Eliza argued. "You don't know what you're up against. I fear that if you chase this thing too far, you'll find only death. Think about Corvinus. He was older than you, stronger, more subtle. He staked it all and lost. Why don't you settle here until this blows over? Or take sanctuary with CrossTerPol, the Union, or Emerantha Pale if you're not comfortable here?"

"The reason I live in CrossTown is because of all it has to offer," I told her bluntly. "If I can't settle with Fetch and the Whitesnakes, I'll have to give up everything I've worked for. I'll never be able to live freely in CrossTown, or walk the Ways without always looking behind me. If I can't live this life I've chosen, that's just as good as dying."

I thought about that. Even if I did not have an obligation to my late master, I knew I had no choice anymore. I had to resolve this problem with the Fae and the Whitesnakes if I meant to go on living in CrossTown. At the same time, I suspected that there must be some connection between Corvinus's murder and my present troubles.

"NightTown isn't enough for you." She caught and held my gaze. "Staying here with me isn't enough."

I looked her in the eye for a long moment of silence. "No," I said at last.

Until we had talked, I had not fully realized where I intended to go or when. I hadn't thought that far ahead. But then I felt it, an itching need to investigate the causes of Corvinus's death while the event was still fresh. I wanted to find out who killed him, and why, not only for him but for myself. Emerantha had been right in one respect—if Corvinus had been killed for his research, then the killer probably figured, like Emerantha, that I had knowledge of it too. If someone had set me up deliberately for the vendetta and the trap in Faerie, then my bet would be that the same person would prove to be involved in Corvinus's murder.

And if that were the case, maybe the murderer was not so much interested in stealing Corvinus's research as suppressing it. That ugly thought gave me considerable pause: with the number of things the Raven had been investigating, almost anyone could have decided that he had begun to dig in forbidden areas. Knowing the nature of his project might inform me as to the nature of his killer or killers. If I could track my troubles back to the root cause of Corvinus's death, I had a chance of dealing with my own problems and getting my life back on track. As long as Fetch could legally hunt me for defaulting on a contract, as long as the Whitesnake bounty hung over my head, and as long as unknown forces thought of me as a threat because of what they believed I knew about Corvinus's research, I was a fugitive in CrossTown. Hell, I would be a fugitive anywhere I traveled along the myriad Ways, if they were motivated enough. I couldn't dodge all those bullets forever.

I considered my possible courses of action. I could investigate Corvinus's activities and check out his abode and the workshop there, as well as his study in the caves above DeepTown. I could also track the money the Whitesnakes had posted—fifty golden hours sounded like quite a bit for the ragged lot of cultists I remembered. It also seemed odd that all of it would have been put on my head. They had other sacrificial knives to grind— why not thirty on me and twenty on Anthony Vayne? Even ten golden hours gets a fair amount of attention in the CrossTown market. That focus on me reinforced my suspicion that more lay behind the Whitesnake bounty than simple revenge.

Tracking the money wouldn't be easy. The Bank of Hours wouldn't tell me squat if confidentiality were involved, unless I could pay the disclosure price, which I doubted. My best bet there would be getting my hands on a Whitesnake in the know, like one of their priests. I knew where one Whitesnake priest had lived, but I had retired him myself (permanently), so that didn't help.

I wished I could have found an analogue of Corvinus, or talked to a past self who could tell me what I needed to know, or journeyed to a timeline wherein I could warn him against his impending death. But subjective time is a constant in Cross-Town. In addition, the more we travel the possible Ways, the more the probability waves of our alternate selves collapse into our subjective past and present. I might have been able to find an analogue of Corvinus down some strange Way, but as a powerful user of the Ways, Corvinus would have absorbed all of his closest analogues into his personal probability.

Analogues of initiates of the Ways were so rare as to be virtually nonexistent. If I did find an analogue, the experiences would be divergent enough that any information I obtained would be unreliable. Each subjective past is fixed. Even trying to scry into a place as tangled as Corvinus's home would be beyond all the experts I knew and trusted. Certainly it was beyond me, though I might have some luck picking up traces once inside. Although, given what Pale had told me about how the killer had left no traces for CrossTerPol to find, I had my doubts.

"You're going to approach this thing the way you always do, aren't you?" Eliza sounded amused and a little melancholy.

"And how's that?" I asked.

"Head on." She smiled. "You could stay here with me a little longer. I think you're afraid that if you stayed long enough, you wouldn't want to leave."

That had more than a little truth in it, so I kissed her and said nothing. We sat together in silence for a while, listening to the wind in the trees and watching the shadows dance.

To break the mood, I changed the subject. "Who was your uninvited guest at the party?"

She cocked her head, and then laughed. "Emory? My half brother. He managed to get himself turned a few years back, freeing himself of his master."

I raised an eyebrow. "I didn't think that happened often."

"It doesn't. Most masters are more careful than that. Still, it was careless to turn Emory in the first place."

"He's dangerous?"

"To himself and everyone else. I don't expect him to last long."

I grinned. "And what does a masterless vampire do?"

She chuckled. "Whatever he wants, as long as it doesn't involve sunbathing." She gave me a quizzical look. "Do you think he's involved in your present problems?"

I shook my head. "Just a stray thought. Should I?"

Eliza shrugged. "Not to my knowledge. But then, I don't always know what he's up to these days. Word has it he's hired himself out to nobility. I wouldn't have expected that. Put it this way: if he finds out that you have a bounty on your head, it wouldn't surprise me to find him trying for it."

"He's not concerned about your reaction?"

"That aspect of it would amuse him."

"I knew I didn't like him for a reason."

Eliza plucked fastidiously at my ragged shirt. "You need to burn these before you go. I can give you new ones. There's a stream not far from here, for your bath. You need one."

I gave her an impudent look. "You didn't seem to mind before."

She arched an eyebrow delicately. "That was before. And you had the excuse of fatigue."

Truthfully, I needed a bath. "Lead on."

We left the remains of the picnic under the broken trees. Eliza led me to a narrow stream running between smooth rocks and down to a clear pool hemmed in by dark, crooked trees whose roots curled snugly under a thick blanket of moss. Long-stemmed roses with midnight petals ringed the pool, nodding gently in time to the unseen rhythm of a gentle breeze only they could feel, every movement wafting a delicate, musky scent into the air. Fresh clothes and thick towels lay folded at the base of one the trees, nestled in the midst of roses.

"You're nothing if not prepared," I commented as I stripped.

She laughed. "Teila was happy enough to bring the clothes and towels down."

The water had the cold, clear bite of purity. I thought about a great many things as we bathed, and when I rose from the water I had considered my course of action. I needed to deal with the Whitesnake bounty. Until I did that, every move I made would provide some joker with the opportunity for making some fast cash. I needed a plan, and I had the beginnings of one smoldering in the back of my mind. But first I needed information, both on the Whitesnakes and on the details surrounding Corvinus's recent demise. So I needed to hit the crime scene while the evidence was still fresh. I needed to see if Corvinus had left anything for me there. I doubted it. I expected that he would have left any valuable information at the more secure workshop "down by the sea," but I couldn't afford to pass this opportunity by.

I picked up the clothing Eliza had prepared for me, and found three small chains nestled in the folds of cloth. The links of the chains had been fashioned alternately out of a bright metal and a dull metal. I held them up. "Iron and silver?"

She nodded gravely. "You never know."

I fastened the chains around my throat and wrists. They would slow certain NightTown predators with particular vulnerabilities. "Thanks for thinking of me."

I drew on loose trousers, a long-sleeved and high collared shirt, and low boots. All fit well. Everything had been cut from fine cloth, and fit as if it had been designed for me. All of the clothes quite possibly had, Eliza being the way she was.

I turned my attention back to strategy. All of my planning, of course, ignored Fetch. He motivated me to move, in the final analysis. Even at Eliza's place, if Jack found me, he would take me. I couldn't present anyone with a stationary target. I had to stay away from any and all of my places and regular contacts. I needed to shift from the defensive to the offensive.

"It's dangerous," Eliza told me quietly. She stood behind me, her hands tracing the line of my spine.

I had almost become accustomed to the way she could read me. "So is staying here. So's life."

"And that's what you love about it."

"There's a measure of truth to that. I'm going to keep this thing out of your backyard. I think that my best chance is to keep moving."

She turned me and carefully smoothed my collar as it lay against my neck, covering the chains at my throat. "Don't get caught."

"Not if I can help it."

With Shaper's help, I pulled the guise of age back over myself. The wind stalked gently through the trees as I set my feet on the path out of there, my mind open to all the possibility I could reach.

CHAPTER XIII

I TRAVELED on crooked paths, wary and alert for traces of the hunters. I intended to make my way to Corvinus's place, then on to set other wheels in motion. I needed information and I needed to confound the bounty on my head. I knew a bounty hunter I had worked with on a couple of occasions, and perhaps I could use him to stymie the Whitesnakes' efforts to see my imitation of John the Baptist a la Salome.

But first, I bent the Ways of NightTown toward the high-rent district of CrossTown's native users of power—a place known as the Folded Quarter. The Folded Quarter housed more Shapers of the Ways than any other area of CrossTown. The Ways there turned in on themselves, Worms Ouroboros of infinite possibility. Powerful users of the Ways could go almost anywhere from the Folded Quarter and reel themselves back in even more easily, given appropriate markers. Most dwellings built there took advantage of the peculiar nature of the place to increase their lebensraum; closet tesseracts were a dime a dozen. More flagrant uses of the Ways could be seen in that place by paying a fee and taking a walk through one of the works of the

Folded Quarter's most expensive architects, a man by the name of Escher.

Corvinus had designed his own home. It looked conventional enough on the outside. A large, walled palazzo—a concession to the Italian origins of Corvinus's family—built in a circular design that curled around the central white spire of a fifty-foot tower like a sleeping dragon wrapped around the trunk of an ancient tree, Corvinus's home lay on the conservative side of the Folded Quarter's dwellings. The reality of the place, as with so many of Corvinus's works, turned out to be something considerably more interesting than it appeared at first glance.

I could feel the light presence of CrossTerPol interdicts on most of the obvious approaches to Corvinus's estate. I had expected that. It was a crime scene, after all. There would be wards inside, as well. But I had planned this approach with exactly those safeguards in mind. I intended to observe, not interfere enough to set off any alarms. So I turned down the branch of a Way that tended to deny its existence to all but the most persistent observers.

As I had expected, no CrossTerPol traces lay across that Way. I had not expected, however, to see that Corvinus's security remained in place. I entered the backdoor Way, only to stop in a featureless gray room. A closed door set in the wall across from me barred my path. A bulky, inhuman silhouette stood in front of the door, like an ivory statue.

My eyes widened in surprise. "Shaw. I thought you would be gone."

Eyes like icy pits opened to regard me. "Not yet, Zethus. The bonds weaken slowly. Corvinus's strength fades with his death, but has not yet broken."

He raised one hand in warning as I stepped forward. "You may not pass."

"What?" I asked sharply. "I never had a problem before."

"Corvinus tightened security," Shaw told me flatly. "I had to check with him before allowing anyone to pass. He no longer replies. I can allow no one to pass."

I bit back curses. Shaw had always been overtly hostile to his binding, and as such, had never been trusted with any flexibility in interpretation of his orders. I would have to destroy him or loose his bindings to pass. On the other hand, I could use this opportunity to my advantage. "Did you see the murder?"

"I look outward, not in."

"Did you sense anything?"

His eyes darkened. "I felt the ones who entered. I felt the Master die. I felt the one who came after."

I leaned forward, suddenly interested. "Tell me more."

The pits of his eyes caught and held my gaze. "You don't command me," he said flatly.

"I don't. Yet. I could."

"Could you?" Without moving, his aspect became threatening.

I said nothing as the Legion stirred within me. He sensed the Captains rising to look him over with hungry interest, though, for a touch of sickly green painted his white flesh. I thought about my digestion problems. I didn't need to add another threat to the already volatile mix, but he didn't need to know that.

"I offer a bargain."

His eyes narrowed. "What bargain?"

I pulled out my pack of cigarettes. "Tell me what I want to know and I'll try to break the bonds that hold you."

"And if I refuse?" He asked the question with deceptive calm.

I lit up. "Then I bind you, and take the information anyway."

"If you were strong enough, you wouldn't have to bargain."

I grinned. "Don't think to test me. I may change my mind. Do you really doubt my strength?"

He paused to consider, then sighed. "No. Not really. But I don't have much to tell."

While I spoke to him, Bright Angel and Bane rose to monitor Shaw. If he lied, I would know. Digestion problems or not, I would have the information out of him if I had to consume him to get it.

He flinched as my Captains' attention fell upon him, but he spoke steadily. "Something smashed Corvinus's defenses. Something powerful, something old, something wild. Then someone came through while the walls were down. A visitor with the stench of NightTown on him. Felt different than the power that took down Corvinus's barrier, but I didn't get a clear feel for anything other than the power. Then that old, wild power took Corvinus's personal defenses down, and the NightTown visitor killed him. The old, wild power sheltered the killer from Corvinus's death curse. After they had gone, something else came in. Something so subtle I wouldn't even have noticed it except that it cleansed the place of all traces, psychic and otherwise. Even most of the last bindings Corvinus had in place vanished under that touch. I wish it had reached me here. Once all the traces and psychic resonances had been eliminated, it left. Everything seemed normal in the house, except that Corvinus was dead."

I thought about that. The NightTown connection I had heard from Pale, but I hadn't believed it as anything other than a ruse. But with Shaw's story, I didn't have that certainty any longer. "Anything more specific? About the power that protected the assassin, or the one that came after?"

"Nothing more on the last. I only knew it indirectly, by what it did. The escort had so much power, so much wild strength. It kept Corvinus's power locked up while the assassin killed him."

My attention sharpened. "Wild? Anything more specific about the nature of the power?"

Shaw shook his head.

Bane and Bright Angel spoke to me together. "Truth. Or so he believes."

I frowned, considered the bindings holding him, then frayed them away to nothing with the sharp edge of my will. Shaw's bonds fell without too much difficulty since Corvinus no longer held them in place. Over time, they would have decayed away. Shaw would have been able to escape then without any outside aid.

Shaw rose and twisted as the bindings weakened, then he snapped them in a sudden surge of rippling power. He studied me for a moment in silence. I smoked and returned his gaze. I felt the Ways respond to his will, and he vanished.

"Think he told us everything?" The White Wolf asked.

"Probably not." I stood there for a moment, thinking. "Titania, possibly? Wild power is a good description of the feel of her workings."

"Perhaps," the White Wolf growled dubiously. "But she seems bound by place. And what of the NightTown connection?"

My lips tightened. "We still don't know enough. It could have been Fetch. He isn't bound by place. And stop playing devil's advocate."

"You know someone better suited to the part?"

Bright Angel chuckled. "A touch. A definite touch."

I ignored them both, drew a last hit from the cigarette into my lungs, pinched out the ember between thumb and forefinger, dropped the stub into a pocket of my coat, opened the door and stepped through into Corvinus's uptown workshop. The room stretched around me in an octagon, like the tower that housed it. Gray catwalks connected the black metal stairways that stretched into the workshop's upper reaches. Floating globes of pale light provided illumination. Corvinus had varied the shade and intensity of the illumination as needed. I expected to see tall cabinets of dark wood holding everything from vials of hydrofluoric acid to neatly baled cockatrice tongues. I anticipated long tables standing around the walls, every bit of a considerable and eclectic set of equipment neatly in place.

Emerantha told me the place had been torn apart, but I hadn't believed it in my gut until I saw for myself.

I hardly recognized my old master's workshop. A whirlwind had ravaged the lab, leaving nothing untouched. Equipment had been smashed, furniture torn to pieces, papers scattered to the winds. The sharp chemical smell of spilled reagents fought the pitchy scent of freshly broken wood. I had to step carefully to avoid losing my balance amidst the debris. Despite my care, the crunch of broken glass, the rustle of paper, and the gritty protest of shattered ceramic accompanied every step. I could have spent days cataloguing the destruction, but I wouldn't have been able to discern whether anything had been taken.

Not that it mattered. Corvinus had never kept anything important in his public lab anyway.

The house itself did not react to my presence. Everything around me felt quiescent, as if waiting for the Master to return. Except that the Master would never return. Did sorcerers leave ghosts? Often. Unless killed by another sorcerer.

I shivered. The house didn't understand that the Master would never return. As I stood there, it seemed to me that I could almost hear his voice in the distance, speaking to someone in another room, ready to be furious as a thundercloud when he discovered the wreckage. It felt as if I stood just beyond the place where the echoes of his presence fell away into nothingness.

I didn't spend much time there. I had planned only a cursory examination on the workshop in the main house. Only the haunting echoes of the voice of the newly dead held me, caught in the moment like a fly in amber. Corvinus had another workshop in DeepTown for higher security projects. I'd hit that one next and check it out thoroughly. I valued the residence more as the scene of the crime.

I eased my way up the main curving stairway of rose marble, where I carefully pushed back the heavy brass door. It swung open soundlessly into a cave lit by dancing apparitions of beautiful men and women. The walls glittered with the sheen of polished jewels. Thick coils of pure gold ran out of the cave walls and down over the floor in ropy loops thicker than my waist.

I chuckled and stepped through the door, feeling the twist of a guided Way. Instead of stepping into the cave, I found myself standing on a balcony made of smooth, green stone. I leaned over the rail of the balcony and looked down to see amber clouds curling like surf around the length of the jade tower. I pulled back, smiling, to watch the diaphanous sweep of a Death Angel's wings as it spiraled indifferently down to circle the tower. Above, the crowded sky blazed with the clear, cold light of countless stars—a jeweled curtain holding more colors than I could name with a light that danced as it refracted through the Death Angel's translucent body.

I stepped back through the archway before the Death Angel became tempted by my presence and set my feet on the jade steps that wound down and around inside the tower. I passed a window with every complete turn, glancing through them at scenes at once foreign and familiar. Here lay endless possibility, the recreation and entertainment of one of CrossTown's finest WayShapers. Glancing through any window, one might see veils of swirling golden sands parting to reveal a city of sweeping ivory towers, or perhaps the view might look out from a half circle of stone built in the shelter of an undercut cliff of dark red rock, tall and beautiful people with bronze skin farming and living and loving and conducting their business in the bright golden light bathing the river below. Then another turning of the stair and the view could open through cut crystal into soft darkness holding the rage of a seething red giant sun like a ruby in velvet, and then another turning, and another, down through a long gallery of infinite views.

I reached carefully, touched the Way of the stairs lightly, and stepped off the last stair and into the deep blue luminescence of bright sunlight filtered through a few feet of seawater. Deep red wood framed walls of thick, clear glass. The light and life of the ocean came pouring into the room through these ports. Rainbow schools of fish swirled like clouds whipped before a quick gust of wind, then flickered and vanished as bright torpedo shapes flashed into view and out again. Thick cushions lay piled around the room, placed strategically near long, low tables filled with everything from handheld computers to paper notebooks, inks and quills, heavy telescopes and delicate telesonde equipment.

I turned round and round about, to a doorway hidden behind the slope of the jade steps. I walked through the doorway, felt the gentle twist of a Way moving beneath me without my guidance, and then I looked out into the long sweeping curve of Corvinus's main entry hall, where he had displayed a motley collection of artifacts and curios picked up from diverse places during the course of his long and checkered career. Most of those curios held little intrinsic value, but he'd had a story for each, a memory tied to place by some oddly carved stick or twisted lump of clay.

I walked around the long arc of the corridor, my footfalls as soundless as I could make them on the polished marble floor. I kept my senses open, knowing that Corvinus's simple entry corridor had been fashioned from a Way that bled subtly beyond the confines of his home. And while I could feel the distant traces of the CrossTerPol monitors across many of those Ways, none seemed to stretch inside the house.

Despite the temptation to make the trip short, I refrained from using the entry Way, figuring that it would be more closely monitored than any other. Instead, I walked as would any burglar, slipping quietly between pedestals and display cases, watching for sentries. When I found one, I nearly tripped over the damned thing.

They had shaped it to look like one of the pedestals, supporting a bust of a stern-faced dignitary whose nameplate read Daniel Webster. I didn't recognize the name, but I knew that the bust and pedestal didn't belong. Corvinus hadn't been one for half measures, especially in statuary.

A bit of discreet examination revealed that the monitor had been set along this Way as a supplementary passive detector of possibility manipulation. I only hoped that it hadn't picked up my entrance into the workshop or my impatience in Corvinus's Gallery of Worlds. I continued down the corridor, more cautious than before, encountering no one. I knew that I had come close to my goal when the smell came to my nostrils.

Someone had set preservation effects over the entire scene. CrossTerPol must have discovered the killing not long after it had happened. Maybe Corvinus had prepared automatic notifications, and an alarm had managed to get through to someone. While I had considerable insight into Corvinus's security layout, even I hadn't known everything he'd held in reserve.

At any rate, the rich copper scent of blood didn't hold the slightest trace of decay. When I came around the curve of the corridor, I saw the scene and bit back bile. Blood splashed everywhere, pooling on the floor, the walls, even splattering the high ceiling. Bits of flesh, bone, and muscle had been scattered like chaff. The largest trace of Corvinus I saw was a bloody chunk no greater in size than a closed fist. Someone had been more thorough than I would have thought necessary.

Someone had enjoyed the killing.

The scene of the crime covered a larger area than I expected. There was so much blood . . . I opened my sorcerous senses, but I found only the power that held the area aloof from the process of decay. CrossTerPol would be going over everything forensically. If anything of the killer remained, they would find it. I had no doubt of that. I also doubted that they would find anything.

When I say that I felt no other traces of power aside from the preservation effects, I mean that all signs of Corvinus, who had worked in that place year upon uncounted year, had been scrubbed clean. I had never seen that done. I would not have imagined that it could have been done. But in that place someone had swiftly cleaned all traces of power from the scene. Anyone with that kind of skill and finesse wouldn't have left any physical traces behind, either.

My senses open, I felt the entry Way twitch subtly under me. I looked up to see bulky figures in official dark uniforms trot into view. I fled out into the wild Ways. Shrill whistles cut the air behind me. The slap of flat feet echoed on the stones of the hallway.

I took the wildest Ways I could find, rocketing through a whirling sky of kaleidoscope light on a RoadWay that writhed under my feet like a snake in its death throes. I lost them in a maze of living rock, where doors opened and closed like yawning mouths, jagged stalactite teeth could come crashing down on an unwary traveler at any instant, and howling winds pushing a violet froth of hallucinogenic spores cut through the opening and closing Ways like the breath of a mad god. I pulled my sleeve over mouth and nose, and ran, breathing as shallowly as I could manage.

The pursuit fell away behind me. By the time I walked out of a cave mouth and onto a beach of white sand, my lungs burned and the lights of the glass towers above me throbbed and pulsed in time to my heartbeat. The sun left visual echoes of itself as it passed across the sky at the pace of a boat leisurely rowed.

I waited for the sun to slow, and for the echoes to fade, and for the lights to steady, as the effect of the spores faded. Fortunately, no disgruntled CrossTerPol patrolmen showed up to continue the pursuit. Traveling the Ways while in an altered state of consciousness could be dangerous for everyone involved, but I couldn't afford to be caught, questioned, held, and made into a stationary target. It was not so much that I didn't trust CrossTerPol, it was more that I didn't trust anyone much at that point. I understood their desire to keep the crime scene clean, but I wasn't going to let a few bureaucratic regulations stand between me and any information I needed to get to the bottom of this.

Evidently, I had missed a CrossTerPol monitor, or the one I had found had been more sensitive than I realized. But I had discovered at least some of what I had gone there to find, and that was enough. More than one individual had worked to kill Corvinus. One had come from NightTown, the other commanded some of the most considerable power I had yet seen, probably of a sorcerous nature. What did that tell me?

It told me that I didn't have enough of the facts yet.

CHAPTER XIV

I KNEW of only one individual who had more than a snowball's chance in an Evangelical Christian hell to glean any information at all about the origins of the Whitesnake's gold. And that seemed to be the next step. Although "individual" wasn't entirely accurate. The Wraith seemed to be both more and less than an individual.

The Wraith, being an old friend of Corvinus's, might also have information on Corvinus's latest project. That would be the good news. The bad news consisted of the simple fact that the Wraith happened to be a good friend of my late master's, not a good friend of mine—which meant I'd have to be as persuasive as I could manage without strong arm tactics.

Unfortunately, my powers of persuasion have always been at their best when I have the other guy by a sensitive portion of his anatomy.

The Way from the sea towers ran (with a little encouragement from me) back through the edge of NightTown to a long spiral stairway formed of black marble that disappeared into the earth. I nodded to the tall figure that stood before the stair, the moonlight gleaming off his tufted ears and shining off the silver blade he held casually in his left hand.

He showed me his teeth. He had too many of them, all too long, all meant for meat. "Have you permission to pass this way?"

I looked up at the height of him. "Do I need it?"

"Probably not." He cocked his head. "Nice disguise."

"Thanks," I said modestly. "Can't say it fooled you, though."

He chuckled. "You didn't really expect it to, now did you?"

"Not while you're on sentry duty. Trying to keep the undesirables out, or the game in?"

"Little of both, little of both." He looked off toward the horizon, red eyes distant. "I hear they've put a bounty on your head."

I nodded.

"Shame about that. I might be tempted myself, if it weren't for our friendship."

I kept a straight face. "And the Tindalans."

"Aye, there's always that," he said thoughtfully. "There's always that."

He stood aside from the head of the stairway. "You know, one way to get around that problem might be to partner with someone who doesn't know about your pet swarm of private vengeance."

I grinned up at him. "Maybe that would keep you clear. Then again, maybe not. I understand that Tindalans track by intent and are a hungry bunch. As far as they're concerned, the more prey the merrier."

He grunted in reply, apparently losing interest in the conversation, so I walked on past him and down the stairs. The black marble, veined through with threads of crimson, silver, and white, throbbed under my boots with the pulse of the living earth.

The stairway dropped down into velvet darkness, lit at every full turning of the spiral by a globe radiating a cold, white light.

A distant scream, cut off abruptly, floated down from above, but that was nothing new for that place. I held to a steady, unflagging pace, passing down through geologic layer after geologic layer of earth—wending my way back through forgotten ages. The white skeletons of ancient animals lay embedded in the rock, occasionally close enough to be visible to pedestrians like myself. They offered mute testimony to the variety of life, and in their broken bones, jagged teeth, curving claws, and sharp spines could be seen the signs of past violence, ancient Darwinian arms races, and a silent plea for remembrance.

A solitary cloaked figure passed me on the stair, winding tirelessly up into the darkness, holding the small bundle of a babe in its arms, but other than that I made my journey alone. Despite the numbers of travelers in and through areas of Cross-Town, the less commonly traveled Ways can be quite deserted, due to the effort and danger involved in anything less than a skilled manipulation of those tricky paths. So the lack of traffic didn't surprise me. But the steady noise of clicking claws behind me did.

Bright Angel brought it to my attention. The sound had been stealthy enough that I had not noticed it consciously, but as Bright Angel played back the unconscious, lower level hindbrain recordings of my perceptions for the last few minutes, it became obvious that this light noise of distant pursuit had been teasing me for some time. It could have been another pedestrian, but the distant rasp of claws on slick marble seemed to be keeping pace behind me, speeding up as I increased my pace, and slowing as I slowed. I became suspicious.

I had a Hound on my trail.

Below, at the foot of the stairs, white sands covered the length of a beach that stretched beside the dark waters of the river. That place had always been used as a boat landing, but would provide no cover. I suspected that my Hound had this beach and the lack of cover to be found there in mind.

Rather than fear, a dark hostility grew in my heart. I didn't particularly like being hunted. I much preferred to hunt, instead. I kept my pace steady and extended my otherworldly senses behind me. I found only a diffuse darkness, an absence of discrete detail, and I nodded to myself grimly. It was cloaked against probing. A denizen of NightTown with natural (or unnatural, depending on your perspective) defenses against sorcery had decided to try for the Whitesnakes' bounty.

Simple hunger could also have been its motive, but by that time I had abandoned any trust in coincidence.

A NightTown Hound could be bad. Ordinarily I might have sweated getting to a WanderWay quickly enough to escape, but the river that waited below provided one of the most powerful and wild Ways in CrossTown, and I had reached the point where escape did not interest me as much as discouraging some of the opposition. I maintained my pace. The clicking slowly became louder. Knowing that most of the NightTown predators had unhealthily wide sadistic streaks, I stopped as if listening, and the steps shuffled clumsily and audibly to a stop half a heartbeat after I did.

Yep. It was definitely looking for a fear reaction. Which meant that it didn't know me very well.

I began descending the stairs once again, pushing the pace this time, making my steps a little quicker, a little more hurried, a little more evidently nervous. The clicking of claws resumed, a little softer than before, a little further behind than before, but moving a little quicker as well, closing the distance between us. I could almost hear the thing above me salivating. I had Shaper relax the disguise slowly. I figured that I might need all of my strength for what lay ahead.

I kept the pace brisk, risking a glance down to see how far the beach might be, and turning what I hoped looked like a worried expression upward. I saw nothing below but darkness, though I caught what might have been the first whisper of the voice of the waters. Above, a deeper darkness could be seen against the shadows of the stair. As I watched, the shadow slowly and insolently pulled back out of view.

Eyes narrowing, rage growing, I resumed my descent at an even brisker pace. Above, my stalker made no effort to conceal the ticking, rasping noise of its pursuit. At the same time, the sound of the river began to rise around me. I smiled. At my urging, Bright Angel focused my rage and anticipation in a sudden burst of adrenaline and I bounded down the stairs in a rush.

I hit the sands and saw no boats, but that didn't particularly bother me—once I'd found out about the hunter, I'd had no real intention of taking a boat. I had a wilder ride in mind for my new friend.

I ran out along the strand, stopped by the rushing flow of the river, formed a quick contact to the Way in the waters, and turned to see the thing that hunted me descending the stairs. It moved in a cloud of visible darkness, which made its form difficult to discern, but as I watched it rose from all fours (or sixes, I couldn't say for sure) and the shadows spread around it like countless pairs of wings. Blood red eyes gleamed at me out of the shadow surrounding it, and the rasping sound, like one claw moving against another, formed rough words. "Man most mortal . . ."

"I'm working on that mortal part, actually."

I had the impression that it cocked its head. "I am of the Wild Hunt, Blood and Bone. Does your life mean so little to you that you will not beg for it?"

I reached for a pack of cigarettes. The wind had changed, or it had a lousy sense of self-control, since I had just gotten a whiff of something sour and fetid. "I'd rather not," I said mildly as I lit the cigarette from an arc dancing between my fingers.

It took a step toward me, moving with delicacy and natural, predatory grace. "Are you so eager to die, then?"

I took a puff and rolled my eyes. "Look, let's get on with it, shall we? You're here to kill me. I'm here to keep that from happening. Wanna dance?"

I think I offended its sense of propriety. Whatever else it was, it certainly didn't seem very bright and it had been clinging to a formula.

It charged in silence, moving with the kind of flickering speed that almost made me pay for my irresistible desire to bait the opposition. I stumbled backward, toward the river, dropping and rolling as it leapt through the space I had just occupied. It sailed past me and landed half in the water. I dove at it as it turned, hitting it about belly height.

I fell into the embrace of what felt like everything from arms to tentacles. I locked us into our destination as the current pulled us downstream. Claws ripped at a thin barrier of force held in place by Bright Angel, as my will built a barrier against a swirling psychic attack. It had strength, viciousness, and power in plenty, but I was gambling that it didn't leave its regular haunts all that often.

Some inhabitants of CrossTown have more tolerance for wild environments than others. And I don't mean the usual vacuum/hard radiation/distorted gravity environments. In many of those, if you're prepared, you're fine, and if you're not, you're dead. Those environments won't change you, they'll just kill you.

I had something less pleasant in mind.

I took my snarling adversary to a place where the self, the soul, the ka, the complex of the ego/superego/id, the "I"ness of the individual, manifested itself, while the body vanished. In that place the senses changed. I translated what I perceived into something I could handle—a visual and tactile metaphor.

Each self could be perceived as a liquid in suspension of another liquid, a self held within an all-pervading self like the soul of the universe. In that greater self, the soul had two choices: become a tightly contained sphere, or dissolve, lose cohesion, and mix in with that overwhelming, all-pervading self.

Kabbalists describe the Sephiroth, the worlds of creation, as bubbles floating in the mind of God. I became my own Sephirah, holding within me the many smaller spheres of the members of my Legion. Through that I could see the milky web of something else spreading through my Legion like cancer. For the first time, I could see the problem brewing within, and it was like nothing I had ever encountered before. I wanted to trace that web back to the spider that spun it, but I had other problems.

Beyond my periphery, I sensed the stretching, twisting geometry of my shadowy hunter. A constellation held together by the chains of a powerful will, it had clung to me during transit and had begun to mount an attack on the borders of my Legion.

Instead of resisting, I pulled my sentries back. My attacker followed eagerly. The Legion pulled back further. More of my assailant rushed into the gap. Some small members of the Legion fell under the rising tide of the opposition, fighting furiously before sinking into isolation for later digestion. I fed my attacker memories I could afford to lose as well, parting reluctantly even with such small parts of my life as closing a bathroom door, or waiting in the cold of a stone antechamber on my master's pleasure, or inventorying cockatrice tongues. My assailant took the bait, plunging further after the retreating line of the Legion, until the bulk of it had passed beyond the extending wings of the fiercest members. The two wings, led on the right by Bright Angel and on the left by Bane, closed behind the shadow creature's attack and completed an englobement of its forces.

The retreating front of my Legion suddenly stiffened, Blade at the fore. I drove my will into the center of my enemy's mass like a falling hammer. The NightTown creature's personality shattered like glass. I took the mass deeper into the thunderous tides of that place, where I let the power of the Way work with my forces to extend our advantage as we freed the few small ones who had fallen early. Together we consumed the essence of the shadow creature's self.

Parts of the creature's essence slid through mine, as the Legion crushed every last piece of resistance. I sorted through the fragments of my assailant's self, trying to find its memories. As I moved and assimilated, my Legion accompanied me, feeding like remora on the flotsam and jetsam that I ignored.

It was a little power in its own right, a thing of the dark Fae, a Shadow Hound and a Hunter, an old weapon in forgotten wars roused from its slumber and sent hunting. This had been no chance encounter. Though I could not identify the one who had sent it in the wreckage of its memories, the Faerie linkage gave me strong circumstantial evidence. Titania was not content to rely on Fetch alone.

As I studied its memories, riffling through them like a pick-pocket with a freshly stolen wallet, a reference to the Wild Hunt stirred my own memories. "I am of the Wild Hunt, Blood and Bone," it had told me. Another had used a similar phrase—the Jigsaw Man, Vincent's ghost, had also spoken those words. They were brothers, these two, paired weapons with a clear maker's mark. Titania had been hunting me even before she had set Fetch on my trail. But again, I didn't understand the need for the charade when Fetch had taken me to Faerie. Had she feared the Tindalans so much? They were alien to the Fae, but she had so much power at her command. Or had it been a matter of timing? Had she been weakened in her attack on Corvinus?

If it had been Titania. I had no hard proof, but doubt was fading fast. And if it had been, I still didn't understand her motive.

"Is it safe?" the White Wolf asked, "to take this one as well? The infection in your Legion spreads even now. The last member of the Wild Hunt surely lies at the root of that problem."

I let him sense my own bitter amusement. "I'm certainly not letting him go. And last time I let you feed, someone was sloppy. This one I'll take myself."

The White Wolf drew back as I pierced the last defense of the heart of my enemy, and drew forth the dark, savory core of its power. I fed on that power, consuming it as the Legion churned below me, snapping up pieces of memory and personality drifting in the currents of that place.

Later, once I had fully encompassed the last of the Shadow Hound, I slid free of that place at last, stepping comfortably back into the familiar restriction of my body. I had with me the faintest slip of an apparition, a manifestation of the power that had stood at the heart of the dark Hound. Its appetite had been relentless, consuming, a bottomless well of hunger. As I came out into the dim light of a back alley in the port of DeepTown, all that remained of the Hound hid in my shadow. The vast cavern that cradled the trading community burned with countless points of light, holding back the return of the patient darkness.

The Shadow Hound had become nothing more than a small, mewling, weak ripple of shapeless power, a mindless movement of distant hunger. I trapped that last restless trace of power in my shadow, binding it easily while its resistance was broken. When my shadow faded, the power faded; and when my shadow grew dark, its strength grew. But the Shadow Hound had no self left to it. I had taken that. The strength that remained had become an extension of my will.

I thought about the infection I had seen spreading through the Legion in a web of pestilent influence. I knew that something would have to be done. I didn't need to call up the White Wolf or Blade to feel their agreement. Bright Angel's passion burned like a thousand watch fires at the towers of the fortress of my soul. What I had seen attacked the very natures of the individual members of the Host, something I had always left alone. That disturbed them deeply, and left them all hunting, one through the other, for the source of the infection. Though the Legion roiled unsteadily within me, I took this for a good sign. Perhaps they could deal with it independently. Perhaps they would root out the infection without my supervision.

I didn't have the time to deal with it in any event.

I called on Shaper, once again pulled the distasteful cloak of age over myself, left the alley, and set my feet on the main thoroughfare of DeepTown. I needed to come up to where the Wraith made his abode. From there I would hit Corvinus's workshop, which happened to be in the vicinity.

CHAPTER XV

MANY OF DeepTown's avenues were waterways, stretching between buildings built on the flat-topped cones of huge stalagmites thrusting up out of the dark, fathomless waters of the inner sea, sometimes on pilings that stretched down to anchor to deeper stalagmites. Above, lines of light from hanging bridges snaked across the distant roof of the cavern, casting pale reflections into the dark waters. The main thoroughfare consisted of a floating causeway that cut through the center of Deep-Town and ran out to the suburbs and through the nearest wall of the great cavern that harbored the inner sea. I avoided that Road, preferring to snake my way through side streets and along swinging footpaths.

The crowd around me stank of fish or money, the former the more honest scent. DeepTown, like most of the other areas of CrossTown, thrived on trade. Anything could be found in the markets and on the wharves of DeepTown, including some things that could not be found elsewhere. Considering that and the various hunters and traps that sought my blood recently, I stopped in a small shop set between two large import houses, its wooden doors marked by a single, curious sigil.

I pushed through the thin wooden outer doors and walked past the open, armored inner doors and into the shop, which seemed much larger than it had from the outside. Knives, swords, and other bladed weapons of all conceivable sizes and shapes covered the walls. Racked out from the walls stood long arms—some recognizable, some not.

The man who met me in the middle of the floor of that first room wore a plain, gray uniform, which matched his skin, hair, and eyes. "What do you need?"

"A great many things," I told him briskly. "But I'm in this place for a weapon."

He nodded abruptly. "This is the right place. Powered or not?"

"Doesn't matter. I need something that disables machines."

"Damage to organics or not?"

"Nothing lethal to organics, I think."

"Ranged or not?"

"Ranged, preferably."

"Capacity?"

"At least five shots. Reusable. Reloadable. And I'll need additional ammunition."

"Concealable or not?"

"Concealable."

"Price range?"

"Reasonable."

"I have three weapons in mind that will fit your needs." The shopkeeper turned, and I followed him deeper into the shop. He stopped before a large rack of handguns of various shapes and sizes, and picked up a large unit with a bulbous head at the business end. "Pulsegun. Focused electromagnetic pulse. Fires in a cone, strongest near the weapon, broadest coverage at the far extent of the range. Effective range fifty meters. Largest diameter of the cone approximately two meters. Some advanced shielding will diminish or eliminate the effect. Fifty shots per rechargeable clip. No immediate damage to organics. No Cross-TerPol interdiction. Five silver."

He turned, led me deeper into the room, stopping to pick up a thick cylinder about a foot and a half long. "Multi-strand Power Whip. Effective range three meters. Area of effect three cubic meters. Ten minutes of continuous use before needing a recharge. Power arcs will fry most electronics, takes longer on certain shielding. Lethal to most unprotected organics. Limited CrossTerPol interdiction. One gold."

He turned again, led me yet deeper, and stopped before a glass aquarium. I looked in at a thick layer of mud, and saw the surface twitch. "Power lampreys?"

"Not a personal device." He stooped, opened the cabinet under the aquarium, and pulled out a pouch filled with round objects the size of marbles. He poured several into his hand, and I saw mottled, gray spheres with irregular, creased surfaces. "Spores. Dormant form of driller worm colony. Driller worm is a smaller cousin of the power lamprey. Works against machines with an electromagnetic power source only. Harmless to organics. Must be thrown or placed within one meter proximity of a powered machine. Depending on configuration of target, may result in some delay before target is rendered harmless. High level of CrossTerPol interdict in certain districts. Carrying driller worm spores in TechTown is a capital offense. Three bags for one silver."

I hesitated. "How much to exchange funds through the central billing location?"

"Price doubles," he responded without hesitation.

"Done. I'll take three bags." I recorded my permission for the exchange with him. He completed the transaction through the central billing location for the weapon shops. I had no doubt that any transaction I made would be traced by someone through the Bank of Hours. All they would have to do is pay the fee. By making the transaction through the weapon shop's central location, they would be able to determine the general nature of my purchase with ease, but my location and the specifics would be more difficult. That degree of anonymity was well worth the additional cost.

I tucked my dormant worms into separate pouches on my belt for easy access and exited back out to the thoroughfare. I felt better about any machine ambushes, and as long as I stayed away from the anchored WanderWays I would be fine for virtually anything else. I disappeared back into the cavernous depths of a path between two looming buildings and touched the possibilities of the Road. It took me a snaking Way, up and around and over, until I came to walk amidst a jungle of twisted seaweed strands far above DeepTown, following a path leading into one of the upper entrances of the caverns.

Bats glared down at me from where they hung on the supports of the rope bridges, but I received no second looks from passersby, even though straight human stock seemed to be a minority in that place. I did see plenty of bodymod types, most adapted for the water, others for flight—wings or fins or gills, or long, articulated limbs flattened and streamlined for swimming all made the bodymods obvious. Those were the backbone of DeepTown; the ones who wouldn't or couldn't absorb the price of the inflated real estate below, but who commuted in for a quick copper or for the pleasures of the deep.

I pushed my way through the crowd and into the mouth of the caverns, where the traffic lapsed a bit. Smooth granite passages embraced me, lit by blue-green luminescent strips running at waist and ankle height. I traveled more swiftly at that point, snaking along the long single Road of the intertwining corridors on a ripple of possibility.

I stopped before an opaque archway; the space under the arch filled with something darker than the surrounding stone. I touched the shadow under the arch and it rippled into motion. The face of an old man formed in the smoky substance, sneering at me. "Zethus. What do you want?"

I gave him my best, delicate irony. "Alistair MacWraith, as delightful as ever. I need to talk to you."

He seemed unimpressed. "So? Why should I spare the time?"

"For Corvinus."

He paused. "You are a bastard. Come in."

The smoky barrier faded to light. I stooped under the arch and stepped into a domed room. Recalling the numerous strange artifacts and machinations the Wraith collected, I paused to leave my coat and the driller worm spores in the antechamber. From that room, I came into a technosage's workshop. Odd devices had been strung together all over the open expanse of the floor. The ones I recognized ranged from a teletype to several models of home computer, some extremely advanced, some extremely primitive. Banks of larger machines enclosed the crowded space and extended some distance into the darkness. In the center of this space, in separate cases with lines and cables leading to and from them, stood some objects not usually associated with technology, such as stones for geomancy, bones for osteomancy, one fanged skull the size of a pony, a cracked plastic Ouija board, and no fewer than three perfect spheres, each a bit larger than a man's head—one made of clear crystal, one polished to mirror reflectivity, and one that reflected no light.

In the midst of those three spheres stood a table and chair, a tower of sparks dancing before the chair. As I entered the room, the pinpoints of light curled together and drew upright into the form of a tall man with a stern face. "Zethus. What do you want from me?"

I went straight for the throat. "You knew Corvinus had died. Did you know that he had been murdered?"

"I didn't know that anyone knew for sure that he had been murdered. Did you kill him, to possess such certainty?" he asked offensively.

"I thought you knew him better than that."

He simulated a sigh. "You do have a way of cutting to the heart of the matter. No, I don't think that you're responsible. What did you come here for?"

I stepped closer. At proximity, the illusion crumbled; the Wraith's form trembled with the individual motions of the millions of tiny photoelectric animals that made up his (its) corporeal self, and housed his (its) collective intelligence. The Wraith had always exhibited the form and personality of a crotchety old man to me, though not for the purpose of concealing his condition. "Did you know what Corvinus was working on? Emerantha Pale gave me the news. She wanted me to take shelter in the loving arms of the Union. But she also told me that Corvinus was working on something that might have gotten him killed. She insinuated that I knew more than I do. I came to you to see what more you might be able to tell me."

"One of Pale's theories is that you killed your master for his research," he snorted. "She just doesn't know you very well. The fact that someone's put a price on your head is more indicative of your personality or lack thereof than a common motive for murder. Besides, what makes you think he would tell me something that he wouldn't tell you?"

"You didn't answer the question."

He turned his head away from me, though of course he was as aware of me as he would always be. At any given time, at any given angle, thousands of his eyes would be looking in my direction. "You're quicker than you used to be. Tell me, did you ever beat Corvinus at chess?"

"Once." I smiled in spite of myself. "Oh, I won the game a couple of times, but I only beat him once."

The Wraith nodded in satisfaction. "Once you would not have known the distinction. Corvinus and I are both old. You're new to this game. Corvinus played chess like he lived his life, always planning ten or twenty moves ahead. If you managed to catch that, you could deliberately break his strategy, rather than bumbling into victory. I will tell you this much: Corvinus was working on something, and that something was valuable enough to kill him for, and I don't know what that something might have been. He never talked about it; I never pried. Anything else?"

"I could almost agree with you regarding the motive of the Whitesnakes, but the price they posted for my head and the involvement of the Fae do not seem so easy to explain away," I said mildly.

"You're beginning to think," he said. "In some cases it takes a while. You don't have the luxury of time. Corvinus planned in advance. His history in CrossTown counted centuries, not years.

Whoever killed him had to be able to plan for that. They must be able to play at Corvinus's level. Odds are, the Whitesnake bounty is only one move made against you. When were you poisoned?"

"Huh?"

"Poisoned," he repeated impatiently. "You and your Legion. It's obvious to anyone with eyes to see. Surely you knew."

"I'm having problems with some recent conquests," I admitted.

"That's an understatement," the Wraith said dryly. "You've been attacked at the foundation of your power. If you believe that's anything but a deliberate strategy, you're fooling yourself. Did it happen in Faerie?"

"No." I spoke slowly, thinking about my recent past. "I'm beginning to believe now that it came before the meeting with Fetch. Vincent asked me to take care of a problem for him. A nasty spirit with a horror fetish. The Jigsaw Man. My troubles seem to have begun about then. On the other hand, I've been attacked since by a Fae Shadow Hound, and both it and the Jigsaw Man referred to the Wild Hunt."

"How difficult do you think it would be for someone to discover that Vincent knew you well?"

"Not hard, if they went to the trouble." I sighed. "It all goes back to Corvinus and points to Faerie. Silverhand is out for my blood, after all, but something doesn't ring right with that. Not his style. I fear that Faerie might be another blind."

His head bobbed nervously. "I heard about the contract. Fetch should concern you more than Silverhand. You do realize that Corvinus was killed while you were waiting for Fetch."

"I thought of that," I said. "The amount offered and the timing strike me as more than coincidence, but is it a distraction? Can you track the Whitesnake's gold? Find out where it originated? It will probably be several layers deep, and of course, it's in the hardest nut to crack, the Bank of Hours . . ."

"Don't try to manipulate me, boy," he interrupted. "You're so clumsy it's ridiculous."

"Maybe so." I grinned at him. "But . . ."

"But you knew I'd be interested. I also see your theory. But who in Faerie? Silverhand had a grudge against you, not a grudge against Corvinus. I don't see Silverhand attacking Corvinus to get to you. And once he had you in Faerie, I don't see him letting you go. The Wild Hunt is Fae, but not commonly linked to Silverhand. It's too old and too wild to fall under Silverhand's control."

"Maybe so, but Silverhand didn't trap me. Titania did."

His features grew suddenly indistinct. I realized that I'd shocked him. "Titania's moving again?"

"I suppose so," I said indifferently. "I'd never seen her in the Faerie courts, or heard her referred to there . . ."

"They wouldn't mention her," he cut me off brusquely. "No one would speak of Titania in the courts of Lugh's liegemen. She's a separate power, and Lugh doesn't like that. When the Fae betrayed their allegiance to Danu, Titania alone remained faithful. For most of the interval before what you would call history, she remained in the time beyond time. She set up a permanent residence in Faerie when the Sidhe Lords began to isolate it from mainstream possibility. She has appeared infrequently at best since that time, rarely involving herself with anyone or anything beyond her own demesne, and few are welcome there. A number of Sidhe Lords have never met Titania. The link to the Wild Hunt isn't strong with Titania, but she does have the resources to call on some of those old powers. Titania is an old, wild power herself."

I licked suddenly dry lips. "She was . . . impressive."

His outlines blurred. "You saw her?"

He didn't pay any attention to my nod. His voice had taken on an odd timbre, an inhuman tone. That vanished when he spoke again, his outlines once more settling into the smooth façade of humanity. "Humans are not among her favorites. She must have planned to discard you from the start. You're right in one respect—the contract was a sham covering an attempt on your life. But a strange attempt. She could have killed you herself, even with your Tindalan insurance. Something deeper is at work here. Perhaps she felt she could not afford the time it would have taken to recover from the attack of a Tindalan Swarm. Perhaps she did not mean for you to die just yet. Perhaps she means to use you for something before she kills you. And now that you've broken the contract she made with you, Fetch can take you anytime, anywhere without stepping outside CrossTown laws."

My eyes narrowed. "I hadn't known there were powers in Faerie separate from Lugh's dominion. She sounds as powerful as Lugh, at least. Did she kill Corvinus?"

"Who knows?" The Wraith shrugged. "She could have," he said. "It would have been within her capabilities, but it would have been risky. She would have had to act through agents, for she is bound to Faerie, and that increases the risk of discovery. Whoever killed Corvinus did cross the line. They will be hunted. CrossTerPol is persistent. Emerantha Pale and the Practitioner's Union has sufficient resources that even Titania would have difficulty operating within CrossTown ever again, even indirectly; and the penalty could even be more severe, since CrossTerPol can't afford to let someone in the suburbs get away with casually

murdering prominent citizens. I will do this for you. I will follow this Whitesnake's gold. If it is Faerie . . ."

"Then we'll have more questions than answers. Again."

He nodded in agreement. When he spoke, his voice softened, surprising me. "Have you thought about turning away
from this obligation? Corvinus is dead. What does he care if
you find his killer? Your own life is at risk. And at this point,
smart money is on the opposition."

"Thanks for the vote of confidence," I said sourly. "Look, I'm
not ready to abandon CrossTown. There's no guarantee that I
could stop these attempts by leaving CrossTown anyway. So it's
in my own interest to pursue this. More importantly, an obligation doesn't end when a friend dies. If I walk away, I'm not just
walking away from my old teacher, I'm walking away from the
foundation of my own principles. The life I'd save in doing that
wouldn't be worth having."

The Wraith had nothing to say to that. His human form became something resembling a column of smoke. I lifted a hand
in farewell as I turned and slowly made my way back to the antechamber and picked up my belongings. Corvinus's workshop
seemed the next logical place to hit, and given its proximity that
would be easy. After that—depending on what I learned—perhaps it was time to deal with the Whitesnakes.

CHAPTER XVI

CORVINUS HAD owned two workshops. He kept one for low security or high profile projects: the lab at the base of the tower in his home in the Folded Quarter. It served as an excellent blind for any high security projects that he might have been pursuing elsewhere: "elsewhere" generally meant in the four thousand or so square feet of finished cave that he owned in one of the upper caverns of DeepTown. That one he kept for high security, low profile projects, which meant research done for his own purposes as opposed to research done for hire.

Corvinus had always been cautious; in this case, his ownership of the DeepTown cave passed through at least one corporation and a couple of dummy identities. It would have been difficult and expensive for anyone to link him to his activities in the DeepTown caves. He had chosen an isolated, nearly deserted section of DeepTown for the lack of honest traffic and for the lack of neighbors. Some research is less savory than others. His security measures could perhaps be best described as draconian.

I had several advantages, however. As the Raven's apprentice, I had been keyed to all but the most restricted of his security levels. I had assisted on a number of projects. I knew the place well. I had no fears of being unable to penetrate the security, even though Corvinus might have changed the accesses again before he died.

I followed the passage around the last bend. What I saw stopped me in my tracks. The broken slabs of granite that normally concealed the inner doors of interlaced composite fell away to each side of the lab entrance. Of the composite doors I saw no trace but black powder. I wouldn't have to worry about breaking through Corvinus's security. Someone else had done that already.

I felt a tingling in my extremities. I remembered the Wraith's warning that Corvinus's killer had to have significant resources and knowledge. The evidence of some player, whether the killer or not, with more resources and knowledge than I had anticipated lay before me. I couldn't afford to stay behind in this game.

Concerned, I began to examine the area carefully. I didn't want to be taken by surprise. Through a gray haze of interference, I tasted no hint of power in the area.

I worried about that haze on my senses. I thought about the lack of power traces at the scene of Corvinus's murder. That haze could be a less sophisticated version of the same technique, covering any traces of whoever had broken into Corvinus's workshop. Bright Angel stood ready when I called. "Have you seen that kind of interference before?"

"No." She said mildly. "And there's a reason why."

The White Wolf answered before I could ask the question. "It's from within."

"The interference? A side effect of the digestion problem?"

"This is a bit more serious than a digestion problem," growled the White Wolf. "You need to give this a higher priority. Remember what the Wraith said about spiritual poisoning. Indigestion doesn't change tactics. This is definitely a change in tactics. You'll notice that you're communicating with us without interference. This thing, this poison, now seems to be trying to cut your senses off from the outside. You need to deal with this in a hurry."

"Look, dammit!" I snarled. "I understand. I'll deal with it when I have time. If I slow down now, I run the risk of Fetch catching up with me. First we deal with the workshop, then I try to find a safe place to deal with this thing."

"You need to make the time—" the White Wolf argued.

"And now is not the time," I told him flatly, cutting him off.

His voice dropped to a muttering growl. Fortunately for both of us, I couldn't make out the words.

Blade broke in at this point. "I have to agree with the White Wolf. You must make this a priority. If you allow this poison to continue to work unopposed, I fear it will seriously impair your ability to function."

I turned my attention to him. "Have you and the White Wolf discovered anything?"

"Some. The problem is centered on the Captains of your Legion, and the White Wolf."

"I like that!" the White Wolf said with an affronted snarl in his voice. "If I'm not a Captain by now, I should be."

My eyes narrowed. "I thought it was spreading through the Legion."

"It is," Blade said patiently. "It's spreading through the Legion, but it's spreading outward from the Captains. Including me. And I can't feel it."

I looked from one to the other. "So. How do I deal with something none of us can sense? Tell me that."

Silence.

I thought about the workshop. "Keep working on it."

"Purge the Legion."

I turned back to the White Wolf. "What?"

"Purge the Legion." He settled back comfortably on his haunches. "Confine all possible sources of infection and already infected members of the Legion. Wait and see what happens to them."

Blade nodded grudgingly. "It would be the best way."

"It would also strip me of my defenses." I considered that. "This isn't an accident. The effect is too convenient. The Wraith was right. I've been poisoned, spiritually speaking. Or you have. This eliminates the possibility of the Gold."

"The Jigsaw Man," the White Wolf said flatly.

"Seems like the logical choice," I said. "Vincent called me. I made no secret of the fact that I knew Vincent, and he knew my work. Any problem of that nature in the abode of a friend would result in calling me in. It would have been an easy trap to set for anyone who knew my habits, or did a little research."

"It would fit the facts the best. Elements of darkness . . . infecting the Captains and the White Wolf, who all fed on it," Blade agreed. "All of us had begun to suspect. We just hadn't faced it yet."

"Knowing its nature should help." Bright Angel shifted uneasily, her discomfort more evident for being foreign to her nature.

"It should. Hopefully it's enough." The White Wolf couldn't leave it alone. I glared at him, but he met my eyes without flinching.

"I'm starting to believe the Faerie theory," Blade said. "As much as it pains me."

I sighed. "I don't believe in that much coincidence either. The timing . . ."

"None of us do, at this point," the White Wolf said acerbically. "What would you like to bet that the Whitesnake bounty is ultimately from Faerie as well?"

I thought about that. "I don't know. There's still something off. Faerie doesn't seem to want me dead. At least not yet. They seem to want something else. If they had wanted me dead, they had plenty of opportunities to kill me. I almost have the impression that there are factions involved."

"Which could all still be Faerie," the White Wolf insisted.

"There's one way to test the Faerie commitment," Bright Angel interjected.

"And what's that?"

"Go home. See if Fetch is waiting there for you. See if he refuses to take you."

I shivered. "I don't think that I want to test my theory quite that far, yet. And I don't have time at the moment."

"You'd better deal with it soon," the White Wolf said bluntly, "or you may lose access to the Legion altogether."

"I know, I know." The conversation was taking us nowhere. I felt the growing urgency, but I had too many problems to juggle. I was at the workshop. I needed to find what I could while I had time, then find a place to work on cleaning up the Legion. I didn't like the idea of a purge, and I didn't like the idea of isolating my Captains. I didn't have a strategy for dealing with it. So I decided to keep dealing with one thing at a time. I had too many things that demanded my immediate attention, but I had the feeling that choosing the wrong course might mean that I would never have the opportunity to choose anything else again.

I ended the conversation abruptly by pulling out of the conference and taking the time to study my surroundings with both conventional and sorcerous senses until I was satisfied that no one had left any signs of passage, deadfalls, powered traps, or spirit guards. The interference from the spreading cancer within had not diminished, so I took longer than usual, scrutinizing everything as carefully and as closely as I could. The impairment of spiritual senses emphasized how urgently I needed to deal with the poison within.

I didn't find any traces of active or bound power. Of course, someone could have been waiting inside, their power pulled in on themselves to keep their profile low, but I doubted it. There aren't that many users of any power out there who could hide from my careful attention at such close range. The ones I knew of who had enough subtlety to conceal themselves from me even when I was actively searching wouldn't bother with stakeout duty.

The place looked empty of any sign that sorcery had ever been used there. I did not take this as a good omen. Corvinus had shielded it, but the shields leaked at least a little bit all the time, due to the magnitude of power he would call up and bend to his will in the midst of his research. But now the doors had been cast down, the shielding had been destroyed, and the workshop felt empty, cold and dead.

Everything about that supported Emerantha Pale's theory. But who else had known about, or would have been able to find, Corvinus's secret workshop? He had died a terrible death. Perhaps his killer had tortured him. Perhaps Corvinus had given all of his secrets up before the end.

On the whole, I doubted that he had given anyone much. He had been tough, had Corvinus; no one who had survived as long as he had doing the things he had done could be anything but tough.

I thought about Pale as well, as I stood there in the corridor. It couldn't have been an official raid; otherwise the place would still have been guarded by representatives of CrossTerPol. If Pale acted legitimately, she would move only with the sanction of CrossTown's finest. But Pale could have been acting independently. She seemed to be convinced that Corvinus's research had been important enough to kill for. How badly did she want it for herself?

Thinking about CrossTerPol made me realize something else. This damage hadn't been done long ago. As soon as a local happened by here and called the authorities, the place would be crawling with narrow-minded public servants. I had things to do before that occurred. Even though traffic had never been heavy in that area, passersby that would eventually call the authorities could stroll through the corridor at any time.

I entered cautiously through the broken doors. I thought about the force displayed so casually there, combined with the subtlety necessary to work through Corvinus's security precautions unscathed. If the perpetrator had been unscathed; I hadn't yet seen any body parts or copious amounts of precious bodily fluids that would indicate some serious scathing had occurred.

Subtlety and strength always make a bad combination for the opposition. In this case the opposition meant me. I can't say I was happy about that.

The place had been reduced to a ruin. Corvinus's equipment had been ground to powder—no pieces big enough even to be considered rubble remained. The walls and floors and ceiling showed signs of damage on a large scale. It looked as if some-one had become a bit frustrated when they found nothing. For-tunately, the section of wall with Corvinus's Keystone hadn't taken much more than surface damage and the Keystone itself hadn't been so much as chipped. I loosened it carefully, pulled the long stone out of its place, turned it around, and slipped it back into the wall.

Corvinus had designed the Keystone well. I knew the the-ory, but I didn't have the craft. He had taken his skill with the WanderWays and built a small, specialized, and conditional AccessWay into a limited space. That access only existed when the Keystone and the wall were in a harmonious configuration. When the Keystone slid into place reversed, as it had been when I came into the workshop, the AccessWay collapsed and was nearly undetectable.

The Keystone warmed under my hand. I touched it light-ly, manipulating the Way within, and it opened into a narrow stone room. My nostrils pinched at the dead air moving past me, mixing with the fresh air of the lab. The room couldn't have been more than five paces wide, ten paces long, the ceiling within easy reach of an outstretched arm. Burning white crystals placed in tall stands made of twisted iron illuminated the room with harsh, unforgiving light. The floor, walls, and ceiling were all seamless and smooth. Corvinus had hollowed out or found a perfectly rectangular pocket deep in a thick layer of bedrock. The dark stone always felt cool to the touch. The air always tasted stale. I knew that place. I had been there before. It was Corvinus's cache, his safe place, his hidey hole. And it was nearly empty.

The only contents of the room aside from the lights were three objects resting on a long, plain, waist-high wooden table at the end of the room. Everything else had vanished. Considering the hoard of monetary and sorcerous objects that Corvinus had kept there, I wondered for a moment if it had been a robbery. Approaching the table slowly, I discarded the idea that this had been a robbery, since no thief would have left all this so neatly for me to find.

I studied the table and its contents. In the center lay a dark lump of stone the size of a child's fist. A multitude of tiny crevices marred the misshapen surface, giving the stone the appearance of petrified flesh. On the right side of the stone lay a spirit trap in the form of a crystal. It glowed brightly, occupied. To the left of the stone lay a small, glossy brick of stiff material. I recognized that glossy brick. I'd used one before for Corvinus, when he'd sent me on an errand that required traveling through a radioactive wasteland. It was a nanotech recovery suit. I could survive high pressure, temperature extremes, radiation, or even hard vacuum for a time. The suit would sustain me by using my waste heat and sweat and breath as fuel and building blocks. Evidently, Corvinus had been making plans for an errand. Without a doubt, he had left these things for me.

I pocketed the suit, careful not to disturb the activation tab. I picked up the stone, and realized that it had been resting on a folded pouch of soft leather, tied with a long thong. I slipped it into the pouch and hung the pouch around my neck, inside my clothing. With my coat closed, it might be tough to notice, but with just a shirt it made a sizeable lump. Still and all, it would be more difficult to lift from my person without my knowing while hanging around my neck.

Corvinus's spirit trap I didn't touch. I probed it cautiously, noting that it had been sealed with Corvinus's characteristic style. That didn't reassure me any. It wouldn't have been beyond Corvinus to supply a little insurance to his cache by leaving this behind, perhaps containing a Tindalan Swarm or something worse.

I probed further, still cautious, and received a light touch. I sat back, shocked, before recovering and opening the trap quickly. Sapienta tumbled out, her sparkling cat eyes amused. "Careful, but not careful enough. Another that knew you well could have used my signature."

I grinned. "Anyone hostile that knew me that well wouldn't need to go to such lengths."

"Matthias told me that you would open the trap for me before any other."

"Was he wrong?"

The green eyes danced. "Of course not."

I thought about the trap and frowned. "You know that Corvinus is dead?"

Sapienta radiated assent and a subtle mixture of emotions. "I felt him go."

"I'm sorry."

"Don't be. He had his time. He pushed too far, in the end. He paid for his greed and his hunger for knowledge."

I paused awkwardly. I didn't know what to say.

She sensed my hesitation. "I'm sorry you lost your teacher. And I remember many good times with Corvinus. He treated me well. But I was still a slave. He was my master. I will not weep, now that he is gone. I am free."

The thought came to me, as it would to any sorcerer, to bind her, and take her into the Legion. But she was not some wild thing to be tamed or consumed. Sapienta threatened no one. She had often acted during my apprenticeship as my instructor for the small things, the things Corvinus couldn't or wouldn't spend time on. With some regret, I reined in my instincts. "Do you have a message for me, then?"

"My last task. To deliver a message for a dead man."

I heard a bitterness there I had never heard before in her, and I wondered again about my own Legion. Of course there were those like the White Wolf who openly chafed at their bonds, but what of Blade? How many held rage and hate against me in their hearts? How many would aid the Jigsaw Man if it meant destroying me, and so breaking the chains that bound them? What member of the Legion would not turn against me in the name of freedom?

Would the Legion be my salvation, or would it destroy me in the end?

I concealed as much of this sudden concern as I could. "What message?"

Sapienta blossomed into a green flame, and within the flame the familiar outlines of Corvinus's face took shape. "Zethus. If you're listening to this, then we've had our talk, or I'm no longer able to talk. Take the heart of stone . . ."

The message never made it any further than that. The flame broke apart into green smoke, smashed under the spiritual blow of a figure filling the doorway behind me.

I turned to see an almost familiar presence. I recognized Fetch easily enough, but he had changed. A second skin of power as gray as death and as pale as a winding sheet clothed his limbs and features. The eyes in the mask of his face crawled with the inhuman strength and hunger of pure entropy.

I had an "oh, shit" moment then as pieces fell into place. Titania's invite to Sidelines Altaforte had effectively isolated me from Corvinus during his murder. Fetch could have broken Corvinus's defenses, though that didn't explain Shaw's Night-

Town killer. Perhaps Shaw had sensed Fetch on multiple levels. Certainly, Fetch and Titania looked much better as Corvinus's killer, which meant Fetch had come to me at Sidelines Altaforte fresh from murdering my master.

I suddenly understood why Titania wouldn't have wanted me dead, at least not right away—I doubt she would have shed any tears had I happened to fall to any of the hunters she'd set on my trail. Pale believed Corvinus's research had been the motive for the murder. Say that was so. If Titania wanted Corvinus's research badly enough to kill him for it—maybe to keep it, most likely to make sure it was destroyed—then she would keep on after it if she or her errand boy Fetch didn't find it once he'd killed Corvinus.

Corvinus would have been tough enough that taking him and squeezing him for information would have been difficult. He had probably forced Fetch to kill him without giving up any information on what he'd hidden. That would leave Titania still in need of the research. So she'd dangled me out there in Faerie, knowing she could take me at any time, but holding me as insurance, as an alternate path to my master's research. She could motivate me by keeping the pressure on. If I happened to be good enough or lucky enough to survive the first few attempts on my life after the bounty had been posted, she had to figure that I had the best chance of uncovering what Corvinus had concealed.

Fetch had probably been dogging my steps since I'd left Faerie. Since he was enforcing a broken contract, neither Fetch nor Titania would have to worry about CrossTown authorities, as my death would have been sanctioned. She'd covered the traces sufficiently well during Corvinus's murder, so neither of them would have to worry about paying the piper for the deed. Titania and Fetch had played me like a wild card in a game where I didn't even understand the stakes. What the hell had the research been? What could have been so important that Corvinus and I both had to die?

Whatever the answer to those questions, now that I had opened Corvinus's hidden vault, Fetch's motivation for keeping me alive had vanished. He had his orders. I owed him a life.

My first thought was flight. I had touched Fetch's strength. I feared him. The only Way out led past him, but when I tried to move, I found that my limbs responded only sluggishly. My intended lunge became a drunken stumble. Instead of evading destruction, I bumbled toward its embrace.

I tried to call to the Legion, but only silence greeted me. Fetch. Or had the internal corruption finally struck? Either way, I stood alone. When I looked into his face, I saw Death looking back.

He moved against me in an inexorable but leisurely way. I felt his will closing over me like the fist of a giant. I caught myself hoping that the Tindalans stuck in his craw like a fishbone in a dog's throat when I realized that he stood just over the threshold of the room. A thought came to me then. If I could force Fetch back far enough, I could break the link to this place and escape him for a little while. Even Fetch would have a difficult time finding Corvinus's random pocket of air in all possible beds of stone. I didn't have any idea as to what I might do after that, but it seemed to beat dying.

All this flashed through my mind as I threw everything I had into pushing him back one step. One step would be enough. He began pulling me down into that deepest darkness. Color leached out of my vision, leaving me in a flat world painted in shades of gray. I drew on reserves of strength I had not been forced to tap in years. I fought his strength as it closed over me, lifting my head and turning my stumble into something more coordinated, pushing at him physically and psychically. I sensed his amusement as he took one step back to stand at the halfway point of the passageway. I became intimate with despair as the last ties began closing over my will.

Then my outstretched hand touched a familiar rock face. I hit the Keystone with a single desperate stroke along the Way, pulverizing it, destroying the lynchpin that had held the Way open. Caught halfway between both locations when the Keystone shattered, Fetch's grip on me fell away, brushing me with the agony of being torn between two overpowering forces. Color and life and warmth flooded back into me as he drew back. I scrambled away, watching as for a moment it (in that moment I could not think of Fetch as anything other than "it") stood there, holding the bridge open by will alone. Fetch seemed to be trying to work his way back to the ruins of Corvinus's workshop.

Then the bridge slammed shut. I lost all touch with the workshop. Bits and pieces of cold power flailed across the unrelieved stone of the chamber before fading like the memory of a hallucination. I sat for a moment, breathing heavily and trying to recover.

My mind was already working overtime, attempting to find some means of escape from the trap I had closed around myself. I had only a few hours of air at best. I had permanently shut the only Way out of Corvinus's chamber. I had traded immediate certain death for a slightly delayed certain death. Of course, I could always use the suit to extend that, but at some point I would be just as dead if I didn't figure out a way out of this. I found comfort in the thought that I had faced Fetch and hurt him badly. Perhaps I had even killed him, if that was possible.

A small consolation, at best.

Worse, a delayed reaction from the fight or fatigue or something else had seized the opportunity to drag me into unconsciousness. I was slipping into darkness, despite my desperate attempt to focus. I only hoped I would wake up before I consumed all of the available oxygen.

CHAPTER XVII

I FOUND myself walking down a long, straight road lined with tall, bare trees. The bark of the trees was as white as bone. Bodies hung from the trees like enormous, misshapen fruit. I avoided looking at the faces. I feared that I would recognize them. The air tasted like corruption. The stones of the road felt unnaturally hard under my feet, bruising them with every step.

A tall figure walked beside me. He wore a serene expression on his pale, bearded face like another man might wear a mask. "You grow weaker," he said.

I looked him in the eye. "You grow bolder." Despite his change of form I recognized him as the spirit I had given to the Captains of my Legion in Vincent's apartment building. "I took you once. I can take you again."

His expression never changed. "May the second taking bring you more joy than did the first."

I looked back, along the road. Behind us stretched a line of bloody footprints. I looked at his feet and saw that the laced sandals he wore were full of blood, every step sloshing fresh blood down to the stones of the road.

Remembering the dreams of the children, I reached up and caught him by the beard. The skin of his face sloughed off into my grasp. The thing beneath the mask grinned at me. I recoiled in spite of myself. The Jigsaw Man put one hand on my chest and gave me a single hard shove. I fell backwards, slamming into the ground hard enough for my teeth to pop together like ivory castanets. Then I sat bolt upright, once again in the sealed room of my prison, the bright light of the crystals glaring down at me.

My feet hurt. So did my teeth.

The White Wolf and the others had been right. I had been terribly wrong. The Jigsaw Man had gained strength. It might have become strong enough that I would not be able to defeat it. I called to my Legion, but received no answer. I had been afraid of that. Fetch hadn't cut me off from my Legion. I had allowed the Jigsaw Man to cut me off instead.

For the first time in all the years I had been a sorcerer, I feared entering the stronghold of my soul, but I knew that I could not escape this thing so easily. I had to face it, or it would consume me from within. I withdrew to the fortress of my spirit. Open gates yawed before me. A gloom of gnats swallowed the courtyard held by the high walls, the grounds, and the central ring of towers. The buzz of their presence wound through the warm air like the heavy stink of rotting flesh that met my incorporeal nostrils. I pulled the cloth of my shirt over mouth and nose, knowing that it wouldn't help, but unable to resist the impulse to try. Saliva filled my mouth. I fought spasms of retching as I entered the gates cautiously. I saw no sign of the Legion. I took my time, easing toward the single tower at the heart of the fortress, stumbling in the gloom.

I found the first signs of the Legion at the entrance to the central keep. Statues of black basalt I had never placed stood at the open corridor and lined the passages. The faces of the statues contorted with rage and pain and fear and hate. The gnats covered everything like a heavy blanket, breathing with unholy life.

I counted the statues as I passed. I recognized each of them, of course, the soldiers of my Legion bound in torment. I wondered where he had put the rest. I did not see nearly enough to account for the entire Legion.

I came at last to the great hall under the central tower. I moved inward toward the high seat at the center of the room, stepping carefully to avoid the rivulets of blood that ran from the fountains and overflowed to soil the white flagstones. My enemy had set the Captains of the Legion in place around the throne like an honor guard. The White Wolf crouched at his feet. All of them were bound in stone. They stood silent, unmoving, accusing.

My adversary lolled on my throne, the shape of a man covered with countless wounds, blood flowing from the wounds to run down into a pool at his feet. Rivulets of blood snaked out across the floor of the hall from the pool of blood. "So, you've come at last. This place is mine, Blood and Bone. I give you one chance, mortal. Kneel."

I gave him the fig, then a couple of other nasty gestures I'd picked up over the years. "Up yours, cupcake."

He blinked. I think that the last thing he'd expected was insolence. I had pegged him as taking himself too seriously anyway.

He came up off the throne with a roar. I tried to avoid him as he charged me, but he snagged me with a long arm and pulled me close to grapple. He had a stronger will than I had anticipated. I had relied on the Legion for many years. I had also been a sorcerer for more than one mortal lifetime. I ripped free of his grasp and hurt him. He turned and flexed a finger, and Bane came rippling to life.

I sneered at my adversary. "I should have taken you myself."

He laughed at me. "Fool that you did not. Now it is too late."

He stepped back. Bane moved past him, silver eyes gleaming, pale limbs rippling with long ropes of muscle, claws flexing against the stone underfoot as he advanced.

I met Bane's silver gaze. "He can't force you."

"But he can offer a better deal," Bane responded. "He told me of the road you'll be traveling. I want no part of that. I've decided to accept his bargain."

I threw myself back from the strength of his reaching hands, caught his silver eyes, and drove him to his knees. I had taken him in the beginning, after all.

But I looked past Bane as he knelt before me. I saw Shadow rippling to life. Behind him I could see the movement of myriad small others, edging closer hungrily. I knew then where the missing members of the Legion had been. They had gone over to the Jigsaw Man's side, rather than fall to his hunger and strength.

I couldn't fight them all at once, so I fled that place, my adversary's laughter burning in my ears. I slammed the gates shut behind me and braced them as heavily as I could, to slow the pursuit. I opened my eyes to look around the doorless, windowless cell in which I was trapped. I stared at the right angle joins of the walls, floor, and ceiling. I could not escape my own Legion, of course. The Jigsaw Man had subverted enough of my own forces to hale me down from within. So I had to take the initiative.

Acting rather than reacting would be a pleasant change.

Studying the angles that pent me, a desperate plan came to mind. And yet, in its desperation it could solve more than one problem. It could lead me out of the vault, as well as cleanse the Legion of taint, but the cost would be high. I would lose my Tindalan insurance and a significant portion of my Legion.

Still, it would be better than losing my life.

I searched my pockets frantically for a marker of some kind. I found none. I shattered Corvinus's spirit trap against the stone table. I used a sharp crystalline shard to draw blood from my left hand. With my blood I inscribed a small circle. I used exquisite care, for though the size of the circle did not matter, the smallest flaw would render it useless.

I put my hand in the circle, triggered the curving runes that covered my arms and upper body—runes I had never planned to use—and poured the Tindalan swarm into the circle. I pulled my arm and hand out hastily as they rose before me, a tightly meshed formation of sharp angles, barely visible to the eye. My senses were so clouded by that time that I could perceive hardly more than that, though with the Tindalans that was perhaps more blessing than curse. The Tindalans's spiritual appearance had never been recommended for the faint of heart.

They spoke to me in one voice and many. "We are freed too early. You still live."

"I bring a new bargain."

"Dangerous. What if we choose not to accept?"

"Then I call on what power I have left to remove every angle from this place," I said flatly. "I will die in any event, but I can choose the manner of my going. In the process I will leave you trapped here for eternity. Once the Legion is gone, what will feed you?"

The swarm paused. "What do you offer?"

"I offer the lives of my rebel Captains, their hosts, and the one who corrupted them. I offer freedom after the task is done."

"And what do you ask?"

I closed my eyes. "Take me and all of mine from this place. Bring us to the Crossroads at Dulchen Fen."

They hesitated, conferring, weighing options. The peripheral psychic static from their conference buzzed against the walls of my mind like raging hornets. Then they spoke. "Done. Free us of this circle."

I broke the circle with my thumb. Howling, they descended on me. They swept me up into their midst and carried me with them as they drove down toward the fastness of my spirit. A tide of wild, voracious power swept me along. In that place the sharp, angular clash of hellish forms hungry for prey took on a solidity like transparent crystal, pieces of their bodies catching the light with the flowing clarity of wet glass. Jagged tongues flicked against needle teeth with a sound reminiscent of crackling ice. Clawed feet rose and fell against the rock with the light, unforgiving patter of frozen rain. They led me on, all purpose and power and appetite. I followed along, hunting amidst my hounds. They took the scouts first, the small impatient ones swarming over the closed gates I had barricaded behind me when I fled. Those scouts were devoured so swiftly that most never had a chance to cry out. It would not be the end of them, I knew; Tindalans digest with a very deliberate lack of speed.

We burst through the gates. The most powerful and the most intelligent rebels fled when I led the Tindalans into the new wilderness of my spirit. We hunted down through the inner courses of my soul, tearing the darkness asunder with the sickly, eldritch light of Tindalan rage. The small ones ran before us until they were caught and consumed. A larger group swept into view. I saw Shadow's wings stretching up into the darkness. I picked Bane out of the group as well, his silver eyes flaring as he saw my hunt riding down upon them. Bane and Shadow put their backs together, surrounding themselves with the remnants of their hosts. Bane lifted one pale hand in grim salute as I rode the hunt closer.

The Tindalans hardly paused as the swarm swept over my rebel Captains. Nothing remained when we passed.

We found my adversary, still wearing his jigsaw form, in the heart of my fortress. He waited for me. The frozen forces of the loyal Captains and hosts surrounded him. (It almost surprised me to find the White Wolf still frozen, still loyal.) The Tindalans picked their way through the statues with the delicacy of an avalanche and threw themselves on him. The Jigsaw Man fought well, better than I would have guessed, throwing Tindalans back, hurling them to the flagstones of the keep. But each fallen hound rose again, endless, boundless hunger driving them back to the attack. I did not hang back from the battle. I struck past and through the Tindalan storm repeatedly, hamstringing my enemy spiritually, smashing his armor and breaking his weapons as the swarm overran his defenses and took him down.

We paused there. I felt the satisfaction of the swarm, the momentary satisfaction of a hunger that grew with each conquest. I heard another crackling grow as stone figures twisted to life, the power of the Jigsaw Man falling with him. The Tindalans turned to regard me. I returned their regard. I felt Bright Angel stepping up to my right shoulder, Blade stepping to my left, and the White Wolf coming round to stand before me. My remaining Captains marshaled their hosts as the bindings of the adversary dropped away. Those hosts gathered to stand with them, giving the reduced Legion a solid sense of power that gave even the Tindalans pause.

They had a cohesion the rebels lacked. In their rebellion, in their pursuit of individual freedom, the rebels had fragmented enough to be easy meat for the swarm. The unified loyalists presented a different kind of game altogether.

Then the Tindalans swept forward and through us. I felt the curious, exquisitely painful, and entirely wrong sensation of being turned inside out. I opened my eyes, looked up into the sunshine, and heard the wind murmuring around me. In the distance a great cairn, overgrown now with grass, marked the dead of an ancient battle. In a few more centuries, it would be nothing more than a hill, slumping to join the texture of the landscape around it.

I stood in the center of the empty Crossroad at Dulchen Fen, said to be the site of the first battle between Faerie and Men, a place avoided by all. I felt the freedom of the Ways calling to me. Within, the Legion settled into watchful silence. I would have to be careful. I had been considerably weakened by the loss of nearly half my Legion and the insurance of my Tindalan swarm was gone.

And yet I had faced down Fetch and beaten him. I had destroyed the Faerie power that had been poisoning my soul. I had recovered important information. More than the things Corvinus had left for me to find, the fact that he had left them told me that he had been prepared for something to happen to him. And the fact that he had called on me was undoubtedly the reason that someone had it out for me. Not so much because his enemies had known that he had prepared something for me, but because they had been confident that he would do something that involved me. And, of course, Bane indicated that the Jigsaw Man had known something of my future course, strengthening the Faerie tie. If the Jigsaw Man hadn't lied to Bane, and if Bane hadn't lied to me.

I called to my remaining Captains, including the White Wolf. I felt a restlessness in them I hadn't felt before. "Did he try to turn you?" I asked.

"Yes." Blade looked me in the eye as he answered. The others refused to meet my gaze.

"Did he tell you anything?"

"He said that to save yourself, you would devour us all," the White Wolf said. "Better to fight for our freedom now and throw our lot in with him, than to be sacrifices to your doomed attempt to survive."

"You didn't believe him?"

"You were a better choice," Bright Angel said softly.

I thought of Sapienta and her animosity toward Corvinus. I winced. I let the contact fall away and sent my Captains back to the fortress of my spirit. What pride could I have for such an accolade? I reminded myself that sorcery is about domination, not love. The reminder left a bad taste in my mouth. I was better than the Jigsaw Man, at least. Wasn't I?

My thoughts turned again toward Sapienta. I hoped that she had escaped Fetch's attack, but I feared that she had not. I thought of the bitterness she had held toward her former master, the bitterness of a favored slave, and I winced again.

Understand that I knew slavery of old. I had grown to manhood in the Hellene city-states, in a culture that took slavery for granted. Slaves were property. Who wasted time considering the feelings of slaves? Slavery was a better alternative than death. The natural order of things dictated that the victor should benefit from his victory, and that the vanquished should serve the victor's purposes.

Why didn't I feel much like a victor at that moment?

I had fought hard and I had won past battles, as well as this most recent. I had my spoils to show for those efforts. But the bright sheen of victory had been tarnished. I had less confidence in my Legion than I'd had in a long time. I saw weaknesses there I had never seen before. Cracks under the Legion's façade had been exploited once, nearly killing me. What other vulnerabilities lay hidden in the heart of my forces?

I had not accomplished all that I might have. I did not have Corvinus's message to go along with the items I had retrieved from his lab. Instead, I had a recovery suit and a rock, and I needed to talk to someone who could tell me something about what I had found. I thought I knew just the person who might be able to make sense out of something as obscure as a heart of stone without the corrupting influence of ambition or greed for Corvinus's possible research. The time to follow up would be as soon as possible, while the opposition was reeling from what had surely been an unexpected defeat.

If they weren't reeling, then I was really in trouble.

CHAPTER XVIII

I TOOK my time, though I had things I needed to do. I had thought of Dulchen Fen for a number of reasons. Isolation and lack of inhabitants I ranked as perhaps chief among them. The Fae opposition should count me as dead, though the Whitesnake bounty would still be in effect. I didn't want to risk that advantage through early exposure and identification. I needed to muddy the waters further and shake the hunters off my trail.

At the same time, there were places in Dulchen Fen that could heal wounds not physical. I knew of a place where perhaps I could recover some of the strength that the Jigsaw Man had ripped from me, a place where I could heal injuries still fresh from the recent struggles and regain my focus.

I roused myself and wandered off the road, detouring around the massive cairn. I climbed up the gentle slope, the long grasses whispering around my legs. I drank the fresh and untainted breath of the trees as I walked. There on the rising slopes of the winding hills, the trees grew thickly. No underbrush rose to choke the clear spaces between the trunks. Only the long grasses danced under the spreading boughs.

Down in the deceptively thick and deep grass of the narrow valleys that ran between the hills, the dead lay sleeping. Human and Fae lay mixed there, as together in death as they had been opposed in life. An unwary traveler, thinking to rest himself on that inviting turf, would find himself quickly mired in a bog of endless depth, sucked down to lie forever in the arms of the dead.

Above, the trees veiled their faces in long streamers of leaves, fleeing the terrible burden of memory. Light faded in the dusky colors of the leaves, and under the canopy of Dulchen Fen's forest lords even memory faded into the thick rolls of deep green moss that covered the earth.

I walked further into the wood, stooping occasionally to gather seeds fresh from the trees. I needed those seeds for a bargaining chip. They could buy me some aid; buy me some time. And I needed all the time and aid I could get.

By the time I had a handful of seeds packed away in a coat pocket, I came to a small meadow. The grasses there lay in the embrace of the gentle murmuring of the leaves and the wind. As I had walked through the wood, I had caught occasional glimpses of ghostly white flashes. That dimly glimpsed shape could have belonged to a deer, though it stood larger than any deer I had ever seen. It could have been a horse, though it moved soundlessly, like a ghost. Bright glints of light glittered from the length of horn jutting straight out from her head. That pure presence paralleled my course. I smiled, pleased to see her waiting for me. Dulchen Fen had become a place where memories fell away. The keeper of that place could ease the burden of memory without consuming the self. She could treat those wounds that remained when the scars on the flesh faded. All she asked for this service was trust.

I laid my tired body down in that place, alongside a thick trunk bearing the marks of a single ivory horn more precious than silver or gold, and sought sleep.

In that place the darkness of recent memory rose within my soul, clothed in nightmares. As the darkness came upon me, it lost power, swallowed by the deep peace of the forest and the flowing, white strength of the forest's keeper, impaled and carried away by the keeper's bright horn. No poison could survive that touch, not even a poison of the spirit. I slept a long and peaceful sleep, untroubled by dreams, cleansed of taint. And when I rose from my slumber, I found the circular impressions of dainty hooves in the grass all around where I had slept. Refreshed as I had not been for some time, my mind relieved of rage and hate and fear and other personal demons, I followed the slope back down and out of the trees, and set my feet upon the crossroads.

I needed information. I already had someone in mind.

Chimereon lived not too far from my place, though farther out from the city and deeper in the wilds. My most significant fear would have been Fetch waiting for me in ambush, but after recent events, I would never have a more favorable opportunity to slip in and out of Chimereon's abode undetected. I had to keep the Fae off balance, keep them thinking that I slept with the dead, or at least unsure whether I walked free among the living. They had to believe that I still lay safely sealed in my early tomb. I never would have risked Chimereon's place before the struggle in the cave because it lay too close to my own abode. The Fae would be watching for me there. In the aftermath of my recent encounter, the risk of detection had dropped considerably. And I needed all the information I could get.

I took a slow, methodical approach, following paths through the wild Ways that threaded between towering forest giants wound about with thick, furry vines. The colors brightened, flowers opening petals of crimson and orange and yellow, the greens shading toward emerald. A muttering, chittering, rustling susurrus grew in the closing space between the trees. Faceted eyes sparkled like crystal in the shafts of sunlight, flicking to the cover of shadow as the bright blur of feathered wings swept through the columns of light in predatory arcs.

I eased my pace. If I were to encounter any watchers, it would be on the borders of Chimereon's territory. Blade moved restlessly within me. I turned my head to stare directly into the slit, considering eyes of a great cat. I touched its spirit lightly, blunting hungry desire. It wrinkled its lips over its long teeth, fanning its whiskers, and chuffed disgust. It turned and slid noiselessly into the brush, a sinuous curl of dappled fur, a moving shadow, and then nothing the eye could see.

That surprised me. I had expected to work harder to deflect its intent. Generally, cats were not so reasonable.

I took my slow, easy time, walking gentle Ways to keep my traces as minimal as possible, and so heard the sibilants of soft conversation before I happened upon the speakers. I eased to a stop, listening. I worked my way forward and listened again, repeating the process until I had a clear idea of the speakers' location. I worked my way cautiously around the bole of a great tree until I caught sight of a flash of movement, then crouched behind a leafy burst of vine which had the admirable combination of cover and visibility to serve as a hunting blind. I spotted two men quickly. I looked for but didn't see signs of any others.

As I watched the two men, both relaxing against the weathered flank of a boulder, I hoped the vine I had chosen as a screen didn't possess any propensities to secrete unpleasant toxins.

Both of the men wore robes covered with dark sinuous patterns which blended well in the half-light under the trees. Both carried stubby long arms with wide bores. I couldn't identify the make from the distance, but weapons like that fit into an unpleasant range of possibilities. I couldn't see their faces, but knew from the robes that they would have snakelike characteristics: possibly scales, fangs, reptilian pupils, flattened noses, or some other bodymod granted to reflect devotion and status within the cult. Given the darkness of their robes, I pegged them for low-level members of the Whitesnakes. Their presence on a back Way into Chimereon's abode indicated either a penurious reluctance to pay out on a bounty for prey they might take themselves, or a dedication to my termination above and beyond all reason.

Granted, cults and reason have never gone together.

A small device crouched between them on spidery legs. I could see the light glow of a screen facing them. A sudden chill swept over me. They had a monitor. My precautions in using the Way had paid off, or they were baiting me while a squad of heavies trotted eagerly toward me from some other post.

As I considered the risk of sliding out of there, keeping a low profile and hoping for the best, an itch grew between my shoulder blades. I turned slowly, examining my back trail. Nothing moved in the undergrowth, save the dance of leaves and wind, birds and insects. I froze, glanced casually upward, and spent a long moment listening to my heart thunder in my ears as I returned the interested gaze of a recumbent feline peering down from a broad branch over my head.

"I'm disappointed in you, Blade." My internal voice had a controlled, warning mildness. I didn't vocalize the thought, as I didn't intend to trigger any unwanted activity on the part of the cat.

"It doesn't have any detectable hostile intent," said Blade. "And it seems to be able to screen on some level. I didn't feel it before you saw it."

"Let's hope it doesn't change its mind," I replied sharply. I didn't continue the thought, which had threatened to blossom into a lecture, as I thought of the possibilities. That cat, with sharp predatory reflexes and at least four times my mass, had considerable potential for mischief.

I reached out gently, touching the cat's mind with my will. I watched its reactions, minding Blade's comment about its ability to screen on some psychic level. Its ears pricked forward as I made contact. I saw the tip of its tail twitch against the trunk of the tree. Cats are contrary critters. I had apparently blunted its appetite but piqued its curiosity. I thought I'd take advantage of both.

I nudged its attention across the clearing, to where the two men reclined. It didn't want to cooperate. I occupied its thoughts for the moment. It wasn't taking my word that something else might be more interesting. I wheedled, I persuaded, I made my case in images and shades of emotion. Cats were territorial. Wouldn't it want to know what these interlopers were all about? It took a bit, but slowly the great liquid eyes blinked, and the gaze shifted, sharpened. Then I concentrated on the potential deliciousness of rare Whitesnake: the hot savor of the blood; the marbling of the meat; the sweetness of the marrow. I waxed a bit enthusiastic. By the time the cat drew itself up with an elaborately casual yawn, dropped from the branch, and slid into the cover of the brush, its eyes never moving from the two sentries, I had to wipe my mouth and spit. I didn't even like those damned Whitesnakes. I felt certain I wouldn't like one rare, but I still fought sympathetic drool.

I pulled back, into the brush, and made my way on toward the border of Chimereon's lands. When the first scream cut the air, I picked up my pace. The screams followed me longer than they should have. I had to clear my mouth and spit frequently.

I really didn't like Whitesnakes, but I almost felt the stirrings of sympathy for those two. In a hungry sort of way.

I came out of the edge of the trees and crossed into Chimereon's environs without further encounters.

I hate influencing another mind. I prefer brute force. I don't have to get so close.

Chimereon's temple sat on the edge of a granite cliff. Neatly tended gardens bordered the path that wound up the edge of the cliff. Ordinarily, not so much as a blade of grass or a single pebble dared be out of place.

I winced as I saw shrubs trailing broken branches, places where gravel spilled across the path, and the dried stains of old blood. The blood would be especially bad for the goblins, since only Chimereon spilled blood in her environs without paying a price for it.

The temple rose above me, the edges of fine marble shining a delicate rose color in the light of the setting sun. In Chimereon's area, the day itself passed quickly, but sunsets and sunrises seemed to last forever. Various scripts had been cut into the steps of the temple: Chimereon's effort at cross-cultural recognition. I couldn't remember whether each script had been laid down in the language of each new culture from which she drew a worshiper, or each script had been laid down by a race she had conquered.

Either way, it would be much the same with Chimereon.

I stepped through the rising columns, waiting politely in the throat of the temple. Torches flared to life before me, lighting the long hallway of white marble that gradually blended into the rose-tinted granite of the cliff. I took the invitation, descending down the long slope of the hall. I took the only lighted corridor of the many passages that opened around me.

The place had all the silence of a tomb. The hollow resonance of my footsteps faded into the shadows like echoes of mortality. Whatever else Chimereon had, atmosphere she had in plenty. I stepped at last into a brightly lit, circular room. The long curving walls shone with the purity of unsullied gold, matching the two seats and two low couches, also covered with cloth of gold. Marble tables stood at intervals around the room, each displaying a particular object: on one table, a ruby the size of a man's head; on another, a chess set of onyx and alabaster; on yet another stood the carving of a clipper ship in full sail, jade waves furling around the prow.

Chimereon stood in the middle of the chamber in human guise, her white hair long and uncombed, dark eyes smiling. "Wipe your feet."

I did so instinctively, then looked down at the throw rug. Pale and blotchy and oddly shaped, I couldn't remember having ever seen anything quite like it. "My apologies."

She laughed. "No need to apologize. I simply like to make sure that my new rug gets used. Goblin skin has a certain durability, though it does go surprisingly well with the decor. I'm considering adding more to my collection. What do you think?"

I looked again at the "rug," stepping carefully away. "I think he still looks surprised. Where are the wolves?"

"Tsk. Wolfskin simply would not do." She grinned, displaying a mouthful of pointed teeth. "Besides, I hold the riders responsible, not the wolves. If the riders want to tame a beast, then they had best be able to control it. Wouldn't you agree?"

I grinned back at her. "Would it matter?"

"Not really." She waved one hand toward a low couch, and lay bonelessly back on its mate. I took my own place more gingerly and with considerably less flexibility.

"You've been busy, from what I hear lately. You must be, to have left my message unanswered." Her expression was carefully neutral.

"I haven't wanted to access the house or any of its services. Fetch is waiting for me there," I responded.

One eyebrow lifted delicately. "Fetch? Really? I'm afraid I can't help you with that."

"I know. And I didn't drop by to ask for help with Fetch."

She cocked her head. "Why did you drop by?"

"To be neighborly, of course. And to see if you might be able to tell me what significance this has." I pulled the pouch out of my shirt, freed the stone from the confines of the pouch, and passed it to her.

She considered it in her hand. "You know that I do nothing for free. Even for good friends like yourself."

I steeled myself. "What price do you ask?"

She winked at me. "Let us not be hasty. I also enjoy a challenge."

She closed her eyes, brought the fragment close, sniffed it, and flicked her tongue against the rough surface. Watching her reminded me of her inhumanity, and how well she wore the human form. Then she glanced back up at me, a delighted smile on her face. "I haven't come across this in quite some time!"

I wondered how far her pleasure would carry her. "What is it?"

Her eyes narrowed. "Not so fast, my boy. What do you offer me?"

I spread my empty hands. "What do you want?"

Her eyes sparkled. "Years of service?"

I started to stand. "I don't . . ."

She forestalled me with a hand. "Sit down, sit down. Relax. The bargaining has just begun. What about specific services? Tasks?"

"Predefined?" I asked warily.

She threw back her head and roared with amusement. "I love a good haggle. Let me go this far. I'll tell you the first part of what I know. This is a piece of a place and time. It still has some connection to where and when it arose."

"So it can be used as a guide. Or a map."

She nodded grudgingly. "So I confirmed a suspicion. Fine. That you get for free. But what about the nature of the place? Eh? How much will you trade for that?"

She handed me back the fragment, and I bobbled it in my hand. "I could simply use it to go there and find out."

"You could. Might be dangerous. What if there are obstacles? What if the environment is hostile? I will tell you this much: what you have there is very old, and what it leads to some would kill to find, and others would kill to leave lost."

My attention sharpened at that. She saw it.

"Three tasks, any nature, for as long as we both survive," she said quickly.

"One task, of a predetermined nature, that I must agree to in advance."

She leaned forward. "The fragment you hold in your hand is a motive for Corvinus's death. I'm not saying that it is *the* motive, but it is a possible motive. Two tasks, any nature, for as long as we both survive."

I frowned. "Two, predetermined nature, agreed to beforehand, for as long as we both survive."

She made a clicking sound with her tongue. "You should have been a lawyer. So many clauses. One favor. I swear I will not ask for anything outside your principles."

"Including the principle of self-preservation?"

A hint of melancholy clouded her expression. "I will not cause harm to you and yours. I thought you knew that." A quick smile flashed across her face. "Good neighbors are hard to find."

I caught a hint of something I had seen in Chimereon before, a touch of regret at her continual solitude. Even Chimereon's worshipers feared her, and rightly so. Fear tends to be a barrier to intimacy. I nodded, wondering how badly she was taking me. "Done."

"In your travels, have you ever heard rumors of the Nephilim?" she asked.

"Doesn't sound familiar."

"Not surprising," she said. "The world's changed since the days of the Nephilim. There's no need for them anymore. The entire project had been so cloaked in secrecy that knowledge of them just . . . faded away. Back in the early days, before possibility had split along its many paths, humanity fought continuous battles for survival with a multitude of powerful forces. You can still see many of these forces in NightTown, UnderTown, and of course in Faerie."

She leaned forward. "Humans had sorcerers then, naturally. They had a little of everything. Everyone else tended to be specialists. Specializing was a winning strategy. Humans needed an edge. They found the edge in the Rites of the Nephilim. Men and women gave their lives trying to become Nephilim. Only a few succeeded."

I began to ask, "Why?"

She forestalled me with a raised hand. "Human leaders found a desperate answer to a desperate situation. Who's to say that they didn't save humanity by acting as they did? The Nephilim fought against all of the enemies of mankind. Those wars divided reality. The various races fled from the fury of the Nephilim down the newly opened paths of myriad possibilities."

My brows shot up. "You're saying that the WanderWays didn't exist before the wars of the Nephilim?"

She nodded. "That's exactly what I'm saying. The Nephilim had power never before seen. Each, alone, was like unto a god. Together . . . only legends remain of them, and in them the Nephilim are angels and the sons of angels, gods and the sons of gods, giants in the earth and demons. Most of those tales come from the time after the Possibility Wars, when their foes had fled to the far reaches of possibility and the Nephilim turned on one another. The power that made them more than human also passed the bounds of human definitions of morality . . . and sanity. The Nephilim were weapons, you see, and a weapon with a will must have something to fight. All of this took time. But the Nephilim had time—all of time. The process that made them Nephilim gave them immunity to the passage of years. They became immortal."

"Then where are they?" I said. "I can see why some would kill not to have the Nephilim released, and I can see why others would kill to have the secret of the Rites, but why did it fade away? Why are there no more Nephilim?"

Chimereon's dark eyes pulsed with the beating of my heart. "Only a few humans could control the power. Only a few could survive the Rites. Those few were enough. The other races fled, or became furtive. The Nephilim who survived the wars of possibility locked away the knowledge of the Rites. Nothing remained to oppose them. And so they opposed one another. When all the enemies of mankind had retreated from the ferocity of the Nephilim, they turned on themselves in a battle so cataclysmic that only dim memories remain of the times before the battle. Echoes of those memories survive in myth and legend. Though the transformation made the Nephilim immortal, they perished in the Wars of the Brethren. Knowledge of the Rites faded with them, destroyed accidentally or deliberately through the wars."

"Knowledge of the Rites, or the Rites themselves?" My voice sounded sharper than I intended.

Chimereon smiled. "Perhaps the Rites no longer exist," she said. "Perhaps they remain. If they do remain, they would be at the birthplace of the Nephilim . . . at the Fane of the Nephilim. Given the power involved, it would be difficult to do more than isolate them and make the Fane difficult to find."

I leaned forward. "Do you think that's what Corvinus was trying to do?"

"I can't say," she said. "But echoes of that time are around us still. Some of the Nephilim's descendants remain, the power and madness in the blood diluted but still potent. My father was such."

"What about the original Nephilim?" The topic had swept me beyond my earlier caution, but Chimereon didn't seem to mind the probing.

"If any of the original Nephilim survived, they conceal themselves well, along with all traces of their origin," she said. "The Hebrews who wrote the Bible called them the Nephilim, and believed that they were the bastard children of the angels. The Norse called them Aesir and Jotun. The Greeks called them Olympians and Titans. The alchemists' search for the Philosopher's Stone was a mask for their attempt to recover the Rites. The Nephilim were a living power."

Chimereon had just given me a glimpse of the stakes in Titania's game. They scared the shit out of me. I held up the fragment, my hand shaking. "And this?"

Her eyes had brightened during the discussion. Her pupils had lengthened to slits. "As far as I can tell, it's the heart of one of the Nephilim. It'll take you to whatever Corvinus was researching. I wouldn't be surprised to find that Corvinus might have been searching for the Fane. If he found the Fane, then the heart could act as a kind of key to the Rites."

That brought me up short. "A key? Shouldn't finding the Fane be the hard part?"

Chimereon didn't blink, and hadn't for a long time. "You don't understand. Even if you found the Fane, you'd have to make it past the security surrounding the Rites. A key probably can't even get you through all of the barriers, but it should help. Expect no easy entrance. The security in that project will last."

"But where would he have found such a thing?"

That question had been more rhetorical than anything else, but she took me at face value and answered seriously. "Where Corvinus came across that stone, I have no idea. I would guess that investigating the Rites would be the project that proved so dangerous for him. Something in me doubts that he went through the Rites. If he had, he would not have died so easily. Are you planning to pursue this thing?"

"They're already after me," I said. "They were after me before I found it. I really don't have a choice, do I?"

She didn't answer. I sealed the heart of stone back in the bag and secured the bag around my throat. It felt heavier than it had before.

I began to rise, saw a flash of loneliness in Chimereon's dark eyes, and settled my weight back onto the divan.

Surprise flickered across her face. "Aren't you leaving?"

"If you want me to. It's been a while since we talked. How long has it been since you've played a game of chess?"

She smiled suddenly. "A long time."

"Would you like to play?"

She sat up straight. "I believe I would."

She didn't really need help with the tables or the chair, being considerably stronger than I, but I offered, and she politely accepted. As we settled in over the chessboard, she looked up at me, the pleasure fading from her face. "One last thing."

"Yes?"

"Something you should consider." Her tongue flicked out from between her lips in a quick movement not at all human. It looked split at the tip, but it moved so fast I couldn't be sure. "Just because one never hears of the Nephilim anymore, doesn't mean that they're all gone."

I stared at her for a long, still moment. "Do you have anything more solid than that?"

She gave me a slight shake of her head. "Just the thought that if one of the Nephilim were still around, then he or she might not want anyone else delving back into that old power."

"Now there's a reassuring thought."

We turned our attention back to the chessboard. I won the first game. She won the second. The third we stalemated. We dined between games on bread and wine. I carefully refrained from touching any of the meat she offered me unless she identified it first. Her eyes twinkling, she never obliged me. I ate vegetarian.

On some level, we all choose how we will nourish our souls as well as our bodies. Consider Eliza Drake and her fellow creatures of the night. Consider how the choices they had already made had locked them into a narrower and narrower set of possible choices. They must nourish themselves on the lives and hearts and minds of others, as must we all; but by their nature they must take without giving in return. Such an existence must be a hollow torment.

For that very reason I am cautious about the choices I make. One step leads to another, and another, and the final destination winds up being a place you would never have chosen to go when you set out on your journey.

Consider Chimereon. Chess partner, pleasant company, and carnivorous goddess. Whole civilizations had given themselves to her. She avenged the most insignificant slight with spilled blood. She had a side to her nature beyond my comprehension and beyond my approval. Did that mean I should bar myself from her company? Did it mean I couldn't trust her? Did my association have to be restricted to people whose whole selves I could describe, and number, and mark down as meeting my requirements for moral behavior, whatever those might be?

I wouldn't have many associates left. I probably wouldn't enjoy the company of the few that remained.

Consider Anthony Vayne. I didn't meet Vayne's tough standards. But then I doubted that Vayne met Vayne's standards. I'd always had considerable respect for him because of his ability to befriend even a cheerful pagan like myself. It said something about Vayne that earned him my respect.

I have always had enough difficulty trying to live my own life well. I didn't have the time or inclination to try to live the lives of others for them by forcing them to conform to my own standards. My advice for anyone burning with the desire to show the world the right path is first to find it, then to walk it. Let anyone who desires to seek the same destination find their own path. Truly, isn't anyone without a little danger, without experiences and perspectives beyond our own, just a little bit less interesting to be around? How much can we learn from someone who already shares our point of view?

I slept there that night, on one of the low couches, resting up for my next step. I slept well and dreamlessly. I had a plan. I intended to carry it through. I needed to sow as much confusion in the enemy ranks as possible. I expected a certain bounty hunter named Jack Duncan to help me to carry it out.

CHAPTER XIX

JACK DUNCAN lived out on the fringes of TechTown in a small orbital habitat that circled over a blasted and slowly recovering planet. The owners and builders of that orbital habitat had apparently gone the way of all flesh by the time Duncan had found it and taken it for his own. On the world below the habitat only bugs and plants and fish throve in the wake of that particular apocalypse.

An orbital habitat is one of the most Road-secure locations I've seen, an alternative much fancied by the more paranoid technocrats and those without much trust in the Ways. It takes a great deal of effort and skill to reach an orbital location by WanderWay. I'm not saying it can't be done; given the virtually infinite variation of the Roads, one can find a place where the rules are different enough to bend oneself into existence in such a location, but it wouldn't be fun. That's a large part of what Duncan had always relied on for security. I won't say that Duncan was paranoid, given his profession, but then I won't say he wasn't, either.

It so happened that I had been to Duncan's place once before, when he had hired me to remove a curse that had been laid on him by a Shaman (as I understood it, the Shaman had been a brother of someone that Duncan had taken for bounty, so the curse had been nasty and driven by all the fuels of a blood feud). I remembered enough details that I knew that I could make it there through a translation zone without too much difficulty.

I had no intention of doing so, however.

One thing about traveling by WanderWay is that if someone else is good enough, they can place triggers to announce visitors. Dropping in on Duncan that way would have been like hiring a crier to run before me to spread word of my impending arrival. I didn't plan on being so direct. Besides, I didn't have the need.

Jack Duncan, like everyone, had passions. Some were undoubtedly cleaner than others. I knew Duncan tolerably well, had worked with him on a couple of occasions, and so I knew of at least one passion of which I could take advantage. I knew a place on that world of his he frequented regularly, and I knew the Ways and seasons of that place and how they played into his passion. I had no doubts of finding him there. But before I did seek him out, I needed a safe place for the heart of stone.

I walked the Ways to a land off the beaten path, where willows wept silently into a dark and winding river. I waited there on the banks of the river, watching the trees move and whisper despite the absence of wind. As long as I harmed nothing and made no threatening moves, the trees would tolerate me. At least, they would tolerate me until their master arrived. If he decided to remove his protection from me, it would be an entirely different matter.

He came upon me almost before I saw him, moving like a ripple of wind through grass. He came to stand before me, regarding me with patient hazel eyes. "Zethus. It's been a while. What do you want from me?"

I grinned in spite of myself. "You know me too well. I have brought you gifts." I pulled the seeds I had gathered from Dulchen Fen out of the pocket of my coat and poured them into his cupped hands.

Pleasure suffused his features, bringing an almost human glow of warmth to his pale cheeks. He had never worn the human form well, though I would not be the one to tell him so. "I have not heard the voices of the trees of Dulchen Fen for some time. Thank you. I ask again, what do you want?"

His tone had gentled. He treasured the gift, as I had known he would. He didn't travel any more than his charges did. "I need you to keep something for me until I return for it."

I gave the environment suit and the heart of stone into the keeping of the shepherd of the trees. He took them from me in silence, his eyes warm and deeply alien. I knew he would keep the heart safe. More importantly, he would return it to me when I came again.

I had paid in advance, so I left that place feeling as secure as I could be. I didn't trust anyone much with the heart, but it would offer no temptation to the shepherd of the trees. He didn't have much use for the quarrels between fauna, including the human kind. If it didn't impact his world, he didn't care.

I kept the driller worm spores. I planned to stash them outside Jack's immediate area, but in a place close enough to lay my hand upon them should the need arise. I didn't want to take them close to Jack, since he was a technophile and would be most unhappy if I ruined several years' earnings in machines.

I felt ambivalent about the heart of stone. I needed to confirm what I had learned from Chimereon. I needed to discover whether or not Corvinus the Raven had been killed for prying into the ancient Rites of the Nephilim, and who had killed him. Titania had certainly implicated herself, but had she acted alone? Had she truly been at the heart of Corvinus's death? And was she the only player involved? What of the last of the Nephilim, if any still lived?

At the same time, I had no desire to follow my late master's path too far. The Rites sounded dangerous. People died trying to become Nephilim. I counted that as a bit more risk than I wanted to take for a reward I really didn't understand, despite the temptation of immortality that lingered in what I had learned from Chimereon.

I didn't wonder if that tidbit about immortality had been deliberate. Everything Chimereon did was deliberate. I simply didn't know what her exact motive might have been for dangling the bait in front of me.

Shelving those considerations for later, I took a direct route, fast and short and hard, running through wild and deserted Ways. Duncan's choice of abode, fortunately, made deserted routes easy to take. Outside the area where I expected to find him, I tucked away my bags of driller worms beneath a small, twisted tree with long reddish leaves. No other large plants grew in proximity to that lone monument to arboreal hardiness, so I figured that I should have no problem locating it again in the rolling grasslands.

Duncan had set out monitors, which I had expected, so he didn't even turn to face me as I walked down the long slope of a river wide enough to have been the Nile, thin blue grasses sliding along my legs as I approached the shore and the fisherman standing there.

His wrist flicked the fly pole in a steady rhythm that did not change even when he spoke. "Zethus. Foolish of you to come to me with a price on your head."

"Nah." I halted beside him. "Our friendship is too good and too old for me to worry." I grinned as he shot me a skeptical look. "Besides, you're on vacation."

"There is that," he said wryly. "So what's your proposition?"

"You know me too well."

He laughed.

I watched one wave curl into the next. "The bounty has been offered by the Whitesnakes."

His mouth twisted. "I know. One of the reasons I haven't been chasing it."

"Some have." I bent, picked up a rock, and weighed it in my hand.

He shot me an evil look. "Don't even think about it. Scare away one fish and I might not care about the Whitesnakes."

I hid a smile. "Fine, fine. The money does have possibilities, though."

He favored me with a sidelong glance. "What now?"

"How would you like to have the benefit of that money?"

"You don't look depressed enough for suicide," he said mildly. "So you must have something else in mind. What is it?"

"You have cloning tanks still, right? For organs and the like?"

He nodded slowly. "I see where you're going, but I don't think . . ."

"It'll be dead. Eventually. And I can give it enough of a psychic imprint to pass all but the most dedicated scans," I told him.

"Maybe so," he said. "But you have to realize that a bounty hunter lives by his reputation. I take in something like that for the cash, you crop up later, and my rep's blown. No one will ever trust me again."

I winked at him. "That's the beautiful part. I remember you talking about the competition in less than favorable terms in the past. You've never turned down an opportunity to make life difficult for someone else."

A slow smile blossomed on his face, vanished as the pole jumped in his hand. His reflexes responded for him, setting the hook, and then the fight began. After about fifteen minutes of what I'm sure Duncan would later report to other fishermen as an epic battle, he brought a long, sleek fish up to shore, carefully drew it out of the water and held it up for clear visibility to his monitors, cleared the hook from its mouth, and released it back into the river.

I shook my head as I watched it dart out into the rolling current. "I will never understand a man wasting his time and effort catching a fish that he's only going to release immediately."

He gave me a jaundiced look as he collapsed his rod. "You'd rather I tortured it for a while before I let it go?"

I shook my head, chuckling. "No, but it seems that you'd at least eat the thing."

He shuddered. "Oh, no. I hate fish. Besides, the fish in these waters have learned to live with poisons that would kill me quickly and painfully."

"But you love to catch 'em."

"It relaxes me. I can't say that about much else." He picked up the rod and began walking back up the slope. "The ship's this way."

I followed, watching the blur of his monitors as they rose whining from their hiding places in the grass and fell into escort formation around the two of us. The monitors' chameleon cloaking technology made them virtually invisible when they weren't moving, and made an observer a little queasy when they were. "Are they armed?"

He looked back at me. "The monitors? You know I never talk about methods. Besides, would you believe me if I told you?"

I laughed. "Probably not."

"There you are."

His ship had the same chameleon cloak as his monitors. Essentially a long, sleek, aerodynamic dart, Duncan's ship floated just above the tall grass, a hatch in the side of the ship opening as the ship itself ghosted into view. Duncan, the monitors, and I boarded without preamble. The monitors stored themselves in vacant niches while Duncan and I strapped ourselves into the cockpit. Apparently an ex-military craft, the ship hadn't been designed with the comfort of the crew in mind, but it responded to Duncan's commands like a living thing, leaping up and into the dusty, golden sky.

I watched the ground drop away and swallowed heavily. Duncan glanced over at me and grinned. "Still not a flyer, eh?"

"Maybe I just don't like giving someone else that much control over my fate."

"You could always become a pilot."

"I'd rather walk."

"Like I said."

Darkness grew around us as the craft drew itself up, beyond the reaches of the atmosphere. Though I've been in space a few times, I will never tire of the exquisite clarity of the light of the sun, moon, and stars, just as I will never grow accustomed to the endless nausea of free fall. Fortunately, the moments of true weightlessness were brief as the ship followed an intersecting course with Duncan's habitat.

Duncan reached into a pouch set low on his seat, took out a couple of chocolate bars, and waved one in my general direction. I shook my head feebly and concentrated on controlling my rebellious stomach. Duncan made no attempt to conceal his amusement as he peeled the wrapper back on one and ate it, the son of a bitch.

Fortunately, Duncan's station had been built by a relatively conservative bunch who knew the value of simulated gravity. The station had been constructed as a topless and bottomless cylinder. A hollow shaft ran through the center, connected to the interior wall by several rigid tubes. The interior of the shaft, the tubes, and the sealed, hollow wall of the cylinder provided pressurized passageways and living space. The entire structure spun around the central shaft, providing a comfortable illusion of gravity in the living quarters located within the cylinder's walls.

The ship docked at one end of the central shaft, matching the rotation of the station until the station stilled to rocklike solidity and the Earth, sun, and stars spun around us. None of that helped calm my stomach one bit. We disembarked through a narrow tube that led through the central shaft, pulling ourselves along by means of regular handholds set in the walls of the station. Duncan took his slow, easy time, so I pulled myself on past him, virtually diving down the first available shaft that led out to the interior wall of the cylinder, flipping in mid-flight and putting my hands on the side rails of the long ladder that stretched up the shaft. As the pull of gravity increased, settling my nervous stomach, I tightened my hands, slowed myself to a stop, and proceeded downward at a more leisurely pace into the steadily increasing pull of the station's centripetal force.

Duncan was waiting for me at the bottom, undoubtedly having taken advantage of an elevator. I didn't care. My mood had improved as my stomach settled. I looked at the velvet blue of the walls and grinned. "You've been sprucing the place up."

"I finally managed to figure out the controls on the wall displays. It's more comfortable like this."

"The effect you're looking for is something like night-blindness?"

"I like it dark," he said defensively.

"I noticed."

"So what's the plan?"

I sat down and drew out the details for him. He corrected and added a few things. I went along with that, since he knew the habits of our prospective dupe better than I did, though I had at least heard of him. The man whose reputation Duncan had decided to destroy had not spent his time endearing himself to anyone. He called himself Edward Harvest, and he preferred to take bounties that did not specify the condition of the target after capture. Edward Harvest apparently found it easier to deal with dead bodies than live ones.

Edward Harvest was not a nice man.

His predisposition for killing, however, made him perfect as our patsy. He also had no talent for sorcery or psi or any of the other esoteric trades that might have made the deception more difficult. He used a variety of weapons, most of them high tech. As a result, he crossed paths once in a while with Duncan. Duncan didn't like the competition, and Duncan didn't like Harvest. Because of those dislikes, Duncan did like the plan, and that was the important part.

We began that night. I donated a few drops of blood to one of Duncan's more advanced machines and we settled down to wait. I took the opportunity to eat and catch up on some needed rest. Even at its most accelerated state, the machine would take three days to complete its task. With my cells, it would be able to grow and age a clone to what we needed. I'd have to take it from there.

I would have challenged Duncan to some chess to pass the time, but poker was his game of choice, and he chose not to play with sorcerers or any other of the more esoterically skilled, which I thought a bit narrow-minded of him. So I used the time to rest and to go through the Legion, paying attention to every minuscule detail of my waiting host. I didn't want to take any chances on losing control of that situation again. The White Wolf, Blade, Bright Angel, and the White Rose all passed inspection. I could detect no trace of taint on any member of the Legion. I did note that my forces, though less numerous, had gained in strength, undoubtedly due to the power gained from the Gold.

I made the White Wolf's role as a Captain of my Legion official. I had doubts that it would do anything but increase his arrogance, but he deserved it.

In the shadows of Duncan's station and in the boredom of waiting, I noticed that I had begun to see with far more clarity than the conditions should have allowed. What should have been the dim outlines of walls had sharp contours, and in the pools of darkness where the light faded, I could see more clearly than in the direct light. Once I became aware of this clarity in the darkness, I thought of the Fae Hound I had taken into my shadow. Its power had been linked to the darkness. I had absorbed its power with its memories. That power had become mine. I should not have been surprised as it began to manifest itself. I decided to take a more active approach to exploring my new abilities.

I worked with the darkness. I found that in the corners of deepest shadow in the station, I did not need line of sight to be aware of what passed there. I grappled with this new strength, stretching senses through darkness, until I came to see shadow as a gateway and took my first cautious steps through the station from room to darkened room without using the hallways in between. The power of the Shadow Hound had opened a new kind of Way.

Duncan had plenty of shadows for the dweller to move through, so I used my new power to explore his abode. No other living soul occupied the station. Duncan had put away considerable stores. He had also converted several storerooms to holding cells. More of the station seemed to be active than I remembered from my previous visit. In other words, I found nothing surprising. Still, the empty shell of the Shadow Dweller's power responded easily to my will. With practice it could become a useful tool.

When I ate that night, I explored the selection available in Duncan's stores. I had broken into my third sealed box of rations when I realized that I felt physically as tight as a drum, stretched and bloated and hot and sweating, and yet I still could not assuage the gnawing hunger at my core. I worried then, remembering that the power of the Shadow Hound had carried with it a hunger as well. I put down the rations and retired, turning the lights of the bedroom up to full brightness. I could afford no distractions. I would grapple with the hunger of the Shadow another time, but first I would wear down its power. Trying to sleep in bright light left me nervous and irritable, but the hunger did diminish. It didn't fade entirely, but it became something I could ignore. I wasn't sure what it would take to assuage that new appetite. I didn't really want to find out. I had enough bad habits as it was.

Of course, given the weakening of the Legion and the absence of my Tindalan insurance, a fallback couldn't be entirely bad. After all, my head had become a popular commodity in recent times. I wouldn't turn away from the prospect of using the power of the Shadow Hound, but I didn't need to embrace it and all it carried with it too eagerly, either.

On the third day, Duncan came for me and told me that his machine had completed the accelerated growth of my clone. I followed him back to his medical facilities. The machine had opened to a featureless, white table, revealing a recumbent form lying as if in deep sleep.

I felt an eerie sensation as I looked down at my doppelgänger, but there were obvious differences between it and the body I wore. The skin of the clone had the pink, soft, new texture of a newborn baby. None of my wrinkles or blemishes existed on that blank parchment. Fortunately, I wasn't known for having large identifying marks, but everyone picks up a few white lines of scar tissue over the years, even if they're minuscule. The clone had none. It breathed evenly, but of course the eyes were empty when I raised an eyelid. That new brain, neurons unwired by experience, would be a tabula rasa on which I could write enough basic controls and commands to make this body give a good enough performance to get killed for my sake. Considering my empty twin, I smiled.

I've always thought highly of family loyalty, particularly when I reap the benefits.

CHAPTER XX

DYING DIDN'T seem like a habit I wanted to acquire.

It had taken us a week to set everything in motion. Duncan spent his time tracking down Harvest and establishing his movements. I worked on my doppelgänger. The White Rose provided tremendous help, offering a purely technical and encyclopedic knowledge of all things living. In the end, though, I decided to do the deed by direct control.

It proved to be more of a task than I had thought, making the body respond robotically to programming. After a while, I reconsidered my original plan to provide set instructions for the clone. At the White Rose's suggestion, I prepared the brain of my clone as a vessel. I took enough time to strengthen the paths of the central nervous system to the point that walking the body around didn't make me look like a bad imitation of *The Night of the Living Dead*. Possessing my clone proved remarkably easy, particularly with the assistance of the White Rose. After all, she knew my body from the inside better than I did. I only used it; she kept it running in spite of the hazards of my lifestyle.

I started slow. While the clone bathed in ultraviolet to give his skin a weathered look that at least approached my own, I sat next to the machine, closed my eyes, detached myself from my physical form, and reattached myself to the clone's physical form. As I thrashed the body of the clone around in a bed of light, the White Rose busily mapped nerve clusters to my attempts to control the body. The ether grew heavy with floral sweetness, until I finally asked the White Rose to tone it down. She did what she could to moderate the intrusive byproduct of her power, but she could not stop and I needed the power she provided. The cloying sweetness clogged my mind until I began to wonder if I could develop a psychic head cold to escape the impression of working in a flower shop.

The process of mapping the nerve clusters in my clone resembled the thrashing of a newborn who flails wildly in that initial attempt to gain control over his or her new limbs. With the aid of the Legion, I could accelerate this process considerably. In the meantime, Blade practiced concealing all signs of my remote consciousness, while the White Wolf and his forces guarded my original body.

It took a certain amount of time and effort, but after a few days of neural mapping, I had the body doing laps around the station in a loose suit of clothing laid out for me by Duncan. The muscles, even with everything sorcery and technology combined had managed to accomplish, were pathetically flaccid compared to my own battered vehicle. On the other hand, all this body had to do was simulate me long enough to die. How many muscles did that take? The White Rose worked constantly all this time, refining the physical processes of the new body to match the old one.

An interesting thought struck me while we engaged in all this preparation. A more permanent link would provide a cumbersome method for pursuing longevity. I'd have to be sure that I had plenty of bodies available. An active lifestyle probably wouldn't be recommended unless I became quite a bit better at possession. But obviously transfer after transfer could be made. Using the next clone as a replacement when the first one wore out could keep a man going for a long, long time. I hadn't felt any soul in the body to displace, so I didn't have any nasty ethical conundrums. Still, I did have an emotional attachment to my old flesh, but as an alternative to dying, body jumping could be something to keep in mind. I wondered idly how much Duncan's equipment would cost to acquire.

I felt confident that after a few more days the clone would perform well enough. I had no fears about jumping back to my old body from a distance, though I didn't want to keep my original body in the orbital. I wanted to be close to a Way in the event that I struggled more than I expected to return to my original body. I hadn't had any trouble transferring between the two on practice runs. The distance didn't concern me too much, since I did exercise a similar skill every time I looked ahead on a WanderWay, pushing my awareness out through varying possibilities to seek my path.

When I had a Way to work with, I felt much more secure.

When Duncan's shuttle docked, I met him in the clone. "Find him?"

"Harvest is always easy to find," Duncan said contemptuously. "He leaves a trail of blood wherever he goes. He has this particular bar he likes in the underbelly of TechTown called the One Shot. He's there now. That would be the place, I think.

Plenty of witnesses who'll talk only for money. Well outside your usual haunts."

"And do I have a reason for showing up there?"

He grinned. "Several information brokers work out of there. I'd suggest that you approach one of them. Ask for information about the Whitesnakes. That ought to get Harvest's attention. If he doesn't take you out before that."

I raised a skeptical eyebrow. "He's already looking for me?"

"You're on his list. I don't like him much, but he is a competent bastard. And the changes in you that can be seen in the clone look like you've been hitting the rejuve again. Your habits are well known enough that it'll be consistent with past behavior."

I resisted a flash of irritation. "I thought the clone looked pretty close."

"Close enough. But still younger. The skin is the biggest reason. It's a tough one to get around, but in your case it'll be to our advantage. I also recommend you take another step. Take a pigmentation treatment from the machines. Take advantage of a couple of other cosmetic changes I have available up here. If you've disguised yourself, so much the better. It adds the right touch." He examined the clone critically. "You've been doing a good job with it, looks like. Add the disguises, and it should pass muster. Any incidental differences will simply add to the impression that you've been keeping a low profile."

"When do you want to set this in motion?"

"As soon as you're done with the treatments, and I get some rest. Tomorrow, probably."

"Sounds good. You program the machines." I fell in beside him as he began walking back toward the medical facilities. "I want my original body down out of the orbital for this."

"Why?"

"Insurance," I told him bluntly. "I want to be close to an available Way. This bar, it's not on an anchored Way, is it?"

He rubbed one hand across his chin. "Yes, it is. But it has an unanchored back alley. Good enough?"

"Good enough."

I laid the clone back down in the machines, retreated to my own body, and met Duncan coming through the door. "I don't know if I'll ever get used to this witchery," he said when he saw me. I could see a shimmer of uneasiness surface in his eyes for an instant.

I grinned at him. "Don't think about it too much, Jack. Are you still planning to contest Harvest's right to the reward on the basis that he doesn't have the right man?"

"I don't want to be tied to this," he said, shaking his head. "I know I won't see any direct return that way, but Harvest will have to pay when you show back up again. You know he won't be happy with you."

"One more cross to bear," I said with a shrug. "If I live that long, I'll worry about it."

"You could always move out of CrossTown. Give up the life." He watched me out of the corner of his eye.

"Would you?"

"Nope."

"Exactly."

I spent the night sleeping and dreaming. My mind needed the rest even if my body didn't. My dreams were wistful things, running across the darkness of my mind like thin clouds racing before the wind. In the darkness, I felt a hunger growing. One thing that had disturbed me about transferring between bodies was the fact that the power of my shadow dweller followed me wherever my consciousness went.

I woke from a troubled sleep, brought both bodies to the ship, and left the clone comatose and strapped down in a berth. I took the copilot's seat again in my old body. The cosmetic treatments had changed the clone's appearance considerably, but not enough to pass more than a casual inspection. If Harvest had any sophisticated analytical equipment, he'd have my DNA fingerprint faster than you could say Crick and Watson.

Once we landed I roused the clone and rose from the ship in my borrowed body. As we had practiced, the White Rose managed the connection to the clone, Blade concealed the connection, and the White Wolf guarded my body, while Bright Angel continued to hold the fortress of my spirit. It wasn't that I didn't trust Jack Duncan. It was simpler than that. I didn't really have much trust left for anyone.

I followed Jack's directions, taking a straightforward Way for a while, and then angled off, following back trails until I found the alley stretching behind the One Shot. Jack had been correct. It was an unanchored Way. Good.

Social strata in TechTown were reflected in the architecture of the towers: the closer to the level of the street you were, the lower on the social ladder you had to be. The One Shot turned out to be little more than a shack, a motley collection of various alloy plates salvaged from the nearest available junk pile and riveted to a metal frame, all done up in late rust and early decay. The people in that neighborhood didn't so much walk as skulk, and they didn't do that without someone to watch their backs. Even the rats scurried about their business in groups of three or more.

I found that this body responded much the same as my old one when it came to nervousness and fear. After all, I planned to walk in there and get myself killed. The plan was to travel back down the conduit provided by the White Rose and the connection to the rest of the Legion. Even with the distance involved, given the presence of an anchored Way and my time spent practicing, I had every confidence that I could do this. It wasn't an idea that my less than rational side agreed with in the slightest.

On the positive side, things went much more quickly than I expected.

I opened the door, strolled in, and looked around. The harsh and naked light bulbs hanging from the rough, uncovered rafters above my head lit the room far too brightly for a comfortable bar. I didn't see any information brokers off hand, but I figured that Harvest must have been the slight man in loose clothing who rose from his table and hurled something at me as I walked through the door. I had just registered that the object looked like the illegitimate child of a Klein bottle and a Möbius strip, and that it had a negative spiritual presence, when it struck me lightly in the chest. Abruptly, the White Rose and the link tying me back to my body vanished.

At the same time, Harvest leveled two excessively large caliber pistols at me and fired. I didn't have time to see much more than the flash, but I was already frantically trying to extricate myself from the body when Harvest blew my head clean off.

CHAPTER XXI

DON'T LISTEN to what any optimist tells you. Dying hurts. It's painful. All those nerve endings slowly and randomly firing during the eternal moment when the body hasn't yet settled into the idea of death create a uniquely tortuous experience. Then you feel gravity and entropy and the other natural forces that you've been denying all the days of your life begin to step in and take over.

Not an experience I wanted to have even once. Certainly not more than once.

I couldn't jump free. That was the worst of it. Harvest had cut all of my ties and effectively blocked me in the body with a Spirit Tap. I hadn't expected that. The damned things weren't easy to acquire, and had much the same effect on the spiritual and psychic phenomena as an EMP wave had on unshielded solid-state electronics.

I shouldn't have had the sorcerous strength to even remain in the body. I should have been dead, finished, complete, worm food—and the body was, no doubt about that—but my consciousness still survived, trapped in that useless slab of meat. I had become a ghost without a place to go. I could feel the dark roots of the Shadow Hound's power twining through my consciousness. It had stayed with me. And apparently it had some resistance to the Spirit Tap's effects. Even the little while I remained caught in that dying body, like a wolf in a trap, nearly drove me mad. Some would say I wasn't entirely sane when Edward Harvest made his first mistake.

He had been cautious, staying well away from the body while it dropped to the ground, twitching, voiding its bladder and bowels. He stayed away far enough to make no physical contact with the body, but as he reached across my leg to retrieve his Spirit Tap, his arm blocked the light.

I felt that shadow cross me like a sinner feels the doorway to salvation open. More darkly, through that shadow I felt the essence of Edward Harvest. I raced through that open doorway and into the soul of the man who had killed me. I took him so fast I didn't even have time to consciously absorb his memories.

The gnawing hunger that had been with me since I had opened the Ways of Shadow in the station abated.

I didn't really need Harvest's memories, though. I already knew that Jack Duncan had betrayed me. Harvest had been too prepared.

As I pulled Harvest down into the darkness, his body stood, having picked up the Spirit Tap reflexively. The presence of it didn't drive me out of my newest body. The Spirit Tap dangled absently from one hand as I looked out through Harvest's eyes. His body had a different feel from my own: much more powerful, poised as if ready to dance, a coiled spring awaiting the release of killing. Harvest had a wiry strength far above that portion natural to a man, and his reflexes were apparently the finest TechTown could manufacture. I seemed out of phase with the world around me. A nearly dressed catbreed waitress seemed to float from step to step as she backed away from my still-leaking corpse. In Harvest's body, I found myself looking up at the world, which seemed just a little larger, as Harvest had been physically shorter than my original body as well as that of my clone. With great deliberation I crushed the Spirit Tap in my fist and walked out the back door, the ruin still in my hand. No one tried to stop me. I imagine they were too confused.

At first I found myself staggering like a drunken wastrel. It took some time to acclimatize myself to Harvest's body, particularly with the augments, but I found it an easier process than I should have. I had the echoes of Harvest's recent occupancy to guide my possession.

Not that Harvest himself remained. The hunger of the darkness and the desperate rage of my betrayal had consumed his personality and self in the first flash of contact. I did have most of his memories left, though.

I hit the alley moving fast, reached for the Way, and felt it respond sluggishly to my touch. I didn't know if that sluggishness came from some remaining backlash from the Spirit Tap or the adjustment period for my possession of Harvest's body. I didn't really care. I threw myself into the effort of using the Way, casting myself on a long route back to Duncan's ship. I wanted to walk long enough to become accustomed to Harvest's body. Accustomed enough, at least, to pass for Harvest long enough to get close to Jack.

The path I took paralleled the darkness in my heart. I shambled through visions of blasted earths filled only with ruins, desolate wastelands, barren plains, and shattered mountains empty of life—all monuments to the folly and stupid, bloody-minded ignorance of mankind. As my control of Harvest's body firmed, his/my spine straightening, his/my steps becoming sure and quick, I turned my attention to the stolen memories so I could look out through his eyes into his recent past.

Jack had come to him/me with the proposal while I had been gaining control over my cloned body. Harvest had been surprised to see him enter the One Shot and settle directly into the seat across the table. "Jack Duncan. What do you want?"

Jack had smiled. "Harvest. Pleasant as ever. How would you like to make twenty-five gold for five minutes work?"

Harvest cocked his head. "Stupid question. What's the catch?"

Jack leaned back in the chair. "You've heard of Zethus the sorcerer? Apprentice to the late Corvinus the Raven?"

Harvest nodded. "The Whitesnake bounty on him is fifty gold."

Jack grinned. "It all spends, no matter what the source."

"It does indeed. You want half."

Jack Duncan shook his head. "I want to cut you in for half. I happen to know that Zethus is investigating the death of his master. I also happen to know that he's been hitting information brokers, lately."

Harvest sneered. "So? I could hit all the information brokers as easy as you. Why should I give you half?"

"Because I can direct him here."

Harvest chewed that over ruminatively. "Why not take him yourself?"

"I don't think so," Duncan replied mildly. "He's a prepared, powerful, paranoid sorcerer. He's ready for anything I try."

Harvest spread his hands. "Why do you think I'd do any better than you?"

"Because you have a Spirit Tap. You can cut him off from his bound spirits. I send him here, he'll be over-extended. You take him out, we split the bounty."

Harvest cocked his head. "What keeps me from betraying you?"

Duncan chuckled. "I'm recording all of this through a Bank of Hours notary. It'll be a legal contract. Even you won't risk breaking a notarized contract."

Harvest nodded slowly. "All right, then. When can I expect him?"

"I'll let you know more when I know more." Duncan stood.

Harvest turned his attention inward. If Duncan were to die, the money would be uncontested, even by the Bank of Hours. If Duncan didn't expose himself, well then, killing the sorcerer would be an easy twenty-five gold . . .

I pulled out of the memory and nodded to myself. Harvest had a certain low animal cunning and damned good reflexes, but he didn't strike me as being the brightest bulb in the box. Jack Duncan had given Harvest no information about the clone, so he obviously still considered the double-cross on Harvest. He was probably holding it back as his ace in the hole.

I had a feeling that Jack had set Harvest up according to plan, then added a few refinements of his own. After all, Harvest had taken Jack's word that the Bank of Hours was recording their conversation. It would be easy for Jack to later ruin Harvest's reputation and collect the reward: even if it were apparent that Jack had duped him, no one wants to use a stupid bounty hunter any more than they want to use a duplicitous one. In fact, a little duplicity can count as a benefit in that business. If Jack had played his cards right, he might even have skimmed twenty-five gold from Harvest, then collected the full amount when the dust settled, leaving Harvest hanging to pay the indemnity on the full amount. Either way, the money had been more important to Jack Duncan than I thought. Evidently, I had a higher opinion of Duncan's sense of honor than he did.

On the other hand, I hadn't trusted him as much as he'd planned. Though he'd done a good job of betraying me, the fact that I had survived would prove to be a fatal error. Fatal for him. Or so I hoped.

I thought about collecting my stash of driller worm spores before continuing on to where Duncan would be waiting for news, but I would have had to rid my stolen body of the plethora of gadgets tucked over and under Harvest's loose clothing. That might make Jack suspect the ruse too quickly. I couldn't afford that risk. Besides, in that plethora of lethal devices I catalogued at least three devoted to electronic counter measures, after shuffling quickly through Harvest's immediate memories.

As I entered the sweeping grasslands around the shuttle, I wondered if some passerby had recognized the clone as me. As I walked toward my rendezvous with my betrayer in the body of my killer, I visualized a massive battle over the dubious prize of my bogus corpse. I hoped it would happen that way. I wished the other side bad luck impartially, and general confusion to the enemy, whoever that might happen to be.

I spotted the storm first. A small whirlwind, complete with arcing lightning bolts, ran erratically across the rolling hills. In the distance I could see the shuttle, floating uncloaked over the grass. I eased my way to the top of a nearby hill, where I spotted the small figure of a man running before the fury of the miniature storm. I saw the glint of metal rising from several sites then tumbling away in the grass, caught in a net of intersecting lightning bolts, and mentally ticked Jack's monitors off my list.

My plan seemed to be streamlining itself with every passing moment. As I watched, the storm ceased its purposeful course and began to disperse. Its quarry shambled to a stop. He stood bent over with his hands braced against his thighs, gulping air.

A delighted grin spread across my stolen face. It looked to me as if the White Wolf held the shuttle and my body. Jack Duncan had underestimated the Legion, and by underestimating the Legion, he had underestimated me.

I pulled myself upright and strolled down to where Duncan stood. "Having some trouble, Jack?" I called down to him.

He whirled, saw me, and relaxed. "Harvest. I hope you have good news for me."

I cocked my head. "Why, Jack? Are you having a bad day?"

"Don't try to be funny, Harvest. It doesn't suit you. Is the sorcerer dead?"

"Oh, I killed him, sure enough." I stepped to within arm's length of Duncan and stopped.

"Shit! Why is his Legion still guarding his body?"

I shrugged.

Duncan's eyes narrowed. "Are you all right, Harvest? Did he do anything to you? Are you going to be straight for this? If you still have the Spirit Tap, we should be able to do this. I'm going to need your help to take command of my ship again . . ."

His voice trailed off as I tossed the crushed Spirit Tap to the ground at his feet. "Jack, I wouldn't trust you with command of a rowboat in a storm sewer."

He scrambled back, one hand darting toward the pistol on his belt, his eyes wide and full of fear. He had begun to suspect, I think, almost from the first. He had either wanted to be sure that Harvest's body had become a vessel for my psyche, or he really hadn't been able to believe that his plan had failed.

I'll give Harvest one thing: the man had been a killing fool. His reflexes had become so hardwired that I didn't even have the opportunity to think about it. Out came the pistols, then the hushed sound of the double report as they bucked in my stolen hands. Jack Duncan fell like an empty suit. He never fired a shot.

I remember Jack telling me once that before he'd taken to wandering the Roads, he had been the man responsible for taking down one of the most famous criminals of his time and place—a man named John Wesley Hardin. The fact that Jack had tracked him, located him, pointed him out to the law, and never came into direct contact with his target always struck me as the most interesting aspect of the tale.

I suppose I should have taken the hint from that. Jack Duncan had been just a little too smart and a little too slippery to ever be fully trusted.

I left that as my contribution to Jack Duncan's epitaph, turned my back on his corpse, and walked steadily toward the shuttle. I came across a trail of broken machinery, fragments of the monitors Jack had used as his escort. They would have worked well enough as bodyguards against someone like Harvest, but they hadn't a prayer against the White Wolf's localized storm.

I saw another weather anomaly rising as I approached the shuttle. I stopped, cupped my hands around my mouth, and shouted, "It's me, dammit! Wolf, stand down! At the least, come out here and check me out!"

The tiny whirlwind continued to build, looming over me, but it didn't move any closer. With some difficulty, fighting the same reflexes of the conjoined psyche that had let me use Harvest's body as easily as I had, I extended my senses, and saw the Bright Angel and the White Wolf.

I sagged in relief. "Angel. When contact with the Legion vanished, I thought the Spirit Tap had been too much."

"It almost was too much," she responded mildly. "If we hadn't been stretched out along the contact line, and if the White Rose hadn't pulled me in, I don't know that I would have made it back so easily."

The White Wolf's tongue lolled insouciantly. "You don't look like you're feeling yourself, today."

"Funny." I weighed them with my eyes. "How's my body doing?"

"Ugly as ever," the White Wolf said cheerfully. "Rose has everything in hand. We were a bit curious, though. With the Spirit Tap, we didn't know how you had fared. We only knew that you hadn't died, for we were still bound."

"When did Jack tip his hand?"

Before me, the whirlwind diminished and collapsed in upon itself as the White Wolf let his controlled power bleed away. Harvest's hair stood erect on his/my forearms and bristled on his/my scalp with the static electricity overflow from the collapsing storm. Bright Angel shook her head. "He didn't. As soon as Harvest made his move and I escaped, the others knew that Jack had betrayed you. The White Wolf struck before Jack did."

"Good." I said it more forcefully than I had intended. Dying had put me on edge.

I stepped past them and into the shuttle. My body remained as I had left it, sitting in the copilot's seat. I let Harvest's shadow slide across my body's shoulder and made the jump back to my old mortal shell. Harvest's body, without me to maintain it, collapsed to the floor of the shuttle. The hunger of the Fae Shadow Hound, though sated, moved with me from body to body. I opened my eyes, settled back into the feel of my native flesh with a sigh of relief, and unstrapped from the seat.

"What next, oh Master?" the White Wolf inquired with mock solicitude.

I stooped and stripped a couple of handy items from Harvest's corpse. It still breathed, the heart still beat, the autonomous nervous system had not yet wound to a close, but no one was home, or would ever be returning home. I had consumed him, after all. All that had been Edward Harvest had become my own. The body he'd left behind qualified as a corpse. It simply hadn't yet figured out how to stop living. "If the enemy's not thoroughly confused by this time, nothing will confuse them. While they're in disarray, I think it's time to investigate Corvinus's research."

I ambled out through the grassland, past Duncan's corpse, and retrieved my stash of driller worm spores. I turned my back on that place and the dead men who slept in it. I set my feet on a Way that would take me to the Shepherd of the Trees. I needed the heart of stone for the next step. With that fragment to guide me, I could search for a Way that would take me as far as I needed to go.

CHAPTER XXII

I DELIBERATELY chose Ways where the traffic would be anywhere between light and nonexistent—preferably nonexistent. So when I crossed paths with a traveler, and a familiar traveler at that, I felt some measure of surprise and concern. I kept my distance. I didn't want the driller worms to awaken prematurely, hungry for any gadgets Vayne might have concealed.

He had stopped in the Road to wait for me. He did not smile. "Zethus. I am pleased to see that reports of your death were premature."

"Knight Commander Vayne. What brings you out this way?"

"I had thought to have a conversation with a bounty hunter. Jack Duncan. I heard that he might have been involved in your death."

I smiled. "He was. He made some bad decisions. He won't have the opportunity to make them again."

Anthony Vayne cocked his head. "Ruthless of you, Zethus. You're changing."

"Not really. I'm just adapting. Being hunted tends to purify a man's goals nicely."

"You're still hunting for Corvinus's killer."

It hadn't been a question, but I nodded anyway.

"Be careful."

I lost my smile. "I'm particularly careful these days." I stepped nearer. "Don't worry about me. I'm close now. I know why Corvinus was killed. Pale had that much right. He was killed because of what he was working on. I just need a little more time, and a little more information, and I'll have the proof I'm looking for. Enough proof for me, at any rate."

Vayne's eyes narrowed. His face hardened. "Are you pursuing the Raven's research?"

"A bit further," I admitted. "But I don't plan on going all the way with it. It sounds too dangerous."

"It's proved to be fatal to him already. You could drop it all, you know. Leave CrossTown behind." He studied my face as he spoke.

"No I can't." My face had become a mask.

He sighed. "I know."

I laughed suddenly. "Don't worry about me. I've made it this far. I'll see this thing through to the end."

"That's what I'm afraid of." He softened the words with a melancholy smile. "Do you want company?"

"No." I said it slowly. "You're a well-known associate of mine. And you'd be missed if you were gone too long. You must have had one hell of a time losing all of the surveillance that had to be on you as it is. No reason to take any unnecessary risks."

"Suit yourself."

I gave him a lopsided smile. "I usually do."

"You always have." He walked past me and faded into a haze of directed possibility.

I continued along the Way I had chosen, thinking about how long I had known Vayne. When I had first crossed over on the back of an errant WanderWay in pursuit of a fleeing spirit, I had been reduced to surviving on the fringes of CrossTown, eking out a living as a sorcerer, but without the knowledge of the Ways needed to earn a true place in CrossTown society—and without the knowledge to return home. I met Vayne then, pulling him out of a particularly nasty situation involving a ghost, a bell, and something that looked like a black dog but wasn't.

When Vayne found that I had no desire to return home without the ability to find my way back to CrossTown, he introduced me to the Raven, who happened to be a Master of the Ways, among other things, and who also happened to be in need of an apprentice. Vayne had known me almost as long as I had lived this new life, over fifty years in subjective time, according to the numbers of rejuvenation treatments I had taken since then. I had no idea how long it had been for him, but he hadn't changed much in all that time.

I had though. I'd seized the opportunities open to me. I'd cleaved unto CrossTown's myriad offerings. I'd embraced immortality, at least in the small pieces I had been able to grasp thus far. I had held on to my skills and training as well as I had been able, though even I had begun to wonder about that. My habits were well known. My Legion had been used at least once to attack me.

I had been a sorcerer since I'd left my home and my brother and took to the Road, herding spirits instead of beasts, making my way by my will and my wits rather than my back. I had never thought of my captive Legion as anything but a set of tools to be used. But I had been perhaps more badly shaken at Bane and Shadow's defections than I wanted to admit to myself. I had come to know them. What had seemed only right, in all the time before the Legion had split, now raised a taint of foulness in my mouth.

Sapienta had said nothing good about her late master. Why did that surprise me? Why did I care?

What would I be without them? If I continued to embrace change, what would I become? When would I lose myself in the changing? Even then, I could not help but wince as I thought of the longing I had heard in Bright Angel's voice when she spoke of freedom. Could I continue to hold them? Particularly if I held them only out of the fear that letting them go would mean losing my grip on my own past, and on myself?

Deep in thought, I hadn't traveled far when I felt the Way twisting, reverberating with sudden movement. I paused, extending my senses, for a moment wondering if Anthony Vayne was returning to tell me something, when I parsed out at least four different sources closing in on my location. I seized the reins of possibility and fled through the most devious routes I could find, toward more populated Ways where I could lose myself among myriad travelers. I didn't move quickly enough, however, or they were more prepared than I had expected, for wherever I went, it seemed that more pursuers appeared.

As I fled I cursed the luck of it. Obviously Vayne had not been as free of surveillance as he had thought. I only hoped that he had not traveled so far that he had no inkling of my situation. I had a feeling that I would need all the help I could get. I sought out my store of driller worms, just in case, and eased a handful into my closed fist.

Probes came crawling down the lengths of the Ways, isolating and tracking me. The probability waves of my hunters converged toward me. The probes increased. As I felt them crawl closer, long and sinuous and decidedly reptilian in aspect, the hairs on the back of my neck stirred in atavistic reaction. I had a good idea who my hunters were, and that didn't make me terribly happy. They would be motivated.

Then one of my adversaries managed to intersect my path and I understood for the first time how devoted the Whitesnakes had become to taking me down. As I had suspected, they had sent their own out after me. From the lightly striated robes, this boy appeared to be a high acolyte or a wandering priest. He raised clawed hands and gestured, but the White Wolf broke his forking lightning strike into sputtering fragments. I felt every hair on my body stand upright as I caught the Whitesnake's gaze and cut his will off from his body.

He swayed, the vertically slit pupils of his inhuman eyes wide and unseeing. Two more came into view then. I sent Blade after the first. The second raised a pistol. I threw my handful of driller worms at him. They exploded in midair, long, thin shapes elongating to coil down over the pistol with hungry eagerness. Two more snaked inside his robe. Evidently he'd been carrying more gadgets. He forgot all about me. He dropped the pistol and started dancing around, shucking the robe.

I grinned. Then I heard a soft report and felt a sensation akin to a swarm of ants biting me all over the surface of my back.

I yelped and turned to look behind me, but my legs had acquired the consistency and firmness of whipped cream. I fell, my clouding vision filled with the sight of another Whitesnake in a dark robe holding a long-barreled pistol in his hands and smiling. I recognized the weapon as a tranquilizer gun. I had a moment of despair. They had decided to take me alive.

Then I fell away into darkness, even the voices of my Legion lost in the silence.

CHAPTER XXIII

O F ALL the places in the world to find yourself when you wake up, an oubliette has to rank as one of the worst. Oubliettes are the most primitive of dungeons, basically low-rent hellholes. That's literally what an oubliette is: a hole in the ground, ordinarily used as a dump for people that the owner doesn't ever plan on seeing again.

I cracked open gummed lids, my head pounding as if I'd had one hell of a good time the night before (which, all in all, I thought a bit unfair: dying is one thing, but dying with a hangover you didn't even earn is something else again) and took a look around. That hole held an old smell of pain and fear and piss and shit and vomit and blood and things even less pleasant.

My limbs felt distant. I could not hear the voices of my Legion. My cache of driller worm spores had vanished. So had my silver and iron chains. So had my other surprises. All my goods had undoubtedly been dumped on the Way before they carried me into durance vile. I had a good idea where. I had been in one of their sanctums before. Less as a guest than an invader, that time around. Beyond me, burning distantly on my clouded senses, I could feel the overlay of the main barrier the Whitesnakes used to secure their privacy.

A tall figure wearing a white, hooded robe loomed over me in the shadows, a lantern dangling casually from one clawed hand. The floor moved in a queasy fashion that did nothing for my already delicate digestion. Then I realized that the man in the hood stood ankle deep in snakes. Even worse, I lay supine on that floor, covered in the living coils of those same snakes. Knowing the Whitesnakes' enduring fondness for poisonous reptiles, I chose not to move.

"Where is it?" The voice issuing from that hood sounded decidedly sepulchral. Like all cults, the Whitesnakes were more than slightly taken with theatrics. On the other hand, the hood kept me from seeing his eyes, those windows to the soul, so I would have to work harder to touch his will. That would take time, and given the snakes . . .

I wished I had a cigarette to light up, just to show him how calm I was about my captivity.

"You can talk," he said impatiently. "My friends will let you move that much. Move any more than that, and I have no assurances as to their behavior."

On reflection, the absence of a cigarette could be seen as a good thing.

He waited. I waited. When I didn't answer, his tone became irritated. "If you don't answer, I might have to ask my friends to encourage you to talk."

I hadn't ever been that fond of snakes, anyway.

He reached down slowly, held out one hand, and a small, brightly colored serpent curled its way down his arm and into his cupped palm. "Take this little fellow, for instance. Interesting venom. It's not fatal to humans, but it does seem to have a particularly distressing effect on the central nervous system. I understand that the level of pain involved is really quite unendurable. I don't believe that I know anyone who's needed more than one dose to be persuaded to do anything. Remember, you are the one who banished the last physical incarnation of our Living God. If you think we might have any merciful impulses that could spare you even the smallest element of suffering, think again."

"What do you want to talk about?" I reached for the Legion but hit a moving, yielding but tough personal barrier—a smaller version of the larger binding over the Whitesnake holy ground, and the snakes tightened around my limbs.

My interrogator made tsk'ing noises. "Shouldn't try that. My friends are sensitive to sorcery. You can't dominate them all. At least, not all at once." He bent down until I could see his eyes burning like coals in the depths of the hood. Not that I could take any advantage of that. "Don't make me repeat myself," he said softly. "Where is it?"

"Where's what?" I did my best to look innocent. The snakes didn't seem to be buying it. They didn't seem to be relaxing, either. I tried for the power of the Shadow Hound, but I couldn't focus well enough to bring it up. That dancing mesh of a barrier seemed to be interfering with my access to my captive darkness as well as my Legion.

He looked into my eyes. I looked back. Despite the snakes, he looked away. "The Raven's Key. Where is it?"

"Under his doormat?" I suggested helpfully.

He shook his head. "You never learn."

"Well, actually . . ." I had begun another smartass comment when the hand holding the small snake dipped down, and the snake slipped his fangs into me. At once the world began to burn. I thrashed and screamed as I felt the venom of it slither through my body like a swarm of tiny snakes engendered by the mother and already feeding on my still-living flesh.

Nature can be merciful.

Systems built into the body, such as the shock reaction, can act to damp out certain levels of pain in extreme circumstances. Of course, not only can this particular reaction prove counter-productive at times, but Nature often chooses to arm some of her children with a nearly limitless arsenal of ways to circum-vent the gifts she has bestowed on other children.

In other words, Nature can also be a heartless bitch.

I don't believe that I ever really understood that until my ex-perience with the venom. I have no idea how much time passed. I only know that as the levels of pain faded, and I could actually begin to perceive the world around me again, I fully understood the Christian concepts of eternity, hellfire, and damnation. Trust me, I wanted to repent. I wanted to be saved.

I also knew that I would have no salvation I didn't provide for myself.

As I came back to my body, I became aware that I had fouled myself. The stench of shit and piss and vomit and blood had become considerably stronger. The Hooded Man had not moved. The snakes still wrapped my limbs. My body ached all over, but that was bliss compared to what I had left behind. I wondered distantly how much time had passed for him. Eterni-ty for me compressed into an inconvenient few seconds for him? How many doses did the snake hold?

I watched the Hooded Man and his little hell spawn like a bird watches, well, a snake. The Hooded Man leaned back down. "Where is it?"

My mouth tasted much like I imagined the oubliette would. "Where's what?" I croaked.

He didn't say a word. Down came the snake. I went to hell for a second eternity.

When I came back, I had all the fortitude of a drowning kitten. If the bastard had been patient, I would have told him anything he wanted to know. I would have invented shit on the spot. I would have become Homeric in my response. But he didn't give me the chance.

I heard the repeated, implacable question, and it almost made sense to me. I stared up through the flickering torchlight at him, trying to wrap my mind around language again, then trying to persuade my tongue, jaw, lips, and everything else to function, when the snake came down again.

It's possible that I died. I'm not really sure. I mean, I'd died once before, but this was a bit different from that. I had gone to a place completely absent of pain. The oubliette and its contents faded to distant transparency. I felt a perfect, unencumbered clarity as I looked around. I floated in the living mesh of a single, unending, fiery snake. It held me in place. I understood that Whitesnake sorcery took this form as it cut me off from my Legion, binding my mind as the exterior serpents bound my soul.

The Whitesnakes had an ugly, hobgoblin consistency in their method. Little minds, and all that.

Through the barrier I could see very clearly the Captains of my Legion fighting against the barrier. Something in me broke as I watched them struggling without any orders on my part. They fought without any hope of reward, without any fear of punishment. As they were not tied to my body, other than voluntarily in the case of the White Rose, the venom would not touch them. If it had, they wouldn't have been able to fight anyway.

I explored the confines of the area in which I found myself and made a couple of interesting discoveries. First, I floated in a suspension of darkness. Everything I did, everything I was, had become encapsulated in shadow. In some ways, I had become shadow. I realized then that in my desperation I had somehow reached through the barrier to touch the captive power of the Shadow Hound, and in doing so, I had fled the only way I knew how. I had fled the same way that I had left my body to possess my clone, and later used the shadow as a link to do the same to Edward Harvest. I also noticed that the barrier I had examined earlier distended where it encompassed me. The burden of capturing my fleeing shadow self had stretched it out of the pattern established to hold me in place without any consideration for my wandering spirit and its shadow path.

I thought again of Bright Angel's longing, of the renegade Captains of my Legion, and of the White Wolf's fierce independence. I thought about all the things I had done and all the things I had been. I thought about what I might become, in the unlikely event that I did survive the next few hours. It was then that I realized that I fully intended to pursue the work of my master, but in my own way.

I had no other alternative. I refused to abandon CrossTown. I refused to abandon my obligation to Corvinus. I would see his work through to the end. If I died, at least I would have the satisfaction of keeping the heart from falling into the hands of someone like the Whitesnake cultists.

And I would not carry slaves with me. I would not continue to compel the Legion to serve me. I had other tools. I had my will, my knowledge of the Ways, and the stolen power of the

Shadow Hound. I could not continue to compel them. I could not continue to carry the risk they represented. I feared what it would mean for me to continue to hold them, when they had stood by me in my time of need. I feared that if I died, they would be taken into some Whitesnake sorcerer's Legion. I damned sure wouldn't have that burden on my soul.

The idea had been growing in the back of my mind for some time. I was honest enough with myself to admit that had I not had an alternative tool in the growing power of the shadow, I would not have been able to let them go. I had depended on their strength. I could no longer afford to do so.

I turned my efforts to breaking through on the inside of the barrier. It gave, but I could not break it entirely. I accomplished what I had hoped, however. Blade noticed my efforts. Soon the entire Legion worked at the side of the barrier opposite from me, attacking in force and desperation. The inner skin of the barrier fell before our combined strength, snapping back around to seal me in with the Legion. The cloak of darkness, I noticed, remained joined with me, instead of separating.

My Legion simply stood for an instant, regarding me numbly. I had managed to shock them.

The White Wolf recovered first. "Tell me that this is part of a plan."

"It's not so easy," I told him. "But I do have a plan."

"Why did you come in?" Blade asked. "You could have fought your way out, where you could have accomplished something against the enemy."

"I'm not so sure that I could have fought my way out. The barrier is strong. And I need you all for a few last things."

"A few last things?" Bright Angel shifted uneasily. "What do you mean?"

"I need your help taking the Whitesnake priest and his little helpers down. Then I want you to carry a message for me, if you can. Chances are you won't make it. If we're in a Whitesnake stronghold, the obstacles raised against spirit traffic will be harsh. If you can break free, carry word to Vayne. Show him where this place is. If he can't pull me out, perhaps he can avenge me."

The White Wolf cocked his head. "You sound like you're preparing to die. Don't you think that you'd have a much higher chance of surviving with us?"

"Possibly." I didn't even sound like I believed it to myself. "But if I fall here, with all of you, some Whitesnake sorcerer will take you into his Legion. I don't want to see that. I'm not comfortable holding you anymore. Do this last thing for me. I'll break the chains that bind you, regardless. If you work with me against the Hooded Man and carry my message to Vayne, then you'll do that of your own free will. I will not compel you. I will not argue if you choose to try and escape on your own, though I'll warn you," I swept the lesser ones lined up behind their Captains with my gaze, "all of you, that you stand the greatest chance of success when you act together."

The White Wolf shook with anger. "Is this some trick? What brings on this sudden change of heart?"

"I think it's been coming for some time," I said. "Even Sapienta chafed at her bonds. I've known that, but I don't think that I've ever truly understood it until now. I've been thinking more and more about it. The Hooded Man's passport to hell convinced me in the end. I can't find it within myself to hold you anymore. Don't get me wrong, there's pragmatism to this as well. These Whitesnake barriers are strong, but designed to balk a single concentrated rush. I don't think that they'll do so well against all of us collectively. I won't be able to divert any attention to direct you, or hold you. It will take all of us to give any of us a chance of escaping. Alas, the compelled Legion has been my strength, but also my weakness. I have been attacked through you time and time again, as I have been tracked through all of my contacts. I'm changing my profile. I'm not eliminating my senses, or my ability to bind spirits, or any of my other basic strengths. I'm simply following advice I heard before. I'm purging the Legion. And I'm purging it in the only way that feels clean."

The White Wolf suddenly grinned. "You don't expect to survive. You want to die with a clean conscience. I get to benefit from it. Count me in. I'll help you here, and carry your message for you. Break my bonds."

Bright Angel sneered at the White Wolf, but I could see her burning even more strongly. "Break my bonds. I will help you."

A chorus of the others followed. Blade answered last, slowly. "It's been so long since I've known freedom, I do not know what it means. Will you object if any of us choose to stay with you?"

"Of course not," I said gently. "But if any stays with me, it will not be because I have compelled it."

In the end, even Blade decided to seek his freedom. Perhaps he had been testing me. Two of the lesser ones took their freedom and refused to help. At least they were up front about it. I didn't care by that time.

I felt curiously clean, cleaner than I had felt in a long time. Together, we turned our attention to the plan. I laid it out for them. Their assent came easily. Having agreed, we turned to the two dissenters and told them that they must not attempt to escape the confines of the Whitesnake stronghold until after the Legion moved against the barrier. If they attracted the attention of the Whitesnakes too early, their ends would be both short and terrible. They agreed easily. I should have taken more notice of that than I did, but I had other things on my mind.

Girding our collective loins, the Legion and I directed our effort against the barrier that held us.

CHAPTER XXIV

W E STRUCK in a focused rush. While perhaps not as focused as they had been in the past, the Legion's new motivation more than made up for it. I had never seen such strength
and such ferocity from them. I had heard that the free always
fight with more conviction than slaves. I believed it then. The
barrier that bound us fell almost as we hit it.

Time bent around us. The Legion diverged to fill the snakes.
I took my own target, possessing the new host easily. No defenses had been raised, no expectation of resistance even crossed its
mind. I didn't adjust easily to the new flattened perspective—
the strange new form, the vastly different musculature and nervous system—but I did gain enough understanding to look up
at the face of the huge creature I had wound myself around. I
opened my jaws experimentally. I felt him twitch. I like to think
that he understood what was about to happen, right there before the end.

Then I buried my new fangs in the base of the Hooded
Man's hand, clenching tighter as he convulsed. I then proceeded to pull out and slam the fangs home again and again, as the

other snakes swarmed away from my supine form and over his writing body, locking him down, burying their fangs in every available piece of his twisting shape. Once I had emptied the snake's venom sacs into him, I killed my host, deliberately burning out its primitive nervous system as I left. Then I walked through the shadows to my own abused corpus.

I rose slowly to my feet, feeling less than human but also steadily better as the White Rose and others rose from the dead bodies of the snakes they had possessed to mend my own battered physical shell as well as they could. I opened my eyes and looked down on the corpse of the Hooded Man and numerous dead reptiles. The hood had fallen back away from his reptilian features. His TechTown-purchased genetic bodymods had changed him enough that his features and expressions could not truly be regarded as human, but the expression on his face—the last expression he would ever wear—had enough human frailty in it to almost satisfy my sadistic side.

In his case, my sadistic side would never be entirely satisfied.

I thought step one had gone off without a hitch. The White Rose completed her work. I thanked her solemnly. She didn't reply. Instead, she swarmed up to join the rest of the Legion as Blade came to stand before me. "We have a problem."

On the end of his sword hung one of the two small rebels who had agreed so easily to wait and join our concerted attempt to escape the confines of the Whitesnake stronghold. It still twisted feebly against the force consuming all that it had been. "Where's the other?"

"That's the problem."

Panic squeezed my heart like a vice as I heard a long, trailing scream. I didn't realize immediately that the scream had not been physical, but I understood what it meant: every Whitesnake around would have been informed by the temple barrier and that scream that something unusual was happening. The other small rebel, the one that Blade had not been able to pin down, had apparently become impatient and tripped the Whitesnake alarms.

"That's torn it," the White Wolf snarled. "Let's hit them now, while they're off balance."

As I nodded agreement, Blade whisked away back into the mass of the Legion. They rose out and up, moving like a living rope of smoke. I fled the oubliette through shadow. I perceived the temple barrier as I rose into a stone passageway through a gateway of shadow. The Whitesnakes had apparently kept their prisons not far from the edge of the primary barrier they used to protect their holy ground. That surprised me. I would have kept the prisons near the center of the compound to make escapes more difficult. On the other hand, I wasn't a religious fanatic. I didn't have a worship area right in the middle of everything I built.

Long florescent lights lit the area above the oubliette, which gave me only a few shadow locations to use to my advantage. Two scaly figures ran by in the direction of the barrier, patterned robes flapping.

I stepped out of the shadows behind them, tripped the first and bound his will, then faced the second as he turned. I felt his own Legion rousing to deal with me, then his buddy (at my internal prompting) reached across and hamstrung him with a large sharp knife.

The sorcerer flailed and fell back, losing his concentration. Apparently he had held his own Legion less tightly than he should have, for they strained at their bonds as his concentration faltered. I took advantage of that. As his buddy (under my control, of course) lifted the knife high for another stroke, I frayed the bonds holding the Whitesnake sorcerer's Legion, and they did the rest.

By the time the knife hit, the sorcerer had already passed beyond feeling it. His roused and newly freed Legion had done him in long before that time. Eyes wide, slit pupils glaring, his hands clenched, his claws stabbing into his palms until red blood trickled out to pool around his fists, his back arched and his muscles locked. It didn't look as if his Legion had been kind to him.

Perhaps he should have been kind to them.

I sent the other cultist off to sleep and dreams. With the dreams I had in mind, he'd be lucky to remember his own name when they found him. Meanwhile, the newly freed Legion joined my old group in their attack on the barrier.

To my spiritual senses, the barrier seemed to be a living curtain of serpents. It not only held against the assault, it counterattacked. Individual serpents would peel out of the barrier to sink long, dripping fangs into whatever presented itself as a target.

But I noticed that where the snakes attacked, they weakened the barrier, so I threw the weight of my will into the area most active, where the Whitesnake's freed Legion had just reinforced my old servants. Aggressive elements of the barrier, representing themselves as snakes, turned their attention toward me, but too slowly. I felt the barrier resist, then give way, snakes peeling back and then dropping out of the net. First one small spirit slipped through, then another, and then the dam broke, and the ether rained smoky snakes as the elements of the two former Legions poured out and through.

That barrier had been quite a piece of work, because even broken it remained a formidable force. The individual elements of the barrier remained active. Every little herpetologist's fantasy seemed to be holding me personally responsible for the breach. As the Legions slipped out, I tried to flee beyond and found my way blocked by massing snakes, so I fled inward instead, back into the Whitesnake stronghold.

I left the barrier behind in something of a hurry. I took to shadow, figuring that the snakes might have a tough time tracking me on those Roads. Once I had enough distance that I didn't hear psychic slithering around every corner, I paused to assess my situation.

You've heard the expression "bowels of the earth"? All of a sudden I had an entirely new perspective on the term.

The passageways twisted and turned around me, flowing over and below one another. Circular, about fifteen feet in diameter, they reminded me of intestines, an organic pneumatic tube, or the obvious resemblance to the tunnel of a snake. A very large snake. A fifteen-feet-in-diameter kind of snake. Of the alternatives, I preferred the pneumatic tube analogy. It was the least threatening, not to mention the cleanest.

The air had a warm, damp, fetid touch to it that made me want to take a bath and change clothes—somewhere else. Since the bottom of the tunnel I had fled had been pockmarked by the open mouths of numerous oubliettes (the taking of prisoners was obviously one of the Whitesnakes' favorite pastimes) the tunnel there had much the same smell as the dungeons. Further in toward the center, the air held a dusty, sharp smell that reminded me of nothing so much as a nest of reptiles.

What a surprise.

I took a quick peek at the spiritual neighborhood. Rather than trying to follow my trail, the ghostly snakes had rather quickly begun to sew the barrier back together with their bodies. I had no chance trying to take that barrier solo, even with it weakened. No escape presented itself that way. I saw no sign of my Legion or the escaped Legion of the sorcerer I had killed.

I missed them even then. Not just their capabilities, though I could have had the White Wolf scouting, and would have felt more secure with Blade manning the fortress of my spirit. I missed Blade's steady support, the White Wolf's acerbic give and take, Rose's gentle touch, Bright Angel's voice of reason. I missed their company. I felt nothing but relief that they had escaped, but their absence left a silence in my head like the echoes in an abandoned house.

Bringing myself back to the task at hand, I extended my senses out along the coiling Way of the cave. Whoever had designed this place had possessed a distinct prejudice against straight lines. The shadows were easier to sweep. I saw cultists in robes shaded from black to patterns of lighter colors. I saw more dark than light robes. I remembered the Hooded Man's white robe, considering who he must have been.

I caught urgent movement through the shadows, a dark robe flapping into a room lit by numerous torches. The inconstant shadow there gave me broken images and distorted sounds, but I heard "High Priest" and "escape" in the breathless report to a tall, scaly lad in a robe marked only by light diamonds across the chest.

I resisted the urge to swear. The Hooded Man had been their High Priest. That would stir them up. At the same time, I had to grin. The Whitesnakes weren't having much luck with me. First their Avatar, then their High Priest. You'd think that they'd be smart enough to leave well enough alone, but I knew better than that.

I had never met any cultist who struck me as terribly bright.

I continued searching the shadowy reaches of the Whitesnake stronghold. I found my awareness blocked from the center by the presence of bright light. Few shadows survived in that place, and the impressions I had through them were scant indeed, but I recognized the gleaming scales of ivory and gold that covered every surface. Whitesnake sanctum sanctorum.

I had been in a similar place once before, in the company of a number of Knights of the New Temple, busily engaged in the business of thwarting the Whitesnakes' efforts to incarnate the demon they worshiped and thus vastly increase their cult's power in CrossTown. The NeoTemplars didn't want that any more than I did. I had concentrated on banishing the avatar, while they had concentrated on putting as many Whitesnakes as they could find to the sword.

I had my talents and specialties; the NeoTemplars had theirs.

Remembering that made me hope that at least some of my old Legion had broken through and reached Vayne. An invasion of NeoTemplars would do wonders for my morale, not to mention brighten my future considerably. In the meantime, I didn't plan on displaying any hubris in my expectations. The gods help those who help themselves, and then only when they're in the mood. Considering the current situation, I'd be just as happy if any gods concerned stayed at a safe distance. The gods who showed would most likely not be on my side.

I explored further along the confines of the labyrinth through my strengthening shadow senses, attempting to discover a Way out not enfolded by the wall of serpents. I didn't find one, but I did find an area behind the Whitesnake Holy of Holies that held something interesting. I counted twelve prisoners chained to wheeled tables in a large room lit by smoky torches.

The torches were for atmosphere, evidently, since the cult had florescent lighting elsewhere.

Trying to reason out Whitesnake motivation would be an exercise in futility from a rationalist perspective. The benefit of those torches, though, looked like a happy circumstance for me. Enough shadows danced in that place for me to see into it intermittently. Fortunately, the torches had been set in sconces to burn above eye level, so under each table stood a large pool of shadow—enough to provide easy doorways.

I searched through the surrounding areas of shadow, hoping to acquire some solid idea of the layout as well as discover how seriously the Whitesnakes took their internal security. I found only two doorways leading into the room with the prisoners. The first door (a concealed, ornate affair all done up in snake scales of gold, silver, and mother-of-pearl) opened out into the Whitesnake sanctum. The only other exit led to a short corridor blocked by a warded, heavy door and full of entirely too many lowbrows in dark robes laden with weaponry. I expected that the prisoners there were meant to fuel an upcoming ceremony, but I also expected their schedule to change with the demise of their High Priest.

I considered three things: first, the Whitesnake schedule had to be as thoroughly ruined as only the sudden death of a central participant of a crucial ceremony can ruin a schedule; second, the Whitesnakes seemed to be deliberately isolating the prisoners; and third, I had no intention of leaving any prisoners for the Whitesnakes to butcher for their own amusement. If those people were going to die, they deserved the opportunity to die on their feet, fighting, with the chance to take some of their captors with them.

If I'm for anything, it's the ability of the individual to resist the imposition of a collective will—particularly when that collective will happens to be driven by a bunch of robed, snake-loving, demon-worshipping, human-sacrificing power mongers.

I considered my strategy carefully before making my move. I would have to free the prisoners quickly, organize them, and then we would need to take something valuable enough to the Whitesnakes that they would be forced to deal with us rather than simply overwhelming us. Fortunately, the most likely place to find something like that would be in the sanctum, right next door to the holding room where the prisoners were kept. If we couldn't find something valuable enough to force them to negotiate, we would at least have the satisfaction of taking out whatever top hierarchy remained in the sanctum and defiling their Holy of Holies. It wasn't much of a plan, but it was the best I could come up with at the time. The more time I spent thinking about alternatives, the more initiative I would lose. Moving fast and keeping the enemy off balance seemed the most prudent course. I had better odds betting on audacity rather than analysis.

The largest patches of shadow stretched beneath the tables. I took the time to build a link between the shadow where I stood and the shadow under a table with a good perspective on the guards. I knelt, opened the Way, sank into the pooling shadows of the cave and rose from the shadows pooling under the table.

One of the guards had good eyes. He glanced in my direction, did a double take, and I trapped his gaze in mine. His mouth, opening to yell a warning when I laid my will upon him, closed with a snap. My will driving his actions, he turned and caught his partner around the neck from behind in a stranglehold. His partner kicked and struggled as I crabbed sideways, freed myself from the confines of the table, and rose to my feet.

Unfortunately, I had taken the smaller of the two guards, who looked to be losing his hold on his partner. I stepped around in front of them, caught the second guard's gaze, and dragged him down into a dreamless sleep after a short, sharp struggle. The first guard I had taken followed more quietly. The followers of madmen and their cults, by nature, tend to be malleable. Cult leaders and other madmen, also by nature, tend to be just the opposite. I wasn't entirely sure if the second guard had been higher in the ranks or just a little crazier than his partner. By that time it didn't matter, since he hadn't been quite crazy enough to stop me from mastering him.

I focused my gaze on the prisoners. I met apathetic expressions of pure misery, stretched over beautiful, arrogant features never meant to display such pain. They were all Faerie, of the high Faerie kind called the Sidhe.

I hadn't expected that particular development. I had more than half suspected that the golden hours put up by the Whitesnakes as bounty on my head were ultimately of Faerie origin. If that were so, what were the Whitesnakes doing with Faerie prisoners? This turn of events played hell with my theory.

Each prisoner lay on his or her back, spread-eagled by four chains attached to each table and terminating in manacles clamped over wrists and ankles. Those bindings had the dull color of iron. The flesh of the captives around the manacles had swollen and cracked, until a thick, clear fluid suppurated out to smear the iron bindings and the surface of the tables.

I didn't see that they would be much help, given the effect of the iron on Faerie flesh. That didn't matter, though. I had no intention of leaving them bound.

No longer restricted to glimpses caught through dancing shadow, I saw that the surfaces of the tables were concave and split by deep grooves that radiated out from slightly off center and curved down past the lip of the tables' concavities. Outrage fought with disgust over the efficiency of the Whitesnakes, who had carefully thought to provide channels for the blood of their sacrifices. Without a doubt, each table would have a place already prepared in the sanctum, complete with receptacles to catch the blood as it spilled.

I bent to examine the manacles more closely. If they had been hammered on by a smith, or welded, or locked electronically, or something similarly paranoid, I would have had problems. But I figured otherwise. The Whitesnakes were nothing if not efficient. They would want to easily remove the bodies and clean the tables for reuse on another set of prisoners. The prisoner closest to me seemed to be suffering slightly less than the rest. Perhaps he had been stronger; perhaps he had been bound last; perhaps he had blood tainted by nasty human vermin like myself. At any rate, he'd probably be in better shape to give me a hand should we be surprised by an impatient Whitesnake.

As I hovered over him, he opened lambent eyes and regarded me. "What are you doing here, sorcerer?"

I glanced at his face. He looked familiar. "Trying to release you."

He shuddered against the pain of the iron. He spoke in a whisper. Yet he managed to keep his dignity. "You are no great friend of the Fae."

I shrugged. The irony did not escape me. I still couldn't place him. "I am no great enemy, either. Silverhand and I have had our differences. Titania's errand boy Fetch is out for my head. But I have never had anything bad to say about Lugh, or the Dagda, or any of the rest, really."

I expected locks—I found instead screw clamp quick releases on the back side of the manacles. With a prisoner bound at all four points, the screw clamps would be unreachable. They'd have to use something else if they ever had a prisoner with more than four limbs. I opened the first and moved to his other hand.

As I freed his second hand, he sat up and cradled his raw wrists in his lap. "What's between you and Silverhand?"

I could feel myself flush. "We were drunk. There was a woman. It was all too damned silly, in retrospect."

He chuckled as I freed his feet. "Maeve likes to start trouble. It's her nature. I hadn't heard that Silverhand had chosen to hold a grudge, though."

My head snapped up as I recognized his voice. "Oisin? Damn! You looked more human at Lugh's place."

He grinned ruefully. "I felt more human, too. I'm further along these days. The land has been changing me."

I turned to the next table.

"Wait," Oisin said. He pointed gingerly at a table further down. "Creyn next. He's a healer."

That made sense. I moved to Creyn's table, began working on his bindings. As I did so I saw that several of the nearby Sidhe had opened their eyes to regard me—some with hostility, some with surprise, a few with hope.

Even as I freed Creyn, I watched the wounds on his hands and feet healing, the flesh closing and smoothing. He turned immediately to Oisin. I focused on the nearest table and began working as quickly as I could. The more than mortally beautiful Sidhe woman I freed favored me with a smile of thanks as the last binding fell away. I saw Oisin further down, working at another's bindings, his teeth set in a snarl of pain. I moved to work with him as Creyn bent to healing the woman I had freed.

As we moved to the next, I watched the pain on Oisin's face, though his hands were steady as they came into contact with the iron shackles. He had wrapped his hands in cloth torn from the robe of one of the sleeping Whitesnakes. It didn't seem to help much.

"The change is even further along than I thought."

"The price I pay," he said between clenched teeth. "If I hadn't let the land of the Fae recognize me and enter me, I would have been dust by now. Before, it sustained me only as long as I stayed in the confines of Faerie."

"How did you come to be here, Oisin?"

He took a moment to reply. "I was taken. So were the others."

I frowned, helped the Sidhe on the table to sit up. We had freed close to half of them by that time, and Creyn moved behind us tirelessly, the skin of his face stretched tight across the bone as he expended his meager strength on healing the captives as we released them. "Were you traveling?"

"We were taken in Faerie. It was a raid, pure and simple."

"I didn't think the Whitesnakes had that much chutzpah."

He shook his head angrily. "They didn't wear Whitesnake colors. They wore the old colors of the Red Branch. Someone had to have given them passage. We were deep in Faerie. Without help, no human band could have penetrated so far."

"You were on Lugh's land?"

"I was visiting Nuada."

My eyes widened. "Silverhand? Do you think . . ."

"No!" A tall Sidhe newly healed by Creyn caught my arm and spun me around. "Someone is working to rouse the ire of the Faerie. But they made a foolish mistake. Nuada Silverhand would not take his own son, even to incite the Lords of the Sidhe against the humans."

I saw his father's angry eyes in his face. I frowned as I thought about what he'd said. "You're right."

He nodded, released my arm. "Of course I am."

"As you say, whoever is behind this raid meant to stir things up between mankind and Faerie," I mused.

Oisin raised his head. "Why? And who?"

I turned back to the nearest prisoner, thinking furiously. I had a suspect. But what would Titania gain by rousing Faerie against the humans? Particularly when relations had been so good of late? She would have had the tools, but how far did her quarrel go? Or did she fear the return of the Nephilim enough to push the Faerie to a war footing?

I remembered what Chimereon had said about Titania's distaste for humanity. What had Corvinus set in motion by catching her attention? She must have feared the Nephilim like nothing else in all the worlds. No wonder she hated humanity. Was she looking for a war, or was she hoping the borders to Faerie would be closed? Perhaps either would suit her.

I raised my eyes to Oisin's, my hands still working to free one of the last captives. "The raid was focused on you as a member of Lugh's Court, and on Silverhand. She doesn't want Faerie to go to war with the humans. She wants the borders closed to human traffic."

Oisin cocked his head. "She? She who? And why?"

I helped the captive to sit straight as Creyn shuffled our way. The strain wore on him visibly: he looked as if he had aged enough to be mortal.

I looked back at Oisin. "I suspect who, though I can't be sure. As for why . . . if I'm right about the person behind this,

I believe that she's afraid war will soon come again. War of a kind that has not been seen for eons. She's trying to take steps to prevent the Fae from being caught in it. She's afraid I'll find what I'm looking for."

Oisin blinked. "What are you looking for?"

"The key to my master's death."

That's about the time a junior priest decided to check on the captives.

CHAPTER XXV

A S WE were talking, a plump little guy in a gold and white checkered robe poked his head through the door to the sanctum. His eyes widened, he managed a little bleat of surprise, and then a dozen hungry hands closed on him and jerked him into the room. As many angry Sidhe as could reach him closed him off from view. Chunks of flesh and strips of robe started raining down through the room.

Silverhand's son stooped, rifled through the silent guards I had bound earlier and retrieved a dart pistol. Oisin shook his head. "I've dealt with them before. Whitesnakes are immune to nearly all poisons. It's why they use the poison dart guns."

Silverhand's son tossed the pistol away contemptuously.

"Damn!" Oisin turned as I cursed. I had forgotten the Whitesnake immunity to poison. I thought I had killed my interrogator. That sadistic swine of a high priest had faked me out completely. I still had a score to settle.

We finished releasing the last prisoner to the sounds of savage violence behind us. It helped to remember that despite appearances, Fae were not human. Creyn looked ready to collapse as he bent to heal the last of the wounded.

The Sidhe moved back from a huddled shapeless mass. They were collectively shivering with rage. Entirely berserk with nothing significant remaining of the hapless priest to vent their rage on, the group lunged for the door to the sanctum. Oisin and I followed in a more leisurely fashion. The last of his brethren healed, Creyn tottered after the rush, looking like an elvish Methuselah.

I followed the crowd out onto the dais where the priests had gathered. Light poured through the room, gleaming from every rich, polished surface. The Whitesnakes had spared no expense on their sanctum. Around the dais, priests stood before stone slabs shaped to take the tables upon which the Sidhe had been chained. Stone mouths opened at regular intervals around the altars. The Whitesnakes obviously had refined the process of human sacrifice to assembly line efficiency, complete with wheeled gurneys built to support removable tables that could be set in place on the altars, where the blood from the sacrifice could be neatly channeled into the stone declivities waiting to receive it.

I had encountered mass production insanity before, but it never failed to give me the shivers. Scale and efficiency made any evil so much more dangerous, I had to wonder if the advantages were worth the potential price. In this doubt lay my ambivalence toward TechTown.

The mass of the Sidhe charged what looked like the full congregation. Every available cultist had apparently managed to make an appearance. They rose from their seats, hissing. Howling, blood-mad Sidhe swarmed over the priests standing at the front of the platform.

It was a sight to warm the cockles of my heart.

Serpentine sorceries flickered at the edge of my awareness. Sidhe sorcery rose to contend with the power of the priests. I coolly stood back by the door and struck the Whitesnake sorcerers down while the Sidhe had their attention. None of them would awaken from the sleep to which I sent them. Like any other total conflict, mercy and fairness had no place in that battle. I had less regard for the Whitesnakes than many of the creatures of NightTown, for each cultist had chosen to follow Whitesnake doctrine, whereas many creatures of the night merely followed the instincts nature had given them.

Screaming, cursing madness filled the Whitesnake Holy of Holies. Bright light lit the chaos as dark blood spattered the silver and gold of the furnishings. The congregation began swarming up the side of the platform. The son of Silverhand led a counter-attack. Priests, whole and in pieces, rained down on the heads of their followers.

I had to admit that the Sidhe were not to be screwed with when their blood was running hot.

As the last of the Whitesnake sorcerers went down and the Sidhe turned their attention to the mass of cultists, a stench of power fouled my mouth and nose. I walked along the edge of the conflict, searching, and spotted a familiar white robe straightening from where he had knelt in a tiny, curtained alcove in the back and center of the platform. A knife and a cup lay on the small table at which he had knelt. Both were covered with dark stains, as was his mouth. The body of a lesser priest lay unmoving at his feet.

His eyes glowed white. He smiled when he saw me. "The blood is good. The god approves."

I could see the power of his god coiling inside him. A snarl twisted my mouth. I had banished the bastard once. I could do it again. The battle raging at my back, I met his eyes as he threw his arms wide and prepared to pour his power into his followers.

The demon incarnated in the flesh of the high priest may not have been a god in truth, but it had unholy strength. I didn't have my Legion to lean upon, to distract it. At the same time, I did not have the distraction of managing my Legion.

I met its strength, holding it in place as the Sidhe slaughtered the Whitesnakes. Losing their sorcerers early in the battle had put the cultists in a bad position. The Sidhe had no intention of easing the pressure on them. The glow in the priest's eyes brightened until he could have found work as a desk lamp. He stood unmoving as the demon infesting him focused more and more of its power on me.

The power of the Whitesnake god wrapped around me with a cold, strangling strength. I stepped forward slowly, as if bearing great weight, fighting as it tightened its hold on me. Each step came slower and slower, each breath came further and further apart, until my heart labored in my chest.

I stepped into arm's reach and struck the high priest as hard as I could in his exposed throat with my right fist. The pressure eased on me immediately as pain splintered his concentration. Then the demon swept him aside and the possession became complete. The glow in the priest's eyes took on a reddish hue.

I used the brief respite to lunge around him and lay my hands on the knife. I appreciated the irony of using the high priest's own sacrificial knife on him even as my fingers closed over the cold hilt. I turned to see the possessed high priest spread his arms and rise skyward. I stabbed him in the small of the back, which was as high as I could reach with him floating toward the ceiling.

He whirled in midair. I hung onto the knife, which ripped free. He screamed like a damned soul. I stabbed him again, this time in the lower belly. I felt a surge of force lashing toward me and turned it aside with the edge of my will. The table behind me exploded, showering me with splinters. I stabbed him again, stepping close to his body, grinning when I realized that his shadow had fallen over me.

I reached up through the shadow to the thing inside and haled it forth. The body dropped like a marionette with cut strings. The demon I held in my will lashed and snarled and raged like a parasite torn from its host. It turned on me, trying to take me, but I felt other wills adding to mine. Caught in forces beyond its strength, torn from the host whose life had supported its presence, and unable to retreat back to the safety of its own plane, the demon died. The Sidhe who lent me their strength smiled with me as we crushed it under the heel of our collective spiritual boot.

I took the moment to draw a breath. Silence fell down around me. I could feel the larger barrier unraveling and fading to foul, ethereal smoke. The wrath of the Sidhe had shattered the Whitesnake sorcerers who had maintained the barrier. Their work followed them into the final darkness.

Creyn limped forth to do what he could for the Sidhe who were wounded. Silverhand's son buoyed Creyn up, nodding to me gravely even as he fed the healer his strength which was used to succor the wounded Sidhe. Watching them, I remembered all the things I admired in the Sidhe—their strength, their joy, their bright and shining power, and their love. They loved as fiercely as they did everything else.

I caught Oisin at the edge of the Sidhe. "Be careful when you return."

"I understand. The Whitesnakes are broken. The other remains."

I nodded.

He cocked his head. "Will you tell me who you suspect?"

I thought about it. I owed him that much, though I doubted the news would be welcome. Had it not been for the Sidhe, the Whitesnake High Priest would have already been examining my entrails for defects. "I believe Titania is behind it. She has the most cause."

Several heads snapped around at that, though I had spoken quietly. Oisin's face hardened. "Do you have proof?"

I shook my head. "That's why I have been reluctant to speak. But she involved herself. She set Fetch on my trail. Who else would it have been?"

"That's a serious charge," Oisin said.

"One I will make when I have the proof I need," I answered. "Once I have dug into this thing as far as necessary, I'll have evidence. Until that time, I make no formal accusations."

"That would be best." Oisin said. "And we will be careful. You be careful as well. If what you say is true, we will be safe once we have reached Nuada's lands. If she fails to prevent us from arriving, killing us there would serve her little purpose. Nuada would be on guard against it. But you have no such refuge."

"I know." I sighed. "She's forcing me to the course she fears the most." I clasped hands with each of them, then I stood with them as they gave respect to those they had lost. Five of the Sidhe had died in the battle with the Whitesnakes, though the cultists had lost far more than that. Any surviving Whitesnakes had departed, leaving their dead to lie as they had fallen. Still, the price seemed high. The Sidhe are not a fecund race.

I watched as they lifted their dead to their shoulders and set their feet on the Way home. I worked myself out through the winding passages, and then found my own Way. First, I thought I'd see if the Wraith had turned up any evidence of the origin of the Whitesnake funds. After that, I intended to retrace my steps a bit, then seek my answers at the root of the conflict.

CHAPTER XXVI

I PASSED swiftly from cave to cave, leaving behind the Whitesnake catacombs for the friendlier environs of Deep-Town. I skirted the populated areas. Though the Whitesnake bounty had lost all meaning, the news would take time to run the rumor circuit. Within a few days the word would hit the streets of CrossTown and I would again be able to travel without fear of anyone but Fetch.

I shivered at the thought of meeting Fetch again. That possibility was bad enough. I'd been lucky last time and he'd underestimated me. I didn't believe that either of those things would happen the next time we met.

I couldn't really believe that he hadn't survived. Fetch wasn't a person. He was a force of nature.

When I saw the archway of MacWraith's abode, the lurking fear in me crystallized into a cold lump of terrible certainty. No barrier danced there to protect the Wraith's privacy. As long as I had known him, I had never seen the barrier inactive.

I stepped through the arch cautiously, my ears tuned for the sounds of a footfall. Only an intruder would betray signs of a solid physical presence. I heard nothing except for a distant buzzing that danced at the edge of perception. I eased through the antechamber, noting the presence of an archway that I had never seen before, opening to my left. Evidently, the Wraith had kept things to himself.

Surprise, surprise.

A small bug like a gnat bumbled by my cheek. I swatted absently at it before the thought of what it might mean blossomed in my mind. Stiff legged, my hands at my sides, I stepped slowly to the main archway and looked into a wild cloud of swirling vapor. The buzzing grew louder. I understood then that what had seemed like vapor at first glance was actually a loose swarm of the same tiny animals that had once composed the Wraith's body.

The Wraith had been disincorporated. The Wraith no longer existed as an individual. Instead, he had been reduced by some terrible blow to his constituent elements: a swarm of tiny flying creatures hovering like a physical ghost over the site of the death of his psyche.

I paused there. How much of him remained? How much could be recovered? If the pieces of the Wraith were pulled back to his original form, would any of his memories survive? Would the single personality I thought of as Alistair MacWraith be resurrected? I didn't know, but CrossTown held an expert on everything.

I paused to pick up the tiny corpse of the piece of the Wraith I had swatted. I drew existing shadow over the opening of the archway like a curtain, then wove a more tangible barrier from the darkness. I didn't want any more of the swarm escaping from that place before I found out whether or not the Wraith could be helped.

At the same time, I searched my memories for someone who might know what I needed to help the Wraith. The only name I knew who might possess that kind of specialized knowledge would not have ordinarily been my first choice. I had a limited amount of currency with the demon scholar Ba'al Sid. I wouldn't use that trivially. In this instance, I didn't see any easy alternative. The request would be anything but trivial.

So I set my feet on the path to NightTown once again, finding my way swiftly into a quiet little suburb on the edge of twilight. Walking the Ways into darkness had become much easier for me, I noticed. I swallowed against growing hunger. Despite the use they had been, I did not feel entirely comfortable with the shadow abilities I had ripped from my hunter. The hunger I had inherited kept gaining in strength.

I had the uneasy feeling that I knew what I would need to satisfy that hunger. I didn't want to become the face of an appetite, driven and corrupted into something I would no longer recognize.

I paused before gates of twisted black iron. They opened onto a long walkway that in turn led to a huge manor framed by squat towers and dark windows. A sense of relief blunted the edge of worry I'd felt since I'd seen the Wraith. The open gates told me that the one I sought would be home and ready to deal.

Long rods with ruby tips bathed the black marble of the walkway in bloody light. Pale grass stretched around the curve of the walkway like a thick carpet. I took the front steps two at a time. The flat cracks of my booted feet slapping jet-black onyx echoed against the granite wall encircling the grounds of the manor. No light penetrated the darkness of the windows, but I knew those windows. The obsidian surface would be perfectly transparent from the inside.

The door opened as I reached for the handle. Bloody light spilled out around the entryway. I looked up, my eyes climbing the nine feet of white muscle and red veins a familiar, fanged grin.

I smiled. "I feel complimented. You answered the door personally."

Flames filled the eyes of the massive head, shaped like nothing so much as the head of a flayed bear. "I always take pains for close friends and the holders of my debts." When he spoke, a writhing mass of movement filled his mouth, like a hyperactive ball of worms.

I raised an eyebrow. "And how many of either do you have?"

"Not many." His voice was the grinding discontent of a glacier, the protest of clashing boulders.

"Somehow I'm not shocked by that."

He turned without answering. I followed him into the depths of the manor.

He led me into a sitting room that could have come straight from Victorian England, complete with leather bound volumes lining the walls, three low stone tables, two divans, and a settee, all covered in the pale hide of some creature. Rugs lay across the floor, thick with dark fur. Animal heads glared down from the wall through thickets of fangs and scales and twisted horns: animals such as those had never been seen in any Victorian England I knew. Stones set in the walls washed the room and everything in it in a surly red glow.

What Ba'al Sid called "home" and "comfortable" gave some indication as to his nature and place of origin. I hadn't ever seen any place in my travels that came close in feel. I didn't really have a strong desire to change that. On the Ways, a traveler can find just about anything. Some things it's not a good idea to find.

Ba'al Sid sprawled on the largest divan, which took his considerable weight grudgingly. "You have a request for me?"

Having long suspected that the hide covering his chairs came originally from an animal that walked on two legs, I chose to stand. I pulled the tiny corpse of the Wraith's wild constituent out of the pocket of my great coat and held it out to the demon sage.

He leaned forward, the long claws of one forelimb closing over it delicately. He held it up before his eyes, opened his mouth slightly, and long whiplashing filaments like multiple serpent tongues churned the air around his claw. Then the filaments withdrew, and his gaze touched mine. "Helbron swarm particle. I'm impressed. They're rare. But you already know that. Take one too far from the host swarm and it ceases to be a component of the greater whole. This one wouldn't have been alone."

"It wasn't," I said. "But the greater whole no longer exists as such. If a swarm's cohesion is broken, can it be put back together? If so, how? And how much of the original personality remains?"

He tilted his massive head. "Is the swarm enclosed? Or are the constituent elements free to roam?"

I shrugged. "Semi-enclosed. In large rooms."

The burning eyes narrowed. "The swarm must be brought close enough together to attain critical mass. I can help you do that. As far as the integrity of the memories and personality of the original composite being, there will be damage. How extensive the damage is depends on the strength of the original personality. It's possible, depending on the extent of the damage, for the swarm to spontaneously generate an entirely new entity, once critical mass is attained. There's no way to know without forcing the cohesion to occur. Do you want what it takes?"

I nodded.

He reached into the air in front of him. A ripple danced through the air and surrounded his claws. I felt a sensation like Ways folding and possibility molding itself to his will. His claws and eight inches of limb blurred into the haze that still expanded in front of him. When he drew his claws back, he held a great sticky mass like a dark ball of honey, swimming behind a thick, translucent membrane. He set it carefully on a nearby table. The membrane deformed slightly.

Ba'al Sid stood. "Fruit of the Helbron Cereb bush. Take the fruit to the center of the current mass. Slice the membrane. Drain the core into a large bowl. The swarm will descend to feed. If enough particles are present, they will attain critical mass. The process takes care of itself after that."

I walked over to the fruit and touched it. The smooth surface of the membrane felt warm and slick under my hand. I picked it up. The fruit must have weighed close to fifty pounds, and it wanted to ooze out of my grip. Carrying it wouldn't be fun. I put it back on the table, and nodded to Ba'al Sid. "Thanks."

He held up one claw. "Answer me this. Is it the Wraith?"

I hesitated, searching my memory for enmities between the Wraith and Ba'al Sid. I could remember none. I nodded.

He studied me for a long moment. "I will send the package to his entryway. Are we square after this?"

I met his gaze steadily. "It's your debt. You tell me. How much do you value your existence in this place? And how much do you fear the Knights? That should put a value on the information I gave you."

The fire in his eyes dimmed. "Not yet. Closer now, I think."

"Much closer. Thank you."

He looked up at me from under his brows. "What happened to the Legion?"

I stiffened. "What?"

"You walk alone now." He cocked his head. "Dangerous given the bounty on your head. But then you've changed, haven't you? Do they even know what they hunt?"

"The bounty is worthless now. The Whitesnakes are gone."

"Mmm," he rumbled thoughtfully. "So. You've acted quickly. Now you take the time to aid the Wraith, though Fetch and his mistress still dog your trail." He held up one massive paw as I started. "Knowledge is my business. You know that. You're changing, Zethus. Be careful on this road you walk. Don't follow too closely in your master's footsteps."

"Why not?" I had meant the question sarcastically, but it didn't come out that way.

"If the toll of the passage means losing yourself, the price is too high. Be careful what you pay, and who you owe."

"What do you know?" I asked sharply. "Can you tell me anything about Corvinus and Titania?"

He didn't respond. He turned his attention to the Cereb fruit, ignoring me. I had little leverage left and I had no desire to be indebted to him. I owed too many debts as it was. When I navigated the Ways to the Wraith's place, I found the fruit and a large, shallow bowl made of beaten copper waiting for me in the silent entryway. It pleased me to see that Ba'al Sid had remembered to include a bowl.

I put the fruit in the bowl, picked the bowl up, dispelled my shadow barrier, and stepped into the Wraith's rooms. The pieces of his swarm flew around me in a fog of wild motion. Holding my breath, I carried my burden through to the heart of the Wraith's workshop, into the clear space in the center of the three perfect spheres, and set the bowl down.

The swarm dwelt most heavily there. I held my hand over my nose and mouth to keep from inhaling hundreds of the tiny animals with every breath. I sliced the membrane with a shaped fragment of darkness, grasped the edge with my free hand, and pulled it around and off. A powerful, spicy, sweet smell rose as the membrane peeled away. The mass of the fruit had the consistency of nearly frozen molasses. It slumped slowly, gravity shaping it to the confines of the bowl.

The swarm began settling down over the fruit. As I watched, the swarm flowed in and down to the bowl like a time-lapse reel of smoke flowing backwards into a chimney. I stepped back as the cloud thickened and settled ever inward. In a surprisingly short time, the air around the bowl for three feet in any direction had become opaque with minuscule flyers. Outside that radius, the air had become virtually clear of any members of the swarm. The swarm fell slowly in on itself. When the critical mass came, it came with the suddenness of a lightning strike. I felt it before I saw any difference. When the rippling darkness of the swarm rose enough to shape the wavering outline of a humanoid head and nearly featureless face, I knew that some memories were intact, and some essence of the Wraith remained.

He spoke in a buzzing whisper. "How long?"

"A few hours at most. Maybe less."

His features blurred, reformed, blurred again. Each time they reformed the elements shifted slightly. Each time this happened the shape resembled more closely my memory of the face of the old Wraith. "I know you but I don't. You brought me back?"

"Yes." He seemed to be verbalizing. The body had not yet followed the head into being. I wasn't sure how well he would do with body language, so I didn't simply nod.

"You asked me for something." His voice became louder.

"Yes. Do you remember what I asked you to discover?"

The face trembled, lost cohesion. "No I . . . I remember . . ."

I saw the face slumping back toward formlessness. "You remember what?"

The head took on a new form, elongating and darkening in color. I took a step back as a ripple passed across the head and the face of Fetch looked up at me before being consumed back into chaos. "I remember pale smoke. I remember white fire."

The head slumped into the body of the swarm, which had restlessly bulged outward, before settling back down over the bowl. The head began reforming. I watched it narrowly, breathing a sigh of relief as the Wraith's features became visible. "I remember pain."

The cloud slowly began to boil inward again, increasing the local density of particles. "I could not find the source of the Whitesnake gold," the Wraith whispered. "I found only rumors. Blood money. Favors given and taken."

I swallowed heavily as I thought of the Faerie captives in the Whitesnake sanctuary. How far would Titania go, if she had sold out her own people? Had she actually supplied the Whitesnakes the money for the bounty on my head, or simply traded some of her own to the Whitesnakes in return for their assistance in hunting me down? In any event, she had miscalculated, or the hunt had gone on too long, for the Whitesnakes had eventually learned enough of the nature of the heart of stone to want it for themselves. There they had parted ways from Titania. Her fear of the return of the Nephilim must have run through her core. I turned my attention back to the Wraith. "I need to let you heal," I said. "I have enough of the information I asked you to find." I turned and began walking toward the door.

"The attack does confirm the involvement of the Fae." The voice was cool and familiar. Not the voice of the Wraith. "Be careful in your assumptions. More have joined the game than you believe, and the players in it can be subtle."

I froze in my tracks. I turned back slowly. A familiar face stared back at me from the moving swarm of the Wraith. The details had been perfectly executed. The black hair, winged with silver, framed a face only lightly touched by the passage of centuries. He smiled sardonically, his eyes glinting with mischief. He winked before fading back into the swarm.

My mouth had become as dry as a bed of desert sand. I had recognized that face, of course. I had spent long years in service to him before I gained enough understanding of the Ways to seek my own path. I had considered that Corvinus might have survived, at least in spirit. Had Corvinus possessed his old friend long enough to contact me?

I scanned for his spiritual presence, but found nothing.

The Wraith had known Corvinus far longer than I had. Were his memories powerful enough to invoke such a sending? The appearance of Fetch had apparently been invoked by memory. Could Corvinus's appearance have been nothing more than the sympathetic reflection of a triggered memory? I didn't know enough to be sure of anything. I had never seen the Wraith as anything but the Wraith. I had no idea what a Helbron swarm could do, or how the collective mind worked. In spite of that, the incident worried me. The Raven was perfectly capable of playing his own game. That game could easily regard me as a piece to be moved, even sacrificed. The thought that Corvinus had managed to survive didn't necessarily reassure me. My primary motivation of late had centered on survival, not scoring points for anyone. Not even my old master.

Vengeance was another thing entirely, of course.

Though if he had survived, I intended to have words with the old bastard.

In any event, I could not allow the possibility to blur my focus. I could not afford the distraction. The next step yawned before me. To navigate that abyss I would need all my strength and all my confidence. I didn't see any alternative now to following the heart of stone back to the beginning of everything. To bring this thing to an end, I would have to seek out the Nephilim.

CHAPTER XXVII

I CAME again to stand on the banks of that dark and winding river, under the shadow of the mourning trees. Once again I waited for the Shepherd of the Trees. I listened to the rustling murmurs and whispers of the shepherd's charges. For the first time in all the occasions I had stood in that place, I felt nothing of the threat in them. I felt a curious peace at having set my course so clearly. For years I had worked through the mysteries of the myriad Ways. I had worked to extend my life but not as an end in itself.

I had always wanted more—more to see, more to feel, more to experience. I wanted to live, not just exist, and I wanted to grow in the living. Those last few days of furious running, working on the mystery of my attackers and Corvinus's death, I had been trying to survive. My life had not been my own. Now my fate had once again come into my own hands, and the object of my reach, exceed my grasp as it might, had again become more than simple survival—it had become a mystery worth the risk of reaching. I would follow the heart and use it to unlock the secret of the Nephilim. Perhaps I would die in the attempt. Perhaps I would survive. If I did survive, I would not be unchanged.

Then again, I was no stranger to change. Not anymore. I no longer was what I had been for so long. I no longer knew what I was becoming.

The shepherd came to me as he always did: all swift movement and fluid grace. He held out one long hand. He gave me the survival suit and the heart of stone. I tucked the survival suit into my belt. I could feel his alien gaze on my back as I turned from that place and laid my will on the heart.

At first I found nothing but stone. Nothing lay beneath the surface of the stone but the cold indifference of the inanimate. Then I looked beyond it, and for an instant I caught a glimpse of a burning line of possibility traced like a thread of crimson through all of the warp and woof of probability that composed the Way.

With that, I understood what I needed to do. I found myself whistling tunelessly through my teeth as I read the Way through the lens of the heart of stone. The crimson thread led me swiftly past lands filled with growing things and into empty places of dry winds and sheer rock faces flecked with brilliant specks of glittering crystal. The chill air there tasted of ice and stone. I did not tarry. The flash of crystal gave way before the paint splashes of mineral rainbows of color, red and umber and yellow and green all running together like leftover daubs from God's own palette. Then the hills and the colors gave way before a long plain of low marshes and tall grasses, where not even a bird or a cloud broke the azure perfection of the empty sky and the sluggish breezes were heavy with salt and rot. I increased my pace, passing through empty realm after empty realm with all the speed I could manage. Some lands flashed by like the strobe of chance reflection, while I traveled for long hours through others on the backs of Ways more stubborn and unbending.

I took one break, stopping at a little charitable place I knew that fed travelers for a small donation. I made sure the detour led me through a land emptied by plague and war in the distant past. That realm lay not far off the empty routes marked by the crimson thread of the heart of stone. The rutted dirt road wound around a gnarled tree. The bare branches of the tree stretched out like a skeletal hand over a buried sack fat with gold coins. I dug in the soft earth for a brief time, thrust my fingers through the rotten cloth of the sack and drew out three coins. I covered over the bulging sack, and pushed on. A pity that it had never been so easy to dig up revenue in CrossTown, but CrossTown rested securely on the foundation of a true service economy, jealously guarded by the Bank of Hours.

The thick adobe walls surrounding the little church guarded a courtyard nearly empty of guests. A homey smell of dust and turned earth and cooking filled the sanctuary. I took thick slabs of hot bread and a healthy stew from a plump little priest in clean brown robes. The bread had the heavy consistency of multiple grains and the stew dripped with fat. As I left, I gave the priest my donation. His eyes bulged in comical disbelief when I dropped two of the gold coins into his hand. I smiled and tipped my hat.

On the Road again, I fought unease. The meal had sated my physical hunger, but sharpened the shadow hunger, honing it to a fine edge. That hunger gnawing at the back of my mind, I took up the crimson thread and pushed deeper into the wastelands.

The air thinned and I decided that the time had come to don the environment suit. I had used nanotech environment suits before. The nanofabric was advanced enough to wear over my clothes. I removed the brick, placed it on my chest and held it there with one hand while I pulled the tab with the other. The brick grew soft and smaller, warming up and dripping through my fingers. I let it go. It slid away from my hand. Where it touched my chest, a layer of gray crawled out over my clothes, down past my belly, and up around my throat. I closed my eyes and held my breath though I'd been through the process before. The nanites felt like a thin spread of oil where they crawled over bare skin, like the lightest touch of plastic stiffening my clothes, but I forced myself to think of open fields and clean fresh air to take my mind off that crawling layer of protective, living slime.

My revulsion toward the suit was reflex and a bit unfair, really. The nanites were smart enough to cover my body completely and at the same time stay out of unwelcome places, flexible enough not to impede my movement and tough enough to protect me from all but the most extreme ranges of temperature and radiation. The suit would feed me air when there was only hard vacuum to breathe and filter poisons out of atmospheres inimical to my physiology. The suit couldn't keep me alive indefinitely, but it could keep me going for days in places where I wouldn't last minutes without it. I opened my eyes. Only ghostly reflections of the rock walls stretching up around me betrayed the transparent layer of nanites masking my face.

I might not be in love with the culture of TechTown, but I have great respect for its products.

Shortly after I donned the suit I passed through a vast, open plain colored white and pale blue, the surface undulating in long swells like a frozen sea. Stars shone down over a scene unfiltered by atmosphere, their light as sharp and steady and impersonal as fate. I kept on through dancing bands of darkness, wandering among shattered ivory towers that gleamed like the broken bones of vast, ancient gods, the hand of gravity pressing down on my shoulders, slowing my step as if with the weight of enforced grief. I bowed my back under the pressure and walked on. Later, from dark to light, the Way led me along the edge of a scarlet cliff so high that only distant, yellow mists could be seen curling out around the base. Rainbow bands of color swallowed me, flashing like a Van Gogh aurora borealis. After I broke out of the bright riot of color, I made my way down a crooked stair that gleamed like diamond in the light of a white sun, the steps of the stair shallower than steps built for a human stride.

I paused at a turning of the stair, watching my reflection shatter in the facets of the cliff wall behind the stairway. I couldn't remember ever having felt the loneliness others spoke of when walking the Ways. These dead realms kindled an ache of loneliness in me, but I knew that I had been feeling it for some time—since the Legion had left.

My own face, slightly distorted by the mask of the environment suit, stared back at me from a thousand broken reflections. I thought of the Legion, and fought a sense of cold solitude. Looking back on my time in CrossTown, I could name many acquaintances, one master, and a few who owed me. My master was dead. I knew no one else closely. I had never felt an absence of companions until I came to lose the Legion. I wondered about them in that moment, hoping they had found the freedom I had denied them for so long.

What did it say about me that I had let no one close except my slaves?

Turning away from that line of thought, I descended at last to a long, narrow causeway. Bleached white like dry bone, the causeway stretched endlessly over a glassy, obsidian plain like the back of the Worm Ouroboros. Points of light burned deep in the rock like captive suns. Still I followed the crimson thread further, deeper than I had ever traveled on barren Roads of forgotten possibility. I passed a chain of worlds burned to their root, hanging in the sky like a vast necklace of sallow harvest moons, the sickly glow of multispectrum radiation providing the only light in the dark waste that stretched around me into an infinite distance, the only sound in my ears the harsh rhythm of my own breath, cycled and recycled through the nanoprocessors in the suit. And still the heart of stone led me further into old places, dead places, until I found myself climbing a long, twisting stair of dark stone that twined around a tall column of basalt like a single strand of clinging ivy.

I crested the column. Harsh, actinic light flared around me. I looked down from the top of the column into a valley lit by the blazing head of a vast comet. It hung tail down over the valley like the gods' own sword of Damocles. No sun burned in the vault of the heavens. The stars could but peek shyly through the azure light of the comet.

The crimson thread of the Way faded into the darkness of the valley. I released the crimson thread and descended the stair of the tower to the valley floor. The survival suit flaked away from my body and swirled down to the hard stone of the valley floor in a light rain of ashes. I shook my head and dusted my clothes with my hat, remnants of the suit coming off me in small puffs of ash.

The Road I had walked had evidently taxed the suit beyond its capabilities, the molecular machines that composed it unable to recover from whatever technological plagues I had passed through. Corvinus had not meant for me to return the same way I had arrived. Why had he not come himself? Perhaps he hadn't wanted to risk his own destruction when he had a perfectly gullible apprentice to talk into making the journey for him. Though admittedly, the journey to that point had been long, but not particularly hazardous.

I could feel no trace of movement in the air. The taste of the air in that place was perfectly clean, perfectly sterile, and perfectly empty. It tasted as if it had not passed through the lungs of a living being for millennia.

As I set my foot on the floor of the valley, I felt the heart of stone throb within my grip. I glanced down, startled, pausing to examine the stone in the light of the great comet. Cracks fissured its surface, like jagged tracks of countless, tiny lightning strikes. Drops of fluid, black in the light of the comet, beaded at those cracks and ran slowly down the surface of the stone.

The heart throbbed again, pulsing in my hand, and more fluid pushed its way up through the fissures. I stepped deeper into the valley, watching the shadows, studying the layout of the valley. Perhaps I would find an entrance to the place where the Nephilim had been brought into being from the frailty of human flesh.

I watched everything as I moved. Chimereon had spoken of security. The Way here had been difficult, but not so difficult that I believed the worst had passed.

The heart throbbed again. I took another step. Points of icy heat touched my hand where I held the heart. Furious, empty hunger tore at the prison I had built for it out of the strength of my will. The stolen hunger of the Shadow Hound strained at the bonds I had placed upon it as scalding, dark blood from the heart of stone ran over my clenched fingers.

The walls surrounding the narrow valley shifted within the shadows that held them. Curious formations of rock, almost like sculptures of the human form, appeared out of the landscape before me in the same way a motionless animal is slowly etched into existence out of concealing brush before the hunter's watchful eye.

I took another step, in time with the next throb of the heart. The icy heat drew itself in lines down my hand toward my wrist. The ache of the sensation went straight to the bone, but faded quickly to numbness. The black hunger within continued to grow.

I looked at my hand—the dark fluid seeping from the heart had covered it over and begun to work its way down my wrist. My fingers were coated, and a network of black traceries wrapped my hand to the wrist and below. None of the fluid dripped down to the ground. Instead, it clung to my flesh.

I didn't like that one bit.

The heart throbbed. I took another step deeper into the valley and the shadow. For the first time, I heard something other than the sounds that I made myself. A deep tone blurred and danced on the edge of perception, a subsonic grumble welling up around me.

Shadow surrounding me, I drew upon my power over the darkness and looked deeper into it, studying the sculptures in the rock. The nearest took the form of a man, his handsome features contorted by great pain, his mouth open in a scream. His legs twined together, joining seamlessly with rock foaming up hungrily from the floor of the valley. In the shadow I could make out the finest detail, and what I saw left me shaken. Everything on the man had been formed in perfection, down to the individual hairs of his curling beard. No mortal artisan could craft so well. No mortal hand or eye had framed that fearful symmetry.

The heart throbbed again. I took another step. I could and yet could not feel the heart as it moved in my relentless grip. I could not open my fingers to release it. The fire and ice of the blood of the heart of stone reached my elbow. My lower arm, from the halfway point of the forearm to the tips of my fingers, was lost to the power of the heart's blood.

I pulled my gaze away from the first statue to look up the considerable dark length of the valley, and felt despair. Hundreds of statues, each as perfect as the first I had studied, each completely different in terms of dress and appearance, stood in ranks along the walls of the valley. All of them appeared to have been carved from stalagmites. The stone of the valley floor reached up around the bodies before they lifted to the clean definition of perfect detail. On some figures the rough stone stopped at the ankles. Others looked as if they had been carved only from the waist up, everything below that point blending into natural, untouched stone. I looked back at the entrance to the valley, and in what I had taken to be a pillar as I had passed, I could now see a face. The length of the stone appeared to have been subtly shaped to form a shroud around a tall, slender figure. Toward the top of the pillar the shroud of stone dropped away from a woman's face of incredible beauty, most remarkable for its peace in the midst of that sea of frozen agony. Her eyes were shut and her mouth was open, as if she were singing.

The heart pulsed again, ice and fire working its way up my arm as if through the bone. The heart's blood crawled past the midpoint of my upper arm.

I did not believe that the lifelike craftsmanship of those statues derived from mere coincidence. I had tried to release the heart of stone. I had failed. I tried to pry open my fingers with my free hand, but my fingers were as cold and hard and unyielding as granite where they locked around the heart. I attempted to turn, to flee that place. The act of shifting my feet to turn my body felt as if I were fighting a mighty rushing torrent of pure force. At the same time, tendrils of pain and cold and heat increased the speed of their relentless advance, spreading to enclose my shoulder in fingers of molten ice.

The heart beat again. I fought and held myself to a standstill. Bloody lines of cold fire touched my chest. The sound at the edge of my hearing grew louder, taking on a deep tone of primal discontent, well past the fuzzy limits of perception.

I tried to reach for a Way, but a roaring, white static filled those senses. I understood then that I had no such option. I could not escape this place so easily. I could not flee the way I had come. I had discovered the nature of the ancient security measures too late. My only course lay ahead, past the statues, toward that immeasurable goal faced by every tormented face. If I failed this test, I would become one of the ranked, silent figures.

I turned forward and set my will to driving my progress. I managed two steps before the next pulse of the heart. Lines of fiery cold crept out over my shoulder and touched my chest below my extended arm. I could not move my arm at all by that time. My arm crooked before me, the heart pulsing in my frozen grip, held slightly below the level of my eyes like a lamp fixed to guide my path.

The heart throbbed again. I had managed three steps. Fire and ice crawled through the framework of my bones, moving through the network of my ribcage to reach my spine more quickly than the lines of power that traced along my skin. The pain and the power of it numbed my chest, filling every breath with icy needles of agony.

The sounds grew louder. The air around me hissed with a continuous cacophony. I turned my head as the first traces of the blood touched the base of my neck. I saw slow movement on the angry lips of the nearest statue.

When the temples of Greece had commissioned likenesses of Zeus, that statue could have been the model for the artist in everything but his face. His face seemed more appropriate to Prometheus. His muscles stood out under his skin as he strained against invisible bonds. Under a mask of pain, his face held an angry, mocking edge. He stood in a pool of shadow, his lips moving slowly.

I took another step as the heart pulsed again and the black tide of blood swept higher. I knew that I would not make it to the end of the valley. I had allowed myself to be distracted. My progress had slowed. I had too far yet to go before I reached my goal.

I made his voice out then, among all the others. The words were still a grumbling mutter of thunder, and impossibly slow, but understandable. "Fool. Where is your Legion?"

The heart beat again as I listened to him and the pain of the blood reached down to my waist and up to the edge of my jaw.

The chorus of voices came in the background, mocking, raging, hating. The nearest statue laughed, almost at normal speed. "Once, twice, and eternally damned. You thought to take the power without lives to spend? Nothing is without price."

I remembered what Chimereon had told me about the Nephilim having been created from sorcerers. I had not fully comprehended until I stood in the valley itself that the finished product might have been something other than a more powerful sorcerer. When the Jigsaw Man had sought to turn my Legion against me, he had not lied to them. He had known more about the trial than I. The candidates had given the members of their Legions to stoke the fires of power high enough to take them through the valley of darkness. They had sacrificed the members of their Legion on the altar of power. Given the choice between sacrificing the Legion and surrendering to the pain, I had a strong suspicion that I would have chosen survival. Truthfully, power would have been a consideration as well. What would that sacrifice have made of me? What of these trapped, damned souls? Had they made the choice not to sacrifice their slaves, or had their Legions not been enough? Once past the valley, what would I find on the other side?

The heart pulsed again, the blood reached up to my temple and down to my thighs, and I had not taken a single step. Shouts and screams and cries of pain and abuse surrounded me. I saw the statues writhing in agony as they mocked me. I saw triumph in the eyes of the nearest, the man who could have modeled as a failed god. "Once you stop it is the end. Here, in this place, the end is also the beginning."

As the blood leached through the bones of my skull, the world became a rage of pain. His laughter surrounded me. I knew then that had I not freed the Legion, I would gladly have given them to the darkness in that place to free myself from the pain. Even the agony of the snake's venom had not been worse than the blood of the heart of stone as it clenched around my skull like a fist of molten iron with fingers of permafrost.

I lost control then, as darkness met darkness. The growing hunger I had pent up slipped its bonds. I raised my eyes to the laughing, mocking, failed god, twisting in his pall of shadow and pain, and my lips pulled back from my teeth in something more feral than a smile. I stretched my hand out toward him until I touched the deepest fabric of the shadow that covered him.

I called upon the darkness, drew strength from him, and life. The pain receded. I managed a step sideways, closer to him.

His eyes opened wide, betrayal and fear displacing the rage on his face as he felt the touch of my black hunger. He screamed and fought as I closed and fed. When I pulled away the fire and the ice had receded from my temple to the line of my jaw. The sounds around me muted and diminished. Crumbling fragments of weathered rock were all that remained where he had been standing.

It had not been enough.

The heart beat again as I stepped deeper into shadow and laid my hand upon the next failed candidate. Another man, he too screamed and fought, but slowly.

With the next beat of the heart, the blood receded again. I worked my way down that side of the valley, pushing the heart's blood further and further back, swallowing the trapped souls of that place into a deeper and more final darkness. I sacrificed them, men and women alike, to prevent myself from sharing their fate. I killed them to live.

Not one of them came to me gladly. As terrible as their existence had become, they clung to it ferociously. The more intense their pain, the more they fought against the end.

I pushed down, through the shadows of the valley. I crossed over to the other side as needed, harvesting as I walked. I reached the deepest place in the valley, where the darkness became absolute. Trapped souls clustered thickly there. I fed richly. The hungry darkness I had held restrained had gained a momentum of its own. I could not stop it. I did not want to stop it.

I forced the last of the blood back to the heart itself, then made my way up the last little slope. Light fought against the shadow of the valley. A great conflagration raged beyond the last crevice of the rock, where the last bastion of the shadows held the light at bay and the light of the crevice kept the darkness of the valley imprisoned.

I had come to the source of the power of the Nephilim, where the Rites had made gods of men.

Behind me, the screams had diminished. Few of the trapped souls remained. Only those I had passed in my initial progress had evaded my hunger, as I had driven continually down and forward. Above and behind their voices, I heard a single voice of great purity singing, making music of marvelous beauty to fill that terrible place.

Fear and shame rose within me. The light oppressed me. I battled fear of the light. My appetite had grown with each taking. My antipathy to the light had also grown as I had descended into the darkness. Somehow I knew that if I left without facing the light I would be giving myself to that darkness. Whatever remained would have been more the darkness than the self I could even then feel slipping away before relentless hunger.

I threw myself into the light in a sudden rush, like diving into a bonfire, in an urgent need to get it over with all at once. The light fell down around me. It burned. The darkness clung to me. Shadows dripped from my body, hissing in the light as they boiled away. I approached the crevice that ended the valley. I looked out onto a vast plain of white stone. Azure light burned in the heart of the plain like a captive sun. I stepped through the crevice and the great flame rose above me like a piece of eternity left from the moment of creation.

The heart of stone beat steadily in my grip as I crossed from the darkness into the light, the rhythm accelerating until it matched the hammering of my own heart. I stepped out across the plain, black trails of shadow streaming out around my limbs.

I walked down to the border of the firestorm, but no heat rose around me. I stood at the edge of creation, but no light touched me. I looked down through the well of time, watching all the myriad days of eternity pass me by.

The darkness and the hunger and the fear within me gave way to something deeper. I could hear the flames calling to me, singing an indescribably beautiful song that blended with the music of the solitary singer at the entrance of the valley.

I hesitated before walking down into the bonfire. A nameless yearning drove me forward despite my fear. A hunger to know, hunger for the root of things, a hunger to see to the heart of things, overcame the darker hunger and the fear that had carried me through the valley of shadows.

The light took me. Gods, the light!

It took me as I stepped into it, its power palpable as a heat I had not felt and an ice I had not expected. It burned through me. A pure brilliance coursed through my skin and muscles, flashing through blood and solid bone without even noticing me. I would have screamed if I'd had the strength. The shadow hunger within me withered and changed under the inescapable force of the light, clinging to me like a weeping child.

Heat seared me, ice shattered me. My body became fuel for the flames. Even the shadow billowed out away from me, a penumbra consumed by the light. The raging flame roared with a voice beyond sound, swallowing all other sound, as the light became a sea of azure fire filling my vision, filling the world of my senses.

The shadow fled me. I had no other lives to give in place of my own. I reached instinctively for the Legion, but I was alone. I turned to my purpose for refuge, my determination to solve the mystery of my master's death, to bring vengeance upon his killers. Compared to the purity of the light, such memories and purposes were a slender reed. They crumbled away beneath me almost as soon as I put my hand to them.

My blood boiled away. My bones crumbled. I stood in the flames a naked shade. I was a flickering candle to the force of the light that burned all around and through me.

I reached further back, into the time before I came to Cross-Town. I looked over the rocky shores and wine-dark seas and wooded hills of my home. I'd been a hunter then. I'd been a herdsman as well, a lover of the chase, and an eater of meat. Then I'd turned to hunting game of a less physical sort and took to enslaving ghosts instead of herding cattle. I'd lost myself on the wild, stormy seas, in the winds and the darkness. Clinging to the wreckage of my boat, I'd fought off the specter of death with a determination and a hunger for life that went deeper than any hunger the Shadow Dweller had brought to me, until I came at last to the shores of CrossTown and made my own way through its wilderness of possibilities, guided always by that lust for life that had preserved me even in the worst of my days.

I touched that hunger for life. I embraced the pain of the light. I moved deeper into the fire. In the heart of the fires of creation, I drank in the light to slake a thirst for living. As I moved toward the center of the conflagration the light changed, sharpening to a diamond purity, until it became a clear, white light the color of the first instant of creation. The pain became something more, swelling to a vast ache for the beauty of creation and a terrible sorrow for all that we had made of the possibilities we had been given.

My will clenched like a fist as I entered the heart of the flames. I hardened myself against even that pain. Pure power, greedy for definition, rose around me. I understood then that the power of the Nephilim had no nature and no definition. It was the raw stuff of creation.

I wrestled the flames into submission. I rebuilt my body out of the light. As I fashioned myself out of will into a thing of flesh and blood and bone, I drew on the hunger and drank of the essence of the power flaring around me as everything else within me fought and screamed and gave itself to survival. I drank of the clean fury of it to cleanse the memory of everything I had done, and all I had become. I drank to go through to the other side of mystery, and discover all I would find there. I drank until the light fell in around me, and the comet itself guttered and fell screaming to be swallowed into the darkness. I drank of the wellspring of the power of the Nephilim until it too failed. And my hunger spread out through the shadow and all that dwelt there, seeking more to fill its endless desire.

I had brought a thing none of the other sorcerers had to the Rites. I had brought the hunger of the Shadow Hound, a power not dependent on a Legion, but one I had taken for my own. I had given the lives of the failed, bound sorcerers to pay my price of admission to the Rites. I had, in the end, become something more and less than those that had gone before. I had tapped into that hunger that had set me on the Road from Greece and kept me alive for many mortal lifetimes, and through that hunger I had drunk the well dry.

At last all became quiet. I opened my eyes and looked around me, into the darkness. I saw the heart of stone lying near my feet. I stood in the bottom of a round bowl, a dry well marking all that remained where the fires of the Nephilim had once raged. I picked up the heart, and crushed it in my fist. The powdered remains trickled through my fingers like sand.

No Nephilim would be made after me. My endless hunger had swallowed the fires of creation. And I, I had become something other than the makers of this place had intended. I had become something for which there was no name.

When I rose up and left that place, no light remained. Within me, the hunger of the shadow had vanished, burned away in the pit. Darkness did dwell within me, but the fires of the Nephilim had tempered it into something vastly different than what it had once been. No longer a remnant of the Shadow Hound, the darkness within had expanded to encompass my own hunger for life. At the same time I had tapped into primal darkness—that first velvety black that was the root of all shadow.

I walked back through the crevice and up the length of the valley. Only one soul remained, still trapped. Only the singer still made music. All the rest had ceased to speak. I had taken them as my hunger had spread to swallow all light. The singer had been untouched, even by the hunger of that raging darkness.

She stood, wrapped in her shroud of stone, singing in a voice as pure and sweet as innocence itself. I closed her eyes with a soft touch of shadow. I took nothing from her. I released her soul to fly away from the prison of stony flesh that had bound her for time out of mind. As she left that place behind, echoes of the music remained, filling the valley, and all the places of darkness that dwelt under the empty sky.

I stayed there, in the darkness, listening to the echoes of that sweet music. It took great effort to shake myself free and turn my attention to other things. My need for vengeance had faded. I no longer held firm to the same passions that once had gripped me. And yet some distant part of me could not let go of everything. I needed confirmation, more than anything else, of who had killed my old master and why. I had firm ideas, but not the whole picture.

I had to face Titania.

With that music still shivering through my soul, I reached through the darkness and betook myself to NightTown. Of all the places I knew, that came to me most naturally. I opened the Way to a familiar estate, my mind on Eliza Drake. Perhaps she could help me understand what I had done, and what I had become.

CHAPTER XXVIII

I STEPPED from darkness into light. The gibbous moon shone down over the charred remains of Eliza Drake's forest. Smoke curled in gray wisps from the ground and from the blackened hulks of the trees. The air weighed heavy with the bitter taste of burnt wood and worse. A bare, cracked ravine of shattered rock snaked down the length of the slope. It took me a moment to recognize it as the stream where Eliza Drake and I had bathed. The vanished flames had eaten every trace of the mossy bed where we had slept.

I walked slowly through the blasted landscape, wondering how Eliza could have allowed this to happen. Her power in her own places had always been nearly absolute.

I understood when I reached the site of her manor.

The flames had raged so hot there that brick and mortar had slumped to shapelessness. The wood had all been consumed. But this fire had been particular. The grove that had surrounded her manor had been left more intact. The flames there had only stripped bark and limbs from the trunks of the trees. The trunks themselves remained.

Eliza and her retainers hung from them.

Someone had nailed them to the trees, using spikes now blackened by the fire. I knew them by their number, for they were unrecognizable, their limbs no more than twisted stumps of charcoal, their heads made featureless by the fury of the conflagration.

I stumbled through the grove, counting the bodies, searching for some sign to identify them. On all of them, long teeth gleamed dully in the moonlight, sullied but not entirely charred by the fire.

This had been no holy excursion. Whoever had killed them had destroyed the lands thoroughly, but limited the flames around the trees to make Eliza and her retainers suffer longer.

I could not tell the bartender from Teila, nor could I isolate Eliza Drake from the group. I searched, but I could not identify her. The long night had at last claimed them all.

The music that had been with me since the valley of the Nephilim faded, leaving only a wrenching emptiness in its place.

I pulled them down as gently as I could. I built a cairn of stone over the bodies. Had I loved Eliza Drake? Our relationship had been both more and less complicated than that. We had filled an emptiness in one another, if only for a while. So many connections were severed by those who chose to make their home in CrossTown. Long associations were rare enough to occupy that space usually reserved for family. Had Eliza and Teila and the rest deserved the torment of their final hours?

Possibly. None of us were innocent.

I stayed in that place for a while, remembering, giving them their due. They had been predators of humanity. Their kind was considered a scourge by all of the righteous.

They had killed to live. We all killed to live.

Shock faded slowly. The cool, gritty substance of the rock under my hand brought my focus back to the moment. Of all I might have anticipated, I had not anticipated what I had found. Why had they died? Who had killed them? Had this been unrelated to my troubles, or had I brought death down upon them by taking even momentary refuge with Eliza Drake? I needed to know the answers to those questions. If I owned any responsibility for their deaths, then I would always carry some burden for what I had done, though that burden could perhaps be lessened with the blood of their killers. Their deaths cried out for vengeance. I needed to discover who had done this thing and why. I needed a release for the bitterness in my soul.

I turned my attention toward the ruler of NightTown. Nothing happened in NightTown without the Master's knowledge. I left that place behind me, and set out through the darkness for NightTown's center.

NightTown's center ran up a long slope of saw-backed foothills to a mountain peak dominated by a sprawling keep. Ruins dripped off those slopes like blood from a knife. Small villages and patches of wild wood threaded throughout the ruins like mildew through a decaying patchwork quilt. Most of NightTown's citizens dwelt in the ruins or the wilds. The villages occupied a niche more akin to a larder than anything else in the NightTown scheme of things.

I took the main Road that swarmed up the crooks of the ridgebacks, though I traveled more swiftly through the darkness than would be considered natural. Eyes glittered in the shadows at the edges of the stone Road. The soft rustle of padding feet escorted me, but not one dweller in the darkness moved against me. Perhaps they realized that the darkness held no secrets from me. Perhaps they could sense that I was no common game.

Nightmarish forms, toothy shapes with twisted limbs, and those who held their most fundamentally alien qualities beneath a mask of humanity were all more evident to me as they lurked in the shadows than when they stood naked in the light of day. The fact that those predators took to the shadows as a shield only placed them more deeply within my place of power. Not one of them gave me cause to move against them, so I wasted my time with none.

I had considered stepping directly into the keep at the top of the mountain, where the Master kept his seat. But Vlad Tepesh had a certain sensitivity in regard to what he considered invaders, and he'd always defined that in the loosest terms possible.

I'm sure he found things more convenient that way.

Since I wanted to save my energy for whoever had burned Eliza and her holdings, I took the less direct path. That Road took me a bit longer, but allowed the word of my arrival to run ahead of me. If the Master decided not to see me, then I supposed I would have the chance to test my new strength against his. I had no intention of being denied.

I passed up the ridges until the slopes flattened to a high plain. Long poles marched across the plain like a denuded forest. Black stains crusted the lengths of the poles and fed the thick beds of moss that humped over the base of the ancient wood. NightTown scavengers had removed all of the larger traces of the Master's cruel entertainment. I saw no sign of the banquet table I had heard that he would set up so that he could feast during the mass impalements and enjoy the music and the dancing his victims provided himself and his court. Perhaps the rumors were exaggerated. Perhaps he had the table in storage, the settings and cloths out for cleaning.

I crossed out of the plain and came at last to the entrance of the keep. The drawbridge lay across an apparently bottomless chasm in the rock. The darkness there, more transparent than any glass to my new senses, held a great deal of empty space, and a myriad of patient lurkers. The lurkers did double duty. The mainstay of their diet undoubtedly fell from the middens of the keep. I felt certain that those lurkers would have regarded any available flesh, living or dead, as a bonus.

A huge figure stood guard at the drawbridge. The tips of his tufted ears passed the eight foot mark. Lips curled back from an impressive mouthful of fangs. Golden eyes glowed in his massive, wolfish head. Thick fur covered his almost manlike body. At an estimated weight in the neighborhood of four hundred pounds, he was the largest wolfbreed I'd ever seen, aside from the Watcher of the silver stair, who wasn't a wolfbreed except in the loosest sense. "Zethus," he said. "Looks like times have been hard. You're a mess."

I shrugged. I hadn't been thinking a great deal about my appearance, but he undoubtedly had the right of it. When I had rebuilt myself in the flames of the Nephilim, I had fashioned my clothes and my body as they had been. I'd been through heavy wear. It showed in how I'd reconstructed myself. "I want to speak with your master," I said mildly.

His eyes narrowed, but his tone remained civil. "Fortunately, this is the Season of Judgment. Any in the Master's demesne may petition him for a hearing."

I smiled without humor. "Good. I'm sure he'll hardly notice me in the press." I stepped past him. One massive hand fell to my shoulder, claws extended. I looked up at him without speaking.

"You would do well," he said softly, "to show more respect."

Shadows of emotion stirred in my soul. Power roused. The mask slipped. His hand fell away from my shoulder and he dropped his gaze. I turned from him and continued across the drawbridge. The heavy wood ate the sound of my footfalls. Raw stone rose around me as I entered the mouth of the keep. A deep chill entered my surroundings, my breath fogging the air. Cold flowed soundlessly out from the mouth of the keep like the breath of a dying man. Two more massive wolfbreeds waited just inside the raised portcullis. I passed them in silence. They remained at their stations, only their yellow eyes moving as they watched me walk by.

Rats, beetles, and other carrion eaters of all shapes and sizes swarmed through the passages of the keep, acting as the eyes and ears of their master. The darkness around me literally crawled with life, every tiny spark of vitality a single note in the Master's personal symphony.

Torches burned at distant intervals along the hallway, a consideration of the Master to mark my path. Shadows clustered thickly around the torchlight, fighting to eat the light. Shadow muted the glow of the torches down to a pale, tired glimmer that faded quickly before the power of the full darkness. The darkness in that place had a rich texture, a sleek taste of silky strength. It moved easily to the touch of my casual awareness. The shadows there had been unchallenged by the light for so long that light itself faltered before the hungry darkness.

I stepped out of the long hallway into a great room. Rich tapestries hung from the walls, depicting scenes of hunts and battles and death. The game in the hunts ran on two legs. A great fire burned in a fireplace that gaped like a hungry mouth. The fire burned without heat, the chill in that place thick enough to layer the walls and floor with a fine coating of hoarfrost. Frozen rushes crackled under my boots as I made my way into the room. Icicles would have hung from every fixture, I felt sure, had the air not been so devoid of moisture.

No other noise rose to meet me as I walked down the length of the great room toward the high seat that faced me from the other end. More wolfbreeds lined the walls of the audience chamber. I envied them their fur. Others stood silently in the darkness, watching me pass. None of them betrayed any signs of normal humanity, other than to the most casual of observers.

The Master had been holding court.

As I walked abreast of the fire, one of the courtiers ahead of me drifted into motion. He came to stand across my path at the edge of the firelight. Scars webbed his face, breaking his heavy features into something like a Cubist interpretation of a mass murderer. "Sorcerer." Jagged fangs glinted at me as he spoke in the cultured tenor of an Anglican choirmaster. "You look as if hard times have found you. What do you want?"

I cocked my head. "I didn't come here to speak with you, Carnifex. I came to speak with your master. Don't waste my time."

"In this place, he is your master as well, human. As are we all. I no longer smell the taint of the Tindalans on you. And the bounty on your head is rich." Cold hunger touched his voice with ice.

My eyes narrowed. The burden of Eliza's death shifted to feed a growing pressure. That pressure was looking for an outlet. Carnifex didn't know it, but with his attitude he might as well have been wearing a placard that read, "Use Me for Emotion-al Relief." The rage I had been holding in abeyance strained at its bonds. Had Eliza been tortured for information regarding my location? Had I brought her killer down on her? "You haven't been keeping track of current events," I told Carnifex. "The Whitesnakes are no longer in any shape to pay bounties. The cult and their demon god have fallen on hard times. Take the hint."

He took a step closer. "Where is the Key, sorcerer?"

I locked gazes with him. I distantly felt him trying to twist my will. His attempt slid off my mind like raindrops sliding down a window pane. "I came to investigate a death, Carnifex," I said. "You know what I'm talking about? Were you involved?"

He sneered. "That bitch is burned. She's not feeling any pain. Worry about yourself."

As he finished his first sentence, all that I had been holding back exploded into full fury. Transparent power blossomed, searching for an outlet. I fed that power into the fire already burning, bound it and shaped it to my will. Carnifex sensed rousing power and lunged for me. He moved with inhuman speed. The power moved faster. A sudden furnace blast of heat broke the cold like a hammer smashing through a sheet of glass. Shadows died as light flared through the room. A rope of bright flame thicker than a man's waist exploded from the fireplace, swallowed Carnifex, and sucked him back into the suddenly raging inferno like a chameleon devouring a fly.

The courtiers flinched away from the blaze of light and heat. I approached the fireplace, picked up a poker, and turned the embers idly. The great logs had fallen away to almost nothing in an instant. No trace remained of Carnifex. The low flamelets that remained to dance sinuously over the embers were beautiful.

"So you opened the door." The Master rose from his seat and descended the steps to stand at the edge of the light. The mask of his humanity was almost complete: only the insatiable hunger of his eyes penetrated the façade.

I straightened, replaced the poker, and turned to meet his gaze. "The Key is gone. The prize is gone."

"And so you are the last of the Nephilim." One hand absently stroked the long mustache that drooped down to his chin.

"What happened on the estate? Who killed Eliza Drake?"

The Master took his turn with the poker, turning the embers, staring into the fading flames. His lean, aristocratic features held as much expression as the stone in the walls of his fortress, but I could tell he wrestled with some unease. Too much humanity glinted through the mask. "I have the one directly responsible. He awaits my judgment." Some signal passed unseen from him to a courtier. The courtier vanished through a doorway. "But there are complications. He did not act alone. And the other is beyond my power."

I bent down, caught his gaze. "I am not bound by place. Who did this thing?"

The mask of his face gave me nothing. "A citizen of Night-Town. And one from outside. One strong enough to strip Eliza Drake of her defenses. Then the killer moved in."

That ran through me like a lightning bolt. The same method had been used to kill Corvinus. Fetch was the first half of my answer, and I had a solid suspicion for the other half. I felt movement behind me. I did not need to look back to identify the prisoner the two Wolfbreeds hauled between them. Emory Drake.

I turned. Emory smiled when he saw me. "Too late to save her. Always too late. And in the Master's hands. You are a fool, sorcerer. Your captive spirits are not enough to help you in this place."

He hadn't been kept well informed. Of course, he had been more of a tool in this game than anything else, and in the confines of the Master's gaol, he probably hadn't been kept up on current events. The power within stoked rage to a white heat. "You killed your sister. Why?"

He laughed. "It was the price I asked. The favor owed me in return for the death of your master. He died screaming like a woman. My sister was even better . . ."

His words ended abruptly. The large, clawed hand of one of his guards had wrapped itself casually around his neck. His toes scraped the flagstones. As a vampire, he couldn't be strangled to death, but it seemed to be an effective way to keep him from talking.

The Master stood abruptly. "I am asked for a judgment. The crime is trespassing and killing without my let." He nodded to me. "He is yours. I give him to you."

The wolfbreed dropped Emory and stepped away from him. His partner stepped back at the same time. Emory straightened his coat and smirked at me, showing considerable fangs. He obviously thought the Master had just handed him my head on a plate. Had this happened before my journey through the valley of shadow, he might have been right.

Then again, maybe not. Emory hadn't shown many signs of brilliance.

His sudden rush surprised no one. I let him come, power within me flaring in anticipation, shaping my flesh to my desire. His movements slowed. The dance of the firelight froze. As he reached for me, I slipped my arms under his, clasped my hands under his chin, set my hip against his pelvis, and broke his back.

I used the moment of shock. I caught and held his gaze, and ripped the identity of his patron from the surface of his mind. I recognized her. She wore the same shape she had when she had brought me into her place of power.

I saw him kill Eliza through the lens of his memory. I saw Fetch take him there, dancing to Titania's command, smashing through Eliza's defenses, stripping her of her powers, and releasing Emory to his work. I saw it as a reflection of a reflection, an act repeating the earlier attack on Corvinus.

It was little more than confirmation.

Shadowy streamers curled out from the darkness covering the wall of the Master's fortress as I dropped him. His mouth stretched wide in a scream of pain and rage. I choked the scream in his throat, locking him in the prison of his own thwarted fury. Guided by my will, coils of darkness caught and bound him, then snapped him back to the wall with irresistible strength. I reached into the flames, shaped the fire with the power of creation and the strength of my will into the form of an eighteen-inch spike. I pulled eight more golden spikes from the heart of the flames.

Then I pinned him to the wall with nails of fire and a hammer of darkness. His blood sizzled and spat as the spikes ate into his hide. His curses became screams that would have torn the flesh from a living throat. I nailed him at wrists and ankles, shoulders and hips. The last spike I put between his eyes. His screaming never stopped. Nor did his screams escape to meet any sense other than mine. I had bound him within himself. I had left him his agony for comfort. In the absence of guilt, pain would have to be enough.

The darkness thickened, covered him over, and faded. When my will eased back from the shadow, Emory Drake could no longer be seen. The stone of the wall bore scars like a tormented face, and nine holes marked it. Echoes of the hammer danced lightly through the hall.

When I turned, the courtiers flinched.

The Master shook his head. "I would have made him last longer."

I gave him a smile full of malice. "He will last as long as his strength holds, and as long as this place stands. I have given him his own private hell. I have given him all he ever deserved."

The Master looked away from me. "And now?"

I stared into the flames. *I give you this*, I told Eliza silently. Would that I could have given you better.

It helped and it didn't. I have ever found revenge to be dissatisfying. It doesn't help with the pain. For me, balancing the scales is a need, not a pleasure. Something within me, though, something old and something new, fed and grew on Emory's pain.

I thought about Fetch, and what I had seen through Drake's eyes. Drake's story of my master's murder matched Shaw's story of how Corvinus died except in one detail—the last visitor, who had cleaned up after Fetch and Drake. Fetch had to be acting as Titania's errand boy still, and Titania was Drake's patron. Titania had reached beyond her limitation of place through her agents. They were nothing more than tools, really, executing her will.

She would be waiting for me. I had no doubt of that.

I could see it clearly enough. She had taken Corvinus, but lost the opportunity to find his research through Drake's clumsiness. So she'd turned to me, and set me on the path. She had Fetch to insure my death, but first, if luck was with her, I might lead Fetch to Corvinus's research and give her the opportunity to destroy the key to the Fane. My evasion of Fetch in the Deep-Town workshop had broken those plans. How desperate Titania must have been, how heavy her fear must have weighed upon her, to drive her down this path to try and close every possible Way that led back to the Nephilim.

And so had she brought me to become what she most feared.

I didn't understand, though, why Corvinus hadn't followed the key to the Fane. Maybe he'd known more than I, or hadn't been desperate enough to take the risk. The knowledge would have been his main goal anyway. For Corvinus, knowledge was the true power.

I considered my options. I needed to think. Revenge alone was not enough for me. I didn't enjoy it as well as some. I harbored no illusion that Titania would leave me be. She had spent centuries sharpening her claws and honing her enmity for the Nephilim. She would not fall as easily as Drake had. Fetch still remained as a complication. I needed time to consider. I needed time to prepare. I decided to take the time to see an old friend and an old enemy. But first, I would take the time to stop by my place to free the ones I had bound there. I didn't want any debts outstanding when I came to face Titania.

I opened a door in the darkness, and stepped through to a starlit evening at the edges of CrossTown.

CHAPTER XXIX

THE WILLOWS murmured together like old women gossiping at a funeral. Wood fragments ranging in size from sawdust with ambition to daggers longer than my hand covered the ground around my house. Of my fence I saw no sign, other than the splinters. Pieces of broken jade glittered in the moonlight amongst the fragments.

My spirit dogs had put up a fight. I hoped they had at least drawn blood.

This had been something other than a couple of frisky dire wolves. This had been someone a bit more serious. A kind of weariness settled over me as I picked my way to the broken door. What Fetch lacked in subtlety he made up for in enthusiasm.

A whirlwind had passed through the place. No fragment larger than a fingernail remained of the contents of the house. Even the walls had been broken and smashed to ruin. The roof sagged dangerously overhead. Moonlight slanted down through ragged breaches in the ceiling. I remained outside, on the steps, surveying the damage in relative safety from having my house collapse on me. My awareness roamed through the shadows. Touching the darkness had become an unconscious act for me.

"Silver?" My voice vanished in the whispering tones of the wandering wind. No one answered.

I closed my eyes. I felt hollow inside. Even if I had wished to let this thing go, they would haunt me. Titania had loosed her hound upon me. I would have to face him.

I considered Titania, and Fetch, and the lands bordered by the Iron Hills, and I set my course. First I would check in the court of Nuada Silverhand, to assure myself that Oisin and the rest had arrived without harm, and to settle the matter that lay between us. Then I would visit Titania, to settle all that remained.

I turned, sensing a presence, to see Emerantha Pale fade into view. She paused at the remnants of the gate. "I thought it might be you. I almost missed your arrival. I had begun to wonder if you would return at all."

I cocked my head. "You're out of your regular stomping grounds, aren't you?"

Her eyes narrowed and her mouth tightened. "My territory is what I make it. Where is the Key?"

I sighed. "I begin to suspect you may have motives somewhat less pure than the driven snow."

"Don't try my patience, Zethus," she said sharply. "Corvinus died for it. You might yet. As well as many others. If the matter of the Key isn't ended, the Ways will run with blood. The old race wars will be on us again."

"It's gone."

"I don't believe you," she said. "How would you destroy such a thing? And even if you had, the prize remains. Enough know of it now, or suspect. They will be looking."

I laughed. "Let them. The prize itself is no more, Pale. No one else will join the ranks of the Nephilim. Not even you."

She sputtered.

I leaned forward. "Look me in the eye. Listen to what I'm telling you. You will find nothing but death in the valley of the shadow. The light is gone. Only the darkness remains. Understand?"

She looked me in the eye. She didn't like what she saw there. Snarling softly to herself, she spun, took a fast step, and faded into the Ways, leaving me alone on my shattered doorstep. I paused a moment to wonder. Had she had a hand in it? Or had she simply been cruising for scraps?

Time would tell. If she moved against me, I would know. I would have cause to act.

Considering the players, I chose to deal with the devil I knew. Shadow opened around me. I rode off down Roads of darkness on a midnight steed of my own making. My steed carried me to the borders of Silverhand's country, where I released my hold on shadow and let the shaping fade back to the deepest darkness. The pall of night faded around me. The directionless glow of Faerie pushed its way into my personal space.

I stood in the middle of a winding river of white stone that cut through a lake of emerald grass. Trees with golden bark and silver leaves walked along the Road, pacing its progress. The Road and its escort of tall timber wound up a great hill, toward a spare fortress of tall towers and open causeways. A pair of riders appeared on the Road, flowing gracefully down toward me.

The Lord of that place would be concerned. I hadn't given him any warning of my approach.

I walked up the hill to meet the riders. Practical scale armor burned with more than reflected light. The lances they carried had heads of pure flame. Long hair whipped behind them as they rode. The faces held the inhuman beauty of the Sidhe, the kind of beauty that rises from an absolute joy in taking every breath. I couldn't help but admire them as they closed the distance between us.

Their steeds whirled around me, and they split to walk at each side. Lances lifted toward the sky, the flames of the heads dancing and sparkling with brilliant colors. Neither of the riders said a word. I glanced at the horses, aware of the power running through them in place of blood. Cut them and flames would wash out to the air. Light sparkled in the eyes of the steeds. Thick, rubbery lips curled back over teeth never meant for chewing grass.

I ignored my escort as they appeared to ignore me while we covered the distance to the keep with deceptive speed. Towers rose before me as I passed through open gates of sparkling alabaster. Tall Sidhe lords and ladies turned to regard me as I walked through the gates and into Silverhand's great forecourt. A fountain of water and light rose higher than the walls in the center of the vast space of the courtyard. Shapes moved in the rippling curtain of mist and bright colors, dancing to the music of the falling water.

I skirted the fountain, my escort falling back, the silvery metal clash of their mount's hooves on the flagstones of the court the only sound other than the rush of the fountain. Shining ranks of Sidhe opened at the far side of the fountain to reveal the tall, elegant figure of a more than handsome man. Light glittered off the crystal in his left hand as well as the animate metal of the hand itself.

Nuada did not move, his beautiful features a blank, passionless mask. Nuada had always been most dangerous when he revealed nothing of his passions. A tall redhead stood at his side. Her green eyes sparked fire at the sight of me. "You look a bit ragged, Zethus. Fallen on hard times?" Maeve's voice had teeth. But then, everything about Maeve had always had a bit of a bite to it.

I nodded to Nuada, ignoring Maeve. Her jaw tightened. "Sidhe Lord. Has your son returned?" I asked.

A familiar voice came to me from my left. "We made it back, Zethus."

I edged around one of my escorts enough to see Oisin raise his glass to me. "No problems on our end."

I straightened as Nuada spoke. "Come to bargain for aid, sorcerer?"

Even carefully neutral and flat in tone, Nuada's words always fell as music. He couldn't help himself. Music was as much a part of his nature as violence. Only Lugh and the Dagda had him beat for the former, and only Lugh and the Morrigan for the latter. Which was why Lugh held the high seat.

That and the matter of the hand.

I smiled. "I don't need aid, Nuada. I don't make any charges. I want this thing between us laid to rest. I want to know that you won't interfere."

He arched a brow. "Between you and Titania? I thought you would be looking for allies, or taking your charges before Lugh. I had no idea you were so foolish as to contemplate confronting Titania in her lair."

A stage whisper came from my left. "Told you humans were crazy."

"I'm not so sure that Titania's crossed any of the High Lord's boundaries," I told him. "Though she may have crossed yours by invading your demesne. If she was behind the raid. I have no proof of that."

Maeve stirred impatiently. "Have done. He's given himself to you."

Nuada held up his right hand. "Patience, Maeve. Patience. Why have you been stirring your troops around my lands, sorcerer? Did you think I would not feel them? I know the taint of your captives."

I had no idea what he meant. "What?"

He opened his mouth to respond and lightning fell out of the sky. Sidhe scrambled for cover. The world incandesced as the first bolt struck. I swallowed the second and the third into rippling folds of darkness as I picked myself up from the flagstones spitting blood and snarling. Wind struck in that moment, driving daggers of ice.

My will lashed skyward, found a familiar lupine spirit, and hurled him to earth. He struck like a white meteor. Gleaming stone fountained skyward and rained down over the crowd. Power crackled over the battlements as the Fae began calling on the forces of the land.

My Fae escorts lunged at me. Power built within me. The rainbow flames of their lances went black. Shadow pooled around me and stretched out across the courtyard. The mounts recoiled from the darkness and streaked back out through the open gates. Their riders dropped their lances but kept their seats. A form rose out of the darkness. Wings of many colors opened before me. A sword of fire struck me through the body. I howled in anguish and a surge of force hurled the avenging angel away from me.

The second stroke followed, as graceful and inevitable as the second step in a dance, taking me in the side. My hand closed around the blade, darkness dripping from my side like blood.

My other hand caught him by the throat. For an instant I stared into the tortured face of Blade.

Then I ripped the sword out of my side. Darkness filled the gap, rolling out around me in pulsing waves. The directionless light of Faerie vanished in the spreading pool of shadow. I tore the blade from his grasp, from the foundations of his self, and wept molten tears as I felt his agony. I bound him in black chains of midnight strength, then I turned to catch Bright Angel's second stroke on Blade's sword.

The impact sent her shivering back. Dark flames crawled up the burning blade to eat the light. Lightning, wind, and ice stormed through my shield of darkness as I closed with Bright Angel. Power turned and folded upon itself as Bright Angel's ragged rainbow wings beat desperately against the hungry dark. I wound her in a shroud of shadows and cast her down into the stone.

I could feel the shielding pool of darkness thinning under the combined efforts of lesser ones. I pulled my strength back, and back again, until I had wrapped myself in layers of compressed ebon power. The broken Legion came swarming after. I took them in groups or singly, binding them with my will and chains of shadow into the fountain that had once been bright.

I felt the White Wolf rise from the earth and turn to flee. I caught him with a black rain lashing down from the same clouds he had once bent to his cause. Winged and clawed shadows, extensions of my will, brought him to me and held him before me. I studied him, tracing the bindings that lay heavily upon him. "Titania?"

He nodded weakly. "Hunted us down after the Whitesnakes fell. I think you have begun to concern her."

Titania had made a terrible mistake. She had bound the ones I had loosed and sent them against me. I would not forgive her for that.

"You never could stay out of trouble," I admonished him. My strength turned back on itself, healing my body of the damage the attack had done. I no longer was what I had been. Now Titania knew that, if she hadn't before.

Tides of darkness slowly rolled back. Light returned to the courtyard. Shades of darkness overran the myriad colors of the fountain. Indistinct shapes writhed where ghosts had once danced.

Silverhand stood facing me, his legs spread, brilliant light flaring around him. His eyes were wide and his mouth had collapsed to a tight line. "What have you become?"

I looked him in the eye. "What Titania feared. Where have you cast your lot, Sidhe Lord?"

The crowd lined the battlements and ranked themselves behind their liege. Weapons had appeared in all hands. Light hunched itself into a defense against the darkness. Maeve edged around behind me, a large axe held tightly in a nervous, sweaty grip. I glanced at her, shook my head, and watched her back off a step.

"Why did you come here?" It took me a bit to recognize the voice. Then I saw Nuada's son step out of the crowd to stand beside his father.

"I came as I said. To see if my fellow captives had arrived. To end this meaningless feud. To see where your father stands. Titania will not let this thing go. Neither will I. If Nuada means to take a hand in this coming conflict, let's get that over with right now." Impatience made its way into my voice, masking the heaviness I felt at the prospect of more blood.

"I will not stand between you and Titania," Silverhand said. "The quarrel we had is as dead as your mortal past, Zethus. You are right in one thing. What you are is not what you once were."

I could read his sincerity. Nuada wanted nothing more than to have me and my troubles off his doorstep and out of his life. I couldn't say that I blamed him for that.

"Good enough," I said. I turned my attention to the fountain and to the captives I had bound there. One by one, I took them out, cleansed them of Titania's dominion, and cast them out through long Roads of darkness to places far from the lands of Faerie.

The White Wolf leaped away without a word, howling his way down the long midnight corridor. Bright Angel watched me out of eyes that burned. "Be careful. She has taken your measure. She is stronger than you believe. And more cunning."

I passed a hand across my eyes. "I know. She has had the initiative from the beginning. I will have to pursue an unexpected course."

Rainbow wings beat against the darkness as she fled.

Blade was the last. He curled in upon himself, a small thing crying in the night. Tearing his blade from him had nearly destroyed him. When I brought them back together, as gently as I could manage, he poured himself into the blade. In my pain and fury, I had shattered the foundations of his self. He had no more independent will. Blade had been the first Captain of my Legion. I had freed him only to tear him apart. He resisted my best efforts at healing. I tried to do what I could. I finished by sending what remained of him to the peace of the far reaches of midnight, a place in comforting darkness where he would be safe and have time to heal. Perhaps he could heal on his own. If I could not bring him back, then perhaps I could lay him to rest.

I had much to discuss with Titania.

I looked past the veil of shadow to see Oisin's cautious salute, opened black doors, and took myself to the border of Titania's lands.

CHAPTER XXX

I WANDERED up through the Iron Hills on foot. I thought about what Titania had told me before setting my feet on this path. Had all this been a test, of a sort? Had she expected me to find someone or something here? Had she expected me to know more than I had?

Darkness covered the hills. The Iron Hills lay close enough to the border of Faerie that night came to that place, after a fashion, unlike the endless day that burned in the interior of the Faerie realms. The stars that swam overhead refused to behave in any predictable way. Watching the night sky in that place bore a similarity to watching luminous fishes swim slowly through dark waters.

I smiled, relishing the darkness. I used my awareness to guide me toward the center of the Iron Hills. I had a plan I felt sure Titania wouldn't like.

I sensed a familiar hunter dogging my trail as I neared my destination. I chuckled to myself in a grim way, and let him close the distance between us. He would be disappointed again in his search for fresh dye for his cap.

He paused well out of what he would have anticipated to have been my visual range, and gathered himself for a rush. I stood at the edge of a level plain of rusty iron, cradled by rolling hills. I turned to face him. "I wouldn't," I said pleasantly.

He froze.

I waited, but he said nothing. "Let's not play games," I chided him gently. "I know you're there. Things have changed between us. You sense the lack of Tindalans. You also sense another difference, but you can't pin the nature of the difference down. You've learned caution, but not restraint."

He growled and tensed. He was working himself toward a charge. After all, it had worked for him before. When he threw himself forward, I reached through the darkness and opened a doorway between us. He threw himself through that door before he even knew it was there. I closed the door behind him.

One good trip deserves another.

I stopped in the center of the plain, where I took a cross-legged seat. I had not measured Titania's strength, but I knew the racial weakness. The nature of the power I had taken lent itself to binding other power, harnessing it, bending it to a certain shape. There, in the midst of the stretching bulk of the Iron Hills, I thought to take up an ancient weapon, and forge it into a new form for the coming confrontation.

I took my time, reaching down through the heart of the ore, down to the core of it, and laid bare the source of the intolerable heat of the bones of the earth. I worked through the long night, spreading the darkness through the heart of the hills, and binding into the darkness something of the nature of the iron itself.

I thought I would die when I pulled the power back. Tainted by the harsh iron, I folded every hard pain and every trace of eternal heat into the fastness of my soul until my spirit ached from holding it. When the gray light of early morning broke over the hills, touched with the life and color of the light of Faerie, I felt as ancient as the power that filled me.

A shape moved in the ghostly light, drifting closer, until it took on the pale and translucent outline of a man, stooped and walking slowly toward me. His features were familiar to me. I closed my eyes against the light. "Corvinus."

His colorless face twitched into a brief smile. "Zethus. You went farther than I thought."

I caught his gaze in mine. "So you managed to escape, after all."

He shrugged. The line of the horizon showed through his body. "Almost. I can't seem to escape this place. I had thought to catch you before our friend the redcap when he came upon you the first time. I failed. Where did you send him, by the bye?"

"NightTown. The Master's private preserve." I chuckled. "He should provide quite a surprise for them. Depending on who's hunting whom, he might even make it out alive."

Corvinus frowned. "You've changed. Was it so hard, then?"

I favored him with an evil look. "How can you ask that? What were you thinking, bringing all of this down on everyone? Me in particular?"

He looked abashed. "Actually, I never meant for things to go this far. It got out of hand."

I snorted. "You couldn't have thought that pursuing the Fane of the Nephilim could have been easy."

"Hey, now!" He held up one hand in protest. "I didn't start out looking for that. All I meant to do was clear up a small matter that had been bothering me. I began investigating the Nephilim themselves, to discover if any might still be walking the Ways."

"And the Key?"

He frowned. "I never thought that such a thing could be used to track back to the Fane. It was a part of my research. I never saw any tie to the Ways."

"What? You expect me to believe that? What about the suit? You were one of the masters of the Ways. How could you not know?"

He paused. "Maybe it was never there in the heart for me to find. If the heart had been a map to the Fane, I would have known. I never saw anything like that in my study of the heart. I had thought that through the Nephilim I could find the true nature of the Ways. But then I had hints that unwanted attention had begun to stir. I wanted you to destroy the heart, or take it out into the most hostile places and abandon it if you couldn't destroy it. That's what the suit was for. I wanted you to be able to take the attention from us, but I didn't realize how far things had gone. I don't think I would have taken the risk of using the Rites even had I known how to find the Fane."

He paused. I waited. When he resumed, he spoke slowly. "I came to warn you. At least one of the Nephilim still walks CrossTown. That's the attention I most feared. I knew there were others, who bear the blood, or who bear memories from that time. Before I realized how much attention I had attracted, Titania moved against me. Fetch cleared the way. The vampire killed my body. Fetch sheltered the vampire from my death curse. But someone else cleared the traces after they left, covered the tracks and confused the trail. I couldn't tell who did it. I've never felt that kind of power before. And I still don't know how Titania found out. I was careful."

I frowned, remembering Shaw's account of the killing. That made sense out of Shaw's account. It meant an enemy unaccounted for. Perhaps more than Fetch had been searching for the heart of stone with destructive thoroughness. "Who altered the heart, if anyone? And who covered Titania's tracks, leaving her and Fetch free to pursue me into CrossTown?"

"Someone close enough to catch on to my project and Titania's intent covered the tracks," he said. "Someone afraid of being revealed by my researches. More than that, I don't know. How did you discover that the heart could guide you?"

I thought about Chimereon. She had the blood. She had the power. She could have set my feet on the path. But why? And why would she have moved against Corvinus, if she had? Chimereon took the public aspect of a goddess. Revealing that she was or bore the blood of one of the Nephilim wouldn't be a threat. And she had no dealings with Corvinus of which I had any knowledge. I shook my head. "I think we're talking two separate events. Chimereon could have opened the Way. She admitted that her father descended from the Nephilim. Who knows what secrets she still possesses?" I watched his face to see if he reacted to her name. He didn't. "Whoever covered Titania's tracks wanted to prevent an actual discovery of the Nephilim Fane. I don't believe that would have been Chimereon. There's another player out there, probably your last Nephilim."

The outlines of Corvinus's shape frayed as the light brightened. "You could be right. Titania and this other both wanted to end any knowledge of the Nephilim. Titania for fear of renewed interest in the power of the Nephilim. The other . . . perhaps also out of fear."

I frowned. "Fear?"

"Fear of the return of the Wars of the Brethren." The light continued to grow in intensity. His voice was fading to a whisper. "Fear of the struggle for the power. Fear of becoming the target of every hungry walker of the Ways."

I spat. It made sense. Though a Nephilim would make a dangerous target, the promise of power or the fear of the threat that person would represent would draw hostile attention. It also meant that perhaps not all ills lay at the feet of Titania. Would this other pursue me out of fear? Even knowing that no more Nephilim would follow in my footsteps?

I met Corvinus's failing gaze. "Is there anything you want from me?"

He laughed thinly. "I'm making my own way, boy. I can't afford to be beholden to any Powers. Not even you."

He faded as I watched. I doubted he was going to his final rest. Corvinus had always been a hungry, restless spirit. Doubtless, he would even then be figuring out a way to claw his way back into the game.

I didn't have anyone pegged for Corvinus's mysterious other player. But I had a couple of suspicions. One had previously seemed unlikely, but was growing on me. And either way, I thought I knew where I'd find the other waiting for me.

Before that, I had Titania and her hunter to confront.

I made my way down, out of the hills. I knew I had come into Titania's Realm when the grass began withering under my feet. Stone glowed where I stepped. The iron burned bright in my blood.

I felt her gather her forces at her keep. The air danced with power there. Fetch stood waiting for me by the side of the water, within view of the keep.

He stared at the water as I came to stand beside him. His reflection stared back at him as if out of a mirror. Steam curled out of the water where my reflection should have been. The water boiled in a shape roughly corresponding to my outline.

He spoke without turning to face me. "You've led me a merry chase."

I regarded him dispassionately. "This doesn't have to happen." I held up a clenched fist. Heat waves curled around it. "I don't hold you responsible. I don't need your life."

He laughed softly. "It's been interesting. The most interesting quarry I've ever run."

He moved with impossible speed. I grunted with the blow, watched him clothe himself in power as pale as bone. A slashing stroke cut me deeply. The heat of my iron blood curled out over him. He screamed and fell back. Black flames licked the air from the wound he had opened in my belly.

I caught him in a relentless grip. I pulled him close and held him as iron fire blackened the air around us. I locked him in place until his struggles weakened, then dropped him back to the earth. The aspect of death faded from his face. He breathed in great gasps, his eyes narrowed against the light. I bent down over him, the gray and stinking smoke of scorched flowers and grasses rising from a circle stretching around my feet. "I don't want your death, Fetch. I never wanted any of this."

I left him there, curled on himself against the pain. I strode on up the path. I stopped at the drawbridge, staring up into the complex, beautiful structure, a working older than humanity. I built careful layers of defense. Beyond, from within the keep, I felt the first cautious probes.

If she had expected me to trot on inside, she had fooled herself. That confident I wasn't.

Power curled out of me, probed down through the earth, carrying the iron taint. Flame burst up around me and clothed my limbs, but did not burn me. My flesh had passed through greater fires. The flames raced toward the keep. The waters of her moat boiled and frothed as the iron fires crossed under it and threaded delicately through the foundations of her place of power.

Brightly colored fish scattered for quieter pastures.

A horde of spirits came roaring out against me then, boiling out of the heart of the keep to descend on me in a furious storm of white power. She had assembled a mighty host and mounted them on steeds of elemental force. Her Legions marched in concert. They rolled down over me in choreographed waves. I was vulnerable: I could not disengage my extended power from the destruction of the keep quickly or easily.

Titania herself followed her host in spirit, her will falling on me as a furious storm of blades. The blow broke through the defenses I had raised and smashed me to the ground, laying me low under a maelstrom of sharp power. But as I fell, iron flames broke through the walls of the keep. The stone itself burst into flame and ran in molten streams down to the waters of the moat. Clouds of steam rose around the site as a scream of pure rage rose from the keep.

I drew the darkness back, trying to build enough power to break Titania's attack as her attention faltered. Her will fell away from me as she fought to hold her fortress in place. Her Legions fought to consume me as I knelt there on the ground.

I built my power steadily, then broke the bindings of her massed Legions in a whirlwind of pale iron flames. Titania remained distracted by the fortress, her body still inside. I smashed her control of her Legions. They surprised me. Fully a quarter of her minions fought on after I had broken their bonds. I cast them out, away from the land of the Fae. I pulled myself to my feet to see Titania come stalking out of the burning ruin of her keep.

Her eyes blazed with rage and white fire. I saw no fear in her. She threw herself toward me, naked but for a bright veil of power, her shape twisting to something all claws and teeth and appetite.

I needed an additional weapon. I laid my hand on the first and best at hand. I sent my strength to the far reaches of midnight. Blade, trapped in his broken shell, screamed like vengeance itself as I brought him out of the darkness. Blade met Titania in mid leap.

She must have been preparing something special for me. A silent roar shook the ground, and all of reality vanished in an instant of hot, white light. Curling licks of power picked me up and gave me a playful toss toward the horizon.

I clung to the shield of my iron fires. When I rose unsteadily from where I had come to rest, I could see no trace of Blade or Titania. Her fortress resembled nothing so much as a nuclear pile in the process of melting down. Clouds of steam rose from the stream for a thousand paces to each side of the keep. I found myself hoping that the fish had been fast on their fins.

I looked back at Fetch, rising from where I had left him, and watched him flee.

I opened the doorways of shadow, walked out along the distant Ways, and set all of the spirits I had recently imprisoned free, even those from Titania's Legion. I could not let my duty to them fail. I had nothing else left to me. I thought of the spirits who had fought on after her bonds had been broken. I wondered what that said about Titania. Then I banished doubt from my mind. I couldn't afford further distraction.

I had one last errand. One last confrontation. And then I would be done with it. Then I could rest.

CHAPTER XXXI

I SEARCHED across all the myriad Ways until I found him. He waited where I had half expected him to wait. Once I located him, disdaining the Ways, I stepped through the shadows to the foot of the spire. I climbed the steps as any man would, placing one foot after the other, but that endless climb passed by in the time between breaths.

He stood facing out over the valley. "Zethus."

I walked up behind him to stand at his back. "Anthony Vayne. I saved you for last."

He turned, his eyes lambent. "Did you think it would be easy for you?"

"I figured out what you must be," I continued without replying. "The last of the Nephilim. You didn't disguise your lifespan well enough. You helped Titania. Your meddling left her and Fetch free to hound me through CrossTown and left me without the protection of the CrossTown authorities. You tried to ambush me with a machine in TechTown, then led the Whitesnakes to me on the Way. Did you let her know about Corvinus's research? Did you set the Faerie onto me?"

The corner of his mouth lifted. "I didn't set the Faerie on you." I started to shake my head, and he held up one hand. "Titania knew you worked with Corvinus. She found out about Corvinus's research independently. I never dealt with her directly. Corvinus was careless. Titania and I both felt his meddling through the Ways, when he found and awakened the heart of stone. The day he died, I wanted to talk to him. I wanted to convince him that the course he was on would be the death of him. I went there to try to talk some sense into him. Maybe I would have killed him if he hadn't abandoned the heart. I don't know. But when I got there I found Corvinus dead, the defenses down. Fetch had already left and taken Titania's vampire assassin with him. So I cleaned up. I confused the trail. I wanted to stop the madness from beginning again."

"Emory Drake did the deed," I said. "He confessed, and Corvinus confirmed. One more sin to stoke the fires hotter for his cockroach soul."

Vayne nodded. "It was quick. Corvinus hardly knew what hit him. Drake was stupid. I don't think Titania meant for Corvinus to die so quickly. I believe she planned to bury Corvinus's research with him."

He sighed, looking past me into the darkness. Traces of emotion ran across his face, too quickly and faintly for me to read. "Who knew Corvinus would hide the heart so thoroughly?" A lightly wry tone touched his voice with color briefly. "Fetch tore the place apart. He searched, but he didn't find what he was looking for. I didn't either. I even searched the lower lab. I needed to find the heart and break the trail. I needed time. Confusion would give me time. I thought I could find the heart before you did. I didn't want you on the Roads that lead to the Fane and the Rites."

I didn't say anything. We stood for a moment in silence, looking out into the valley below. At last he raised his gaze to meet my own. "You have more drive than Corvinus had," he told me. "I couldn't let you get that scent. If Titania knew your master's research had been destroyed, she would not have hounded you. But Corvinus hid the heart too well. I missed it. I didn't know him well enough."

He paused. I waited, looking into his eyes. "Corvinus hid the heart well enough," he said at last, "but he made his mistakes in other things. He was careless enough that Titania and I knew what he was digging into. Neither of us knew the extent of your involvement. We took independent steps. We both remembered what had been loosed in the past. Neither one of us would allow that to be loosed again."

"So she moved against me on her own. What of the ambushes?"

He closed his eyes. "I did nothing to help or hinder you or your opposition. The Whitesnakes followed me looking for you. I let them. I knew nothing of the ambush in TechTown. The bounty was out on you by then. Titania had Fetch dogged your trail, and financed the Whitesnake bounty on you. She wanted you dead as insurance, in case you were involved in Corvinus's research, but she wanted you pressed into revealing that research first if possible. I had hoped you would run out into the Ways, away from CrossTown. I think Titania would have been satisfied with that. But you didn't."

Rage tightened in my chest, fueled by a river of power. "And so you are innocent," I snarled sarcastically.

His eyes opened and he took a step toward me. I felt the hot breath of ancient power swirl around me. "I am not innocent. I have taken countless lives. I have killed gods and monsters. I have destroyed entire civilizations. You know nothing of what I am."

The power of the darkness stretched around me endlessly. I stood at the eye of a storm yet unborn. "You are damned."

He turned away again, unwilling to face me. "I am that. What you have done is nothing compared to what I have been. I am the only survivor of the Wars of the Brethren. I was the first, and I will be the last. God will not let me die."

I could taste his death in the heart of the night. While he hadn't killed Corvinus, and he hadn't set any of the killers on my trail, he could have trusted me in the beginning. He'd failed Corvinus. He'd been willing to kill to protect his secrets. He'd been willing to stand by and let me die. He'd hidden Titania and Fetch from CrossTerPol. He'd made it easy for them to hound me through the Ways. Fury built within me until I could not think. It had become so easy to act through the power. It begged to be used. He would not turn to face me, but waited in silence for the blow to fall.

I couldn't kill him. I didn't have that much mercy in me. It took all I had to fold the power inwards and hold all the fury in check.

I didn't notice when he left. By that time, I had become captive to my own thoughts.

I stayed there for a long time, dwelling in the valley of shadows, listening to the echoes of forgotten music. The beauty of the singer's voice still held me, though only ghosts of memory remained to haunt that place. I thought about all I had seen, and all I had done. I didn't have much cause for pride. Mine had been a selfish life, clinging so tightly to existence as to never enjoy it. At least I had freed those spirits I had held in captivity. Later, I had released all of my captives from the darkness where

I had bound them. Of all my living works, I felt satisfaction with those acts alone.

It can be a miserable thing to write your own epitaph.

My awareness ran out through the shadows and into all of the realms of possibility. If darkness dwelt in a place, then there too did I dwell. If shadow stretched into a time, then that time was home to me. I stayed there, watching over the valley of shadow, watching through the hungry night and into all the worlds touched by darkness. Through all those instants, and in all those places over which I held sway, I would catch sight from time to time of familiar places, and familiar faces: the White Wolf, hunting through the frozen pillars of great trees in a vast taiga; Bright Angel, laughing as she spread her wings and danced with brilliant strokes of lightning; the White Rose at the edge of a still pool of water, softly singing; the Wraith in his workshop, stooping over flickering light burning deep in a great orb, suddenly pausing to straighten and swing his head quizzically, as if he felt the pressure of my regard upon him. All these and more passed by, unknowing; I watched them pass, uncaring. Memory itself faded before the eternal regression of the folded moment, and all that I had ever known came to be nothing more than a distant progression parading behind a wall of glass. Soundless, tiny figures divorced of context or meaning, none of which could touch me. There in the darkness, nothing could touch me.

I had left my humanity behind, and I could not lay my hand back upon it as easily as I had lost it.

I had no conception of time while I remained in that place. Time no longer held any significance for me. So I do not know how long it took her to find me.

I felt her enter the valley, and I paced her as she wound her way up the steps of the spire, though my body did not move from the place where I had left it. The darkness hid nothing from me.

Chimereon's voice spoke from the shadows. "I thought I might find you here."

I didn't move. Settling back into my body sufficiently to converse took grim effort. An endless sea of pain wrapped me in the rough swaddling of flesh. I spoke slowly. "In the end, I let him go."

"I know," she said softly. "I know."

"I feel . . ." My voice trailed off as I struggled for the words.

"You feel." Her voice was firm. "That is enough."

I dropped my gaze back down to the darkness below. "I feel bereft."

Chimereon moved closer. "You knew what it was to be a man. Now you understand what it is to be a Power."

"Other than the power, everything feels the same, so long as I allow myself to feel," I replied slowly. "I still feel all of those things that make me human. I still feel pain. I still hate. I can still fail. I am alone."

She nodded. "Isolation is the nature of power. You have been through the process of becoming the definition of a thing. And that process strips you of all mortal connections. I know that as well as any, and better than most."

I didn't raise my eyes from the shadows. "You knew all along, didn't you? You opened the Way to this place. Why? To end your solitude?"

She looked away, out into the darkness. "The seeds of what you could become had already begun to sprout. If I had not shown you the way, you would have found another, or destroyed yourself on the journey. None of this is easy. But there is solace."

I looked up and met her eyes. They burned with white light. "You still owe me a favor, remember?"

I thought about turning away, back into my solitude. She could not compel me. I had become a thing that could not be compelled. I no longer had the ties of obligation that had bound me through the days of my life. But was obligation merely a matter of compulsion? Or was there something more?

I believed that there was more. I always had. Character meant paying your debts. I considered my power, my independence, and the isolation those things had brought me. I wanted to be able to feel again. I didn't want to remain a thing, and not a man, no matter what that might cost.

In spite of that, I had to go to the limits of my will to bend my neck to accept my debt. It was almost too far for me to reach.

I rose. The darkness thickened around me, taking on a new aspect. Incomprehensibilities opened within it—things I could perceive, but not yet understand. Chimereon stepped out into that darkness. I saw the makings of a Way opening out behind her.

I saw the ghostly image of a coiled snake, feathered wings beating slowly, superimposed over her human form. "Follow me," she said.

The static power I held close fought my first step, an inertia beyond the physical. I rolled that stone back from the mouth of my living grave by the indescribable effort of releasing my clenched hold on the power running through the darkness. That heavy shadow fell away, spread out, and joined with the living darkness of the Road Chimereon had opened.

I followed her, shuffling off the spire and into the looming night. My feet left bare rock and fell on a pathway of deeper darkness stretching through the shadows. As I moved, something stirred in me. I saw Chimereon receding away from me, falling away down the endless length of the Road, and as she diminished away from me her shape twisted, and turned, until great wings beat slowly at the air, long, snowy, and crimson feathers rippling in the air, until her sinuous body became the coiling, emerald length of a great serpent, shining like a beacon at the far end of the shadows.

A second step followed the first. An old, familiar hunger took hold of me. Too long had I charted my course between narrow boundaries. Too long had I cut straight to the bone. The Road lengthened before me, quickened under my foot, and the shadows stretched out, reaching for eternity. I lost sight of Chimereon then, but it didn't matter. The Road had a hold on me, the endless possibility of the journey.

Paths branched before me and branched again. My mind spun down distant channels, and my body followed. Power ran like a current under my feet, buoying my step, but my memory turned toward other Roads, and my next step fell on stone. A high roof of stone arched far above my head. I breathed in dry, cool air, as if I stood in empty lungs, rather than deep in a cave. In the distance I heard the poink! of a single drop of water, falling, destroying, building, reshaping. The rocky floor of the cave sloped down. Through the darkness I could see, as if I stood there again in the daylight, that the cave would open to a pool of clear water, surrounded by climbing vines covered in white and purple flowers. The flowers perfumed the air. The spirit of that place, revered locally as a healer and gentle oracle, carried that light, sweet scent with her even after I took her into my Legion.

I didn't want to disturb the White Rose if she had returned, so I took another step on the Road of darkness, and the stone shifted to a thin, thin veneer of slick mud over river rock. A chill, clean breath of fresh rain caressed my face and moistened my lips. Bare trees jutted up into the night. Dead, rotting leaves warring with red mud covered the riverbank in a layer of slime. The place felt empty. Bane would haunt it no more. He had made his last choice. He had fallen to his own betrayal.

Shivering, drawing my coat around me, I stepped again. Gravel crunched underfoot, sharp stones turning together under the soles of my boots, an ordered chaos breathing warm dust with every step. The roadside shrine hadn't changed, it seemed. Monks from the abbey on the hill still groomed the river-rock surface of the Road, tending the stone like a garden. A patchwork of shadows picked out the coiling pattern of the low, shaped trees that lined the Road and framed upright posts. Angular characters slashed down the broad faces of the rectangular posts, catching the prayers of that alien land and binding them to service. It had been a special place, but the genius loci dwelt there no longer. I had taken the guardian spirit that drew pilgrims from distant lands in search of a warrior's blessing. He had fallen at the last as I chased my empty vengeance to Titania's door. I hoped Blade had found peace, but I feared I had brought him only destruction.

A deep, enquiring hoot followed me as I stepped again down a Road of memories, still traveling through the reaches of shadow. An uneven surface tripped me, and I stumbled. Even without starlight I saw the straight lines of long grasses thrusting up through the cracked, tilted slabs of gray concrete that surfaced the Road. Towering oaks lined and roofed the lane. The concrete buckled under the slow, inexorable grip of the roots of the trees. Shadow had taken that place for his own, a feral echo of an older time. He had held that place as his own until I came along and bound him and took him away. Moonlight fell on the grass past the leafy roof of the oaks. Light would prosper in that place more easily in Shadow's absence, while the roots continued their slow, destructive work on the Road. I could hear small movements in the grass as the animals crept back to make that place their home.

Another step and a pale sun tried unsuccessfully to pull itself over the sharp line of the horizon. I stood on a bare outcropping of stone surrounded by blowing streams of white, powdery snow hustling along beds of ice. I thought I heard the distant call of a wolf on the wind as I paused to listen, shivering, but it fell away, until I heard only the voice of the wind, endlessly calling through the vast, empty desert of ice and rock and snow. If anyone made his way home, it would be the White Wolf.

Chilled by the absence of life, I stepped to another cold place, a high place. I stood on a stone peak. The sun lay low in the sky, his light burnished orange by thin clouds. Under a blue-velvet firmament, lush green jungle sprawled out around the peak like a verdant sea. White feathers of mist rose from the long stream of a high mountain waterfall dropping from the cliff across from me. In the borders between the clouds and the mists flashed the brilliant broken arches of rainbows. I searched the morning light for the bright sweep of wings, for a familiar shout of laughter, but if Bright Angel had returned to her home, she was hiding from me.

I couldn't blame her.

In the end, I fled that place, those memories, turning even deeper into the past until I came to the beginning of the journey that would bring me to CrossTown. My hands still rough from laying the stone foundation of the walls of the city that would become Thebes, sweating in the hot Mediterranean sun, I'd watched my brother sing and shape the final stones into place, and I'd sworn to Amphion then that I'd find my own magic, instead of breaking my back while he made his music. I had found magic, too, but not in the captive spirits I'd enslaved, nor in the fires of the Nephilim. I'd found it first in the mystery of the Road, in the wonder of discovering what lay over the next hill, and around the next bend. I'd lost that mystery some time during my sojourn in CrossTown, when in my desire to extend my life I had forgotten how to live.

I ran past Thebes before I arrived. I came at last to another high place. I stood at a crossroad, marked by a lightning-shattered oak overgrown with ivy, and looked down over the City below. CrossTown lay below me, pulsing and breathing and growing like a great sprawling beast. TechTown and Night-Town, DeepTown and OldTown, the beating heart of the Fold-ed Quarter, all these and more danced and shuddered and lived down there. Roads ran through the City like the threads of a vast tapestry. Even the darkest Road sparkled with possibility, and even the tamest harbored in its secret heart the wild desire for freedom.

More than the lifeblood of CrossTown, the Road was the lifeblood of all us traveling fools, all those looking for what lay over the next hill, around the next bend, or over the horizon. My brother chose the City, but I, I chose the freedom of the Road, the freedom of the hunt, the freedom of life without walls, until I had built walls around myself, narrowed my course, limited my choices, and ultimately severed all connections but the empty ties of power and coercion. I had built myself a prison I could carry with me, and so could never escape. And once I'd settled my last debt, I'd let all that stolen power and all those endless days drop down around me until I could no longer find the promise of the Road. I'd nearly lost myself in the barren comfort of empty power.

The wind turned chill against my exposed hands and face. My breath puffed to a frozen cloud. A flash of color caught my eye. I turned to see Chimereon step into view in a bright, ghostly glitter of almost seen feathers. "You've traveled far, but there is further yet to go." She held out a hand. "Come," she said. "Dance with me."

I took her hand. Memory still lay heavily upon me. I was in no dancing mood. I could hear no music, yet I followed her, shuffling out down the dusty Road and into looming shadow. Walls of darkness closed around us. I felt no fear. Darkness held nothing that I feared. But I felt something akin to wonder as our feet left the dust of the Road and she led me, stepping lightly out into a black, infinite place so vast I had not the words to wrap around it.

Then I heard the music, softly at first but swelling in volume until it reached down through flesh and blood and bone to the spirit beneath. I had never known music so pure. In it I could hear every note a man could make and more, all arranged in perfect balance.

As I heard the music, I fell into step with Chimereon. I had to do no more than cease to resist, for if I allowed it, the music moved me. I followed Chimereon's lead, whirling further out into the deep. As I looked at her, sometimes I saw the woman I knew, other times I saw a vast serpent, feathers red and white gleaming against the blood-red scales, the enormous wings beating in time to the music. And no matter what form I saw, I knew her as she was.

Then the darkness paled. The shining face of the moon swung by, smiling and gently swaying. The sun rose from behind mother earth, roaring his vibrant song in endless waves of brilliance. We waltzed through the courses of the worlds as they swept around us in their stately dance, singing swelling songs that followed the sun's lead and blended seamlessly to the whole. Nodding to the giants crowned with bright rings, we swept further out, the children of the dark spaces playing at our feet.

We whirled and stamped, sweeping through a growing multitude of brilliances, stars and their chorus of planets, all dancing, all singing, all filling their roles in the celestial chorus, not one ever missing a step in the dance or a note in the score. Brilliant solos flared in supernovae as stars gave everything they could give to the symphony, filling the void with all that was themselves so that they might live again as pieces of the myriad others lining up to join the dance.

Again we spun outward and upward, swinging in one another's arms as galaxies pirouetted and came together in the soft darkness for brief moments of fire and passion only to sweep on again, changed by the brief touch of another, stars trailing out between the parting arms like distant tears.

Then again out and up, we stepped lightly down promenades of empty spaces lined by endless standing throngs of living light. Beyond the walls of galaxies moved a brilliance that we could not see, the master of the chorus, the lord of the dance. And when the dance ended, as all dances must, we knew it would be in an outpouring of glory so vast that it could not help but start the music all over again.

Then we whirled to a close, stepping down out of the light and the darkness to the cultured perfection of Chimereon's grounds.

I kissed her deeply, still filled with the glory of the music.

She laughed. We settled in the garden as the stars whirled around us, and the moon bowed out of sight. Fire defined and then broke the horizon with surprising delicacy. As we turned our faces into the warmth of the sun, she laid one hand over mine. "You understand, now. There's more to living than wrestling death, or waiting for your heart to stop. Even for us. Even for the Powers. Eternity, vast as it is, should be swallowed in sips, a moment at a time."

I grinned at her, flushed with life as if I had just been born. "Next time, I lead."

We stayed there in the garden, watching the splendor of the sunrise. Past the stairs that led to the path that wandered through Chimereon's gardens, past the ruin of my house and the grove of willows, the rising sun painted the sky in shades of hot flame and velvet shadow. Below the magnificence of the sunrise, CrossTown burned with a grimy vigor all its own, the lights of TechTown blending into the morning glory, the shadows of NightTown settling into the deep places to drowse away the coming day.

All the many folk of CrossTown could not see beyond the rough beauty that embraced them. As they fumbled toward the mysteries that beckoned from beyond the horizon, following Ways bounded only by their own desire and imagination, the inhabitants of CrossTown, travelers all, were too busy with all the matters of living to raise their eyes and look up into the naked face of creation. That was as it should have been.

They knew, but did not remember, as I had once known but forgotten, that the journey is more than the destination. That was also as it should have been. Those who had the capacity would see through their own heart's desire in time.

As for myself, I had set my feet on a new path. New worlds awaited me. I could not say what the morrow would bring, but I found myself looking forward to all that lay beyond my horizon.

I turned my attention from CrossTown back to my companion. I had living of my own to do.

ACKNOWLEDGMENTS

All the folks in the Whidbey program, without whom this book would not have been the same. And less formal first readers, Garth, Gary, Jeff—I miss the time spent idly building worlds.

BIOGRAPHICAL NOTE

Loren W. Cooper is the author of three novels, one short story collection, and one nonfiction work. He is a member of the SFWA. He won the 2001 EPPIE for Best Anthology (*The Lives of Ghosts and Other Shades of Memory*), the NESFA short story contest in 1998 for "The Lives of Ghosts" (title story of the anthology), and placed in the Altair short story contest with "Lanikaula and the Powers of Lanai," a fantasy short story based on Hawaiian myth. *The Gates of Sleep*, his first published novel, was nominated for the Endeavor award in 2002. Other novels include *A Slow and Silent Stream* (2003) and *A Separate Power* (2004). *The Lives of Ghosts and Other Shades of Memory* appeared on the Real Best Seller's List in 2004. He holds a Master of Fine Arts from the Northwest Institute of Literary Arts, with degrees in English, physics, and Russian Studies. Currently he works as a Global Systems Engineering Manager at HP Inc. Loren is married with two daughters and lives in Cedar Rapids, Iowa.

CPSIA information can be obtained
at www.ICGtesting.com
Printed in the USA
BVOW09s0410121017
497441BV00001B/1/P